THE VERMILION BOOK
OF OCCULT FICTION

EDITED, TRANSLATED

AND WITH AN INTRODUCTION BY

BRIAN STABLEFORD

THIS IS A SNUGGLY BOOK

ISBN: 978-1-64525-104-0

THE VERMILION BOOK OF OCCULT FICTION

Brian Stableford's scholarly work includes *New Atlantis: A Narrative History of Scientific Romance* (Wildside Press, 2016), *The Plurality of Imaginary Worlds: The Evolution of French roman scientifique* (Black Coat Press, 2017) and *Tales of Enchantment and Disenchantment: A History of Faerie* (Black Coat Press, 2019). He has translated more than three hundred volumes from the French, mostly in the genres of *roman scientifique*, *contes de fées* and Romantic and Symbolist fiction. His recent fiction includes the visionary science fiction novel *The Revelations of Time and Space* (2020) and its sequel *After the Revelation* (2021); the last in his long series of "Tales of the Genetic Revolution," *The Elusive Shadows* (2020); and the comedy fantasy *Meat on the Bone* (2021), all published by Snuggly Books.

SNUGGLY BOOKS

CONTENTS

INTRODUCTION

THE FRENCH OCCULT REVIVAL of the nineteenth century and its literary spinoff were closely connected with and rooted in the Romantic Movement of the early decades of the century. It was initially fostered by historians and other scholars who were interested in the investigations of their predecessors into the "occult sciences" that had thrived in the sixteenth and seventeenth centuries before being subjected to disenchantment during the supposed Age of Enlightenment that dominated the eighteenth century, supervising a gradual weaning of chemistry from its alchemical roots and of astronomy from its astrological associations, and thus ushering in a new era of rationalism and materialism. That new era was not uncontroversial, of course, experiencing strong opposition from the Church, which was naturally determined to preserve its own brand of supernatural belief from corrosion while condemning all others—a stern opposition that, like all controversial oppositions, had a polarizing effect on popular conviction, encouraging a common notion among dissenters that the progress of rationalism and materialism was "going too far" in its sterner philosophical manifestations, which were most extremely represented in France by the philosophy of "positivism" developed by August Comte under the partial influence of his sometime employer, the unorthodox social philosopher Henri de Saint-Simon.

The Romantic Movement was, in essence, a kind of counter-Revolution directed against supposed ill-effects of excessive rationalism, suggesting, in particular, that recently revised accounts of human nature tended to neglect or devalue aspects of human thought that were not inherently rationalistic and calculating. Influenced in part by developments in German Idealistic philosophy, Romantic writers put more emphasis on sentiment than calculation, and the historians associated with the movement began to pay more earnest attention to the role played in history by the evolution of ideas, connecting and narrativizing the supposedly objective chronicling of facts and events in a particular fashion. History had always been a kind of story—in large measure a concatenation of interested distortions of actual events—but in the decades prior to the Romantic era new ideas had emerged as to what kind of story it was and what lessons could be drawn therefrom. There was only slight dissent from the thesis that the fundamental story was one of gradual "progress" but disagreements had become sharper as to exactly what that progress consisted of, what forces were driving it, and whether it was headed in the right direction. The social implications of that philosophical dispute had recently become much more clearly manifest, more sharply polarized and more urgent when they had reached the crisis point of 1789, when the French Revolutionaries attempted to seize history by the scruff of its royal and clerical neck and drive it in the direction they wanted, with the aid of the guillotine.

Romantic historians had little difficulty finding heroes for their narrative of unsteady progress toward liberty, equality and fraternity, going all the way back to antiquity. Their anticlerical sentiments helped to promote a certain sympathy on their part for paganism, and for neo-Pythagorean and neo-Platonic philosophies that had been rudely stamped out by early Christians and condemned again as heretical in the seventeenth century, when some scholars interested in pagan documents had elected to ignore or defy Church dogma. Many agents of the Enlightenment dismissed such defiance as stupidity and superstition, but some of the advocates of Romanticism refused to take that judgment as an item of faith, and gradually began to put together and alternative history of ideas in which the supremacy of rationalism and materialism were not only not to be taken for granted, but actively, imaginatively and creatively opposed.

The process by which various oppositional ideas were collated, and to some extent combined, was inevitably untidy. It is characteristic of nascent convictions, especially unorthodox convictions, that they are defended fiercely, not merely against supposedly-obsolete theses and the prevailing orthodoxy but also against alternative theses and rival unorthodoxies. Nevertheless, unorthodox thinkers of various stripes often do develop a certain sympathy for other orthodox thinkers, enabling them to operate tacit truces if not to make explicit alliances. For that reason, birds with somewhat different exotic plumage did begin to flock together, hence forming what came to be considered as a multifaceted but general "occult revival."

It is difficult to compose a summary account of such a heterogeneous and calculatedly perverse process, but relatively easy to select out the most influential writings, which became unsteady foundation stones of the rickety French revival. They did not spring fully-formed from the national zeitgeist, and the particular investments made by prominent scholarly fantasists deserve recognition as significant and original works of art appealing to esoteric minorities.

The first renascent creed to catch on sufficiently to become and remain a significant element of the French occult revival, and to make a serious bid to be recognized as its core, was Martinism, a mystical offshoot of freemasonry, named for its founder, who called himself Martinez de Pasqually (c1725-1774), but philosophically sophisticated and popularized in

Paris by his chief disciple, Louis-Claude Saint-Martin (1743-1803). It was Saint-Martin who produced the first classic novel of the tradition that is celebrated in the present anthology, in the surreally bizarre *Le Crocodile* (1798; tr. as *The Crocodile*), nowadays reviled by earnest Martinists who consider it far too playful, but admirable from the viewpoint of ideative anarchists (or, in more recently-fashionable terminology, Discordians) more concerned with subversive esthetics than the construction of pretentious convictions, and providing a striking illustration of the complex but intimate relationship between literary fantasies, scholarly fantasies and lifestyle fantasies, which is abundantly illustrated by the background and contents of the present volume.

Martinez de Pasqually and Saint-Martin were contemporary with the Swabian physician Franz Mesmer, who developed a theory of "animal magnetism" and attempted to develop therefrom a medical practice based on the stimulation of "magnetic tides" within the body. He moved to Paris in 1778, where his therapeutic method achieved a fashionable success, and soon became extremely controversial—to the extent that Louis XVI appointed a committee of investigation to assess its merits, whose members included the chemist Antoine Lavoisier and a notable visitor from America, Benjamin Franklin. The committee's report was negative, but only proved that all publicity is good publicity, and that bad publicity is sometimes the best of all. Mesmeric medicine took firm root in France, especially within the Romantic Movement. Félix Bodin's pioneering assessment of *Le Roman de l'avenir* (1835; tr. as *The Novel of the Future*) assumed that it would be the medicine of the future, while mesmerism became the central motif of a new species of occult fiction, celebrated within the Romantic Movement by such works as Frédéric Soulié's novel *Le Magnetiseur* (1837), and Alphonse Esquiros' novella *Le Château enchanté* (1846; tr. as *The Enchanted Castle*).

Among the historians who began to produce radically new narratives of past events was Antoine Fabre, who preferred to sign himself Fabre d'Olivet (1767-1825). A polymath of sorts, intensely interested in Biblical hermeneutics and neo-Pythagorean philosophy, he also loved music and engaged in amiable controversy with Lord Byron after comparing and contrasting his own drama *Cain* with the English poet's. His fanciful interpretation of the apocryphal *Vers dorés de Pythagore* (1815) and his sweeping *Histoire philosophique du genre humain* (1824) had a powerful influence on later French occultists and their key notions were syncretically combined with Louis-Claude Saint-Martin's ideas by the founders of a new Martinist Order in the 1880s.

Fabre d'Olivet's slightly more orthodox contemporaries included Augustin Thierry (1795-1856), Edgar Quinet (1803-1875) and Henri Martin (1810-1883). Thierry, who served as Saint-Simon's secretary before being replaced by August Comte, did not write romances himself but provided fuel for many writers who did—his fanciful history of England after the Norman conquest was largely responsible for the modern mythology of Robin Hood—and his nephew Gilbert became one of the most prolific novelists of the occult revival, adding his uncle's forename to his own by way of a memorial. Quinet, however, did write Romantic historical epics of his own, following up the vaulting ambition of his *Ahasuerus* (1835; tr. as *Ahasuerus*) with the more intimate *Merlin l'enchanteur* (1860; tr. as *The Enchanter Merlin*), the latter produced in competition with the work of Théodore Hersat de La Villemarqué (1815-1895), whose adventurous interpretations of Breton folklore helped lay the groundwork for the "Celtomania" of the latter part of the century. Quinet was close enough to the core of the French Romantic Movement to duplicate Victor Hugo's insistence on remaining in exile throughout the Second Empire, refusing to accept the amnesty offered to both of them by Napoléon III.

Henri Martin was equally close to the heart of the move-ment, and also wrote poetry and fiction, although his primary focus was on his historical studies; he worked briefly as an editor for Émile de Girardin and published abundantly in Girardin's periodicals, alongside the likes of Honoré de Balzac, whose principal work of occult fiction was the Swedenborgian *Séraphita* (1834), the mercurial Théophile Gautier, and the folklorist and fakelorist S. Henry Berthoud, who had a partic-ular fondness for tales featuring the Devil. Martin collaborated with "P. L. Jacob le bibliophile" [Paul Lacroix] on the early volumes of his popular history of France (1833-36 in fifteen volumes; subsequently expanded to nineteen), which became controversial for numerous reasons, including its identification of a largely-hypothetical "Druidism" as the essence of primitive Gallic thought and identity—a notion that was taken aboard by many historical novelists, who were not shy about improvis-ing details of hypothetical druidical magic and mysticism. The writers who got into the act included the godfather of French Romantic prose, René de Chateaubriand, in *Les Martyrs* (1809; tr. as *The Martyrs*) and Eugène Sue, in the first novelette of his epic *feuilleton* story-cycle *Les Mystères du people* (1849-56).

Martin's narrative of French history also took considerable inspiration from the work of his friend Jean Reynaud (1806-1863), the author of one of four key texts of the French occult revival published in quick succession between 1854 and 1862, during the Second Empire, all reacting in perversely imaginative fashion against the severe censorship of that regime. The first of those texts to appear, a curious amalgam of cosmology and metaphysical speculation, was Reynaud's *Terre et ciel*, [Earth and Heaven], initially advertised as a work of religious philosophy, which has considerable analogies with Edgar Poe's "prose poem" *Eureka* (1848) and with the extraordinary hypothetical cosmol-ogy set out by Nicolas Restif de la Bretonne in *La Philosophie de Monsieur Nicolas* (1796), previously dramatized in *La Découverte australe par un home volant* (1781; tr. as *The Discovery of the Austral Continent by a Flying Man*) and *Les Posthumes* (1802; tr. as *Posthumous Correspondence*). *Terre et ciel* proved to be a very influential text among unorthodox thinkers, greatly inspiring Camille Flammarion, who became France's leading popularizer of the science of astronomy as well as a vocal spokesman for the doctrine of Spiritism, which he combined under Reynaud's tacit guidance in the novel *Stella* (1897) and the short story reproduced in the present anthology.

Spiritism was the brainchild of "Allan Kardec" (Hippolyte Rivail), whose early scholarly work was on the theory of education, written under the influence of his colleague Johann Pestalozzi; he embarked on his new obsession after attending a séance held by a medium importing the methods of American "Spiritualism," but he was always keen to distinguish his own pseudoscientific doctrine, first set out in *Le Livre des esprits* (1857; tr. as *The Spirits' Book*) from the more religiously-inclined American fad. External observers have usually considered the two movements to be slight variants of the same fundamental belief and the same practices, but the most evident difference, in the early days, was that Spiritism accepted the notion of the routine reincarnation of souls—a key aspect of Reynaud's and Martin's philosophies—whereas Anglo-American spiritualists mostly did not. Kardec's work was enormously influential on literary and lifestyle fantasies alike.

Le Livre des esprits was rapidly followed by a sweeping *Histoire de la magie* (1860; tr. as *The History of Magic*) signed "Éliphas Lévi," which followed up his earlier scholarly fantasy *Dogme et eituel de la Haute magie* (1854; tr. as *Dogma and Ritual of High Magic*), providing the earlier text—an invaluable handbook for lifestyle fantasists—with an elaborate largely-fictitious history of the supposed "Hermetic tradition," liberally spiced with invented doctrines of "Rosicrucianism," the mythology of which had originated in a scholarly fantasy constituted by

13

a series of pamphlets published in the 1614-17 and probably written by the Protestant utopian philosopher Johann Valentin Andreae (1586-1654). The book was enormously influential, recklessly plundered by writers of imaginative fiction as well as neo-Martinists, who produced their own elaborate versions of the Hermetic tradition, the most widely-read popularization being *Les Grands initiés* (1889; tr. as *The Great Initiates*) by Édouard Schuré (1841-1929), a fellow-disciple of Fabre d'Olivet who wrote several occult novels, including *L'Ange et la sphynge* (1897; tr. as *The Angel and the Sphinx*). Lévi's English translator, Arthur Edward Waite, also recycled and elaborated his ideas in a series of scholarly fantasies, and exercised a powerful influence on many contemporary poets and fiction writers, including W. B. Yeats, Arthur Machen, Aleister Crowley and "Dion Fortune" (Violet Firth), all of whom became occult lifestyle fantasists to a greater or lesser extent.

It is perhaps unsurprising that the ideas in Lévi's *Histoire de la magie* thrived in the context of Romantic fiction; his real name was Alphonse-Louis Constant (1810-1875) and while still writing under that name he had produced an occult novel of his own, *Le Sorcier de Meudon* (1847; tr. as *The Wizard of Meudon*) and had actively courted Théophile Gautier and his coterie of Romantic writers. Constant was married for some years after 1848 to Noémi Cadiot (1828-1888) who went on to become a successful writer of naturalistic fiction under the pseudonym "Claude Vignon," after producing a notable collection of supernatural fiction that was banned by the French censors but printed in Brussels, *Minuit!!* (1856), the contents of which were probably penned before the couple separated.

Histoire de la magie was swiftly followed in its turn by another of the seminal classics of modern scholarly fantasy, *La Sorcière* (1862; tr. as *Witchcraft and Satanism*) by Jules Michelet, a close friend of Edgar Quinet. Like Henri Martin, Michelet spent the greater part of his life producing a monumental comprehensive history of France, rarely letting mere facts get in the way of his progress-celebrating narrative; he took over where Augustin Thierry had left off in further elaborating the hero-myth of Jeanne d'Arc, the fantasization of which had begun almost as soon as she was dead, in the interests of political propaganda, during the latter phases of the Hundred Years War. *La Sorcière*, an account of the seventeenth-century witch panic whose lyrical celebration of persecuted witches as members of a heroic feminist resistance movement against Church tyranny, took such fantasization to an entirely new level, assisted in its anecdotal section by stories concocted by the maverick Romantic novelist and prolific faker of memoirs who styled himself Étienne Lamothe-Langon (1786-1864), whose *Histoire de l'Inquisition en France* (1829) was long taken seriously but eventually proved to be mostly fictitious. Michelet's book, apparently written tongue-in-cheek but taken seriously by many readers, has remained an extraordinarily prolific stimulant of lifestyle fantasies until the present day.

By 1862, therefore, all the foundation stones of the nineteenth-century French occult revival were in place, ready for appropriation by a new generation of occultist lifestyle fantasists and exploitation by a new generation of literary fantasists, who rejoiced in the relaxation and eventual abolition of Second Empire censorship. Another important new element initiated outside France was, however, added in the 1870s by the advent of Theosophy, the brainchild of the Russian-born occultist Helena Blavatsky (1831-1891), who had relocated to the U.S.A. in 1873, where she practiced as a spiritualist medium before founding the Theosophical Society in 1875. Her esoteric philosophy was first summarized in English in *Isis Unveiled* (1877), a syncretic amalgam of Leviesque Hermetic mysticism and ideas drawn from Hindu and Buddhist mysticism, many of them obtained via popularizations by the French writer Louis Jacolliot (1837-1890), whose study of *Le Bible dans l'Inde*

(1869) and its sequels were liberally spiced with quotations from an imaginary Sanskrit text of his own invention relating to the legacy of a sunken "lost continent" in the Indian Ocean, which he subsequently moved to the Pacific. Jacolliot eventually became a prolific writer of fictionalized travel books and adventure stories.

Isis Unveiled was also spiced with borrowings from the fanciful occult novels of the English mock-Rosicrucian Edward Bulwer-Lytton, *Zanoni* (1842), *A Strange Story* (1862) and *The Coming Race* (1870), which had also influenced the author's French fan Éliphas Lévi, and thus became a highly significant pipeline to French Occultism. Blavatsky visited France in 1883, traveling from Marseille to Paris in the company of the founder of the French branch of the Theosophical Society, Maria de Mariategui, Countess of Caithness (1830-1885), previously a key disciple of Allan Kardec. Mariategui went on to be one of the founders of the French branch of the Society for Psychic Research, originally founded in London in 1882, whose most prestigious French member was the physiologist Charles Richet (1850-1935), an enthusiastic researcher of Spiritist and other "paranormal" phenomena, who also wrote fiction under the pseudonym Charles Epheyre. *The Secret Doctrine* (1888) further elaborated the imaginary history of Blavatsky's bold but mostly second-hand scholarly fantasy, both borrowing from and contributing to the French occultism that was by then in its heyday.

The pace was set for the emergent generation of Parisian lifestyle fantasists by Joséphin Péladan (1858-1918), who preferred to style himself "Sâr Péladan," thus claiming descent from ancient Babylonian royalty, when he appointed himself the leader of a new masonic cult combining Rosicrucianism with Martinism, although his first job, after he arrived in Paris in 1882, was working on Arsène Houssaye's neo-Romantic periodical *L'Artiste*, and he soon established a Salon de la Rose + Croix, which became a briefly-significant showcase for

Symbolist painters. Péladan's didactic novel *Le Vice supreme* (1884) was the first of a long series proclaiming the necessity of saving humankind from cultural decadence by means of a rebirth of allegedly ancient Eastern magic and a spiritual evolution toward "androgyny"; many of the volumes included lyrical interludes of visionary "prose-poetry" which became models for similar exercises by other lifestyle fantasists, including François Jollivet-Castelot, who developed his own metaphysical thesis of "hylozoisme" to support his active research in alchemy, and helped to prompt a whole subgenre of neo-alchemical romances in France in the late nineteenth and early twentieth century. Although the literary merits of Péladan's and Jollivet-Castelot's work are rather dubious, they represent a significant thread of occultist literary fantasy.

Péladan's first convert to his syncretic lifestyle fantasy was the poet Stanilas de Guaita (1861-1897), who became his partner in a renascent Rosicrucian Brotherhood, and who amassed a considerable research library of occult texts, frequently consulted and mined for inspiration by such neo-Romantic writers as Édouard Dujardin, sometime editor of the *Revue indépendante*. The Brotherhood was rapidly joined by Gérard Encausse (1865-1916), who signed himself "Papus," a childhood friend of Guaita's, and by his fellow poet Victor-Émile Michelet (1861-1938)—no relation to Jules—perhaps the most seamless synthesist of occult notions with his literary endeavors; much of his occult fiction was collected in *Contes surhumains* (1900; tr. with additional material as *Superhuman Tales*).

Papus joined numerous other occult societies, including the French branches of the Theosophical Society and the Hermetic Order of the Golden Dawn, and made practical as well as philosophical attempts to draw them together. He demonstrated his eclecticism in his editorship of the Rosicrucian Brotherhood's periodical, *L'Initiation*, and organized a Congress of Occult Organizations in Paris in 1889, to which many organizations sent delegates, establishing a vague community of interest in spite of fierce doctrinal disputes, particularly between Spiritists and Theosophists. Other occultists that Papus brought into the loosely-knit fold and whose work he helped to popularize included Alexandre Saint-Yves d'Alveydre (1842-1909), a disciple of Fabre d'Olivet and a prominent Hollow Earth theorist, who followed the example of Madame Blavatsky in making alleged telepathic contact with "Eastern masters." Their supposed revelations—including the assertion that the Sphinx had been constructed by refugees from Atlantis—became a key component of several subsequent scholarly fantasies.

L'Initiation included a literary section which boasted of employing a panel of prestigious editorial consultants, including the popular *feuilletoniste* Jules Lermina. In 1880, Lermina's eldest daughter, Marie-Pauline, had married a *bouquiniste* specializing in occult exotica, Henri Chacornac, for whom Lermina rented a shop, where all the occultists in Paris soon began to hang out. Charcornac and his brother Paul then launched a specialist publishing venture, in imitation of the one operated by Lucien Machuel, alias "Chamuel," with which it soon merged. Later issues of *L'Initiation*, its sister publication *Le Voile d'Isis* and many other occult publications, including many of Péladan's works, were issued under the Chamuel imprint, which also published other works of fiction, including Lermina's collection *La Magicienne* (1892) and early collections by the prolific Frédéric Boutet, including *Contes dans le nuit* (1898; tr. in *The Antisocial Man and Other Strange Stories*). Although Lermina was a skeptic, Papus persuaded him to chair the 1889 congress, and the author penned several occult novels and shorter works, following up the feuilleton *La Comtesse Mercadet* (1884), some of them under Papus' acknowledged influence and with his collaboration, including the novella *À bruler* (1888; tr. as "Burn This").

Most of Lermina's literary contemporaries who dabbled in lifestyle fantasy under the influence of Péladan, Guaita and

Papus only did so briefly, but sometimes intensely, notably Jane de La Vaudère, who participated enthusiastically in Spiritist séances and cultivated a more general quasi-academic interest in esotericism—the produce of which she channeled into her lurid best-selling historical novels—and Gabriel de Lautrec, who published an interesting pseudoautobiographical account of his involvement with the Movement and his adventures in drug abuse in *L'Initiation*. Only the first part of Lautrec's "confession" was advertised in the literary section of the magazine's contents page, the rest being indexed in the "philosophical section" and presented as non-fiction. In the present collection I have placed Lautrec's article in a separate appendix with two other twentieth-century items, which belong to the same curious hybrid subgenre, illustrating the aftermath of the nineteenth-century revival. Other members of *L'Initiation*'s literary advisory panel, including Boutet, Maurice Beaubourg and Charles de Sivry, were careful to maintain a skeptical distance from occult lifestyle fantasy even while drawing upon its influence in their fiction, for inspirational purposes.

By far the most loudly-publicized contribution to the literature of the Occult Revival was Joris-Karl Huysmans' carefully-researched novel *Là-Bas* (1891; tr. as *Down There*), which helped to popularize the notion that Satanism was alive and thriving in the occult underworld of contemporary Paris—a fantasy assisted by the fact that some of its characters were drawn from life and assisted in making their models notorious. Its hero, Durtal, went on to feature in several other quasi-autobiographical novels, while his enigmatic lover, Madame de Chantelouve, was a transfiguration of Huymans' sometime mistress, the Junoesque artists' model and would-be poet Berthe Courrière (1852-1916), and the renegade priest who conducts a Black Mass was modeled on Joseph-Antoine Boullan, a friend of the prolific writer Jules Bois (c1868-1943) and an adversary of Stanislas de Guaita in a much-publicized feud. Courrière had a longer relationship with

Remy de Gourmont, and his association with her is reflected in some of his mystical fantasies. Although Huysmans' novel maintains a stern opposition to its bugbear Satanism, its notoriety tainted his reputation, and much of his subsequent literary work and his own idiosyncratic lifestyle fantasy (he dressed in a monastic habit and became a somewhat half-hearted recluse) seems to have been a conscientious reaction against that unwarranted suspicion.

Jules Bois' acquaintance with Huymans and Boullan was reflected in a book of his own on *Le Satanisme et la magie* (1896), but he was not a specialist in occult material, in spite of being extensively quoted in that context by Gilbert-Augustin Thierry and others, and he also became well-known for his writings on feminism. Another of Huysmans' friends, Jean Lorrain, cited Madame de Chantelouve as a prominent member of a set of contemporary literary archetypes—"Princesses of Darkness"—echoing Jules Michelet's *sorcières* in making tacit Satanic pacts; Lorrain cited examples from the work of Paul Adam and Rachilde (Marguerite Eymery, later Madame Alfred Vallette). The novel cited by Lorrain as a key example of the new Satanism, *La Princesse des ténèbres* (1895; initially intended to be published under anagrammatic alternative pseudonym misrendered by the printer as Jean de Chibra) remained a relatively obscure work, as did Paul Adam's historical novel *Être* (1888), but Lorrain was correct in identifying them as representative of a gathering trend of fiction putting a new spin on the notion of quasi-Satanic *femmes fatales*, in which *Là-Bas* was merely the tip of a considerable iceberg. By the 1890s the image of the witch as redefined by Jules Michelet had become standardized, especially in neo-Romantic fiction; the exemplar included herein—Théodore de Banville's "Le Philtre" (1881; tr. as "The Philter")—was one of the earlier examples of what soon became a flood.

Another writer who flirted briefly with occult lifestyle fantasy at the beginning of the twentieth century, Maurice Magre, credited Gabriel de Lautrec with introducing him to what was rapidly becoming a thriving Parisian "occult underworld," of which he later became a somewhat unreliable retrospective chronicler, under the pseudonym "René Thimmy," in *La Magie à Paris* (1934). He also mapped that underworld out briefly in retrospect in his classic occult novel *Lucifer* (1929; tr. as *Lucifer*), which carried forward Huysmans' notion of a secret but thriving French Satanic worship in a stirring fashion. Magre wrote several other novels and essays drawing upon the modernized version of the Hermetic tradition, which he did not hesitate to modify for his own narrative purposes in his survey of *Magiciens et illuminés* (1930). By that time, however, many of the ideas embraced by the Occult Revival had become familiar commonplaces of cheap popular fiction—an aspect of the staple fare of thrillers and crime stories—and writers of occult fiction of the class and enterprise of Magre had become rare. There is a quasi-nostalgic note to Magre's fake reportage and fantastic novels that reflects an evident consciousness that things had moved on since the end of the Belle Époque. The most prolific era of occult "horror fiction" was yet to come, but its age of relative innocence had gone, and the loss of that relative innocence was not without a certain cost.

In the aftermath of the occult revival that unfolded between Lautrec's and Magre's exercises in pseudoautobiography, various other quasi-confessional works appeared, some of them—like the example by Renée Dunan included in the appendix—marketed as fiction but others pretending more earnestly to be "real," and thus helping to found a subgenre of masked occult fiction that continues to thrive to the present day. All autobiography is, of course, essentially dishonest, its purpose being self-glorification, self-justification or self-protection rather than accurate revelation, but autobiographies into which supernatural claims are inserted become particularly problematic in their relationship to truth, and it is very difficult to draw a line between fake reportage and the purely literary devices of first-person narrative, by means of which invented characters put on a show of verisimilitude, also in the interests of a kind of "truth"—a show further complicated by the fact that the adventures of such striking fictitious autobiographers as Robinson Crusoe, David Copperfield and the unnamed narrator of *Moby Dick* really were based to some extent on real experiences.

The boundary I have drawn between the stories in the main body of the text and the appendix is a temporal one rather than a categorical distinction, illustrative of a particular evolution within the larger body of occult fiction, the foundations of which had been laid long before the likes of "Éliphas Lévi" and Madame Blavatsky, let alone Gabriel de Lautrec and "René Thimmy," got in on the act. The present anthology is manifestly an anthology of occult fiction, as advertised, but the implications of that classification are not as simple or obvious as they might seem. All of its contents are fictitious but not all of them are "honest fiction," and the degree and precise character of their dishonesty are sometimes hard to assess.

The whole point of occult fiction is, of course, to hide its true nature and motives—that is what "occult" means—and the challenges that it provides to reader credulity are an essential component of its appeal to its readers and the esthetics of its composition, including its production of pleasure and stimulus to the imagination. There is a sense in which the true purpose of this anthology is to be enigmatic—because, by definition, it could not be otherwise—and the simple adoption of a skeptical attitude, although undoubtedly necessary, does not provide an answer to the enigma, but rather a commencement, whether of psychological analysis or of wonderment, or both. Amen—or, in the pretentious jargon more typical of the occult revival, so must it be.

—Brian Stableford

THE VERMILION BOOK
OF OCCULT FICTION

NINETEENTH-CENTURY TEXTS

THE DHARANA

by Edouard Dujardin

"IT'S the mental operation known as Dharana; the spirit, emancipated from the world, is fixed in the meditation of Vishnu; then the spirit grasps a sensible form of Vishnu; and, as a fire blazing in the wind ignites thick grass, so Vishnu, seated in his heart, consumes the Seer."

One such seer was Alexis Pranne, the Magician.

One day, Alexis Pranne, having had his mind fixed in the meditation of an idea, saw his ideal Vishnu.

Magic. It is necessary not to disdain anything; it is necessary not to laugh at anything; it is necessary to contemplate everything; science lives outside time and place; seekers are of all the ages; the truth hides from whoever does not desire it with a grave, free and superb amour; the austere truth does not like those who mock. Study things. Study things, for the Word remains eternally. Wisdom was not born yesterday, and for one reasonable century, ours; twenty and thirty centuries could not have been ignorance and folly. Consider the succession of races and empires, peoples and scholars; those thirty centuries of scholarly and popular history; think about human history; all that cannot have been vain, and all is not false of that which has always been. Meditate on what has been; study things; study respectfully, and see.

See what the thought of times was; savants think and people dream; and the thoughts of the former are the image of the dreams of the latter; now, the crowds dream and the sages say one thing; amid human history, one belief; under various forms, religions are the same, and philosophies are the same; all lands, in all ages, are enlightened by the reflections of one light; there is only one truth. Asuras, the principle of things; devas, the inhabitants of the distant Sansara; Izeds and Ferouers; Bel and Sin; angels, servants of Jehovah and demons, servants of Samael; Zeus and his cortege of gods; the infinity of Latin powers; the vague spirit tenants of Scandinavian rocks; mysterious existences, worlds, emanations of Being, which extend, as genii, alternately above and below humanity, in unlimited regions, were the belief of the fetishistic savages of the Nile and the ages that cultivated the Pierian Muses. Jesus taught the expulsion of the evil spirits and the satisfaction of the good; and like the Haoma that gives its faithful its flesh as daily nourishment, Christ offers his body and his blood to humans in sacrifice. Then, those grandiose pressures, the metaphysical divagations of the first heresies, on the fringes of the new faith; the theurgy of Alexandria, the last and most sublime flower of the old trunk of antique religions; Christianity built on the debris of vanished cults; and, from the seething amalgam of universal doctrines to the Middle Ages, the sums of monstrous anxious philosophy, of spiritual agents.

Humans live among invisible spirits, the causes of visible phenomena; that is human belief; Alexis Pranne believed it.

Human being itself is the middle of a chain; nature's work is incomplete therein; it does not conclude with humankind, nor the flight of human being to god; but human being is the median in which, in unified and infinite nature, amid the infinity of the manifestations of one substance, the eternal dissolution of existence into essence, the reflection of the All. Humans are at the admirable point at which the two worlds sensible to human being touch, the two manifestations that human being contains of the manifest infinity: matter and spirit.

Thus, in the world of our realities, there are two appearances of being, which humans unite sovereignly; and something is beneath human being, matter, and something is above it, spirit: below, the inert object, then the animal, in which thought is embryonic; then human being rises, and from the terminus of the body, body and spirit, spirit departs; and higher up in the vague spirit, serene being, and pure spirit. An unlimited sequence of beings: beneath us we see them via our senses; above us, thought sees them; the body sees the body, and thought can see the phantom that commences the spiritual chain, obsessing the human soul with its immaterial wings, the spirit of imponderable form, the subtilized spirit, and all the spiritualities that float outside space, surrounding the human spirit, which matter and the bond enclose.

The spirit knows spirit; the spirit can speak to spirit; the spirit can command spirit. The beings that live without form above our heads can be constrained and subjugated; since the human arm can force obedience from matter, the human spirit, similarly, can force the obedience of fantastic spirits; they are dominated by a powerful will; they bow down to it, and I have them in my servitude if my thought knows the imperious and magisterial word; both material and spiritual nature are open to human will.

Thus, the old science, the primal and universal science, is not vain; it is the sublime science that embraces and contains all others and has engendered them, the eternal magical science.

✳

Alexis Pranne had not known his mother, who had died bringing him into the world. She was the last child of ancient noble families of the Franche-Comté, vanished races grave and meditative. The extreme survivor of generations of other faiths, she had been a frail, dreamy young woman, pale and sad, and was said to have been very beautiful.

Alexis Pranne had been brought up in a solitary patrimonial château in the Franche-Comté, almost primitively; he was ignorant of the noisy joys of the early years; a pensive seriousness grew in his brow, like an ancient hereditary legacy. As a child he spent days alone in the solitary plains, while his father dreamed, irremediably taciturn, beneath the vaults of great halls.

Toward his tenth year, Alexis Pranne, having lived in insouciance of the mother he had never seen, thought about that vanished mother. One day, by chance, he found the portrait of a young woman between two pages of a book. His father said to him: "That's your mother..."

The book was a Bible; the child read the lines, and having read them, holding the book in his hands, he gazed at the portrait, which gazed at him. He commenced dreaming about the things that one sees, and the things that one does not see.

He had shown an exclusive taste for study at an early age; gradually, he became passionate about it; he did not like any amusement; he was never seen to laugh; there was nothing but study. It soon became relentless toil, without distraction; he never mingled with society. One day, in his fortieth year, he retired to his château in the Franche-Comté and did not emerge again; he lived there alone, finishing his work.

The spirit must respond to the evocative spirit. Thus, there was no book that he had not read; he had learned all languages in order to read all books, and he knew histories, religions and philosophies. He studied all the sciences, and nothing that is human was foreign to him; he knew everything that a man can know; the experience of human generations was reunited in him, and he held knowledge in his hand. Oriental, Hebrew, Arabic and Medieval magic were open to him; he lived the ceremonies of the churches of all lands.

All modern sciences are familiar to a Magician, and he also retains the formulae of the alchemists, the signs of necromancers and the litanies of exorcists. He follows the recent discoveries of astronomers; he reads the movement of heavenly bodies like Leverrier, and the astrological mysteries are unveiled to him. He has repeated the experiments of Claude Bernard, Berthollet and Pasteur; and he has stirred the philters of sorcerers, founded metals, mixed the juices of plants and all the venoms of serpents, and caused sparks to spring forth from stones, like souls. He has known physiological lives and the swarm of inspirations; nature and the demonic world. He has raised himself above the arcana of human psychology and he has repeated the terror of mental invocations. Everything: and in the funereal solitude of his laboratory, amid the impenetrable silence of nocturnal wakefulness, he reiterates everything, seeing the law of supernatural evocation appear gradually, during assiduous nights—possible, then probable, and then certain—looming up before him slowly, ever nearer. He follows, from the beginning, the entire chain of universal Magic; one by one, he pronounces every formula and founds every mixture, and in the sublime order of his conjurations, he recites, from the alpha, all the way to the omega, the immense sequence of the prayer that is commandment. And when the final combination appears, the final word, the fatal gesture, the somber unknown of thought will shine, evocatively. Thus, he will have found; Magician, he will be; spirit will obey him.

And Alexis Pranne murmured these words:

"O pitiful human beings, in your ambitions; flesh in which stifled thought groans. To you, money, power, amour: tomorrow, I shall have the world. To you, the rich, the adored, those embraced by women, I abandon my wealth, I live solitary, I have not known woman; virgin of your joys and your desires, alive with the unique spiritual vision, tomorrow I shall have before me my dream made real: the awakened phantom."

Thus spoke Alexis Pranne; and, grave, austere, tall and thin, his head straight and very brown, his pale cheeks shaven, his eyebrows broad and salient, his eyes profound and dark, superbly arrogant in the fixed and vague gaze of a disdainful visionary, when he retired at forty to conclude his labor in the solitude of the final isolation, he had the obsession of the idea marked on his visage, as in his soul.

One evening, Alexis Pranne had stayed awake, and all night he worked doggedly, as he had all day. The end was near.

In his eyes, circled with black, was the increasing anxiety of an immense expectation; his mind, overexcited, embraced infinities of thought in a minute; and it was as if the breath of magical centuries were in his lungs.

Dawn was about to appear on the horizon, but in the laboratory, behind thick curtains, in the shadow of grimoires and retorts, was there any day or night? The pale oil lamp suspended from the ceiling cast gray reflections over everything.

The term was approaching; the idea was about to open. And he thought about his hopes, he thought about the page once open of the very divine Merkabah[1] in confrontation with the maternal portrait, while his hand turned the pages of the final volumes and traced symbols on the walls. Oh, how he had always had, living and ardent, the certainty of the thing! Oh, in that achievement, what anguish and joy there was! And his being was exultant while the term drew nearer: Magician, he

---

1 The Hebrew Merkabah (Dujardin renders it Mercaba), in the context of mysticism, refers to the chariot of God seen in prophetic visions, most notably the one featured in chapter 1 of the Biblical book of *Ezekiel*. It became the symbol of an entire school of Mysticism.

would have spirit, the superhuman world, before his sovereign will; spirit, the material, manifest, phantom . . . .

The lines joined; the mystic triangle was closed, circumscribed in the circle; visible in the entanglement of signs, the letters expressive of Thought gleamed . . .

Acrid vapors, in green-tinted gusts, floated in the great nocturnal silence with a faint crackle. Having no more to do than rise into Thought, he paused momentarily and before completing the action, during a second of dream, he stood still, leaning lightly against the wall, under the fear of what he was about to do; all his life, all the life of the universe, came into his soul.

At that moment, outside, dawn broke, virginally perfumed, at the tops of green April trees; in the distance the railway line was designed between the clumps of bushes, and the night train from Paris to Belfort drew nearer. In the little station, a troop of hunters descended; they were arriving unexpectedly, cheerfully, having planned to surprise Alexis, a friend who had forgotten them, and to depopulate his forests. They made haste, with the cries of awakened sleepers, counting and calling to one another; gripped by the morning air, they were laughing in advance at the astonishment of the tenebrous fellow; they inhaled the spring breeze and considered the rosy whiteness of the dawn joyfully.

And in the night, the night of aromatic mixtures, fuming crucibles and open grimoires, in the bleakly lunar night, and the silence barely troubled by a faint crackle, by the prodigious terror of magical preparations, the Magician, very pale, with flamboyant eyes, very feverish, with dull eyelids, had straightened up, looking straight ahead, into the void of the shadow, and he took a step forward; with his left hand he touched a Biblical book, where words were ringed by a line: "I see visions . . ." And with his thumb he brushed the portrait of a young woman—pensive, pale and sad, and very beautiful—and in his mind, heightened by the power of the will, obstinately fixed, he pronounced the thought of evocation.

Then his short black hair, having become whiter than the snow of the mountains, stood up upon his head; his eyes protruded from their frightfully dilated orbits and his breathless breast capsized; his abdomen tightened; his throat became suddenly dry; his heart stopped beating and his spirit was petrified, for a minute that was a million centuries, outside time.

For if, later, after breaking down the door, they found, near the wall, a living corpse devoid of thought, an inert being devoid of will, it was because he had had his hallucination: in that moment, standing, motionless, his gaze in the profound void of space, suddenly, he saw, he saw with his eyes, before him, present, real, without error, without illusion, he actually saw something, distinctly, clearly, certainly, a shadow, a phantom, a spirit devoid of form but sensible, devoid of color but apparent, an upright specter that was gazing at him.

THE SUCCUBUS

by Jules Bois

I

WHEN Nahema felt the approach of death, she had the calm smile that irritated me so much, the smile that she wore on her lips during her days of health when she had accomplished some cruel sacrifice. This time, I did not have the strength to be angry; in supreme moments an imperious fluid spreads out to appease the sensibility of the nerves when the soul is profoundly troubled. I did not become angry, even though that smile entered me like a sharp point. Oh, I divined that she felt happy because she sensed that she was dying . . .

I approached, my hands haggard and my speech unsteady, trying to belie what was my intimate conviction:

"Tell me, don't you feel worse? This beautiful day must have put a warm radiance in your heart; and then, you wouldn't want to quit me like this . . . If you want to, I know that you can avoid dying."

And Nahema said: "Don't worry; I'll never leave you, but I am going to die . . . Don't call anyone; I don't want anyone around me. You alone will see my soul flee."

I looked at her eyes then, and I received a shock in the epigastrum on seeing them so full of amour—of a superhuman amour.

Within them there was the glimmer of a distant hostelry that one divines on the highway beyond the mist and the darkness. Her pupils were appealing to me like voices, caressing me like hands; they drew me like phantom arms toward a beyond that I sensed to be more terrifying than death.

She stammered, again: "I can die, but I'll never leave you."

Then, slowly, heavily, like an iron curtain falling on a stage henceforth and forever empty, her little eyelids folded, no longer leaving any but a narrow gap still open between the lashes, as if death had taken pity and suspended the irreparable for an instant.

She had just died.

II

Days and months have passed, but I have not been able to forget her eyes; the sound of her speech remains clear to me, slow and profound, like something abnormal and yet truthful, with the obstinacy of a prophecy. Now, I flee from darkness; it seems to me that after dusk, when I am still in my study, arms folded, without a lamp, in the numbing quietude of the rising night, it seems to me that those eyes, those eyes that death could not close completely, are suddenly going to open before me like the doors of a furnace and that the last words that expired on her lips, the words that I repeat sadly, words that only my lips pronounce, are suddenly about to be exteriorized around me, and that I am going to hear an unknown throat pronounce: "I can die, but I'll never leave you."

A few days ago, I wanted to extract myself from the funereal voluptuousness of my torpor; ungraspable bonds enchained me, so to speak, to my armchair; and when I finally stood up in a start of revolt, it seemed to me that a hand—or, rather, the translucent form of a hand—tried to retain me, to make me ashamed of my fear.

I went out, my breast breathless.

In the street, the amorous prowlers were whispering.

They crept forward, with seductive inclinations of the head, phrases of soft tenderness, and their gestures produced the effect on my excited sensibility of an electric shock. Dishabituated to embraces, my flesh was anguished by the contact of that offered flesh; I trembled slightly, overtaken by that gross intoxication, as if I had drunk some horrible alcohol on the zinc.

One of them was persistent.

She had large, soft eyes, stupid and magnetic. She took me by the arm and, I don't know how, lulled by the banal chant of her promises of pleasure, I allowed myself to be drawn, without responding, along a corridor of bitter odors. In the chamber illuminated by the redness of an inflamed grille, I got undressed while her hands palpated my pockets. My brain was vacillating in my skull; the walls of the chamber drew closer and drew away as if for a fantastic quadrille, and then I fell upon her with hungry lips . . . eventually, everything darkened. It seemed to me that I was about to faint.

When I came round it was late. A heavy shame rose from that weary and blue-tinted cleavage. She was asleep, surprised by that unhealthy warmth, while a candle was melting on a little table beside the bed.

I was exhausted, but the sleep that I now desired fled me in the fever of my profaned memories, in the disgust of my slaked desires. And of my remorse a fear was born, small at first: the fear of the dead woman I had betrayed in those opportunistic sheets with an unknown woman. I wanted to leave, but my legs disobeyed me; a cowardice also prevented me from confronting the cold, solitary street. But my fear had increased of a slight breath on my forehead, as if of a mouth very close to me, which almost spoke but dared not, touching me with an unexpressed, silent reproach. An insupportable haunting! I had raised myself up on my elbow, trying to escape, when my companion raised her head and opened her eyes—the eyes of a somnambulist for whom the invisible had become real, the pupils dilated by horror, her fingers splayed to repel a threat—and she gasped, in muted phrases:

"Oh, the eyes, the eyes! But I haven't done anything to you, Madame; it isn't my fault . . . Pity! Oh, she's too close, there . . ." Her index finger designated the empty air above my head. "She's above you, there! She's malevolent! Oh, defend me, she wants to do me harm . . . and you too. She says that she'll never leave you . . . She wants to kill you."

Then a stifled scream; her head fell back on the pillow, her body shivered, gradually calmed down, and normal sleep, interrupted by that nightmare, resumed, calm and crushing, similar to oblivion and death.

When she awoke in the morning she did not know what to respond to my anxious questions. Her large soft eyes of a passive beast stared at me, stupid and magnetic. She had forgotten everything.

But I understood the wrath of the dead woman, who was still alive there, imperiously, at my side!

III

I have the certainty now that She will no longer quit me, the certainty that She exists.

I have seen her . . .

On the first evenings, it was her eyes that appeared to me when I was about to fall asleep with the lamp extinct, like bright shadows against an orange background, which one might have thought the distant light of a setting sun. Her eyes have a beauty now superior to that of before; her suffering eyes speak to me like a mouth, but it is not words that they proffer, it is thoughts, thoughts that penetrate me through the epigastrum like a spear of pale light. I'm sure then of not being asleep, but I'm immobilized by those eyes; they're placed rather high, forcing me to stare at them, and their power thus subjugates me more; in spite of myself, I remember then the procedures of magnetizers, who oblige their subjects to place themselves lower than them in order to dominate them by means of their gaze . . .

Every morning I wake up exhausted, as if a vampire had drunk from my veins during the night.

Now her visage is becoming more and more precise. Further doubt would be madness. Her face, a bright shadow, is stamped on the distance of a horizon of orange light. And her body, her body, that feast of my senses, her body that I knew as a mother knows her son, as my caresses once ran over and searched it, her fluid body, every closer to me, intoxicated my immobile pupils with its reality of the beyond, more tempting than all previous realities.

I have seen her; she speaks to me . . .

What I hear—always via the epigastrum, my epigastrum pierced by that spear of pale light—I could neither say nor write, so mysterious is its rhythm, so ineffable is the sensation! More and more, she holds me, conquers me, penetrates me, but every morning, I wake up, bleak and crushed, as if an abominable orgy had ravaged my nerves, my pale gaze as empty as that of a moribund. And I remember vaguely these words, which I do not understand:

"I am *avid* for you," she tells me.

IV

Yesterday, she embraced me!

My lips of flesh were creased beneath the devouring weight of her translucent lips. I suffered the most horrible joy. That phantom body slowly leaned over mine, brushed it with her electric epidermis . . . and that kiss, that kiss above all, in which I felt the saliva of death, is the supreme delirium. I'm scared . . . it seems that her eyes want to tear me away from the earth, that her lips want to inhale my soul . . . My God! My God! If that's true, if I'm going to die . . . I don't want such kisses . . . I'm scared . . . !

And other words surface in my memory, words that She pronounced after that terrible caress:

"I want you entirely . . . I alone shall possess you; I shall destroy your body," she told me.

V

When I drag myself from this bed, where I am agonizing alone, when I drag myself into the street, I am so pale, so fleshless, that people turn away when I pass by, and women scream . . . they believe that they have seen a ghost.

All life horrifies me now that I see Her day and night; She eclipses the sunlight from me and the colors of things. The phantom has devoured me, I no longer have any more than a spark of life; but I'm strong, I'm no longer afraid; I've understood . . . I'm consoled!

Last night, she said to me: "I'll come again tonight, but for the last time. And I'll be your wife, as in the time when I was alive. There will no longer be the kisses of lips, there will be the supreme embrace, possession; there will also be death . . ."

Yes, yes, that's it. Our spasm will break entirely this torn prison where I am etiolating . . . Am I afraid? No, I'm no longer afraid . . . the last embrace will set me free . . . We'll rediscover one another out there, in the realm of souls, as if after a long separation . . . Ah! Night's falling . . . finally! It's death . . .

"Nahema!"

REDIVIVA

by Gilbert-Augustin Thierry

EVA

I

MAY 185*

My friend, Doctor Marcus, emerged from the room where Eva was sleeping; I followed him. Slowly, he went down the staircase of the château, and went silently to lean on the balusters of the terrace.

Dusk was falling. Below us, at the bottom of the hill, the town of Vauvilliers, with its gray houses and its red roofs, appeared flamboyant in the blaze of the setting sun; in front of us, the hills of Faucilles, black with woods, licked the plain with their immeasurable shadow; and further away, over the "balloons" of Alsace, in the pearly vapors, the first stars were already showing, pale and seemingly fearful. A few more moments, and one of the earth's days would sink into the past of worlds.

I broke the silence first.

"Well, Marcus, what do you think of the unfortunate Eva?"

He turned round and looked me straight in the face. "Be happy, Monsieur de Tréan. Eva will not see tomorrow's dawn shine."

Marcus was no longer addressing me familiarly; his face was hard and his lips were tremulous with anger. He seized my arm, and said, in a dull voice: "Be happy; Eva will die tonight. The death-throes have commenced. Oh, that's agreeable news, isn't it true, Monsieur? Tomorrow, your liberty will finally be recovered, and all the life of facile pleasures will be reborn; tomorrow, it's gambling and prostitutes! With what embraces the gallant girls will salute your return, Monsieur debaucher of honest women!"

Insensible, but shrugging my shoulders slightly, I let the flood of unseemly and words and banal moralities erupt.

Marcus released my arm and became solemn. "Do you know, Jean, that blood, from now on, will cry out against you . . . Eva's husband is dead."

"What do you mean, dead?" I said, rolling a cigarette.

"He has killed himself. Read."

Marcus took a newspaper from his pocket and held it out to me. In the Parisian news I perceived an item ringed in red pencil, and I read:

> *Very sad news: we have just learned of the death of Monsieur Yves Mériadec. That premature end was due, it seems, to a suicide. The unfortunate was found yesterday morning lying in his bedroom, lifeless. He had plunged a dagger into his throat. Family chagrin had motivated that fatal determination. A letter that the dead man was holding between his fingers left no doubt in that regard.*
>
> *It is well-known that Yves Mériadec had acquired a certain public notoriety by virtue of his studies in theurgy and spiritism. He was one of the great pontiffs of the Occult. Another poor man whom the omnipotence of the Spirits has not been able to preserve from the petty accidents of humanity!*

"Yes, poor man," I said, tranquilly, returning the newspaper to Doctor Marcus.

Now, the latter went on, "would you like to know his last adieu and his supreme thought? Listen!" He opened his portfolio, took out a piece of paper, and read me these simple words: "*Eva, I forgive you.*"

In spite of myself, I lowered my head, and a profound silence fell between us.

Marcus spoke again: "The poor woman! To have deserted her duties for love of a man who is incapable of love!"

I tried to protest, but he went on: "Shut up! You never loved that woman, you who, knowing that she was doomed, only called me in order to confront me with her cadaver. It's all over now. There's nothing I can do but go. Adieu!"

He went down the steps of the perron without me making a gesture to retain him. However, when he reached the last step, the doctor turned round. Was it an effect of the dusk, was it an illusion of my disturbed mind? It seemed to me that his tall stature had increased further. The sun's last rays enveloped him like an aureole, and his long hair and black beard appeared to emit strange reflections.

Marcus extended his arm toward me, and said: "Mériadec, my venerated master, was able to forgive, but the One who hates Evil, because he appeals to the God, does not forgive thus! Woe betide the two of you, then! Sooner or later it will be necessary for you to expiate, in the Inferno of down here—and perhaps expiate together . . ."

He left. For a few moments, I saw him going down the winding path that leads to Vauvilliers. Night had fallen, but I could perceive Marcus distinctly in the shadows. He was walking at a feverish pace, stopping, turning round to look behind, and resuming his course. Finally, he disappeared.

The wind from the Vosges had risen, putting shivers into the foliage of the old trees in the park. And again, traversing the murmur of the great chestnut trees, I thought I heard these bizarre words: "Woe betide you, then! Sooner or later, it will be necessary for you to expiate . . . perhaps for both of you to expiate together . . ."

"Had Marcus told the truth? Free—I was free! So, death was bringing the rupture so much desired; it was about to break the chain that weighed more heavily every day upon my twenty-three years . . .

Free . . . ! But also, what a vulgar and stupid adventure! To abduct a woman from her husband, publicly! And who? A petty bourgeoise, the wife of a man almost ridiculous. To impose a burden on myself, almost a duty, and to know one's own heart so poorly as to call a simple caprice passion! Oh, how they laughed in society at my sad escapade! What epigrams at my club! What bursts of laughter at the Grand Seize and the Moulin Rouge! Little Vitray had laughed at my simplicity; even Raoul d'Amance, the dearest of my friends, had shrugged his shoulders, and in her old town house in the Rue de Varenne, how my mother had wept over my sin!

Free . . . !

Eva was dying. For twelve hours, a frightful torpor had enchained her limbs, annihilated her thought.

The night had become dense in the bedroom. I lit a candle and approached the bed on which the young woman was lying. For a long time I gazed at her in the tremulous candle-light. I gazed at her long blonde hair spread over the pillow, the motionless large blue eyes, the convulsively clenched lips and the meager cheeks, which two creases hollowed out at the corners of the mouth. The discolored face had taken on an ivory tint, but two tiny pink patches stood out against the mat whiteness of the face above each cheekbone.

Oh, how familiar that sign was to me, where consumption had engraved its imprint. How many times in the hours when I thought I was in love, had my lips posed upon it for a long time, and how many times, too, shivering under that caress had Eva said to me with a heart-rending smile: "Love me well, Jean, for you have so few days to love me . . ."

And I gazed at her, pensively.

I placed the candle on a table near the bed, and, taking a chair, I sat down. On that table there were a few volumes, bizarre books with truly strange titles: Porphyry's *Theurgy*; Iamblichus' *Egyptian Mysteries*; a French translation of the Bardic triads, with commentaries; Swedenborg's *Arcana of Heaven*; and the famous work by Jean Reynaud, *Terre et ciel*. I riffled through them by turns and pushed them away one by one. I took possession of one last volume, but I shivered suddenly, unable to repress a start of surprise.

It was a pamphlet of a hundred pages, the fatigue and wear of which attested that Eva had read it and meditated upon it many times. The cover bore a single word: *Redemption*, and the book's author was Yves Mériadec . . .

Yves Mériadec, Eva's husband, yesterday's suicide!

I opened the book at random, and I read:

> *And I, too, want to cry to you, O Death: "Where, then, is your victory?" Yes, to die is to be reborn, and to be reborn, to expiate.*
>
> *O law of Redemption by the necessity of reincarnation and the torments of the Inferno of life—implacable and yet merciful law! You are the supreme reason or the moral progress accomplished by humanity. Thanks to you, the fraternity of all men, brethren in death, will one day reign over his poor*

earth. No more exploitation of poverty, no more monstrous egotism of opulence! Henceforth, the evil rich man will tremble to refuse the crumbs of his table to Lazarus the pauper, since he will know that the dung-heap of Lazarus awaits him in his turn. Thanks to you, again, no more slaughter by war, no more extermination of men by men! Dare, then, Napoléon, to launch people against the mouths of cannons, if you, an obscure soldier, must fall one day under the bullets and you too are to utter the great cry of thirst on the evening of the battle. Never has a more terrible meaning been given to the words: "Woe betide you who laugh, for you will weep!"

At that point the sick woman had underlined a passage and written a few words in pencil in the margin. The book continued, in its mysterious and tormented style:

Amour, life of worlds, you whom the great Being created to become the morality of all beings; you who put happiness into duty and sensual pleasure even into suffering, Amour, who makes the wife, Amour who makes the mother, woe betide those who abuse you!

"Jean," a voice suddenly murmured in my ear, "why have you never loved me?"

I sat up with a start. Eva's hand had settled on my shoulder, and her breath was burning my cheek.

She extended her finger toward the pamphlet. "He loved me so much . . . the man we've betrayed, the man we've killed!"

A tremor agitated her body; she went on, her breathing labored: "Yves Mériadec is dead, Jean, we have killed him. For long hours I've just seen him, there . . . . . . there, beside my bed!

46

He had his eyes fixed on mine; he was very pale, very bloody, and had a hideous wound in his throat. He looked at me for a long time without addressing a single word to me; then, twice, he extended his hand toward my neck. Finally, he disappeared. Jean, he ordered me to follow him. He and I will be summoned to judgment. Oh, I'm afraid! To what punishment of the Inferno of life will I be condemned? Yes, I'm afraid!"

A smile, nevertheless, parted her lips. "And yet, I don't repent, I don't regret anything . . . I've loved!"

She approached her face to mine, and, lowering her voice, spoke so quietly, so quietly that I could not hear . . . and yet, yes, I affirm it, I understood . . ."

"Jean, a little more time, and we'll see one another again, doubtless to expiate together and then to love without remorse in the life of space . . ."

Eva placed her hand on my shoulder again. Under that feeble pressure, as if under a crushing burden, I fell to my knees.

"Listen," she said to me, "and remember . . . Wherever on earth you will encounter me, and in whatever human form my soul is clad, this is the sign by which you will recognize me!"

Very slowly, her hand moved over my forehead, my eyes and my lips . . . and suddenly, I felt an atrocious pain that gripped my temples and wrung my heart. I uttered a cry, and she started to laugh.

"Remember!" she said, again.

At that moment, her head slumped. I heard a long sigh; her hand released me, and fell back, rigid. I got up, threw myself upon her and wrapped my arms around her. Her pulse was no longer beating; even the death-rattle had ceased; her face was as white as a shroud, and upon that whiteness, the two roseate patches appeared more visibly . . .

And for two days and two nights I called to her, striving to reanimate her with my kisses, howling in pain, but not weeping.

I was in love . . . I was in love . . .

Several times, it seemed to me that my domestics were trying to tear me away from Eva's room; I struggled; I clung to her bed, to her body . . .

I was in love; yes, I was in love . . .

When, on the morning of the third day, the nascent dawn let its first light filter into the room. I looked, and saw this:

Eva, still motionless; her eyes were vitreous; her swollen face had livid tones, and the open mouth designed a frightful rictus . . .

Then, uttering a scream of fear, I fainted.

II

June 185*

For seven days they thought that I was in danger of death; for seven days my mother, having hastened to my bedside, kept anxious vigil, and the physicians made dubious gestures.

And for seven days, my Eva, you remained with me constantly; for seven days, I spoke to you, I heard you. Enlaced together, we traversed space! Oh, the strange sensation of coolness when you placed your cold hand on my burning brow! What sensual pleasure throughout my being when you placed your lips on mine. My Eva!

But on the eighth day, you didn't return, and when I opened my eyes and looked around in the morning, I heard a voice saying: "He's saved" and I perceived my mother, who was smiling through her tears.

Now they affirm that I am cured; my mother is no longer weeping; the physician has returned to Paris, and when he left, he said: "I no longer have any fear for his reason."

My reason!

Yesterday, beloved, for the first time in a long time, your name emerged from my mouth. I took my mother's hand, and, interrogating her with my gaze, I only said a single word: "Eva?"

My mother went very pale, got up and left my room without responding. But Vincent, my old servant, has told me everything. Your remains, alas, are far from here. You repose among your family, out there in the little cemetery of Baden, in the region of Auray. So far away, and yet so close! It's there that I must go, beloved . . .

I'm going there . . .

✻

July 185*

I have seen the narrow Breton cemetery where your remains lie, my Eva, out here on the shores of Morbihan, in the shadow of old oaks. They have not even engraved your name on their tomb. For long hours, embracing your sepulchral stone, I have murmured my oaths of amour to you and lent my ear to listen to yours. But only the distant rumor of the ebb-tide and the great sob of the fir trees tormented by the wind responded to my voice.

Not a word from the beloved!

And yet, this time, again, I haven't wept. Why, then, do my eyes seem to be forever empty of tears?

✻

July 185*

No, I can't tear myself away from this place, in which her body resides and her spirit doubtless ought to haunt. Everywhere it might be granted to me to glimpse the dear soul, I go, pushed by my desire. Oh, if, while passing close to me, she only deigned to brush my face!

Often, a boat transports me to one of the isles of Morbihan, which seem consecrated to eternal mourning, where all the women are clad in black, all weeping for some father, son or husband. There, I sit down on a reef and, silent and motionless, shivering at the slightest sound, I plunge into my hope.

Many times also, I climb the tumulus of Saint Michel, the sepulchral mountain that covers the plain of Carnac with its shadow. At my feet the fantastic menhirs extend and stretch, gray on the yellow heath, which seem to have sprung forth from the earth . . . emblems of life engendered by death. Before my eyes, the moving blue of the ocean extends as far as the immobile azure of the sky; and in the distance, sinking into the mist, the tongue of land fringed by the foam of the waves that is the sinister peninsula of Quiberon.

On fine summer evenings, when the setting sun sets the horizon ablaze and makes the waves catch fire, one sees a pale and dubious glimmer appear in the vapors floating over the sea: the little lighthouse that signals the reefs of Port Aliguen. Its light is tremulous and timid, as if ashamed of showing itself in the radiance of the day's end. Gradually, however, the crimson disk of the sun sinks into the ocean, diminishes and disappears . . . dusk blurs everything, and the shadow, gray and then black, envelops it all. The gleam of the lighthouse seems to increase then; its light grows, and soon illuminates the night.

It is thus, beloved, that as your image darkens in the night of my memory, amour grows in my heart and hope shines there.

Yes, I hope and I have faith. I wanted to know the mysterious religion in which you believed. Now, I know and I have understood. I have understood your words of terror when you said: "What chastisement does the hell of life reserve for us?" And I have understood the cry of joy that emerged from your lips: "Jean, we shall find one another again."

O my Eva, I am waiting.

✳

August 185*

Nothing, still nothing. I'm despairing!

✳

August 185*

Was that you, my Eva? No, I can't believe it.

Yesterday, the boatmen transported me to the narrow islet of Gavr'innis. I was sitting on the summit of the enormous tumulus whose green roof shelters the long-inviolate sleep of the Brenns with jade necklaces. The heat was stifling. In the cloudless azure of the sky, the sun darted rays that dazzled as the sea reflected them. No breath of air traversed space. A lugger, trapped by the calm, was reposing on its anchors, entirely asleep. No human sound reached me; only the great rumor of the currents silvered by foam troubled the frightful silence. I was waiting; and always, still, that same uncontented desire for tears . . .

I felt my head curbing under the weight of the day . . . and suddenly, in my ear, feeble but distinct, the chimes of a bell resounded, ringing in some distant church. But what were they ringing? Sometimes, the bell wept a death-knell, slowly. And sometimes it beat with rapid and urgent strokes, as for a baptism.

At that moment, seeming to respond to that appeal, a bright cloud rose into the air. Was it a cloud? No, for as it drew closer, I distinguished a human form clearly. It had all the characteristics that doctors in Occult Science have described many a time: the second envelope of the soul, visible but impalpable, immaterial matter . . .

51

Oh, I wasn't asleep, since I wanted to weep . . .

It wasn't you, Eva. The woman was blonde, like you, she had blue eyes, like you, but her features weren't yours; and yet, on the whiteness of her cheek, I could perceive very clearly the two roseate patches, the memory of which will never be effaced from my memory. She stood before me, silently, and her harsh gaze, her eyes charged with hatred, chilled me with terror.

Effortfully, my numb tongue stammered a name: "Eva!"

The woman started to laugh—yes, it was the same laughter that I thought I heard on my beloved's death-bed. She extended her hand toward me—and then it seemed to me that I was suffocating. An unknown force gripped me by the throat and squeezed violently. I wanted to cry out, but in vain, and I fell to the ground.

When I opened my eyes again, I was in the bedroom of my inn at Auray, and a physician was standing at my bedside.

"Your cares are superfluous, my dear doctor; the malady from which I'm suffering is not one of those that human science can cure."

October 185*

An appeasement has taken placed in my thoughts. My friend Raoul d'Amance has come to find me and I have allowed myself to be taken away like a child. Now, I have resumed my old life. We all laugh together at my dementia—everyone except my mother. Yes, I was mad, and what is worse, ridiculous . . .

And yet. I was so happy in my madness!

MADELEINE

I

That day, 25 June 187*, our dinner at the cabaret of the Moulin Rouge had been very cheerful.

The evening was magnificent. The concert of the Champs-Élysées sent us the confused rumor of its strollers, drowned out at intervals by the splendid sound of brass instruments. At dessert, Raoul d'Amance got up filled the glass of the joyful Vitray and mine, and then made a solemn gesture.

"Messieurs, I propose a toast. I drink to the forty-five years accomplished today by our friend Jean de Tréan!"

He put down his champagne glass, and, becoming almost serious, he went on: Forty-five years since this morning, and you're the youngest of the three of us!" He sat down again. "Bah! it's unnecessary that it afflicts you. Forty-five years, you see, Jean, is the fine age, the age when a man is finally able to love."

"Yes," I replied, in a melancholy tone, "doubtless because it's the age when one no longer wants to love."

Vitray put on a slightly piqued expression, and darting a glance at the mirror, said: "You're not speaking for us, I suppose . . . even less for you, tenebrous beau, for whom all the women are crazy! Sell me the secret of our elixir of youth, Jean; you scarcely seem twenty, my dear! Only yesterday, in the foyer of the Bouffes, Violette said, talking about you: "Tréan is an amour." Lauzun, go!"

He looked at himself in the mirror again, while humming a popular tune, and added: "My dear Jean, I know a woman who, like so many others, is very smitten with you."

"With me?"

"Yes, with you, my dear, and an ingénue in the theater, as well. Come on, you must have noticed her? When you're in the audience, she only performs for you; when she laughs, it's for you alone that she shows her teeth; when she sings, it's for you alone that she spins out her trills. You can't guess? Léa . . . little Léa de Coucy."

"Who is Léa de Coucy?" I asked, indifferently.

"Oh, my dear, don't show so much distaste. Léa is a very pretty woman, even though, according to Violette, she lacks breasts and puts in fake pads . . . and then, a true artiste, although she drags out the high notes too much and stammers when she talks. First honorable mention at the Conservatoire de Toulouse. And with that, a good family, Her father was a professor at the lycée in Agen—professor of gymnastics, Forgivable! It's agreed, then—I'll introduce you!"

I shook my head and, half-joking and half-serious said: "Pointless."

"Why?" retorted Vitray. "Léa's very nice . . . a girl who would do you honor, and . . ."

"Don't persist," Raoul interrupted, squeezing his arm slightly. "Jean's been smitten with someone else for a long time."

"Bah! He should have said. With whom?"

Raoul took my hand. "Poor fellow! He's in love with a phantom . . . a dead woman."

I sensed myself going pale. Twice I filled my glass to the brim, and twice I emptied it in a single draught. Then, launching a burst of laughter: "How appropriate, Raoul, for my birthday, to remind me that I have been mad . . . fit to be tied." After a slight pause I continued: "Yes, I loved a dead woman, a phantom, as our friend Monsieur d'Amance has just said. But, dead or alive, women are all the same: ingrate, forgetful of their promises, perjurers of their oaths. In twenty-two years, Madame the Corpse has not deigned to honor me with a single visit. So, it's agreed; tomorrow you can introduce me to Léa de Courcy."

But Vitray had become grave. "No," he said. "You talk about your dead woman, my dear, with your lips taut and your eyes shiny, as a furious and desperate lover would. Personally, I don't know why, when one has loved a woman, one shouldn't want to see her again … even if she's dead … especially today, when it's so easy to see the dead again!"

A great silence fell.

"Yes," Vitray continued, "I, who am speaking to you, Messieurs, chatted with a woman a week ago, who has been asleep for more than ten years, far away from here, beyond the sea, in a cemetery in America. Oh, don't laugh like that, Raoul, you irritate me with your skeptical airs. I tell you that it was her. It was her hair, her eyes, her mouth. She repeated a secret known to me alone. I'm still sick with fear."

For the fourth time I emptied my glass, and, replacing it noisily on the table, I cried: "Infamous conjuring tricks!"

Vitray stood up, and said, in a dry tone: "Monsieur de Tréan ought to know that I scarcely allow myself to be tricked. Anyway, go to Passy, and at 25 Rue de Ranelagh, ask to see Doctor Allan."

I made no reply.

In the distance a clock chimed ten.

"Ten o'clock!" exclaimed Raoul. "Let's go to the Circus. It's Saturday, when high society goes. Are you coming, Tréan?"

"No thank you, your dinner and stories have muddled my brain too much. I need to sleep; I'm going home."

We quit the Moulin Rouge and found ourselves in the Avenue d'Antin, already almost deserted.

"Goodnight, Monsieur de Tréan," said Vitray. "Above all, no bad dreams!"

And they both drew away in the direction of the Circus.

Left alone on the sidewalk, I headed for the Pont des Invalides, desirous of returning home; but my head was heavy and my stride laborious. I was definitely a little drunk.

An empty cab was just passing. I climbed into it.

"Where is it necessary to take Monsieur?"

Then, in a low voice, as if strangled by emotion, I said: "To Passy, 25 Rue de Ranelagh."

II

It was a house of elegant appearance, an odorous cottage, which laburnum and wisteria coated with their variegated draperies. A small garden planted with rose-bushes and lilacs extended before the façade. The entire abode suggested a reposed, perhaps happy life.

In spite of the advanced nocturnal hour, the gate was open and the windows of the house were brightly lit, scintillating in the shadow. Motionless on the sidewalk of the street, I dared not approach; a sentiment of shame held me back. What would I say to Doctor Allan? How could I explain my visit? I wanted to run after my cab, which was drawing away . . . but no; my feet remained nailed to the ground, and the vehicle disappeared into the night. Oh, how violently my heart was beating! What feverish sounds the blood was making in my ears!

For twenty-two years you have wanted to know, Jean; are you going to know, finally?

At an unsteady pace, I traversed the garden and climbed a perron. Like the gate, the entrance door was open. I went into the vestibule. No one . . .

For the second time, shame seized me, but less forcefully. Not daring to call out, I looked around; everything seemed strange to me.

On the walls of the antechamber I perceived, suspended in large numbers, drawings of human figures in black or blood-red, of a truly fantastic aspect. Whether deliberately or by virtue of the inexperience of the artists, the features, confusedly traced and scarcely visible, seemed to be lost in a diaphanous fog; but more bizarre still were the captions inscribed below the portraits:

Apparition of 1 January 187*: Pierre (still refuses to submit to expiation.)

Apparition of 2 November 187*: Phryné (will submit to her redemption.)

In the midst of those drawings, on the white wall, the following lines stood out in red letters: *By virtue of three things humans fall back under the necessity of Adred (the Inferno of Life): the absence of effort toward knowledge; scorn of the good and the practice of evil. Triad XXV.*[1]

While observing, I listened.

The sound of voices reached me from a neighboring room. A man was pronouncing words, interrupted at certain moments by murmurs of approval. At times, too, a plaintive melody interrupted the orator's speech or accompanied it mutedly.

Weary of waiting, and making my decision, I tapped my cane on the floor-tiles and called out. A door-curtain was raised and a black-clad domestic came toward me.

"Doctor Allan?" I asked.

The domestic examined me suspiciously for a few seconds. "Monsieur," he said, "is doubtless one of the new adherents invited this evening?"

I nodded my head slightly.

"Well, hurry up," he aid. "The mystery has commenced," And he stood aside to let me pass.

I went in.

In a room of vast dimensions, abut thirty people were sitting in chairs arranged in rows. At the back of the room a rostrum had been set up at which a man was standing, speaking while making solemn gestures. He was a tall, aged man with a strange face. Long white hair fell over his shoulders; a bushy beard

---

1 The quotation is from the "Bardic Triads" of Iolo Morganwg (the Welsh antiquarian Edward Williams, 1747-1826), who is now believed to have authored the mystical works that he passed off as translations from Medieval Welsh.

framed his face, and dark eyes glinted beneath thick eyebrows. The man was not unknown to me.

Sitting by his side and almost at his feet, I perceived a young woman of about twenty. Oh, that one, yes, I had already encountered on the path of my life. But where? Where had I seen that blonde hair, that thin and pale face, those steel-blue eyes? Where? Her head raised toward the old man, she was contemplating him with an amorous admiration, and seemed to be in ecstasy under the charm of his speech.

A place was free in the last row of chairs; I sat down there.

I looked at the woman.

Almost immediately, she turned her head slowly, apparently looking for someone in the audience, and her eyes met mine . . . but with a visible effort, she closed her eyelids and raised her face again toward the man with the white hair.

One of my neighbors murmured: "An unfortunate mystery. What's wrong with Allan this evening? He isn't as brilliant an orator as usual."

Doctor Allan was evidently troubled. However, with his left hand applied to his heart and the right extended toward the assembly, he continued his speech.

"Yes," he said, "death is only a vain word, a syllable devoid of meaning. All of us here present have already experienced successive incarnations, and the Inferno down here will seize us again until our complete redemption. O Death, you are but a renewal of life; O tomb, you are but a cradle. And I, taking inspiration from Saint Paul, want to issue my challenge to you, as my master Yves Mériadec once did, and cry: 'Sepulcher, where is your victory?'"

The name of Yves Mériadec, suddenly thrown into my memory, caused me to shudder. Instantly, the young woman felt a similar commotion; then, turning her head toward me violently, she riveted her gaze to mine again. Now her eyes were staring at me obstinately. But Allan had interrupted himself abruptly. He tried to resume his improvisation but he could only stammer. Finally, his brow inundated with sweat, he was obliged to sit down.

An orchestra composed of a piano and harps started to play a bizarrely modulated harmony.

"The music of a composer who no longer belongs to our earth," my neighbor said to me, again.

In the meantime, Allan, very pale, was examining the young woman fearfully, but she, insensible to everything, still kept her eyes fixed on mine.

Finally, shaking off the torpor of his thought, Allan got to his feet again, and spoke emphatically to invisible beings: "Innumerable spirits of the dead," he cried, "you who surround us, among whom we walk, whom we respire, in whom we live, listen with benevolence to the prayer of your servant! Let one of you deign, for a moment, to unite yourself with the flesh of this living being and become incarnate in her!"

He designated the blonde-haired young woman.

"But no!" he said, interrupting himself. "Such prodigies have been accomplished many times. I sense that the moment has come to attempt something more. Allow, for a moment, the body of this incarnate, this living being of today, to resume its anterior form! For a long time, I have been trying to realize that impossible dream. But a voice has resounded within me, which has said to me: 'Dare!' I want the blind to see! Yes, I want it," he added, forcefully, "Even if my heart must break! Before being a man, I am a priest!"

On hearing those jerky, incoherent words, the assembly was shaken by a long frisson. But Allan, dominating the rumor with a gesture and abruptly extending his finger toward me, he cried: "Monsieur, you whom no one here knows and who have slipped into the temple like a thief in the night, stand up!"

As if struck by an electric shock, I stood up; the woman also stood up.

"Approach!" the doctor ordered.

I marched toward the stage; but at each of my forward steps, the woman took a step back, and, still looking at me, she went to place herself against the wall.

"Of what did you come here in search?" Allan asked me, harshly.

And I replied: "I came in order to know."

He started to laugh, an angry laughter. "So be it! You shall know!"

Paper and a pencil had been placed on the rostrum in advance.

"Write a name," Allan said to me. "Yes, the name that is the lust, that is the torture, of your heart."

I traced a single word: "Eva."

"Now," commanded the doctor, addressing the young woman, "it's me that it's necessary to obey. Resume your place!"

And with his finger, he pointed to the armchair.

The woman did not budge, still looking at me.

"Well, so be it, Monsieur," said Allan. "You're the stronger—order! You doubtless don't know it, but God has made you a redoubtable medium."

Then, at the mute injunction of my thought, the woman marched toward me. For a moment, she beat the air with her arms, as if she wanted to drive me away, but, her strength exhausted, she sat down heavily in the armchair.

I placed the piece of paper on which Eva's name was written on the woman's breast, and I waited, quaking.

Immediately, an amazing phenomenon was produced. A livid pallor invaded her face; her features contracted and her cheeks, hollowing out, traced two profound pleats around her mouth; an oppressed respiration emerged from her parted lips, succeeded by a cough—the cough with the bloody mucus that precedes death. Finally, the woman uttered a great sigh, and her head fell backwards.

"She is dead!" cried Doctor Allan. "Her heart has ceased beating. Is there a physician here who can certify the fact?"

A member of the audience climbed on to the stage, examined the subject, and declared that the heart had, in fact, ceased beating.

Soon, however, it seemed to me that life entered into the cadaver again. The cheeks colored slightly; a respiration, weak at first, and then regular, lifted the dead woman's bosom; the dead woman came back to life. And then—was it a hallucination of my senses?—oh, then . . . yes, I saw it: her face was transfigured!

Suddenly, I recognized in the pale face the same pink sign on which I had placed my lips twenty-two years before. Eva! Eva herself was before me!

I fell to my knees.

But the dead woman straightened up slowly; she extended her arms toward me, and gently ran her fingers over my forehead, over my eyes and over my mouth.

A very faint voice murmured in my ear: "Jean, it's me . . . it's the beloved."

I uttered a cry of terror and stood up. Allan placed his hand on my shoulder, and said, in a dry tone: "Are you satisfied, Monsieur de Tréan?"

And I, my eyes rendered haggard by fear, stammered: "Marcus!"

III

Oh, what a night, frightful and delectable, full of voluptuous terrors . . .

Eva, finally rediscovered!

IV

The following morning, at ten o'clock, I rang Doctor Allan's doorbell. I was introduced immediately.

Marcus was alone in his study, surrounded by books, working. When I entered, he stood up and bowed slightly, but did not offer me his hand.

"Monsieur de Tréan," he said, "I expected your visit; you had to come."

I took a chair and sat down.

"Do you know, Monsieur," Marcus continued, "that you are a medium endowed with a formidable power? Yes, formidable. What brought you here, good or evil?"

I did not reply.

"Good, doubtless," he continued, after a brief silence. "Your intervention in our mysteries has already produced useful results. Several of yesterday's incredulous are believers today and henceforward."

He then started speaking to me about a small Spiritist church of which he was one of the priests. Fifteen years before, he had devoted himself entirely to his apostolate; he had quit the name of Marcus in order to take that of Allan, in honor of one of the prophets of the good news, Allan Kardec. Oh, they had suffered a great deal, masters and disciples, ministers and adherents. In Spain, the Catholic clergy had burned their books in public squares; in France the tribunals had thrown several of their pastors in prison. Every day, abominable mockery was heaped upon them; people sought to kill them with ridicule. And yet, their church was growing in strength. Allan estimated at several hundred thousand the followers distributed in Europe; they were even more numerous in America. Eminent men in letters or the sciences adhered to the doctrine: poets, novelists, playwrights, historians, philosophers, astronomers and mathematicians! But it was above all among the disinherited by fortune that the faithful were recruited.

"What other religion," Marcus exclaimed, enthusiastically, "can give a logical and yet consoling explanation of poverty and hunger? Christianity is impotent henceforth to moralize the masses, and the masses are abandoning it. O Nazarene, how did you dare to say: 'There will always be poor people among us'?"

While he was declaiming his sonorous phrases, I listened with a distracted ear. Time was passing. What, was *she* not going to come?"

The door opened. Shivering, I stood up. It was *her*.

She stopped, as if frightened by the sight of me, closed her eyes, placed her hand swiftly against her heart, and turned her head away.

"Oh, that man!" she stammered.

Marcus had approached, and said, designating me: "Madeleine, Monsieur de Tréan."

She seized his hands and bore them passionately to her lips, murmured a few words in a very low voice, and then ran outside.

"Do you know, Monsieur," said Marcus, when we were alone, "what my wife just said to me?"

His wife! *Her* ... married! *Her* ... Marcus's wife!

"Madeleine said to me: "Send that man away; he is bringing misfortune here."

I remained motionless, stupefied, and faint. Finally, mastering my emotion, I dragged myself to the door.

"I shall never come back here," I said, as I left.

And as I closed the gate of the house, Marcus, who had accompanied me that far, exclaimed, dolorously: "So it was for Evil, then!"

V

I July 187*

Why, then, had the physician affirmed, twenty-two years
ago: "I'll answer for his reason"? My reason! It seems to me, alas,
that it foundered a long time ago. And now, the poor madman
is turning into a credulous simpleton. What a farce! What a
master charlatan that Marcus is! Great pontiff Allan, and you,
Madame Madeleine, his worthy spouse, look elsewhere than in
the house of a Tréan for your dupes!

But Eva? I sensed myself gripped with shame, as well as self-
pity, and the sensate lines of the ancient poet returned to my
memory:

> *Love a shadow as a shadow, and of extinct ashes*
> *Extinguish the memory.*

10 July

This morning, Vitray erupted into my bedroom.

"Well, Jean, what's become of you? It's two weeks since anyone has seen you, my dear. The entire club is in mourning. Are
you ill? How pale you are! Fifteen years more on your head in a
fortnight! By the way, have you been to visit the miracle doctor
we talked about the other evening?"

I shrugged my shoulders.

"No?" he continued. "Skeptic! Personally, I have a more
cheerful excursion to propose to you. After dinner, I'll take you
to the Bouffes-Parisiens. Young Léa de Courcy is making her
debut, and believe me, it's a big event, as the members of the orchestra say. You have to come. The girl is absolutely mad about

you; you'd be ashamed of causing chagrin to her little heart. You'll see what a pretty muzzle she has when she's throwing her enticements into the stalls! An adorable foxy face! And the comic! How they laugh in the hall when he looks the ingénue up and down and cries: "That's immense!" Don't protest; the box is booked. Even the sage Raoul is in the party. Above all, don't forget the tea-rose in your buttonhole—your lady's colors! Until this evening, dear chap—I'll come and pick you up."

And Vitray went out, repeating: "Immense!"

✳

Same day

In truth, what do they have in their hearts, my friends? Personally, I can't live like them . . . no, I can't do it.

I want to flee France; I want to extend the distance between my memories and me. Out there, far away, I'll doubtless find a corner of the vast world that will render me repose, forgetfulness of myself.

I'll leave tomorrow.

VI

Naples

I have traversed peoples; cities have passed before my eyes. Always myself, alas! Italy, the land where nature lavishes such charming smiles on people, no ray of your sunlight has been able to descend into my heart.

Further away, further away!

Jerusalem

Jerusalem! O Jesus of Nazareth, you who, you who accord, my mother told me, the tear that purifies, the blessed tear, I have bowed my head over your sepulcher. Why, impotent God, have you not given me tears?

Further away, even further!

Calcutta

Finally, calm will enter my spirit! I have set foot on the old soil of India. This strange world pleases the monstrosities of my thought, and in this ossuary of so many civilizations, in this land of the dead, I hope to die myself.

What have I just learned? Among the letters that were waiting for me in Calcutta I have found one from my friend Vitray. He relates thousands of foolish trivia, but this is what I read:

The séances in the Rue de Ranlegah have ceased. It appears that Madeleine Allan is very ill.

Ill... Madeleine? Well, what does it matter to me?

A ship is leaving tomorrow for Marseille; I shall embark in an hour.

Oh, yes, I want to see her again! I shall see her again...

※

May 188*

Ah! I've seen her again!

VII

May 188*

Yes, I've seen her again. What irresistible power, then, has driven me toward the detested house, and what is that Madeleine making of me . . . Madeleine Allan?

The night was well advanced when I arrived on the Rue de Ranelagh, already in May, still warm, brightly illuminated by the moon. In that remote corner of Paris, all was solitude.

The Rue de Ranelagh, half-built, is bordered by empty plots enclosed by wooden fences. Opposite Allan's house I slipped through a gap in one of those fences. I found myself in an area full of long grass, with a few trees here and there. An old cedar, the debris of a park that had been parceled up, spread its roots over that abandoned garden. I went to lurk in its great shade, and then watched, with my eyes fixed on the house.

Why that absurd escapade, poor Jean? Why that self-degradation?

Everything in Allan's dwelling seemed to be asleep; only one window on the first floor allowed a faint light to pas through.

Ardently, I concentrated my sight and thought upon it.

Time went by. Three o'clock chimed on the distant clock of the church of Passy.

Suddenly, the window opened quietly and Madeleine appeared, clad in white, her hair scattered over her shoulders. I uttered a small cry and, emerging from the shadow that enveloped me, I contemplated her passionately.

She turned her head toward me, undoubtedly perceived me, smiled her same distraught smile and fixed her eyes on mine.

For a long time, we looked at one another thus in the silence of the night, by the light of the stars. And when dawn spread its nascent light over the horizon, Madeleine made an effort to extract herself from her ecstasy. She closed the window again and disappeared.

✳

Amour, rapture of my soul, intoxication of my senses; amour, again you have come to invade my entire being!

VIII

June 188*

For a month, the two of us have been plunged thus into the great ecstasy of grand amour, making our eyes talk and exchanging the words of our hearts from afar. I'm happy! O voluptuousness of suffering, bitter enjoyment of unslaked desires!

Madeleine . . . Eva.

IX

July 188*

Everything has been accomplished in accordance with Eva's solemn promise; we are bound to one another forever. An immense joy has entered into me, and yet I am afraid.

Yesterday, I slipped away to our habitual rendezvous. The night was hot, strewn with stars, and enervating and voluptuous scents rose from the Bois.

My eyes fixed on the window, I waited, but the window remained closed.

The hours fled, and day was about to break. A poignant anxiety took possession of me, more dolorous with every passing moment, increasing my ardor to see her.

Oh, Madeleine . . . !

And at that imperious appeal of my thought, the door of the house opened, and I saw her, all white, emerging from the shadow . . .

She was standing upright on the threshold of her dwelling, motionless.

Beloved! Oh, Beloved . . . !

Then, as on the night of our first meeting, she made a desperate gesture; then, coming down the steps of the perron slowly, she slowly traversed the garden, opened the gate and advanced into the street . . .

Having reached the wooden fence she hesitated again, turned, and seemed to want to flee . . .

Finally, she came into the enclosure.

I launched myself toward her.

"You!"

Madeleine extended her arms in order to drive me away, and in a muted voice she said: "What do you want with me, Monsieur? Here I am."

I united her hands in mine, drew her toward me violently, and in a passionate enlacement, clasped her to my breast. She threw her head back and closed her eyes.

"No . . . no!" she stammered. "Have pity . . . !"

I brought her face back close to mine by force, and my lips posed on hers . . .

For a long time we remained pressed against one another thus, and for a long time I felt the shivering of her body and the bite of her kisses.

Suddenly, she snatched herself away from my grip. Allan had surged forth before us.

Madeleine fell to her knees, bewildered.

"Kill me, Monsieur; I'm nothing but a wretch. It's me, of my own accord, who delivered myself to this man! And yet," she continued, with a sob, "I swear on my eternal honor that I love you, my master! My lord, I love you! I love you, my husband!"

Allan lifted her up.

"I don't have the right to punish you," he said, "poor debilitated soul, who has twice failed your redemption. But let your destiny be accomplished, and since you have returned down here in order to expiate, expiate!"

Without addressing a single word to me, he took Madeleine back into his house.

I wandered like an insensate all day long.

In the evening, when I went home, my valet de chambre said: "Monsieur, a lady has been here for several hours, who desires to speak to you.

It was Madeleine. When she saw me enter, she stood up.

"Will Monsieur de Tréan deign to give shelter henceforth to an adulterous woman?"

Intoxicated by happiness, I put my arm around her waist and drew her gently towards my bedroom. Then, as we were about to go into it, she uttered a savage laugh, and darting a glance at me full of hatred, she said:

"Wretch!"

REDIVIVA

2 November 188*

The gate of the château grated as it swung on its hinges and the vehicle penetrated into the courtyard.

At that sound, Madeleine, sitting next to me, shook off the torpor of her thoughts for a moment.

"Where are we?" she asked.

"At the Château de Vauvilliers," I replied.

I felt her tremble in every limb, and silence fell between us again. I was terribly emotional; what was soon about to happen was so grave!

*

No, certainly, such a torture could not go on any longer. For six months, I had been united, not with a living woman, but with a dead one. The menacing words that Marcus had hurled at me twenty-two years before had been accomplished in all their horror; Madeleine's hatred increased every day. The first delirium of her senses had soon calmed, but at present she abandoned herself to it, icy and impassive, with the sickening resignation of a young woman prostituting herself. Shutting herself away for entire days in a grim mutism, sometimes she wept. Sometimes she allowed her gaze to wander in space, bewildered, as if she had become idiotic.

"So you hate me fervently, then, Madeleine?" I asked her one day.

"Yes," she replied, "I hate you, you who have abused the weakness of a miserable invalid in order to steal from her everything that she loved."

Another time, seeing her weeping, I asked: "Are you suffering, Madeleine?"

"I'm thinking about him."

"Would you like us both to go to implore his forgiveness?"

"No. He'd forgive me, but I don't forgive myself. In any case, am I not condemned to expiate?" She added in a low voice, punctuated by a sob: "Oh, if only I could die!"

To die! And in a passionate embrace, taking possession of me with her hands: "And me, then!"

Yes, but it was necessary to be sure. What if I were the victim of an illusion? What if Madeleine were not my Eva? If . . . well, I was about to convince myself. Had not Marcus revealed it to me? I was a redoubtable medium.

Vincent, the old servant to whom the guard of the château had been confided for a long time, was on the landing, holding a candle. I helped Madeleine down from the carriage and we climbed the stairs. Having arrived on the first floor, I opened a door and, seizing Madeleine's arm, I went into a room: the room where Eva had died.

"Stay awake tonight," I said to my domestic. "I'll doubtless have need of you."

He bowed and went out.

My orders had been carried out scrupulously. Nothing had been changed in that room for twenty-two years. Extended over the wall there was still the faded antique verdure, the gigantic swans floating between frail trees with yellowed foliage. Two candles were burning on the mantelpiece in fleur-de-lysed brass candlesticks. The old Boule pendulum clock told time with its monotonous tick-tock. At the back of the room stood a large canopied bed with its helical columns and its tapestry curtains; near the bed, finally, on a table, were spread the same books that the dying Eva's fingers had riffled through.

Madeleine paraded a haggard gaze over those objects, and for the second time, a frisson of fear agitated her.

Taking her hands, I constrained her to sit down in an armchair, and, in a voice in which all the passion of my heart vibrated, I said: "Madeleine, it's necessary that you love me."

She sniggered dryly. "I'm your slave, your thing," she replied. "I'll try to obey."

She tried to pull her hands away; I retained them forcibly between mine, and kneeling down before her, I said: "Madeleine, I love you; I want you to love me."

She raised her forehead and replied: "You horrify me. You..."

She could not say any more, and the insult commenced stopped dead on her lips. Her eyes wide open and her pupils dilated, Madeleine looked at me, but could not speak. The power of magnetism that I had once excised so violently on the woman had returned.

Still holding her hands, I stood up, and with an effort of will, I nailed her to her armchair. She attempted to resist, and struggled; it was in vain. Soon, a profound sigh was exhaled from her breast, and her head fell back.

She was now under my absolute domination.

I carried her away in my arms and deposited her on the bed. Then, sitting down at her bedside, I contemplated her for a long time.

Yes, I loved her, that woman who had nothing for me but detestation and scorn. With what passion I observed her large eyes, the color of steel, her pale face with ivory tints, her scattered blonde hair, ad there . . . there, over her cheekbones, the two roseate patches!

And as I buried myself in my contemplation, a distant memory obsessed me. Where had I seen Madeleine before? Through what space, in what world, had we encountered one another?

Suddenly, enlightenment dawned in my mind. Yes out there on the islet of Gavr'innis, when my head was bowed under the burden of my despair, that menacing apparition, it was you! You . . . ? No, but Eva, since I was evoking her at that very instant! You were, therefore, the new form of her reincar-nation. Marcus, in the Mystery of the Rue de Ranelagh, was not mistaken; I was not the victim of an illusion . . . !

Come on, come on, for the last time, it was necessary to convince myself again . . . and then to act!

I approached my lips so close to hers that our respirations were confounded. Then, in a supreme effort, combining all my desire and all my effort, I commanded:

"Eva, become once again the woman who loves me. I wish it!"

Immediately, the terrible phenomenon that I had witnessed before was produced. The woman's respiration became halting; a rattle grated in her throat; her pulse weakened and stopped; her heart ceased beating.

"Eva . . . ! Eva . . . !" I repeated, in a voice that filled the silence of the room.

And slowly, sitting up at my appeal, Eva herself held out her arms to me. She extended her hands toward my face, and gently ran them over my forehead, over my eyes and over my lips.

"Jean, its me . . ."

"Oh, Beloved . . . ! Finally . . . ! Yes, yes, my Eva, isn't that enough proofs . . . enough tortures . . . enough expiations? Let your final words be accomplished: let us abandon this earth in order to love one another forever in the eternity of worlds!"

With both hands I seized the woman's neck and squeezed it for a long time, like a vice. The features of her face convulsed; her eyes looked at me, terribly. Her mouth seems to be laughing.

I squeezed harder. A drop of blood fell and stained the pillow.

Finally, I parted my fingers and released her head; the head collapsed, inert.

The woman was dead.

✳

I precipitated myself toward a revolver hanging in a panoply. I loaded it . . . and then I threw it to the ground. No, that was not the way I had to undergo my punishment.

Then I opened both battens of the door, and with repeated cries, I summoned my domestic. He arrived, fearfully.

"Go," I said to him, "run to Vauvilliers, wake up the men of law. Tell them to hurry. This woman has expiated. It's my turn."

The notes of this journal were given to me last year, after the death of my poor relative, Jean de Tréan, who hanged himself one night in his cell at the lunatic asylum at C***. Three months before, he had passed before the assizes, but the jury, in spite of repeated confessions and a strange desire on the part of the accused to be condemned, acquitted him in the grounds of insanity.

THE DEAD AVENGE THEMSELVES

by Claude Vignon

A numerous society had gathered in the home of Madame
M****, who resides for six months in her château, situated
in one of the most beautiful regions beyond the Loire.

It was All Saints' Day; it was already cold and the yellowed
leaves were falling, impelled by the north wind blowing through
the pathways of the garden. People were no longer thinking of
long walks under the hornbeams; the grapes had been trodden
and the fruits picked. In the large hearth a bright fire was crackling, around which the young and old folk gladly clustered; and
as it was evening, card tables, each bearing a lamp coiffed with a
green shade, had been set up in the four corners of the drawing
room.

However, boston and whist scarcely amused the grandpar-
ents, and even mistigris[1] only had a limited power over young
minds. Near the fire a sulky or morose group had gathered,
whom the mistress of the house had to strive to distract.
Unfortunately, it is often when one searches for an idea that one
cannot find one. She was therefore quite embarrassed when her
partner, divining her perplexity, exclaimed:

"We're being very selfish, we old people, with our cards!
The children are bored, and I can see my young friend Pauline,

---

1 Mistigris is a variety of poker employing a wild card, usually the joker.

gazing at the boston table with an expression that said clearly how little she is interested in heart bids. Come on, Madame M***, we need a game for all ages. Let's arrange ourselves a little in the corners and make room in the middle of the room for playing innocent games."

The proposal caused inclined heads and heavy eyelids to lift

"Will you play with us, Doctor?" asked the girl designated a moment ago by the name Pauline.

"Oh, not me, dear child; I'll watch you, and that will be my greatest pleasure. I no longer have wit enough to reply to 'What shall I put in my basket?' or 'Monsieur le curé doesn't like bones,' and my movements aren't sufficiently agile to defend myself at Blind Man's Buff or Warm Hand."

"Oh, but yes, Doctor," said the mistress of the house. "Since the young folk are playing, it's necessary to play their games with them if we want them to play ours afterward. What age are you anyway, my dear contemporary, to play the old man? Fifty years old, perhaps?"

"Eh! But isn't that the age of serious ideas? You, dear Madame, can play with your daughter; that's always good for you; you're young and cheerful, and Pauline resembles your sister. My humor has always been severe, as you know. I bounced Pauline on my knees when she was a little child, but I've never taken part in the girl's games. All of you play, then, and leave me in my corner, as is customary, to chew the pommel of my cane, remembering the past or thinking about the future. Ten years sooner or ten years later, isn't it always necessary to learn that role?"

The individual who said that, while going to install himself in an old wing-chair by the fire, was a tall, thin man who had once been blond but was now gray-haired, whose hollow temples, sparse hair and stooped figure made him an old man, although he was scarcely fifty, as Madame de M**** had said, had a high and intelligent forehead, and a gaze that was both keen and soft. His left cheek was marked by a profound scar that resembled the mark of a bite.

For twenty-five years Doctor Maynaud had been practicing medicine in the town neighboring Madame de M****'s château, and although he had been a young man when he settled in the locale no one remembered seeing him without gray hair and wrinkles, so invariably severe was his forehead and so calm and retired had his life remained.

Nevertheless, he had become the friend of all the families in the neighborhood, and in Madame de M****'s salon, partly composed of Parisian visitors and partly of neighbors, there was not a single person who was not honored to have him as a fellow guest.

This evening his brow was even more pensive than usual. While the games were organized around him, and as they became noisier, he seemed to isolate himself in order to give audience to reveries or grave, almost dolorous memories. Perhaps the bells that were ringing to announce the festival of the dead were conducting his thoughts toward another world or making him think of beloved tombs. Perhaps he was seeking the answer to a scientific or moral problem. Whatever it was, he was certainly a hundred leagues from Madame de M****'s salon when, after a game, it was a question of settling the bets.

The doctor's absorbed expression struck everyone. As Pauline de M**** was liable to a penance for a pair of gloves that she had left as a hostage, someone thought it amusing to send her to wake the morose old man up with a kiss.

Pauline looked at her old friend maliciously and advanced on tiptoe. Then, when she was before him and she had shown the unblinking doctor's impassivity to the players, she took his neck abruptly in her hands and applied a noisy kiss to his left cheek.

Doctor Maynaud uttered a terrible scream, bounded as if at the detonation of a firearm, looked around madly and, in the midst of general astonishment, ran out of the drawing room.

Madame de M**** ran in pursuit of the unfortunate doctor, called her domestics and ordered that someone must catch up with him, take him to his room, render him all possible aid and find out what had provoked that sudden attack. Everyone set forth on campaign and searched the courtyards, the gardens and the corridors; but it was in vain—he could not be found.

The general consternation suspended all games. People wondered fearfully what pain could suddenly have gripped Doctor Maynaud and caused that fit of madness. A real anxiety soon replaced astonishment, for the character and temperament of the doctor were equally opposed to such violent scenes. The domestics sent forth in all directions returned without having been able to catch the fugitive.

The next morning, naturally, that event was the subject of all conversation. People were sent in search of news all the way to the nearby village, to the doctor's home; but they could not obtain any information from his aged housekeeper, and it was in vain that each of Madame de M****'s guests tried to reach him that afternoon

In the evening, after dinner had been dragged out, and after slowly savoring all the enjoyments of a dessert as opulent as a provincial dessert can be in the autumn, and the coffee drunk even more slowly, everyone went into the drawing room and all possible and impossible explanations for the doctor's flight were discussed again. Everyone gave his opinion and defended it, and the final result was that the thing remained quite incomprehensible.

The conversation finally lapsed for want of fuel, and became sad because it was raining, because it was cold, because it was the day of the dead, because no one had anything else to say, and finally because no one knew what to do to pass the time.

The old men were beginning to fall asleep in their armchairs and the young ones to count exactly how many sections there were in the parquet. For the hundredth time, the regulars in Madame de M****'s salon engaged in long silent conversations with the chubby amours above the doors while following the episodes of the eternal hunt that ran over the tapestries of the walls. How blessed the Melusine would have been that evening who could finally have made the stag leap, set the dogs barking and the hunters running! What would they not have given to see the swings of flowers break under the weight of the plump and joyful amours!

Toward ten o'clock, when everyone was thinking of slipping discreetly out of the drawing room to go to their bedrooms, the door opened and the doctor appeared.

He was still the same man as the night before, and yet they hesitated momentarily to recognize him. Ten years of dolor could not have changed him more than those twenty-four hours. His forehead was creased with new wrinkles, his eyes had hollowed out their orbits and his gray hair had turned white.

"I have apologies to make to you, my excellent friend," he said, in a voice that was still emotional, advancing toward Madame de M****. "I owe them above all to our dear Pauline, for the disagreeable scene that I rendered to her in exchange for the good child's caress. I doubtless appeared to you to be mad, and perhaps I am; but you sensed a horrible dolor under my cries, did you not?"

"Doctor, we here are all your friends, all incapable of experiencing anything but a sincere trouble at the sight of your suffering. We didn't know..."

"You didn't know that I was subject to such fits? Reassure yourself, dear soul," said Doctor Maynaud, striving to smile, "it was the first time, and doubtless the last—for," he added, "you can see in my face, my dear Pauline, that another kiss like that would no longer leave anything but a cadaver."

"In the name of Heaven, Doctor, what's the matter with you?" cried the young girl, even more frightened by the doctor's expression than his words.

"I owe you an explanation for that strange scene, my dear child, as well as your mother and all our friends. You're very kind to be interested in the health of a poor old man, who will doubtless no longer sadden you with his presence this time next year."

"My friend!"

"Doctor!"

There was a general cry of sympathy, and yet, no one dared to contradict Monsieur Maynaud, so much had his face changed since the day before.

"I'm old, my friends," he said, "for in 1806 I was twenty years old and a student in medicine with the Faculty of Montpelier. On All Saints' Day that year the weather was magnificent for a day in late autumn. The last sunlight was gilding the leaves that remained in the branches of the trees and dressing the grayest walls of Montpelier with a joyous mantle. We were on vacation, for naturally, there were no lectures on feast days; that's why I departed with three of my friends, three students who enjoyed fresh air and liberty as much as me, to explore the surrounding area.

"Toward evening, after having spent our day wandering through the countryside, we were approaching the town again in order to find a small tavern in one of the outlying districts appreciated by students. We encountered a few of our companions, struck up a conversation, and ordered a copious supper from the landlord.

"The wine was good, the liqueurs exquisite; we talked in the lively fashion that verve sustains, argument stimulates and which throws the mind into a slightly incoherent world of ideas, because all subjects have been touched upon in turn, all questions investigated, and all theses sustained. Half wine and half chatter, perhaps, at eleven o'clock in the evening, when we tried to get up to return to our lodgings, we were stumbling and bumping into walls. Some of us were drunk, the rest tipsy.

"Those of us who were drunk stayed in the tavern on their benches or under the table. Those who were only tipsy, of whom I was one, steadying themselves as best they could, went back into Montpelier in a group.

"The route was settled by common accord and the conversation continued, scattered with interrupted phrases; but there were periodic defections, some recognizing their way home and returning, and a few others dropping behind, leaning on walls and interrogating belated passers-by.

"Personally, I was neither one of those who retained enough intelligence through the fumes of alcohol to guide myself nor one of those who had lost it entirely. Soon, I found myself in the center of the town and was uncertain which way to go.

"First I went straight ahead, without worrying any longer about my goal. The weather was fine and my head was spinning, but gradually, the turbulence of my thoughts calmed down and I tried to recognize the streets and intersections.

"That wasn't easy, for the moon was invisible and the town of Montpelier scarcely suspected, in those days, that it would one day be illuminated by gas. Street-lights of any sort were absent except outside the mairie, the prefecture and the schools. I was therefore groping my way, trying to penetrate both the darkness and the effects of drunkenness.

"Eventually, I thought I recognized a quarter that was familiar. I got my bearings and, my mind floating between wakefulness and dream, I turned into a tortuous little street that I was accustomed to taking. Mechanically, I felt all the doors of the street because it seemed to me that I would eventually find mine and discover the lock into which I had to insert my key. The more I searched, the more I crossed the street from right to left, the more the idea that I was in the vicinity of my house took root in my mind.

"I bumped into a door that was familiar, and without noticing the flag floating above it to designate a public establishment

I inserted my key in the lock. It turned with difficulty at first, but with the aid of a few jerks the door ended up opening.

"I went in, advancing like a blind man with my hands before me, and took a few steps in various directions in order to find the staircase. After a few moments I found an interior door that yielded to the simple pressure of my hand. I pushed it, and scarcely had I crossed the threshold than it fell back heavily, striking the wall.

"My first impulse was to look around, but the obscurity prevented me from distinguishing anything. I only felt that I was not in my own room. An impression of cold made me think that the place was uninhabited, and by the sonorous sound of my footsteps on paving-stones I understood that the enclosure was vast and scantly furnished.

"For a moment, I thought I was in a church, but in churches the lamp of the sanctuary burns night and day, and there was no illumination in that silent and chilly place.

"I wanted to get out and I retraced my steps in the direction of the door, but, either because intoxication rendered my steps uncertain or because the door was not obviously detectable from inside, I could not find it again.

"Then I wanted to know exactly into what place I had wandered, and as I distinguished through the darkness, at the far end of the hall, a large sheet of glass covered by a curtain, I advanced in that direction in order to obtain more light.

"Scarcely had I taken a dozen steps than I collided violently with the corner of an item of furniture or a ledge. I made a slight detour and continued my route with more precaution, but did not take long to be halted by a second impact.

"I extended my hand and felt the cold of marble; then, when I made a second movement, a more intense, more penetrating chill, more repulsive to my flesh froze the blood in my veins. What I recognized, as a student of medicine and surgery, was the chill of death.

"Suddenly, the fumes of drunkenness fled and all my presence of mind returned. I was in the amphitheater where the people who died in the hospice were deposited on marble tables in order to be delivered to study and dissected. I was, however, habituated to finding myself in that place; I was not a debutant to be frightened by the sight of a cadaver. But surprise, the darkness and perhaps the time of year—for I could hear the knell of the dead sounding—all contributed to cause me an invincible sentiment of dread.

"Fear gripped me by the throat and agitated my limbs with a convulsive tremor. I circled those inflexible walls like a prisoner around his dungeon; I applied my hands to each panel, hoping eventually to find the door and make it yield under my pressure, but all my efforts were in vain. The paneling seemed to repel me. Perhaps fear had rendered me impotent even to open a door.

"The bells were still ringing, slowly and inexorably.

"My teeth were chattering; a cold sweat was pearling on my forehead. The moon, which had risen, filtered its pale light through the red curtain of the window. Gradually, objects began to emerge from the darkness. I distinguished the bizarre shadows of surgical instruments extending along the walls, then the black marble tables, whose ridges caught rays of light, then the dispersed scalpels, and then the cadavers.

"There were two—only two.

"One of them was an old man already labored by our hands; I recognized him. The other was a young woman who had died the day before, still fresh.

"The old man, bloody and butchered, his limbs partly detached from the body, was horrible to see.

"The young woman, beautiful with the fascinating beauty of death that consumption leaves its victims, attracted my gaze invincibly.

"Midnight chimed, and each stroke mingled its solemn timbre with the funereal song of the bells. The day of the dead was commencing. My terror became even more intense, it seemed to me that the cadavers were about to hold me to account for my profanation, for on the second of November, in all Faculties of Medicine, the amphitheaters are closed; the dead are respected, as if their souls were watching over their bodies on that day.

"Immobile, frozen, I remained crouching at the foot of the enclosing wall, without being able to take my eyes off the young woman.

"Suddenly, I shivered; it seemed that I heard a stifled groan.

"I listened, my ears pricked, with the terror that makes the senses acquire an unusual acuity. A more prolonged sound troubled the silence.

"I looked around, and I thought I saw the head of the old man shift slowly on its marble bed. I was mad with fear; blood rose to my head and whipped my temples violently.

"I wanted to flee at any price, but my insensate efforts always ended up making me turn in the same circle.

"The bells, as slow at first as the plaints of an invalid, now began to ring at full tilt, their hasty coups resembling gasps of agony. The shaken windows repeated their sound with lamentable notes. At moments, one might have thought that the dead were weeping, asking for mercy and pity, at moments that they were waking up, lifting themselves up in dense cohorts, filling the air with a warrior hurrah.

"I fell to my knees, devoid of strength and reason, my sight troubled, my head lost.

"This time, I really had heard a sigh nearby; this time, I really had seen the cadavers stir!

"And while I felt myself dying, the old man uttered lugubrious cries, for he could not succeed in moving his head, the top of his skull having been removed, nor in moving his limbs, lacerated by the scalpel or sliced by the saw. He was making extraordinary efforts to lift himself from his marble slab, and each movement shook his bloody brain. Finally, he succeeded

in sitting up, and his eyes, half-extracted from their orbits, interrogated the darkness.

"'Today is the day of the dead,' he said, in a voice that resounded in my entrails. 'The dead wake up and avenge themselves! Who is here, with me, in this horrible charnel-house . . . ?
A young woman! Get up, child! Get up, for you still have limbs,
and you're reposing in ignorance of the torture that awaits you!
Today is the day of the dead, and the dead wake up and avenge
themselves!'

"Slowly, in her turn, the young woman lifted herself up and
opened staring eyes.

"'Poor girl! Oh, you've scarcely expired, and you have no
idea of the tortures that the odious living reserve for us! The
dead, they say, what are they? Inert flesh of which the earth will
make a dung-heap. Insensible matter good for the experiments
of the scalpel! And yet, this icy flesh, which no frisson causes
to tremble, it suffers, it feels . . . until the hour of its complete
dissolution. When the trenchant implement cleaves the flesh,
we feel its sharp and agonizing tip; when our entrails are spread
outside our abdomen, we would like to be able to retain them
in spite of the sacrilege that is stealing them; when our brain
screams under the trepan, when our heart bleeds under the lancet, the most intense dolors tear us apart: dolors of which the
executioners, those who can still die, have no idea.

"'Oh, my skull is open! I'm suffering horribly! What are
they searching for in my head? Thoughts, perhaps? It's in the
name of science that the barbarians slice us up, butcher us and
rummage inside us! Ha ha!' he added, with a snigger that made
echoes resonate. 'But they'll be dead in their turn! Today is the
day of the dead, and the dead wake up and avenge themselves!

"'Go on, quit your marble couch and come close to mine . . .
that's it! Come closer, since you can walk . . . good . . . sit down
now and look at all these instruments of torture around us.
Poor child! Scarcely being dead, you think you're asleep, don't

you? Well, they'll come, they're going to come . . . they'll open your breast in order to search there for the phthisis that killed you. They'll part your bones and you won't be able to scream . . . They'll rummage in your heart and your heart will feel the sharp lancet plunge again and again, a thousand times, to the sound of their laughter . . . for they laugh, the wretches, as they rip us apart! They talk about their orgies! They talk about their mistresses . . .

"'And then, when it's all finished, when a part of your being has been thrown on to the rubbish dump, when your hands and your feet, so pretty now, have been cut off and carried away by them to make playthings of them, they'll roll up the remains in a gross sheet—the charity sheet—put them in a box, scarcely joined up, and throw them in an ignoble ditch . . . at random . . . on top of me, on top of yesterday's dead, under tomorrow's, between an old beggar and some debris of shame or crime.

"'You'll feel all that; and the heavy earth, and the pressure of another coffin on top of yours, and the frost and the snow, and the damp of the rain.

"'Then the suffering will last for a long time . . . a long time . . . until the worms have gnawed your bones; until the arid sand has drunk the juice of your flesh in order to make grass and flowers with it.

"'That's what the dead suffer under the tyranny of the living who reign over the earth. But today is the day of the dead . . . and the dead wake up and avenge themselves!'

"And the cadaver, proud of his royalty of an hour, straightened terribly, parading a fixed gaze around himself.

"'But what do I see? Look! Who is hiding over there, under the shadow of a table? A dead man will be with us . . . how those two eyes burn! Perhaps he's alive . . . ! A living man? A torturer? Yes, yes, it's a living man! See how he's folding himself up . . . how he seems to be requesting the walls for a refuge . . . listen to the rattle of fear in his throat . . . Ha ha! It's our turn! Go on, girl, go on! I give the prey to you! Put your hand on his heart and you'll feel it beating...Is it beating? Oh, then avenge yourself, dead woman!'"

The doctor shuddered, and his lips went white; words expired in his throat.

People hastened around him; he was made to inhale salts; but his faint only lasted a few seconds. His eyes opened again; he recovered the power of speech and he added, in a strangled voice:

"Then I felt the dead woman's two hands enclose my neck in an icy circle...and on my cheek—here, where you see this scar, where you kissed me, Pauline—I experienced a pain so sharp that thought can't imagine it. First there was a bite, made with teeth that seemed to be diamonds of ice, and then a horrible suction that drew in my life.

"I lost consciousness.

"When I opened my eyes again it was daylight and I was in my bed with an ardent fever. My friends and comrades were crowded around me.

"'Well,' they said, laughing, 'what the devil were you doing by night in the amphitheater with the subjects? Do you mistake the dead for grisettes when you're drunk?'

"'Today is the day of the dead,' I repeated, mechanically. 'The dead wake up and avenge themselves!'

"'Get away! Have you gone mad? We're going to make a few applications of cold water to your skull.'

"I told them the horrible story, but the students only saw my account as an echo of delirium. 'Vision!' they said. 'Fumes of drunkenness mingled with nurses' tales.'

"Then they strove to demonstrate to me, in the name of reason, the impossibility of the events. They told me all the stories of hallucinations since the remotest antiquity, and for a moment I was ready to believe that I had had a frightful nightmare engendered by wine and fear.

"As I hesitated between their reasoning and my memory, something disturbed an apparatus that I had on my head, and I felt a sharp pain in my cheek. All my terrors returned to me; I demanded as mirror, and removed the bandage and the compresses. On my bleeding cheek there was a gaping wound and the marks of teeth.

"'And this?' I cried. 'Is this a dream too? If my head in delirium heard the dead speak, if the power of my overexcited imagination alone showed me that funereal drama, have I also bitten myself?'

"They had nothing to respond to that terrible proof. My friends doubted, and fell silent.

"They cared for me; I healed—but since that epoch I have never gone into an amphitheater, and I have defended all my dead against autopsy. Young girls, too, when they are pale and tall, like Pauline, have a strange effect on me.

"You understand now what the dear child's unexpected kiss caused me to experience yesterday, on a date and at an hour on which, for thirty years, I've been unable to free myself from my terrors. For a second, it gave me the illusion . . . Pauline, I won't repeat it!"

Madame de M**** and her friends hastened around Doctor Maynaud in order to reassure him. Multiple protestations of sympathy reached him from all directions. There was talk of cure, forgetfulness, of the future . . .

But the following year, the eve of All Saints' Day passed sadly in Madame de M****'s château. At the customary gathering of friends and neighbors the doctor was missing, and no one could avoid a constriction of the heart in remembering him.

REINCARNATION

by Jane de La Vaudère

ACCORDING to Claude Saint-Martin, a man is a spirit fallen from the divine order into the natural order, who tends to return to his original state.

A man senses within him a host of aspirations toward an unknown goal, a thirst for joys that the earth cannot provide. His habitual condition is a kind of anxiety that is almost dolorous, and which increase in direct proportion to his superiority.

Only the occult sciences, without according him complete satisfaction, bring him closer to the luminous ideal that he glimpses when the veil of his habitual darkness is torn by the effort of his thought.

In these times of progress, a few elevated spirits have undertaken to initiate us into the mysteries of theosophy, the supreme science. They have consecrated their lives to the quest for wisdom and the discovery of the secrets of hyperphysical and invisible nature.

Humanity seems to be shaking off a long torpor and marching to the conquest of a veritable conscious state. What demonstrates that with all the clarity of evidence is the great religious movement commenced by spiritualism, under the flag of theosophy and the aegis of esoteric science. It is the studies of Éliphas Lévi, the Marquis de Saint-Yves, Stanislas de Guaita and Papus.

For the facts it is sufficient to consult Richet, Philips and Mesmer; for hypotheses of the ensemble Comte, Stuart, Spencer, Taine and Ribot; for the philosophy Hartmann, Schopenhauer and, going much further back, Spinoza, Leibnitz, Plato, Aristotle, the neo-Platonists and the Pythagoreans. All of them have sensed a state other than the one in which we are living, a kind of human doubling to the advantage of the divine element, an evolution, a spiritualization of human substance.

The most skeptical people are forced to admit certain manifestations that all their science cannot explain. Do we not see in India, "the ancestor of heavy secrets," prodigies accomplished by fakirs that we cannot admit humanly?

"Here," says Dr. Paul Gibier,[1] "a naked, motionless individual, the body in a semicircle, the legs folded, extends his fingers, and suddenly, to general amazement, a small piece of wood placed out of his reach on a thin layer of sand stands up, marches, trots and runs of its own accord, and traces the sentence thought by a member of the audience.

"There, another fakir influences the vegetation in a direct manner and causes seeds taken at random from plants to germinate instantaneously.

"Another folds his tongue into his throat, has his ears and nostrils blocked, enters into lethargy and is put into a coffin in that state. A hole is dug out to receive it, sealed beneath a stone slab subsequently covered by seeded soil, and two sentinels keep watch night and day to prevent any fraud. One, two or three months go by; the seeds have germinated and produced plants and flowers. The man is disinterred, almost mummified; he is warmed up and massaged; his heart resumes beating and the blood circulating in his arteries.

---

1 The physician and bacteriologist Paul Gibier (1851-1900), founder of the New York branch of the Pasteur Institute, who was also interested in thereapeutic hypnotism and psychic phenomena. His book *Le Spiritisme (fakirisme occidental): étude historique, critique et expérimentale* (1887), from which the quotation is taken, compared the exploits of Spiritist mediums with the reported feats of Indian fakirs.

"Another throws a rope into the air and, without anything seeming to hold him, suspends himself from the end, and then disappears from the sight of the bewildered spectators."

Several voyagers worthy of faith have witnessed these scenes and others; do they not prove that anything is possible, when the spirit of a subject is borne by an invincible force and an unshakable will is brought to support it? Unfortunately, we are always drawn outside ourselves by unexpected events, and intelligences powerful enough to resist doubt or folly are rare. Remember the possessed of Loudun and the convulsionnaires of Saint-Médard.

It has, however, been given to me to see the striking triumph of the will over matter. Amour, it is true, facilitated the victory, but is not amour the very essence of our soul, and in whatever manner we experience it, whether for a chimera, for a god or for a woman, does it not give us the power to brave anything and to vanquish everything?

The heart has a thirst for the ideal; materialism has clipped its wings for too long. That is why this story has perhaps come in its time, and however strange it might appear, I do not hesitate to transcribe it.

At the time when I knew him, Ghislain d'Entrames was thirty years old. He was tall, remarkably proportioned, and nature had endowed him with an inflexible will. Over his ascetic forehead, the shadow of a forest of thoughts descended. His elongated visage was mortally pale; he seemed diaphanous, as if the fire of the soul illuminated him from within. In the middle shone two cavernous eyes, as dazzling as two flashes of lightning in two clouds.

He told me that he had always realized what he had wanted, because his desire was able to impose itself in its omnipotence, in the way that whatever is great and strong imposes itself.

People had been docile instruments in his hands; he would have been able to conquer a magnificent situation in the land if his ambitions had not had higher aims.

It is necessary, for the explanation of what follows, to go back a number of years and to recount that which was his happiness, his goal and his reason for living. While very young he had been engaged to a girl whom his parents had seen born, and which a large fortune, a great name and former family relations recommended particularly to their choice.

Bérengère had an imperious spirit, and an ardent and passionate nature; growing up with Ghislain, she was habituated to consider him as her fiancé, the natural companion of her entire life. The young man did not oppose any resistance to those plans, still indecisive in regard to his own sentiments; for the character of a man develops much more slowly than that of a woman, and a man who will one day disturb the world sometimes offers in his childhood a hesitant will submissive to an intelligence surrounded by mists. Bérengère being the only person who was mingled with his intimacy, he experienced some pleasure in seeing her, even though a secret antagonism already put him on his guard. There was no similitude of character between them except the same need for domination, visible in the young woman but as yet unavowed in her fiancé. But while the former was in full possession of her seductive forces, the latter was seeking to disentangle the frightful chaos of his thoughts. Immobile, as if electrified, he tried in vain to coordinate them. He was subject to a sequence of unformulated expressions that were like the imagined representation of his sensations.

Vaguely, he attempted to escape the power of Bérengère, who, using all the weapons that nature had given her, thwarted his resolutions and pursued him with her futile tenderness. Gradually, however, he shook off the yoke; his ideas became broader, his character firmer.

Everything that was simple and vulgar seemed despicable to him. When his brilliant studies were concluded, he launched himself into the complications of theosophy, seeking with a few profound minds to penetrate the mysteries of that science, which had recently become fashionable. With that elite he devoted himself to the triumph of wisdom and the discovery of the hyperphysical and invisible nature. He seemed to be emerging from a long slumber; wonderstruck by the enjoyments of that study he soon progressed to the conquest of his veritable conscious state. His highly assimilatory intelligence smoothed out the first reefs of initiation, and, while being remarked for a few peerless studies, he soon found himself at the head of the new school.

Until then, his work had been sufficient to his existence. Bérengère, whom he continued to consider as his companion, followed him with difficulty in his incessant discoveries, and, desirous of pleasing him, strove to find an interest therein equal to his own. Ghislain, however, was only attached to her by habitude, neither his heart nor his senses attracted him toward that woman of different temperament, with whom he was unconsciously at odds and in conflict, awakening within him the involuntary sentiment of anger and hatred that we sometimes feel in regard to people who cannot understand us. Soon, the dull irritation that he experienced became intolerable; without any avowed motive, he broke abruptly with the young woman and departed for a long voyage across the world.

Bérengère felt a sharp dolor, in which there was more anger than real chagrin. She had fought and built a thousand clever plans to conquer that bizarre nature, and, just at the moment of definitive triumph, her prey had escaped her, without her being able to penetrate the causes of that abrupt reversal. When her former fiancé returned she tried to retie the broken bonds of their intimacy, but he evaded all advances. The reason for that was simple, and a young woman more expert in matters of amour than Bérengère would have divined it easily. Ghislain had escaped her domination because his heart had awakened and was beating for another. Suddenly, he had glimpsed the ardent joys of inspired and experienced tenderness; he had been invincibly attracted, by unknown force, toward a being created for him, and who, it seemed to him, united all physical seductions and all moral perfections.

That marvel, however, was not one in the eyes of the profane, who only recognized in her a great beauty combined with a sovereign charm. Perhaps the young man would not have noticed her if he had not found her there just at the moment when his heart opened, avid for new joys and troubling sensations. A magnetic current was established between them, and they loved one another without ever having spoken to one another.

Djalfa belonged to one of the nomad troops that travel through France singing, dancing, and telling fortunes by means of cards. Barefoot in the sand, her hips tightened by a brightly colored skirt, she went forth leading by the bridle the meager nag attached to a caravan in which clever monkeys, fatal birds and ragged gypsies were piled pell-mell.

The others did not have for her the affection that ordinarily united all the members of the great Bohemian family. Another blood ran in her veins, and her distant memories of childhood traced for her an existence of affection in a regal dwelling, in which she wandered among flowers and silky furniture; but that was so long ago that she was not very sure that she had not had a sweet dream during halts in odorous meadows.

Djalha was an admirable creature. She had the nacreous complexion of a delicate seashell; her forehead was high, her nose slender and her nostrils mobile, and her pale silken hair made her a kind of bonnet of brocade woven with gold. That head would have been angelic if two large, profound brown eyes, scintillating between their double rows of black lashes, had not been animated by an almost supernatural flame. A mysterious smile wandered over her lips, and one divined beneath the slightly frail elegance of her stature nerves of a singular strength and an exquisite sensibility. Her slender body undulated rather than walking toward you, with a smooth serpentine glide.

Ghislain had met her by the side of a road, and he had wondered whether he had before him a human being, a fay or an angel. She had started to dance, to turn and to whirl on an old Persian carpet thrown negligently under her feet, and every time her radiant face passed before him, a double flash sprang from her eyes.

"Oh, dance, dance again!" he cried, as she made as if to repose. And she resumed twirling, to the hum of a Basque tambourine that her pure arms raised above her head. Her flight became lighter, she launched forth, as frail and lively as a wasp, with her golden corsage, his diaphanous skirt and the blonde gauze of her hair spread over her shoulders.

He gave her money, but she threw it on the road with a large bunch of vervain that she took from her belt. Ghislain had departed clutching the fresh souvenir of the gypsy woman, and whatever he did, her image no longer left his thoughts.

Two days later, while going past a small stream in farmland, he encountered her again. The caravan had stopped in a natural meadow enameled with luzerne, clover and sainfoin. Corncockles, bugloss and black xylocopes were intoxicating the bees, and the young woman, lying on the ground, was watching them flying above her head.

Ghislain had felt irresistible attracted toward that meadow and, obedient to the mysterious force that was guiding him, he had arrived beside Djalfa. She had risen to her feet, blushing, and then, without saying a word, she had fallen into his arms, as if she had been living for a long time in the expectation of that blissful moment.

Penetrated by the new doctrines, Ghislain said to himself that he had encountered the woman especially engendered for him, the twin soul that one hardly ever finds on earth, and that it was henceforth necessary to both of them that they live together. Djalfa felt an ineffable shudder throughout her being when the young man's lips had pressed against hers; also learned in the mysteries of the Kabbalah and theosophy, she knew that a stranger would come and that, as one plucks a fruit from a branch by the roadside, he would extract her from her errant misery in order to create an existence of luxury and amour for her.

Throughout their peregrinations, the Bohemians have conserved intact interesting traditions originating from Tibet, which are recognizably similar to theosophical doctrines; the young woman had, therefore, studied the same grimoires as her lover; her mind was open to the same reasoning; her soul, like his, had a thirst for the ideal. She was awaiting the beloved, and when she held him in her arms, she was fully satisfied.

In fact, they complemented one another admirably. In life, human beings, imperfect by nature, march incessantly toward a goal of which they dream, which is equality and equilibrium. In order to attain it, they seek complementary influences capable of perfecting them, of enabling them to cease perpetual wandering. Thus appears the irresistible tendency of two beings to become only one, to enlace one another, to fuse in a physical and intellectual communion.

Instinct, as much as reason, seeks what might bring about that enviable state; from that are born sympathies and attractions, and, when reciprocity does not exist, despairs and follies. The passions, in fact, all flow from amour, the fundamental law of humankind. Do not our thoughts, our decisions and our actions come to us, in their turn from our passions? And if our sometimes hateful passions take on an umbrageous and aggressive form, it is because they result from secret presentiments that perceive a hindrance to the dreamed of and powerfully desired complementarity.

The more equilibrated an individual is in nature and intelligence, the greater his influence will be on others, for everyone will find in him what they lack. Ghislain represented will, strength and power. He was subjective, active and an individual. Djalfa, frail, nervous, ardent and tender, charmed him quite naturally, in the same way that the seduction she exercised on him was immediate and complete. Without argument, without resistance, she abandoned herself entirely.

"Now take me away," she said to him, when they disengaged, unsteadily from that first embrace. "My secret voices have not lied to me; I was born for you, and everything that has happened had to happen."

Plutarch says that incarnate souls have the faculty of predicting the future in this life, but that it is more or less latent, because those souls are obscured by the body as the sun is by fog. In her long reveries during her halts under the alders and the poplars, the Bohemian woman had seen her ideal incarnate; she had loved Ghislain, and when he had come, she had gone to him, knowing that he was destined for her, and that their two dreams were fated to fuse in a plenitude of wellbeing.

He took her away, therefore, to a small property he owned in Brittany, and there commenced an existence so filled with tenderness that there was no time even for reflection. They lived in a sort of radiance, an almost unconscious state of ineffable felicity.

Behind the black walls of their retreat, Ghislain had accumulated marvels: silky carpets, fabrics set with precious stones, large Venetian mirrors with multicolored flowers, and delicately-sculpted golden perfume-burners in the half-light of a tabernacle. At the end of a long illuminated corridor, that magnificence suddenly burst forth, as unreal as something out of a tale of the Thousand-and-One Nights.

Djalfa, semi-naked, clad only in diaphanous fabrics, themselves as soft as a caress, studied with Ghislain the mysterious books that they loved; then, rising with him to unknown altitudes, she seemed to pierce the future, to float in another world populated with enchantment as delectably rosy as a sunrise. She was no longer the same woman. Her instruction was perfect now, and her friend often allowed himself to be guided by her through the chaotic world of metaphysical investigations with which he was ardently occupied. But a sad presentiment often caused her to go pale; her eyes were veiled by tears, and all her courage seemed to abandon her.

"I sense that I shall die soon," she said. "We're too happy." And as he put his hands together in desolation, she went on: "When I am dead, I will not quit you; death only exists for those who do not know love. I shall force the doors of the tomb, for my unique will, my inflexible will, is to remain with you and within you forever. Promise me that you will associate your power with mine, and summon me to you with all the ardor that I shall put into breaking my chains."

"I promise you that."

"Whatever happens, we'll be together, won't we, in death as in life?"

"I swear it," said Ghislain, again, and the young woman, consoled, rested her pretty head on her lover's shoulder. And that was her favorite topic of conversation. Incessantly, like a funeral knell, but very gentle in the sunlight, that phrase recurred: *when I am dead . . . when I am dead . . .*

That idea pursued her. The presentiment of a mission to fulfill beyond the tomb haunted her nights. Sometimes, stiffening in the young man's arms, she uttered a heart-rending cry and Ghislain, livid, tremulous and desolate, implored her no longer to think about anything, to go to sleep in the confidence of his amour.

She almost never went out; the world no longer existed for her since she had encountered the beloved and understood her very reason for being. She belonged to him as the leaf belongs to the tree. They completed one another and were sufficient for one another. The leaf falls and dies detached from its stream; Djalfa did not want to be detached from Ghislain.

※

What about Bérengère?

Bérengère had suffered, cursed and wept. Divining too late that she had not been able to conquer her fiancé's heart, a grim hatred had overtaken her, and, attaching herself all the more the more she was scorned, she had sworn to triumph one day.

A headstrong and spirited young woman is never embarrassed; she had obtained information, had spied on Ghislain and divined a part of the truth. When she found out that the lovers had retired to Brittany she persuaded her parents to rent a property near theirs, and hid in the park, incessantly lying in ambush, and watched her rival's closed dwelling. In a month, she only saw Djalfa go out twice. Her lover gave her his arm and they walked slowly, holding one another tightly.

Bérengère had to admit that the Bohemian woman was charming, with her pale complexion and the extraordinary gleam of her gaze. Until then, no woman had caused her that involuntary sentiment of admiration, and in order for her to feel it, prejudiced as she was against her rival, it was necessary that the seduction exercised by the latter was, indeed, very powerful.

Sensual and willful above all, Bérengère now desired Ghislain furiously. Her brutal and egotistical amour recoiled before nothing. Skillfully, with the cunning that all women have when passion drives them, she searched for schemes and drew up plans. How could she vanquish Djalfa, the accursed and execrated creature who had taken her fiancé? How could she reconquer the place she coveted so ardently?

She wrote to the young man, begging him to return to his former projects, to abandon an intrigue unworthy of him, from which nothing good could come. She appealed to his reason, to his heart, to his rectitude, and, her soul full of distress, she awaited the response.

That response was not the one for which she had dared to hope. Without denying his wrongs, he gave for their excuse the triumphant sentiment that had attracted him toward a woman capable of loving him and understanding him. The stupid prejudices of society did not exist for him, and, in order to consecrate that amour, he was ready to offer Djalfa his name and his life.

That brutal declaration cut to the quick of Bérengère's pride; her anger no longer knew any bounds. What! That schemer, that negligible young women, was standing up impudently between them! That frail creature whom a breath of wind could knock over would be an insurmountable obstacle in her life?

Her lips quivering and her eyes on fire, the young woman looked at herself in her mirror, and saw herself as she was: wild, beautiful and powerful, like an unbroken mare. She twisted her heavy, rebellious tresses over her forehead and attached them with two golden pins, which sparkled like stars in the night of that fleece. Then she smiled, suddenly appeased.

"I shall triumph," she said, "because I have the strength, the cunning and the will!"

That evening, she went to knock on Djalfa's door. The latter's husband had just left her, and, as the domestics were slow to appear, she followed the corridor all the way to her mysterious retreat. The Bohemian, lying on a low divan, was asleep, or seemed to be asleep. Her mouth was still smiling at her amorous dream; her entire face had an expression of infinite tenderness.

Bérengère shuddered to the depths of her heart. The disorder of the cushions and the intoxicating perfumes with which the atmosphere of the room was saturated exasperated her jealousy and troubled her reason. She approached and touched the sleeper, who opened surprised eyes, not understanding how that woman, whom she did not know, had arrived as far as her.

"I'm Ghislain's sister," said Bérengère, without her voice betraying her. "Won't you receive me as a relative and a friend?"

Djalfa threw the ashy curls of her hair over her shoulders, and contemplated her enemy with a soft smile at the corners of her lips.

"Be welcome," she replied. "I didn't know that my beloved had a sister, but you resemble him, and you must be accomplished."

"Truly? I resemble him?"

"Yes, a great deal. You have the same complexion, the same black hair. How he must love you!"

Bérengère frowned, and an imperceptible tremor agitated her hands. "He loves me," she said slowly, "but he would love me much more if you wished it."

The Bohemian looked at her with an incredulous expression. "No one is as good and tender as him. I'm certain that he has given you all of his fraternal heart, as he has given me all of his lover's heart."

An ardent blush covering her cheeks, she extended her hand to Bérengère, who sat down next to her and pressed her to her heart.

Only the soft whispers of the two women were audible in the closed room. An alabaster lamp suspended from the ceiling illuminated them feebly, and the servants, distanced from the retreat, knew nothing of their conversation.

When Ghislain returned, the lamp was extinct, but a tremulous voice called to him in the darkness.

He advanced, groping, and, encountering his beloved, who was also seeking him, he returned her caresses and her kisses.

That night seemed to him the most intoxicating of all those he had spent in Djalfa's arms. She enlaced him and linked herself to him, insatiable, passionate and irresistible. When he finally went to sleep, day was beginning to break.

His slumber was dolorous; terrible dreams assailed him; an unsustainable weight oppressed him, and he suddenly opened his eyes with a cry.

What he saw seemed to him to be the continuation of a nightmare, and, abruptly, he sat up on the bed, wondering whether he was not drunk or mad.

Djalfa was lying in the middle of the room, her face completely bloodless, her pupils fixed and dilated in a frightful expression of horror and suffering, her lips twisted over the enamel of her teeth. A little blood was running over her neck and making a small pool on the carpet.

He leapt forward and lifted her in his arms; he tried to re-animate her, but she was icy, already stiffened by death. There was no trace of a wound on the body. Red droplets, however, remained in the hair, which they had stuck together in little hard locks. Ghislain parted them, and found nothing.

Suddenly, his fingers encountered an obstacle: a golden pinhead gleaming in the blonde fleece. He tried to grip it, but the blood coagulated around it had, so to speak, encrusted it in the hair. At the peak of despair, trembling in every limb, he gripped the shiny little ball and, having drawn it out with some difficulty, a long hairpin emerged from Djalfa's head, which was unfamiliar to him, but which could only belong to a woman.

Who, then, had been in his bed beside him? Who had lavished bewitching caresses upon him all night long?

His forehead inundated with cold sweat, Ghislain turned his gaze in that direction, and recoiled suddenly, as if a snake had bitten him.

Leaning on her elbow, in the disorder of the pillows Bérengère was smiling at him. A slightly ironic expression was curling her lip.

She nodded her head, responding to the terrible question that he addressed to her mentally. "Yes, it was me," she said. "I killed her, because she had taken my place. You thought you could escape me, but my will is equal to yours. I've taken you back, and I shall keep you!"

The young man felt a frightful anger seething within him. He looked around the room for a weapon in order to administer justice; red spots were quivering before his eyes; he was impatient to avenge his beloved Djalfa. As he found nothing, he advanced his taut hands, determined to strangle the miserable creature who, smiling and motionless, was still confronting him.

His fury blinded him; kneeling on the bed, he clenched his hands around Bérengère's neck. She uttered a feeble sigh, and lost consciousness.

At that moment, it seemed to him that the dead woman had made a movement. He turned round, but he had no difficulty convincing himself that he had been the victim of a hallucination. The body was still extended, rigid, on the carpet. It seemed to him, however, that she had ordered him not to commit that crime.

He concentrated his attention on Djalfa, and begged her, with his heart hammering, to let him know her will by means of some manifestation, if that will were that he spare Bérengère's life.

Suddenly, he shivered. The gaze of the dead woman slowly turned to meet his, and fixed obstinately thereon, like those of certain portraits, which always seem to follow you.

That terrible gaze, in that white face, troubled him strangely, and, stirred to the marrow of his bones, he took the young woman's hand, expecting to feel it contract in is own, to warm up, to live again; but the hand fell back inert; the heart over which he placed his ear, remained devoid of a pulse. He put his lips to the blanched lips in order to blow life into them, but the teeth did not unclench; a little mirror that he put to them remained limpid. It really was a cadaver that he had before him: the cadaver of the only woman that he had loved.

His chest tightened, finally exhaling his dolor, he shed abundant tears.

Then, in a superhuman effort of will, he ordered Djalfa for the second time to reassure him, to prove to him that all their research had not been in vain, that there existed a world different from the one they knew, that everything did not stop on the threshold of the tomb, and that the apparent injustice of life ceased therewith. He begged her to dictate to him the conduct that he ought to adopt, and to assist him in his troubles. Had she not repeated to him, often, the sentence that was still singing in his memory: "Death only exists for those who cannot love. I shall force the doors of the tomb, for my unique will, my inflexible will, is always to remain with you and within you."

He heard the vibration of a feeble echo. As his thoughts retraced those consolatory words, a voice, all of whose cords quivered delectably, repeated them within him. He savored that new sensation, that exquisite understanding of the now-wandering soul that he loved, and the voice, whose sonorous waves perceptible for him alone, troubled him so profoundly, continued:

"You promised me to associate your desire with mine, and to summon me to you with all the ardor that I shall put into breaking my chains. The moment has come."

Ghislain knelt down and, his eyelids closed, his lips extended toward mysterious kisses, all his strength directed toward a single goal, he promised to carry out the dead woman's wishes.

When he got up again, he was calm and resolute, a flame burning in his eyes.

※

Bérengère had remained motionless. He lavished his cares upon her, and succeeded easily enough in reanimating her. He said to her then, with a mildness by which she was frightened:

"You can't stay here. Get dressed and return to your parents."

"But I'd die of shame! Keep me, protect me! Have I not doomed myself for you?"

She dragged herself at his feet, vibrant with sobs, more frightened by his forbearance than by his anger or his hatred.

He picked her up.

"Have no fear; I'll protect your honor. When Djalfa's body has received the last duties, I'll marry you, Bérengère. No one will ever know that you spent the night here."

"And my crime? Can you forget it?"

"I forgive you. Go in peace."

She fell upon his hands and kissed them with transports of gratitude, but he begged her to hurry, as the day was progressing rapidly.

When she had dressed, feverishly and had disappeared as secretly as she had come, he laid the body of the Bohemian on the bed; then, having washed way the slight traces of blood that stained the carpet, he summoned the servants.

They all believed, or pretended to believe, that it was a natural death. Djalfa having no relatives or friends, no one was troubled by her decease; the funeral took place without any obstacle.

Only a few curious individuals attended the ceremony, and when Ghislain d'Entrames left the cemetery, he was not subjected to any compliment of condolence or any delicately sympathetic handshake.

For the rest of the day he wandered at random, bare-headed, his garments in disorder. Those who encountered him took him for a madman, so incoherent were his gestures and so wild was his gaze.

At ten o'clock in the evening, he went home, and, after a light meal, he ran to shut himself away in his cherished retreat, still warm with their amour, still embalmed by adorable memories.

The bed was made. Long brocade curtains covered it completely. At the foot, a bunch of white roses marked the place where the coffin had lain. Two half-consumed candles stood on the floor, in their silver candlesticks. Ghislain relit them, lifted a drape at the back of the room and activated a wooden panel, which, as it moved aside, uncovered a secret passage. He went into it, and penetrated into a small dark room of whose existence only he and Djalfa knew, which contained a few rare books, tarot cards, and various magical objects used in their experiments.

The disposition of that redoubt had been modified recently by the young man, and in the place that the bookshelves had occupied at the back of the room there was now a vast divan of black velvet, surrounded on all sides by dark curtains.

Ghislain closed the secret door again and knelt down, trembling. He was very pale, and drops of cold sweat were pearling on his forehead. His heartbeat would have been audible.

After a few minutes of meditation, he spoke aloud.

"If everything is transformed, if the progressive phenomena that we have studied must be renewed until complete perfection, if nothing dies, and if the human initiate to occult powers can direct at will the various evolutions in his life, until the supreme bliss, may my will be accomplished! Your soul is linked to mine, Djalfa, and I can no more be deprived of it than I could be deprived of air or sunlight.

"No, nothing dies; everything simply changes and is transformed, like the chrysalid that will become a butterfly and the flower of the peach a vermilion and flavorsome fruit. Can we not direct at will the transformation of the beings we have cherished? Can we not, by dint of perseverance and energy, find them and recognize them, living by our side? Will the moment of our indissoluble union not come, my beloved, in spite of society and its paltry conventions, in spite of the feeble calculations of human intelligence, which believes that it embraces everything, and only sees the handful of millet that God holds in his hand?

"We have learned that the Earth turns, that the blood that circulates in our bodies in a river that returns to its source, that there are, beyond the sea of darkness, lands covered with trees different from our own, inhabited by men who are also different; but no one has yet recognized that all the creations and all the creatures in the Universe are signs.

"There are divine signs in the sea, in the profound forests, in a grain of sand, in our muscles, our bones and our flesh. Nature speaks to us, at every hour of the day, in an immensely sonorous language, compared with which all our poor science falls into dust and disperses. Those signs demonstrate to us in a manner that does not address our reason but our instinct, our soul and our heart, that we cannot disappear, that our essence is imperishable and that a divine light guides us incessantly toward the eternal light ..."

Ghislain parted the curtains, and on the bed, the body of Djalfa appeared to him, such as he had found it on the carpet after his criminal night. He had taken care to fill the coffin with stones, in order to sustain belief in the inhumation of those cherished remains, and secretly, while everyone was asleep, he had transported the cadaver to this retreat.

Cold and rigid, Djalfa still had open eyes, and her motionless gaze, turned toward Ghislain, had lost none of its luminous gleam.

A profound silence fell. The young man, sunk in his meditations, remained on his knees. He felt himself transported into a different world, rid of his bonds, light and happy. Lost in his intoxicating dream, projected, so to speak, outside of himself, an imponderable body, an astral form, it seemed to him that the force of his vital fluid, thus liberated, attracted Djalfa, or what remained of her, and that she dissolved divinely within him. He sensed her entire being plunging into his as if into an abyss. Her voice spoke to him ineffably, a bell of amour descended from the gods, an echo of the ecstatic prayer of the angels; it vibrated in his most secret fibers, and maddened him.

The whole night passed thus, without him being conscious of it.

The candle went out, entirely consumed; a faint gleam passed under the woodwork.

He closed the curtains that sheltered the body of the Bohemian, and left quietly. His face was fearfully pale, but he seemed calm and resolute.

During the day, he had himself announced in Bérengère's house. The young woman was surprised to see him so soon. She had reflected a great deal; the remorse of her crime weighed upon her; she was gripped by a kind of obscure dreads. Without regretting her rival's death, she feared its consequences. Human justice, although slow and incomplete, could not be blind to the point of absolving her, and in any case, would not divine justice attain her?

Ghislain found her changed, thinner and tremulous, with something anxious and fugitive in the depths of her eyes. He took her by the hand and drew her to him.

"Don't you want to receive your fiancé?" he asked her, with great mildness.

"I dare not believe you. How can you look at me without shivering?"

"What happened had to happen. You were only a docile instrument in the hands of destiny, Bérengère. It has been given to me to read the future; that is why I have come to offer you my name, and I am certain that you will accept it as I offer it to you, with joy and urgency."

"And will you love me as much as . . . the other?"

"Perhaps not at the beginning, but we're young and . . . time passes over everything."

The young woman shivered. "I'm afraid," she said. "A cold breath brushed my forehead, an icy breath like the exhalation of the tomb. Someone is here that I can't see: a specter that is whispering menacing words to me. Can you not hear it, Ghislain, and is it not the soul of Djalfa, the wrathful soul of the one I murdered in a cowardly fashion?"

"Dispel those somber ideas. Those who are dead do not return. Did you not say that to me often when I pored over obscure old books in order to extract therefrom the secret of the eternal mystery in which we evolve? Did you not mock me then for my crazy imaginations, and were you not right, therefore, to take from the earth its sunlight and its dew, like a beautiful insouciant flower?"

There was a little irony in Ghislain's words, but Bérengère, glad to see him so docile and so persuasive, paid no heed to it; she smiled at him, and the cruel flame of triumph lit up in her gaze.

"I belong to you," she said, in a low voice. "Can you love me as I love you, and forget in sweeter intoxications the bloody intoxications of our first night of amour?"

He returned every day, and their engagement was soon announced overtly. Their parents had consented with joy to that union, which fulfilled their wishes, and the solitude in which they lived preserved them from indiscreet commentaries.

Ghislain d'Entrames acquiesced to all of his fiancée's caprices; he was only inflexible on one point: their place of residence. The old château where he had been so happy and so proven pleased him, and all prayers that young woman addressed to him in order to persuade him to sell it remained vain. Djalfa's bedroom would remain Bérengère's bedroom, the dead woman's bed would be that of the legitimate wife, and no change would be introduced to the disposition of their dwelling.

The marriage drew a great many people in spite of the difficulty of communications. A little curiosity regarding the groom was mingled with the eagerness that people put into responding to the numerous invitations that the young woman's parents sent out. People knew about the idyll so strangely commenced and so fatally interrupted by the death of the young Bohemian, and socialites throw themselves avidly on all the romantic adventures that the spirit of calculation and egotism have rendered so rare.

People felt slightly sorry for Bérengère, who, shivering in her white silk dress, lowered her eyes hypocritically.

Entrames attracted the gazes of all the women present at the ceremony. He seemed to have grown in stature, superior to the others, with something cold and willful that was imposing.

Certainly, those preoccupations were far from the one that was leading him to the altar. A different being lived within him, a suffering and anxious being who was feverishly agitated. He wondered whether he might not be mistaken, whether he was really obeying Djalfa's injunctions in giving his name to the criminal woman who awakened in his heart nothing but hatred and scorn.

All his science seemed slender to him, now that he was trying to resolve a frightful problem. Did the books that he had read so often, charmed, contain anything but beautiful lies, gilded and fugitive? Did the stars themselves not lie? Could poor human intelligence comprehend the mystery of the worlds scattered in space like as many turbulent atoms?

He knelt down on the velvet prie-dieu and, while the choirboys were swinging censers and the priest was intoning the words of the ritual, he made a supreme appeal to the powerful being that watches over human destinies. Had that God not said: *let there be light*, in sowing force and clarity everywhere? Departing from that principle Ghislain lost himself in profound reasoning.

Infinity has its ether, the star its light, the organized being its magnetic fluid: the astral body or the plastic mediator. The will acts directs upon it, and by its means, submits all of nature to the modifications of intelligence. Entrames knew that he had an incomparable magnetic power, but he had only made use of that force thus far in pure experiments; might it not abandon him at the decisive moment?[1]

He knew that one could kill by means of magnetism as by electricity, and there is nothing strange about that particularity, which has many analogies in nature. Fluid is matter in rapid motion, always agitated by the variation of equilibria. There is no fluid body that cannot become harder than diamond if its constituent molecules are equilibrated. To direct magnets is thus to destroy or create forms, to produce an appearance or to annihilate a substance, to exercise omnipotence over nature.

That force, insufficiently known in its effects, like electricity itself, can become terrible, and the future belongs to those who are able to employ it usefully. It has presented itself at all times; Hermes and Pythagoras mentioned it; Synesius, who sang its praises in his hymns, had found the revelation in the Platonist memoirs of the school of Alexandria. "One single source, one single root of light springs forth and expands in three branches of splendor. A breath circulates around the earth and vivifies, under innumerable forms, all the parts of animate substance." It is that primal substance that is signaled by the hieratic narrative of Genesis when the Word of Elohim make light by ordering it to be. That light, the Hebrew name for which is *aour*, is the living gold of all Hermetic philosophy.

Our plastic mediator seems to be the magnet that attracts or repels the astral light under the pressure of the will; it is a luminous body itself, which reproduces with the greatest facility the images invoked by the imagination. But cannot that luminous

---

1 The author inserts a reference at this point to Éliphas Lévi, which is garbled in the print-on-demand reprint of *L'Anarchiste*, the text of which has been passed through an Optical Character Reader.

body, instead of receiving its form from the carnal envelope on which it depends, communicate its own to it at length, and progressively substitute one being for another by means of the disaggregation of the constituent molecules?

While Bérengère was praying, her head curbed over her joined hands, Ghislain thought about those things. His mysterious conversation with the dead woman vibrated in his memory. She had reassured him, convinced him and pushed him into that dangerous path. Next to her, he had felt strong and courageous; everything has seemed facile to him. Now, a veil of darkness descended over him. Would the punishment that he was preparing attain the culpable individual? Might it not rather strike the man who was daring to penetrate secrets thus far inviolable?

His entre body shuddered. *Djalfa! Djalfa!* he cried, with the voice of the soul that the ear cannot hear, but which shakes and tears ever being with more force than the clamors of the ocean.

No echo responded to him, but, having turned round, he was struck by Bérengère's pallor. Her fearful eyes encountered his.

"Pity!" she murmured, very quietly.

That evening, when they found themselves alone in the room of the murder, the young woman enveloped him in her arms and drew him toward the divan.

"What I felt this morning was strange," she said. "It seemed to me that my life was escaping me like blood flowing from a mortal wound. An icy cold descended upon my heart, my ideas were obscured; I've never felt such an anguish. Might it be the punishment already?"

Ghislain did not reply. A satisfied smile wandered over his lips; he was certain now of victory.

He lay down alongside Bérengère and his mouth had no sooner touched hers than she fell into a profound slumber. With a few rapid lateral passes, and the more intense projection of the will that he was able to obtain, he plunged her into a complete state of magnetic catalepsy.

Then, bringing the mobile panel of the woodwork into play, he went to Djalfa's body, and there, kneeling down, lost in the intoxication of his desire, it seemed to him that the dead woman called to him, encouraged him, and ordered him to continue his work.

He remained thus for a long time, unconscious, radiant and transfigured.

When he returned to Bérengère, she was lying in the same position; her pulse was imperceptible, her respiration soft, scarcely detectable, except by the application of a mirror to the lips. Her eyes were closed, naturally, and her limbs as rigid and cold as marble.

"Bérengère," he said, "are you asleep?"

She did not reply at first; then her lips trembled, and her face took on an expression of suffering and dread. The eyelids rose up of their own accord, as if to unveil the white line of the eyeball, and, making an effort, she cried: "Where are you taking me? I don't want to die! You've opened my heart, oh, with a needle, and the blood is escaping from it slowly . . . Ghislain! For pity's sake, wake me up . . ."

Imposing his will upon her, he said, gravely: "We have loved one another well, tonight, Bérengère. You'll remember that, won't you? You'll tell everyone that you're perfectly happy?"

She agitated feverishly. "I'll tell them, Ghislain . . . wake me up."

He made a few rapid passes, and her respiration became stronger. She passed her hands over her face, and the iris appeared in the eyeball. Immediately, a smile spread over her features.

"How content I am!" she murmured. "She didn't merit so much happiness. How I love you, and how you love me! We'll have a great many similar nights, my adored. I knew full well that your heart would come back to me, that one day you'd be entirely mine."

She got dressed and went down into the garden. She had never been as joyful. Her parents came to see her, and were astonished by her exaltation. Her eyes had a slightly more feverish gleam, and her complexion was clouded, but happiness sometimes leaves the same stigmata as pain.

The Marquis and Marquise de Sainte-Laure were not overly anxious about the condition of their daughter. Subsequently, in any case, she maintained the same charmed air, even though she had changed visibly. When anyone asked for news of her health, she said that she was very well and fully satisfied, with the result that her entourage soon ceased to worry about the alteration in her features, which might have been attributable to the commencement of a pregnancy.

Every evening, Entrames plunged her into magnetic slumber and put her in communication with the inert body of Djalfa; then, breathless and with his soul swollen by hope, he followed the mysterious work that was occurring in her organism.

Certainly, he hated Bérengère with a grim hatred; all his aspirations, all his tenderness went to the other, the murdered, the only adored. He indulged in orgies of memory. His spirit was burning fully and broadly with an incessantly increasing flame. He insulted the accursed woman and desperately summoned the idolized mistress, as if he could reanimate her and enable her to live again by means of his savage energy and the devouring ardor of his passion.

Bérengère sighed and wept, but her plaints remained futile.

When he interrogated her, she accused him of pricking her heart with a long needle in order to let the blood out drop by drop—and it was a frightful torture! She writhed and struggled;

her fingernails dug into her flesh and her lips twisted in impotent cries; and every morning, a more profound changed was produced in her. Her features now seemed to be melting and diminishing; her complexion was paling in places; her eyes were clouded; even her hair was changing color; her robust figure flexed; one might have thought that she was shrinking.

Her humor, however, was constantly joyful; no worry seemed to affect her. She only spoke to her husband with the greatest tenderness, and reassured her family, who could not understand her metamorphosis and were beginning to become anxious about it.

That state of affairs lasted for several months.

Ghislain acted with the most extreme prudence. The domestics, kept well away from the conjugal chamber, could not discover anything, and when she woke up, Bérengère carried out meekly the orders given to her while asleep. Her memory, moreover, remained mute. She only knew one thing, which was that her husband adored her, that he had given her the most convincing proofs of it, and that every night brought the same intoxication.

Now, every night edged her a little closer to the doors of the tomb, and as soon as the power of her administrator of justice was extended over her she fell into a horrible slumber traversed by terror, anguish and despair. And the invisible and impalpable substance of her being, which constituted her individuality, her energy and her life, was projected outside: the entity that although infinitely diluted, was nevertheless her own being— which is to say, according to the expression of Indian occultists, her astral body, which is to the body what steam is to the machine that it fills and what electricity is to the apparatus that it enables to act.

The young woman, previously the mistress of her carnal envelope, was already no longer mistress of her astral body, which the Hindus also call the Linga Sharira.

Can the astral body that receives its form from the human envelope not metamorphose in its turn, and communicate a different appearance to that envelope? Can there not be a substitution of substance? Could Ghislain, who held Bérengère's life in his hand, not employ his strength to a more complete punishment than death, which destroys and does not repair? Was he not the master of the terrible secret of life and death? Did he not have the power of the adepts who hide in the solitudes of the Himalayas? Is not everything transformed after the last sigh? He was only hastening that transformation and directing it at his whim, like the adepts who have the power to make matter pass through matter. Everything that exists is merely an aggregate of infinitesimal molecules, whose dissociation is not impossible.

Every night, he knelt down before Djalfa's remains, and, his soul filled with an immense hope, concentrating all his strength in his desire to succeed, he listened to the secret voice that led him into that mysterious labyrinth. He had vanquished incredulity and suspicion; everything seemed possible to him now.

Already, although she was inanimate and as cold as marble, Djalfa was visibly changing. In contrast to Bérengère, her features were accentuating, taking on a harshness that they had not had during life; her beautiful blonde hair was darkening and twisting into unsubmissive locks. And Ghislain went from one to the other, establishing the magnetic current in spite of the cries and supplications of Bérengère, who was convulsed by unspeakable suffering, who implored him to spare her, or to kill her immediately. The blood of her veins was always leaking away drop by drop through the imperceptible prick that she felt in her heart, and her rival, like a vampire crouched upon her, gradually penetrated her, gorging on her life.

In the morning, Entrames ordered her to forget the tortures of slumber.

"You will be cheerful, loving and communicative," he told her. Then he woke her up, and the young woman immediately threw herself into his arms around him, thanking him for the happiness that he had given her.

Ghislain's strength, however, was running out; he sensed the necessity of terminating his work of justice. It seemed to him that by concentrating all the energy of his will in a beam, he would triumph over the last resistances of matter. But he needed to act in solitude. He therefore informed his wife, during one of her magnetic slumbers that she had to get rid of her parents on some pretext or other.

The Marquise de Sainte-Laure suffered from chronic bronchitis; the air of Nice had been recommended to her a long time ago, and if she had deferred her departure, it was only to watcher over her dear daughter, whose pallor and diminution troubled her.

Bérengère was so persuasive and so insistent that the good lady no longer hesitated. Her departure was settled for the following day, and everyone employed themselves with it so ardently that she was obliged to take the train at the agreed time.

The heart of a mother has surprising divinations; solid links always attach it to her child, and nothing in life can break them. Enclosed in her coupé, the Marquise wept recklessly and claimed that she was hiding something from her, that a misfortune a hovering over her, that she felt it, that she was certain of it—but Bérengère smiled at her and reassured her.

"What do you fear for me? Have you not always seen me fully satisfied? Did you think that I could pretend to the extent of deceiving you? No, no, Mother, depart without fear. Ghislain loves me, and no shadow of a cloud has ever risen between us."

When the old lady had gone, the spouses returned to their retreat.

✳

"I don't know what's the matter with me," said Bérengère, as they followed the dark pathways. "My thought escapes me now for long hours. A physical metamorphosis is also taking place in me. Does it not seem to you that my hair is lighter in color, that my body is no longer the same?"

"In fact, you now resemble Djalfa."

But she uttered a loud cry. "Don't say that! Don't say that! I'm afraid. Oh, your gaze is cruel—what do you want?"

"I want the resemblance to be complete. I want the dead woman to be resuscitated in you."

The young woman fell to her knees. "Is that the punishment, then? Will you be pitiless?"

"I am as pitiless as you have been."

"But I can escape, flee, return to my patents, ask them for protection from you . . ."

"Try, then. You're feebler than a child, for your will is submissive to mine. Come."

She followed him meekly, incapable of resisting.

He traversed the long corridor, the silent chamber where he had loved and suffered so much, and then, tripping the catch in the woodwork, he penetrated into the secret redoubt.

"Lift that curtain," he said, when her gaze had become accustomed to the gloom.

But she could not obey; she went frightfully pale and collapsed on the carpet. When she came round, her eyes immediately encountered the funereal couch, and she started uttering such clamors that Ghislain put her to sleep and threw her, impotent, on to the cadaver of her rival.

"Oh, Djalfa," he said, "let your astral body, disengaged from terrestrial bonds, melt for me into this palpitating mold. Let this prodigy be accomplished by the power of our amour. Since nothing dies, you cannot be annihilated, and I sense you hovering, like a bird of light You will live again, in all the plenitude of life, by taking possession of this body, which I have liberated for you, and which is already offering itself to give you shelter. Take its strength, its suppleness and its warmth while its impotent thought will go to inhabit our inert cadaver.

Ghislain put the bodies of the two women in contact. After a moment, it seemed to him that a sort of vapor floated over the bed; that vapor was born on the breast of Djalfa, at the place of the heart. It rose up in a blue spiral and extended like a light cloud, uncertain of the direction to follow.

Entrames did not speak; all his power was in the brain, whose lobes were functioning with an extraordinary activity. Upright and motionless, he was thinking of nothing but the miracle that he desired, and the hope of success doubled his strength.

It was that surge of his entire being toward the adored woman that he wanted to revive, he was insensible to Bérengère's suffering, and to the fact that the latter, although asleep, was agitating desperately, making vain efforts to flee. She was experiencing a kind of rip in the region of the heart; her life was flowing away through it, slowly and dolorously. Her empty brain became icy at the same time as a sensation of breath, going from the exterior to the interior, caused her a frightful suffocation.

After a few further passes, she remained motionless. Above her extended a white form, but of a hue so faint that it was scarcely perceptible, a cloudy silhouette of the dead woman. At one moment it was accentuated, and became so clear that Ghislain, frightened, as if before a supernatural manifestation, was troubled, ceased momentarily to project all of his force upon it. Immediately, it vanished. But a further change had taken place in Bérengère, a change so emphatic that she was almost no longer recognizable.

Woken up, she left the room automatically. She did not seem either to see or understand what was happening around her. Obedient and resigned, however, she was submissive to whatever was demanded of her, walking, sitting down, eating, and even responding incoherently to the questions that were asked of her. Her movements had an unaccustomed stiffness, and her features remained immobile.

In the evening, however, when Ghislain wanted to take her back to Djalfa, she struggled with a desperate energy. Consciousness of her wretched situation seemed to have returned to her; her cries became convulsive and heart-rending. Finally, having run out of strength, she submitted; her face was flooded with tears, her breast was heaving with hectic sobs. She fell on the funereal couch, and went to sleep as usual, under the magnetic influence.

From that moment on, Ghislain felt fully reassured. He acted coldly and calmly, certain of the final success. All resistance, he thought, was smoothed out, whatever it might be. He also understood that he had to carry out progressively, by almost insensible degrees, that transmutation of one being into another, for fear of failure, of breaking the fragile instrument that he had in his hands.

His victim, her teeth clenched, her limbs quivering, seemed to be enduring frightful tortures; her nostrils were pinched; a little foam came to her lips. It was necessary to act with excessive prudence, for suffering has its limits, and can become mortal in attaining the limit that nature has fixed.

Bérengère was no longer cataleptic, for she would have remained insensible to Djalfa's influence, and in any case, the ordeal would have been infinitely longer. The limbs had to conserve their flexibility in order to lend themselves to the desired transformation; the blood had to circulate freely, in order to receive the new elements and assimilate them.

Although unconscious, the young woman was suffering in her flesh, gripped by an inexpressible anguish by virtue of the puncture in her heart, through which her life was leaking. The vampire that was obsessing her, gradually taking it, was melting into her, invading her, giving her its form and its thought.

She sensed that confusedly, albeit intolerably, and impotent tears ran from her eyes.

When she left the room, Ghislain was obliged to support her, she was so weak. He dressed her and covered her with thick veils, in order that no one would perceive the new change that had taken place in her.

Her reason now abandoned her. When someone spoke to her, her fearful gaze fixed on them and her lips moved, but then she fell back into prostration. A frightened domestic spoke to Ghislain about the necessity of calling a physician, and that incident persuaded him to hasten the denouement, in the dread of not being able to complete his frightful proof.

The following might, he concentrated all the energy of his will like a beam in order to act upon his victim more powerfully. In the beginning, it seemed to him, for the first time, that his efforts were vain, that an insurmountable wall loomed up between him and her, and that his force buckled as if against armor, bending like a reed.

Then he fixed his thought ardently on the goal that he was pursuing; he evoked the adored soul of Djalfa, and begged her not to abandon him on the threshold of paradise. Had he only succeeded thus far in order to taste the dolor of disappointment more intensely? Must he fall back into the world of darkness, after having nursed the ineffable hope of finding her again? Was he not worthy of that recompense? Had he not traveled his calvary with courage and patience? Had he not obeyed her as he would have obeyed God himself, in the ardor of his respectful amour?

He prostrated himself, with his face to the ground, and from all his being, plunged in desolation and tenderness, sprang a profound cry, a supreme prayer. Immediately, his courage returned, he felt reinforced and sustained. His nerves and his muscles obeyed him; no exterior impression could any longer distract him.

Under the effort of his fluid, the jet of gray vapor emerged from Djalfa's breast, rose up turbulently, folded up on itself and came to float and extend over Bérengère. The latter writhed, and sought to escape it, but an order from Ghislain maintained her motionless.

Then, the mysterious spring still flowing, the vapor took on a vague but recognizable form: the form of Djalfa.

For a moment, she remained hesitant; then she descended, enveloped Bérengère like a light veil, and gradually melted into her.

At that moment, a ray of light slid under the mobile panel, and Ghislain, fearful of being surprised, rapidly made the usual passes to awaken the sleeper. But the latter was mortally pale; her lips tightened and creased, as if in a spectral impression of death, and an extreme chill spread over the surface of the body.

Under the pressure of an inexpressible horror and terror, Entrames sensed the pulsations of his heart stop, and a cry of despair almost escaped him. Had he forced the dose, and had the exhausted organism of the patient been unable to support it?

He threw himself on to her mouth and blew air into her lungs; he dragged her into the bedroom and opened both windows wide.

Finally, a slight tremor ran through the body. However, the young woman could not recover the use of speech; she was confined to bed and remained in the same depressed state all day. Her face was white and drawn, her lips blue, her hair completely colorless. She seemed to be at the utter extremity.

Ghislain hid that condition from the domestics carefully, and, in order to deflect suspicions, talked about a violent migraine and a need of absolute solitude for the invalid.

In the evening, he dared not continue his work. Prostrate before the cadaver of the Bohemian, he remained plunged in painful meditations.

Until then the body had remained, as on the first day, smooth and white, like a beautiful marble; the features had conserved their admirable serenity. That evening, however, a slight alteration was produced, and Ghislain shivered on observing that the gaze was becoming vitreous, and that symptoms of decomposition were becoming noticeable.

There was not a moment to lose, for his proof, so skillfully conducted, might fail, and how miserable his existence would be then!

Brutally, he took hold of Bérengère, who was no longer making any movement, and dragged her to the bed.

Absorbing himself completely in his terrible desire, he concentrated all his will upon her, all the living forces of his being, with such impetuosity that he felt faint, as if the blood were flowing away from his heart in order to ooze out of him in seething waves. His hands were icy and a nervous tremor agitated him from head to toe. He clutched the two bodies in a convulsive embrace, and for the first time, he gave his execrated spouse a long, frightful kiss, which threw him back on the bed, half-dead. A soft caress brought him round.

He almost fainted a second time, under an expression of supreme delight. Bérengère, who was no longer Bérengère but the perfect reincarnation of Djalfa, was smiling at him and holding out her arms to him.

He threw himself upon her and covered her body, whose every sinuosity and all its charming coverts reminded him of his lost love, with mad kisses. Yes, those really were Djalfa's silky tresses enveloping him, like a blonde gauze; they really were her large, luminous and profound eyes, and her moist lips, made for caresses and sweet confessions.

She spoke, and her voice rose up like the echo of ancient prayers and ancient amorous sobs.

"Finally," she said, "our desire is accomplished. I have returned to you, and nothing that is not me can any longer distract us from our enchanted dream. Remember my words: *When I am dead, I shall not quit you for that; death only exists for those who are unable to love. I will force the doors of the tomb, for my unique will, my inflexible will, is to remain forever with you and within you. Promise me to associate your power with mine and to summon me with all the ardor that I shall put into breaking my chains.* We have kept our promises."

"Djalfa!"

"Yes, Djalfa, whom your tenderness has delivered from death, and who has been reincarnated, in order to recommence with you an existence of uninterrupted happiness. Come, let us flee this sinister bed!"

Ghislain cast a glance at the couch. A formless cadaver lay there; a broth of flesh in complete decomposition; a horrible mass of bones and blood.

The two lovers took one another by the hand, and, having closed the door of the frightful sepulcher again, they quit that accursed place for ever.

A TALE OF THE OTHER WORLD

by Charles de Sivry

> Those who do not see the Lord while alive
> will never see him when dead.
> —Fo Hi

THE fearful young maidservant had conducted me to the chamber where I was to spend the night and, as I had anticipated, she only entered it trembling like a leaf, in order to make the final preparations. She hastened to deposit next to the vast fireplace the logs that she was carrying in her apron, made up the bed on the double and fled, darting a "Bonsoir, Monsieur, bonne nuit!" at me full of terror and compassion. I heard her sabots clicking in the sonority of the old staircase and, left alone, I set about studying the famous haunted room in detail.

There was the slight but penetrating odor of damp typical of old wood paneling. However, the walls showed no trace of moisture. The furniture, although somewhat worm-eaten, dated from the last century. The vast bed, whose white paint had taken on the yellowed tone of old ivory, was ornamented with cretonne curtains printed with large red designs, and near the hearth, where a crackling and spitting fire of green wood was burning, two capacious armchairs extended their arms.

The window, with a single flap, was garnished with small panes, some of which were old, green-tinted and blistered, while others had been recently inserted, the putty that held them in place still being new. That detail caused me to remember the fantastic and implausible tales that were told in the locale about the house.

For several nights, it appeared, projectiles of every nature—stones, pieces of wood, fragments of horseshoes, had been thrown at the house, where they had done some damage and broken several windows. Watchmen had been posted and the gendarmerie and the clergy alerted without anyone being able either to lay a hand on the authors of those disagreeable pleasantries or to exorcize the demons naïvely held responsible for the bizarre projections.

I do not know whether I believe any more in the devil than in the gendarmerie; and I got ready to go to bed.

Old legends and nurses' tales of ghosts passed through my mind. I recalled the story of the hussar to whom a frightful specter dragging chains and vomiting flames appeared one night in an old château. The hussar was brave, and, not having died of fear, was conducted by the phantom to a certain paving-stone in a ground-floor room. The following day he lifted the stone and discovered a treasure, of which he took possession, and bones, to which he piously gave a sepulcher.

Now, while the details of that fanciful story were haunting me, I heard—positively—the sound of chains being dragged in the sonority of the staircase. It could not be a fantasy of my imagination. The noise was real and loud. My hosts, honest peasants, farmers of my family for nearly twenty years, were incapable of playing a joke on me—a hoax, as one says nowadays. Was it some scoundrel, then, some vagabond abusing the superstitious credulity of those worthy people in order to lodge himself gratis?

I did not know what to think when, the metallic sounds having stopped on my landing, I heard the latch of my door click and I saw it opening very slowly.

Instinctively, I recoiled toward the bed and took my revolver from the pocket of my overcoat.

When I turned round I found myself face to face with a tall figure entirely veiled by a shroud and carefully bound with enormous chains.

I was about to speak when the apparition said to me, in a very soft and distant voice: "Would you please, Monsieur, rid me of all this apparatus of chains and shrouds in which your imagination is holding me entangled and permit me to warm myself at this hearth?"

Before that courteous fashion of expression, my terror suddenly disappeared, and, although I could not yet divine with what I was dealing, I advanced bravely toward the fireplace and gestured toward one of the armchairs as if to invite my strange visitor to sit down.

In the movement that he made to reach the place I had designated to him, his funereal apparatus disappeared and I saw a tall old man, stiff and upright, with a sympathetic face, clad in a pale blue coat with long basques, a flower-patterned waistcoat, satin culottes the same color as the coat, and chiné stockings.

One thing that struck me was the exaggeratedly faded tone of those old-fashioned garments, and the ensemble of my guest, which seemed so scantly material that I believed I could see through his body the objects placed behind him, as if he were made of horn or unpolished glass.

"Excuse, I beg you, my nocturnal visit, but I'm so bored that I'd be very glad to converse with a living man. All my old friends are dead, like me; sometimes they still come to visit me, but not often enough for my liking."

"But to whom do I have the honor of speaking?" I hazarded.

"I was the Chevalier de Grèges, and I lived in the château of which this farm was a dependency, and which was demolished a few years after my death by the Revolution. "Look over there," he added, "beside the bed, behind the curtain that masks it: that's my portrait, a nice pastel."

I went to look. The portrait was striking, and I noticed that the nuance of the fabrics was exactly the same as that of my singular interlocutor's garments.

"I'm frightfully bored, you see, Monsieur, and I'm always cold since I've been in this bizarre state that people call death. Don't expect any revelations from me on matters of what you call the other life; there's nothing at all here. One gets bored, one does nothing and one is cold. That's it, you see, nothing more."

I immediately put two logs on the fire, and the large flame that sprang up seemed to design a pale smile on the chevalier's discolored lips.

"Your appearance," he went on, "indicates a man of condition. Tell me, what is happening at Versailles? What is the name of the king of France? What is the fashionable amusement at the court?"

"But there isn't a court any more," I replied. "Grass is growing between the deserted paving-stones of Versailles, which has become a museum, and there isn't a king of France any longer."

"Ah!" he said, simply. "In that case, there's no more of anything! People must be very bored. Oh," he added, smiling "you're looking at the window; yes, we're the ones who have recently broken the panes. Romécamp des Saulaies and de Rieux came to see me. We didn't know what to do with our time and made up that game of throwing stones and other small objects we found on the road at the window. We competed to see who could break the most panes; de Rieux won. I regret having caused damage to these poor folk, inasmuch as I'd be very embarrassed to compensate them in any fashion, but what do you expect, Monsieur? I'm so bored, and I'm so cold!"

I added a further log to the fire. I found myself gripped with a veritable compassion for the poor gentleman, defunct and chilly.

"You seem to be a soul in pain, Chevalier," I said to him, "And if a few masses said in your honor could be any relief to you, let it be understood that I'm entirely at your service."

"Oh," he replied, shaking his head, "thank you very much for the gallant intention, but I'm very Voltairean, and it's necessary to confess to you that I don't believe in God."

As he said that, first light blue-tinted the new panes of the window, and my guest, who was no longer saying anything and was warming his hands, suddenly diminished in intensity. He disappeared gradually, vanishing into the light of the matinal daybreak, so completely that a moment later I no longer saw anything but the angle that his faded blue coat made, the color of which disappeared in its turn, confounded with the pale sky of the autumnal dawn.

And the cock crowed three times.

THE MYSTERY OF AN INCARNATION

by Victor-Émile Michelet

Et nunc et semper dilectae dicatum.[1]

IN that epoch, in a vehement fit of misanthropy, I had retired to a grim bay on the Breton coast. The charm of a little village delightfully situated before the sea had arrested my footsteps of a voyager. The group of somber cottages where poor people lived with difficulty by fishing certainly had no special originality, but the soul of the location enveloped with mildness the saddened soul of the passer-by. Woods of oaks and elms isolated from the terrestrial horizon that cluster of huts, whose openings gaped toward that foliage, protected from the west wind by a rampart of abrupt granite ridges.

At that place, the landscape was divided into two antithetical parts. To the east, plunging into the earth, there was the joy of a dense and sumptuous vegetation; to the west, the ground entering as a promontory into the Atlantic consisted of a series of enormous granitic masses of a violent savagery. Camped in that village, I could contemplate simultaneously the two most contrary aspects of multiform nature: her most seductive smile and her most frightful convulsion.

---

1 As it is now and ever shall be, hallowed beloved.

Adjacent to the village, a very small cemetery descended in a gentle slope toward a strand forming a curt solution of continuity between the gaping cliffs of the coast. During high tides the flow came to brush the nearest graves. I shall never forget the impression that my first visit to that meager necropolis caused me. Enclosed in a wall at elbow height, one penetrated into it, as into almost all rural Breton cemeteries, by crossing a stile carved into the granite. An ardent sun made the blue sea shine. Tombstones festooned with brambles and ivy weighed upon the heavy yellow earth. Between them, old pines had grown, the thin bare trunks of which carried the rounded crowns high into the sky, opaque clods in which a few sparrows were chirping. Oh, the adorable cemetery! How delightfully the weary body would repose there, immortally lulled by the song of the waves. To the grandiose sepulcher of Chateaubriand on his solitary islet, I would have preferred a corner in that funerary field, where the angel of death must have smiled when he passed over it.

On the crosses I read Celtic names. A few inscriptions were analogous to this one: *To the memory of Jean-Yvon Guivarec'h, lost at sea.* Thus, several of the sepulchers cited the names of cadavers they had never received, which the waves still rolled on beds of pink algae. But those dead men, so the old men affirmed, came back every year to spend the day of the dead in the ordinarily empty tomb, in order to hear the prayers said for their soul by beloved voices.

One grave was florid with superb red roses, and had an aspect different from the others. It bore an ansate cross sculpted in the granite and charged with the following inscription:

MIRIAME HÉLÈNE
23 November ****-3 February ****
IRRADIAT HAEC ANIMA MEAM[1]

---

1 Irradiate this my soul.

So the person whose remains repose there had only lived for two months! What unknowable destiny casts these beings into a world that they desert immediately? Something attracted me toward that sepulcher of a tiny infant. Why, in that cemetery of mariners, the strange mysticism of that Latin inscription? And was it by chance or not that the ansate cross displayed its form there, unusual in Christian countries and of which theologians, except perhaps for Tertullian, had not glimpsed the very ancient symbolism?[1]

Having returned to the inn, my first concern was to question the landlady about the tomb. There happened to be an old woman of the village there at that moment, old Katell, renowned in the surrounding area for speaking French admirably. Katell, glad to show off her talent as a storyteller to a "city monsieur," told me in her singsong voice a prolix tale from which I succeeded in disentangling the principal facts.

The little being asleep in the tomb for nearly fifty years had lived in an isolated house on the coast, a kilometer from the village. Once, someone who was then, according to Katell, a "young monsieur," had built that dwelling in order to come to it with his young wife and a little girl who had just been born.

"Oh, Monsieur," Katell affirmed, "the beautiful child! But everyone said that she wouldn't live, because she was more beautiful than the angels of the good God. If you had seen her when she smiled! Oh, my God, for sure she heard the angels calling her!"

Of that child, whom she had perceived for a few moments nearly half a century ago, the old woman seemed to conserve an ever-present memory. I was not astonished by that, knowing the indestructible energy with which the memory of those simple folk retains the images it receives in the current of a monotonous life.

---

1 The "most ancient" symbolism of the ansate cross, or Egyptian ankh, is that of eternal life. More recently it symbolizes the female sex; the astrological sign for the planet Venus is a version of it.

A few weeks after arriving, the child died.

"Monsieur," said Katell, "you're not going to believe me. Several times I've recounted the thing to painters passing through here, and I've seen that they took me for an old madwoman. All the same, it's necessary that I tell you. On the earth that covers the poor little body, the parents put armfuls of flowers; beautiful flowers, Monsieur, of a kind that never grow hereabouts. There were roses in the middle of February. They were roses flowered in hothouses, such as one sees in châteaux. Well, for more than a month, Monsieur, the roses stayed as fresh as the day they were picked. However, that winter, there were frosts and rain such as are hardly ever known. Six weeks later, there were still fresh flowers. They weren't new flowers, though, for no one in these parts would have been able to find roses in February, and the parents had gone to Paris. Ask Jean-Marie Elias, the gravedigger, whether I'm lying; he's very old but he still remembers everything I've told you there. And you, Charlotte," she added in Breton to the landlady, who was laying the table, "You're too young to have seen it, but your late mother must have told you about it."

"Ia," replied Charlotte, who did not speak French, "my mother often told me that my older brother, Lomic, who's navigating for the State at present was once very ill when he was very small. The doctor claimed that there was no more hope. My mother took Lomic to the little girl's tomb and said prayers, and my brother was cured in three days."

Candid souls, I thought, for whom all events conserve their aura of mystery; fortunate souls whose florescence has not been desiccated by the breath of sad cities and the evil century.

"But what became of the parents?" I asked Katell.

"The mother is dead, Monsieur. The father still lives in the house, of which you can see the roof from here. He lives there alone, served by the little girl's nurse, a foreigner from Paimpol, who hasn't ever quit her master since that time. Oh, the poor

Monsieur, he was grief-stricken. Such a good man! There's never been an unfortunate in the neighborhood without the Monsieur having been good to him. In spite of that, people are a little afraid of him. He has such a funny way of looking at you. His house is full of books, which he spends his time reading, when he isn't walking along the coast."

"Has he been living like that for a long time?"

"Years and years, Monsieur. Once, when he was younger, he often went on voyages. Now, he no longer leaves the neighborhood."

During my lunch in the inn, Katell, while knitting, told me a host of anecdotes about the old man, trivial for the most part.

"This thing, Monsieur, my late husband could have told you if he were still in this world, poor dear. He'd been a leading seaman and could read like a priest. One day—oh, it was a long time ago—the Monsieur came to our house. 'Pierre,' he said to my man, would you care to take a glass of rum in the house? I have a favor to ask of you,'

"'I'm all yours, Monsieur,' my man replied. Oh, something funny had happened. Monsieur le Vicomte de X, the master of the Château de X, who was then a handsome fellow of twenty-two, had come to spend a few days in the neighborhood. He amused himself shooting the seagulls with his rifle all along the coast. The Monsieur liked the birds, and it caused him chagrin when anyone did them harm. He wrote the Vicomte a very nice letter to ask him not to shoot the seabirds any more. The Vicomte continued hunting them anyway. Then the Monsieur talked to him, and there was an argument.

"That was why the Monsieur came to look for my man. 'The Monsieur has asked me to be his witness,' Pierre said to me, when he came back. 'He's going to fight a duel with Monsieur le Vicomte.' My God! If it isn't frightful that men massacre one another like that! The two Messieurs fired pistol shots on the heath at Bizien, which you can see over there.

"The Vicomte fired first at the Monsieur without hitting him. The Monsieur said to him: 'Monsieur, I beg you, will you promise me not to kill the local birds any longer?'

"'Monsieur,' said the Vicomte, 'perhaps I'll reply when you've fired.'

"The Monsieur said to my man, who was further away than the Vicomte: 'Pierre, raise your hat on the end of your arm and don't move!' And he fired into the hat, which was traversed by the bullet. Then the Vicomte held out his hand and said: 'Monsieur, I promise you to leave the birds that you love in peace.'"

Katell's verbiage, all the details that she gave me about the exterior life of the solitary, piqued my curiosity keenly.

In my walks along the coast I often encountered that singular individual. He was an agile and thin old man, whose face, framed by his white hair and beard, bronzed by the sun and sea breeze like those of mariners, was still handsome. The eyes, very young, shone with a moist gleam similar to one I had remarked in certain vegetarians or a few socialites habituated to injections of atropine.

I had certainly desired to make the acquaintance of the man, but he seemed little disposed to allow his grim solitude to be invaded, and sometimes he was unable to suppress a slightly hostile gaze directed at some passer-by whose silhouette importuned his reverie.

A fortunate circumstance obliged him to emerge from his reserve, and soon, a current of sympathy having linked us, I found myself admitted to the old man's intellectual intimacy. Having sealed his heart, he only opened it by a crack to his thought. I recognized quickly, by the power of his ideas, one of those men of genius, more numerous than one might believe, who, for one reason or another, disdain to work, and concentrate all their energies in the solitary expansion of their personality.

Recalled to Paris, I remained without news for a year of the old man whose magnificent intelligence had dazzled my youth. Then, one day, I received a package containing a manuscript and a letter thus conceived:

When you read these lines I will have quit the earth. I am bequeathing you the secret of the dolor that has tormented my life. A long time ago I swore to destroy the pages in which I was tempted to make this revelation. They are certainly unworthy of the being whose noble apparition they evoke. May they take wing in your hands! I have selected you as my confidant for reasons that you might not understand. Pardon me for speaking this. I have acquired the habit of divining in the present flower the future fruit, and I foresaw in your mind an efflorescence of which you might not have suspected the possibility yourself. You bear on your forehead the seal of the predestined who perceive the radiation of the Light. The last glimmers of my sunset salute your dawn.

I sought information. The old man had been found dead on his child's tomb one October evening.

As for the manuscript, I believe that I am deferring to its author's desire in publishing it in its integrity:

The Mystery of an Incarnation

I have often wondered, with anguish, whether I ought to recount the ineffable event that tore my life into two parts.

Ought I to bury in my heart, as in an inviolable tabernacle, the memory of the being who came to me from the depths of the Absolute? Ought I to deliver a description to the profane human herd, with a sacrilegious pen, of that divine emanation, whose disappearance I shall mourn forever?

As for what it makes of me, what does it matter? Whether, for having recounted with pious exactitude the story of a reality of which the observation surpasses their understanding, I might be treated as a liar, a visionary or a madman, I cannot bring myself to care. I am not accustomed to listen to the stammering of human ignorance. If others, more elevated in the spiritual hierarchy, attribute to me the charm of a deceptive imagination and the futile desire for a literary vainglory, their opinion cannot afflict my indifference.

But I hesitate to deliver to ignorant, vulgar or malevolent commentaries the sacred memory of a being whose mysterious advent could only be sensed by a few rare souls. Oh, frail child, little bird who perched for an hour on the tree of life, angel whose wing of light brushed my somber youth, advise me!

I believe that I discern the response:

"Always act for noble souls. Only think of the others in order to give them your pity. Even if there is only one just man or one genius on earth, think of that one, and remember that you owe him the revelation that you know. Speak: your voice will go toward the ears destined to hear it. When in the human crowd, a great soul cannot hold it in disdain. Every word of Truth or Beauty is a sun from which everyone can benefit in accordance with his ability; the eagle alone contemplates it, but the sparrow is warmed by its radiance. Speak. Why should you fear insult to the object of your worship? Blasphemy only injures those who proffer it. Do you not know that the posthumous strength of martyrs increases in direct proportion to the maledictions launched by persecutors? What would the glory of saints be if evil did not exist? Speak!"

I am obeying.

In the course of my long existence, I have neglected the apparent action. Like all men whose intellect spreads its wings outside time, I could only accord a disdainful commiseration to the sterile agitation of Occidentals in my century. My life was uniquely sentimental and conceptual, and I only sent forth the falcon of my will to launch it into the gulf of the Mystery. For half a century, to the scorn of all minute mortals, only effort toward the Divine obsessed my thought.

In consequence of contingencies that it is superfluous to enumerate, my youth was much involved with society. In citing that detail, I desire to establish that I was not a contemplative hermit whose vision was deformed by solitude. At twenty-five years of age it was given to me to acquire an experience of men capable of challenging that of those miserable old men who take pleasure in the vanity of social intrigue for long years.

I was twenty-six when the event that determined my subsequent life occurred: my wife became pregnant.

Hélène was then twenty-three. She recalled the type of Virgin that certain northern Primitives, like Memling and Jan Van Eyck, cherished. The law of attractions had pushed us toward one another; but her mind, although moving under its native impulsion in the sphere of ideas into which I launched myself, conserved its originality while blossoming in contact with mine. It was certainly impregnated by the emanations of my thought, but without losing the charm of its initial perfume. Her profound soul, a marvelous keyboard with which the fingers of angels, playing thereon, awoke harmonious intuitions, was revealed in her candid dark eyes and in the archaic quality of her beauty, attesting the phenomenon of heredity called by modern physiologists "atavism," thanks to which a being resembles some ascendant, a prototype of its race. But the aggressive energy of the ancestor, a warrior of the Renaissance, a famous Maréchal de France whose family had possessed the crown of Bretagne in distant centuries, was transformed in the young woman into a force of melancholy gentleness.

At the certainty of her maternity, Hélène was gripped by an anxiety that I shared. To summon a soul to life from the depths of the Unknown was a responsibility that our youth did not envisage without trembling.

"So be it," affirmed the young mother. "This child will be my masterpiece. Intoxicated by the Beautiful, my spirit is a bird that flies among worlds from which it returns dazzled, without being able to bring back the smallest flower in its rosy beak as testimony. If I were a man I would be subject to the torture of poets impotent to realize their vision. The faculty of expression was refused me, and sometimes I was saddened to sense myself artistically sterile. Yes, this child will be my masterpiece. I want to create a sublime being, a being of Light and Beauty. And the ideal I glimpse behind a veil of mist, he will contemplate with his eagle eyes, in an integral splendor, with the serene limpidity of genius."

From then on, it was agreed that we would unite our forces in order to awaken to life a magnificent human model.

"But it is not today that that work is commencing," I said to Hélène. "Every effort of elevation, every minute of exaltation toward the Divine pierced under one of its multiple manifestations, every beat of the wing toward the triangle of the Beautiful, the True and the Just, every one of the vanished volitions that constitute the noble part of our past: all that is not lost, any more than the burden of our weaknesses and errors. And it is because you are natally pure that it will be permitted to you to give birth to a superior being.

Hélène delivered herself entirely to her work of creation, with a constant energy, scrupulously following my successive indications.

Of that arrival of a child in the terrestrial world, the mystery of incarnation that disconcerts humans, I could only reveal certain phases to her, but her marvelous intuition penetrated at a stroke arcana on which the meditation of admirable thinkers has labored for a long time.

By means of the enlightenment drawn from my studies I was able to lift some of the veils by which the secret of the Word made flesh is enveloped by modern science, which only knows the modifications of the phenomena of embryology, and by religions, all of which, in the symbolism of the Fall and the Redemption, inform those who can understand of a part of the eternal Truth.

Exoteric science, on the physical plane to which its investigation is limited, has glimpsed, albeit very incompletely, under the name of Evolution, one of the primordial laws that order the world. It has not yet understood that the Law in question is mystically enunciated under the title of Redemption, by all theologies. But it does not know, and doubtless never will know, at the opposite pole, the law of Involution that religions call the Fall, in accordance with which births are operated.

How does a soul, an emanation of the Absolute descending the spiral of Involution, enter into matter? How it is borne away by the vertigo of the Fall, toward the womb of a woman, the first human tomb? Of that mystery, I can only lift a little of the veil here.

By way of Amour, by means of the august embrace of their flesh, the human couple attaches to a parcel of matter a principle of Universal Life. Thus is created a center of attraction, the power of which radiates toward the spheres in which spirits desirous of incarnation circulate. The Word of a couple summons a soul of their race. The higher it launches toward the zenith of Infinity, the more beautiful and more noble is the one that responds to the carnal invitation. But it can happen that the wing of Amour occasionally carries the generative virtuality of a vulgar couple beyond their sphere of customary attraction, and that is why a beautiful woman or a pure genius is sometimes born to a bourgeois couple magnified for an instant by the ecstasy of a spasm.

Like everything else in the world, spirits waiting to put on a corporeal form obey the law of Hierarchy. It is an elementary spirit that enters into the skin of a boor; it is a spirit already florid by virtue of an anterior development that will inhabit the brain of a Dante. "Everything created is a revelation in the Flesh," say all the mystics via the voice of Novalis. And the highest revelation is incarnate in Heroes, the supreme types of humanity that pious Hellas once proclaimed demigods: Phidias, Shakespeare, Leonardo da Vinci, Plato, Saint John, Jacob Boehme . . ."

"I want to be the mother of a child of that beauty," Hélène said.

"Be careful! Every grandeur is expiated by a dolor. Seven swords are reserved for the hearts of glorious mothers."

"Often, alas, those of humble mothers too. Popular belief affirms that during pregnancy, the sentiments of the mother influence the child."

"It is right. The popular soul is the well in which the pure water of Truth is stagnant. Ancient Greece knew an art unknown to moderns, those contemplators of Beauty: callipedia, the art of creating beautiful children."

"Can you reconstitute that art, friend?"

"We can try."

"But first it would be necessary to know the sex of the child."

"That is easy. We can determine it by either of two procedures: that of contemporary physiologists or that of the ancient sages. In the meantime, we can have recourse to magnetic lucidity. All forms are inscribed, outside time, in the sidereal light, as in a succession of instantaneous photographic prints. A magnetized human whose sidereal body is put in communication with that universal receptacle of reflections perceives those forms, inaccessible to anyone who is not in a state of Vision."

I put a young woman to sleep, whose lucidity I had previously proven.

"It's a girl," she said. "Oh, how beautiful she is! She will be born in the first fortnight of December, on a Saturday, before midnight. It's impossible for me to read the exact date, or to know any more. Wake me up."

The sex being known, it was necessary to give the child a name.

To name a being is to consecrate it, to dress it in a cope of silk or a shirt of Nessus; it is to attach a talisman of gold or lead to its neck. Certainly, nothing is indifferent to human destiny, and the eventualities that the vulgar attribute to absurd chance are manifest as the effects of unknown causes. But the will that associates the individuality of a being with the sonority of a few syllables is making an unconscious incantation, the vibrations of which, refracted by the shield of Destiny, fall back upon the head of the living being in waves of curses or glory, sadness or felicity. On that truth, the divination of great poets habituated to manipulating the evocative virtue of words is in accord with the science of the Prophets. It is said in the Vedas: "You shall give your daughter a sonorous name, abundant in vowels and soft in fluttering on human lips." Around the cradles of legendary princes, godmother fays invested the frail godsons with fortunate syllables, and it is not in futility that religions baptize newborns with the already illustrious names of martyrs or saints, beings of a superior humanity that surround the subsequent veneration of races with an occult force.

The child received the names Miriame Hélène, each expressing the feminine ideal of a civilization.

The Hebraic vocable Miriame, the hieroglyphic mystery of which I shall not explain here, designated the woman whose forehead is crowned with the seven stars and whose feet trample the serpent of astral light.

In the Homeric myth, Hélène, the woman whose charming wake the Trojan old men followed ecstatically, bears a name that, preceded by a new hierogram, is attached to the light of the moon—Selene—and of which the root El recalls "immutable," in the initial languages of the Orient, the residues of the mother tongue, the whole concept of splendor, glory and magnificence. If it is for rare seers that the name Hélène awakes the metaphysical revelation contained in its suave sonority, thanks at least to a long tradition, it represents to a greater number of less profound imaginations the idea of supreme beauty, the most radiant form of humanity that nature has caused to spring from her womb.

A name contains within it a representation of the ensemble of thoughts whose correspondences it summons in the person who pronounces it. It therefore combines with its essential virtue that which is attributed to it by the tradition of a human collectivity, and that by which it is magnetized by the will that cloaks a being therewith. A name is a living symbol of the being that it designates.

Bearing in her loins an unknown being, which her maternity was summoning from the heart of the Infinite, Hélène considered herself as a temple that ought not to be profaned by any vile thought or vision of ugliness.

"Spirit of my child, so long as your obscure form fills my womb, you shall live in me as in a splendid palace, in which the genius of great artists has painted the walls with frescoes. I shall never think of you, or any part of you, without associating with it some idea of beauty . . . but," she asked me, "has the soul of a child entered into it while the mother bears it?"

"According to the secret doctrine, the soul only commences to attach itself to the fetus when it has a brain—which is to say, in accordance with the evidence of embryology, toward the eighth month; but it floats around it then. It is only at the moment of birth that it penetrates it, at the same time as the first breath of air, just as, at death, it is exhaled with the last breath. In any case, the essential soul is never allied as narrowly with the body as certain theologians teach exoterically. Irreducible to carnal imprisonment, it is the aura in which form bathes. Your soul is your ideal."

The people who appeared, an adorable missionary, to give our world the most magnificent revelation of beauty, the Greeks, installed noble works of art in the dwellings of women in order that the eyes of mothers, haunted by perpetual images of beauty, might imagine sons as charming as the gods. Like those genitrices, Hélène surrounded herself with an atmosphere of beauty. Living in Paris during the period of her gestation, she spent whole days in the Louvre.

The moderns do not comprehend the harmony of the human body. How can a race habituated to consider nudity as shameful understand the marvelous poem of plasticity? That sacrilegious ignorance of her most admirable masterpiece, just nature chastises in the very flesh of those brutal hypocrites. She fashions them with grotesque torsos, filthy bellies and hideous limbs and launches them into the irony of light, heaps of amorphous meat, in order that one day, some vengeful power, some grim Daumier will whip their ignominious appearance immortally.

Triumphing over time, Greek statuary insults them with its glory and transports with pure joys the human elite, ever renewed, to whom destiny assigns the mission of conserving the flame of the altar of divine Beauty.

Of the Hellenic masterpieces, the one that inspired the most intense emotion in Hélène, the one that twisted all her fibers with a frisson and covered her young face with the sacred pallor that adolescent poets give to a fine verse, was the Victory of Samothrace. Oh, a curse upon the cause that mutilated that sublime body! Certainly, the great hand that sculpted you in marble, O Victory, petrified soul, did not want to make you the monstrous allegory of the massacre of one army by another, the apotheosis of murder and brutality. O august form, I know the desire with which your feet vibrate on your stone rostrum. You are the victory of humanity over Hell, the triumph of the Triangle on high over the Triangle below, of truth over error, of good over evil, of beauty over ugliness; and the lyrical thrust of your loins, the impetuous flight of your large wings, bear you straight toward the climate of your homeland, toward the mystery of your dream, toward the bosom of the divine.

Like all artists loving the spiritualized character of form, Hélène reproached the normal body of woman for the heaviness of the thighs, twin columns supporting the excessively powerful entablature of the pelvis and the rump, a massive architecture whose weight crushes the frail stems of the ankles. Thus the female appears a superb animal of reproduction, all of whose energies are concentrated in the abdomen, a vast temple of fecundity. Veiling that fault, the author of the Venus Victrix was obliged to surround with drapery the legs and the raised knee, in order to cause the flower of the adorable torso to spring forth from the isoperimetric shaft.

The young mother evoked on the horizon of her imagination a slimmer ideal of feminine plasticity, ennobled by the virile elegance of the adolescent, close to that attempted by the sculptors of Hermaphrodites extended in the Louvre on their marble cushions.

Day by day, she populated the memory of her pupils with the most radiant heads that the hands of great masters had caressed. The Virgins of the Italian Primitives, the tapering ovals of those faces ever feature of which reveals and energy of tenderness and amour, the serene candor of those gilded foreheads, had invaded her vision like beloved portraits. It was to those types of feminine beauty, scantly various, that her mind consecrated its sisterly kiss: to the women of Florentines and Umbrians, those whose voluptuous melancholy Sandro Botticelli adored and those whose pink cheeks Perugino animated with a pagan joy of living. But above all, a magnetic attraction drew Hélène to the women of the supreme hero of painting, the divine Leonardo da Vinci. How she absorbed the profound grace and the enigmatic softness of those profiles, which smiled in knowing the arcana of death and life.

Among those creatures of beauty, had she chosen a proto-type after which her voluntary thought attempted to model in her entrails the face of her child? She remembers that one day, in the Academy of Florence, before the archangel soaring with sword in hand in Botticelli's *Tobias*, she had exclaimed in a surge of passionate admiration: "Of, if I had a son, I would like him to resemble him!"

I found a reproduction of the head of the archangel: dense dark curls framing the purity of the outline of genius, enlivening the warm dullness of an even complexion in which an intrinsic ardor is affirmed, directed by will; eyes of a tranquil heroism, a mouth born for the voluptuous kiss of ides; the face of a being capable of putting his dream into action after having conquered it in a superhuman domain. Gentle as it might be, that face is male; Hélène feminized it in her imagination. It was on that flower of archangelic humanity that the butterfly of her dream alighted most frequently. But, an artist without a work, she preferred above all the personal idea of beauty that surged forth in the solitary intimacy of her vision, and which she wanted to realize in flesh.

Every form reveals a soul. To influence the form of a living being, it is first necessary to influence its soul. Hélène extended toward her daughter's soul her thought charged with the genius of great poets and divinatory music. She plunged recklessly into the dream of the highest minds. Celtic in origin, she disdained the mediocrity of the French genius, which, until the dawn of the nineteenth century, had not been able to give the world a single great poet. Shakespeare, Dante and the French Romantics reigned over her ambiance, but above all, she lingered over lyric poets whose dream quivered with an occult vertigo, the chaste ideal of which launched forth like a golden lily from a gulf of shadow, the amour of which flew toward women of angelic essence, such as Edgar Poe and Charles Baudelaire. Around her, companions evoked by her election, matched the likes of

Leonore, Ligeia, Poe's Morella, Balzac's Séraphita and Shelley's Queen Mab, all heroines over which fell the influx of the Moon, the dispenser of melancholy.

That exaltation, which the young woman drank like a sacred wine, those spiritual forces with which she armed her imagination, it was necessary to concentrate toward the unique goal; it was necessary to constrain them to envelop the soul of the child with a sphere of sumptuous ideality. What talisman would have the power of the Flamboyant Star of the magical Pentagram?

The moderns are unaware of the virtue of Signs. They do not know that every symbol contains, living and multiplied, the idea that it represents, and by virtue of the energy of which it can act on nature. Will they ever understand that a man can charge a Sign with the fluid of his will?

Hélène often absorbed herself in the contemplation of the invigorating sign. Everywhere, the design of the Star with five points shone before her thought, which she guided toward the future form of the child as, in occult legend, it guided the three Oriental Magi toward the child of Bethlehem.

A honey-bee of sublimity, Hélène had taken pollen from the purest flowers of human genius. If she thought of some feature of the face that she wanted her daughter to have, she immediately summoned to the mirror of her imagination the special beauty of that feature. For example, if she thought about the eyes, she visualized them, while singing in her memory, a sonorous accompaniment of a realized Word, these profound lines:

> *Large eyes of my child, adored arcana,*
> *You greatly resemble the magical grottoes*
> *In which, behind the mass of lethargic shadows*
> *Unknown treasures scintillate vaguely.*

We decided to place our efforts under the invocation of an intercessor of the elite among the great masters of the Word, among the mild heroes that follow, charmed, the man, the lion, the eagle and the bull. The soul of that dead man, faithful to our appeal, was to watch over our work and caress with his breath the forehead of our child.

Our choice settled on Apollonius of Tyana. The great pagan Mage is alive in a glory that has not been profaned by the vulgar. Only initiates venerate his memory, which has not been sullied by the mud of universal renown. Obscure messiah, no human infamy has been committed in your pure immortal name. In the empyrean of Prophets, where you are enthroned in the presence of your sacred brethren, next to Gautama the Buddha and Mohammed, beneath Jesus Christ, your side does not bleed like theirs, and your serenity laments for them and consoles them. For the truth and justice that their generous hands attempted to bring to humans, humans transmuted into lies and iniquity. Their divine names decorate social ignominy, and that is why, Apollonius, son of God, I preferred you to your sacred brothers.

Miriame appeared in the world on the second Saturday in December,[1] as the seer had announced.

To anyone who can penetrate the mystery of forms, every infant reveals the being that she will be in the maturity of her development. No more than an adult, a newborn cannot conceal the soul inscribed in her flesh.

If Hélène and I had been alone in observing the strange beauty of our child, I certainly would not insist upon it, anxious of perhaps having seen it with the partiality of a father; but no stranger, however indifferent they might be to the prestige of the ideal, passed close to her without attesting an admiration, as if some secret force emanating from that tiny body had

---

1 This conflicts with the date recorded on the tombstone, as reported earlier in the story.

constrained those passers-by to rise toward a domain higher than their habitual thoughts.

In contemplating her daughter, Hélène was swelled by the triumphant joy of creators. She had in her exactly what she had wanted. She had wrought her ideal; she had realized it in life; and that masterpiece was a being that deployed a soul—everything proved it!—a great human soul, one of those that participate most directly in the divine soul.

Certainly, I have never seen, either among the living or among the figures summoned to the virtual existence of works of art, a creature as beautiful as Miriame was a month after her birth. Each of her features had a very emphatic individuality, and yet the ensemble was not marked by the aged character that generally devolves to newborns whose face is less imprecise than usual.

An unusual profundity of feminine beauty, and a charm of masculine gentleness, enveloped that forehead, whose admirable contours announced the rare harmony of equilibrated powers. The artistic type with which Miriame's profile presented the greatest resemblance was the feminine type dear to Leonardo da Vinci, but the child's expression was more superhuman.

A nocturnal splendor emanated from that mat flesh with golden reflections, helmed with thick raven-black hair. The oval was elongated with an elegance that even Van Dyck never knew. One would have searched in vain for an imperfection in any of her features. The dark crimson mouth was designed so purely that it seemed affianced to the kiss of a god; the nose, proudly modeled, revealed a desire of suave authority; the eyes, the large eyes, under the charming arches of the eyebrows, were hollowed out in a vast double abyss of darkness sometimes illuminated by a golden scintillation.

Miriame was one month old when we decided to come and live in our house in Bretagne, in order to bring up the little Parisienne in the best conditions. The wives of the mariners, rude and fecund Breton women, were fascinated by the child, and their naïve ecstasy, their religious admiration and their candid intuition in contemplating in her a mysterious being, astonished me. In the function of her sidereal respiration, every human individual emits an aura, a magnetic atmosphere only perceptible by virtue of its effects, at least to those who have not developed in themselves the faculty of sight that Paracelsus named the sixth sense. Miriame was thus enveloped by an extraordinary power of attraction and beneficent domination.

The strange precocity of the child alarmed me. Perhaps I will be charged with hallucination; what does it matter? In accordance with the methods of my times, in brushing all levels of Parisian society, I had developed a habit of analytical observation whose mechanical function could not be troubled by the most intense emotion; and the testimony of everyone who saw our child corroborates my own.

I remember one improbable event. Miriame was then awakening to the sixth day of her existence. She was reposing in a crib adjacent to her mother's bed. Like all newborns, she sometimes made nervous grimaces in which maternal illusion salutes joyfully the first manifestation of consciousness; but this time—no error was possible—it was not a grimace. It was what popular language, always so accurately imagistic, calls an angelic smile. The child's entire face brightened; a smile so ecstatic, so unfathomable passed over her mouth and her eyes that Hélène, her heart suddenly traversed by a sibylline anguish, uttered a vehement cry, a visceral cry, as if to recall that frail adventurous soul from an unknown world.

A month later, when her mother took her in her arms, the grateful child saluted her creator with that smile, attenuated by a serene expression of humanity; and, extending toward her the inaugural beauty of her hands, she exclaimed, in a painful effort toward speech.

Then suffering fell upon that light prey. A pneumonia and a gastritis combined to torture her. Oh, I always have in my heart that pale dolorous head, that long emaciated oval and the somber lairs of the eyes, radiant, under the crepe of the lashes, with the muted majesty of martyrdom. Oh, little soul of my desperate amour, why did you suffer so much? What is the good of my vain science, which could not protect you?

For three days it was necessary to await the end. It was seven o'clock in the morning, on a Thursday in February—the slightest details of that day will live in me forever—as the moon set. Miriame, at the utmost degree of weakness, was touched by the wing of death. Oh, we sensed her soul escaping from her lips. In vain I had attempted the theurgical miracle. It was the supreme moment.

Then Hélène, in the paroxysm of human dolor, seizing her daughter's hands, uttered an appeal of strange power: "Miriame!" How the sonority of that cry still quivers in my ear! The dying chills—oh, dead already—opened her eyes. An ineffable expression passed into that gaze. And life returned in her as in the daughter of Jairus at the voice of the Master of Galilee. The two little hands clasped the mother's thumbs with all the force of their weakness, in order to draw vitality therefrom. And if Hélène attempted a gesture, a withdrawal of her hands, the infant clung to the thumbs with an unexpected energy, at the same time as her eyes, oh, those eyes of prayer and amour . . .

From seven o'clock in the morning until three o'clock in the afternoon, Hélène remained inclined over the crib without interruption, her thumbs in her daughter's hands, imposing on that tender agonizing body the magnetism of vitality. She was there, insensible, isolated from the world, all the forces of her being extended toward an invincible will: the salvation of her child. And beside her, my will corroborated hers.

At about four o'clock, the physician arrived. He had not hurried, certain that he would find death in the house. He inspected the child with amazement.

"She's saved!" he cried. "Nature sometimes works miracles, but this one, I cannot even seek to understand."

How could he have understood, a poor brain uniquely filled with a meager scholarly science and a few personal observations, that love is stronger than death, and that Hélène's had recalled the animating principles to the dying, to the dead? An intuitive thaumaturge, the desperate mother had triumphantly manipulated the mysterious virtue of the voice and the transmission of vital force via the fingers and the eyes.

Miriame recovered her health. Hope sang within us, but the wings of misfortune were hovering, wide open. Abruptly, three days later—it was exactly seven o'clock in the morning, on Sunday, as the moon set—the child died.

For three days and three nights I did not quit the crib where the dear little body lay among the roses. The serenity of death had effaced the memory of the death-throes from the pale mask. How beautiful she was, thus, in inviolable immobility! Oh, so sadly beautiful! I shall see her eternally, that waxen head with the pale gold reflection, and the vast profundity of the eyes that I did not want to close, and the mouth, the adorable mouth in which that proud color of dark crimson was still resplendent. If you had grown up, O superhuman creature, if the earth had seen you as a woman, what man would have been worthy of your amour? You ought to have been the bride of a god.

Of that mysterious being, one inexplicable detail will trouble me forever. We had wanted her admirable form to be surrounded by flowers. Flowers, those existences of beauty, innocence and perfume, were the only objects in this world meriting the caress of her hands. In order to fortify that vanished soul with the virtue of a sign, Hélène had wanted to make her a cross of flowers herself. To two equal arms, disposed in the form of a

Greek cross, her fingers attached roses, hyacinths and viburnum; in the center she put an enormous tea-rose, for the occult symbolism of the Rose and the Cross.

When, in a harsh February frost, the last spadeful of earth had fallen lugubriously on the little body, the flowery cross was laid on top of armfuls of flowers at the place in the cemetery that has since become so familiar to my knees. Six weeks later, outside the heap of rotten flowers, the tea-rose at the center of the cross still surged forth as fresh as if it were blooming on the bush. Frost, rain and the torments had passed over its petals without withering them. How? Why? That strange phenomenon was repeated several times. The following winter, chrysanthemums remained on the grave for two months without withering.

From you, sweet creature of superhumanity, therefore, such a powerful virtue emanated, such a profound beneficence, that your proximity alone embalmed with a vital energy the chrysanthemums and the roses, flowers as beautiful as you, and like you, so short-lived. Since you charmed the angel of death in their favor, oh, why did you let him carry you away in his arms?

Miriame was born in a year ruled by the Moon, on the fourth day of the new moon. She died, after two synodic months, on the fourth day of the new moon. Several times I had observed a malign selenic influence upon her. And long calculation, later, provided revelations . . .

How many time I have cursed destiny! Daughter of my flesh and my thought, why, then, did you come to earth to fly away so rapidly? The mystical belief of the ancient initiates is true: those who die young are beloved by the gods. The solitary seer of Scandinavia is right: there are souls so pure that for them, the duration of the terrestrial proof in limited to a few days. They only brush the earth; they cannot become entangled with it. They rise again, with an immediate thrust, into the involutive spiral that leads to the increate light, toward the divine entelechy. As soon as they Fall, they soar to Redemption.

However, I revolted. My flesh cried out toward your presence, my child. I have not enjoyed seeing you, I have not seen you in the harmonic development of your strength and your grace. Your mysterious power, which your infantile form revealed, I anticipated without ever seeing it blossom in the triumphant youth of a woman. I had penetrated the soul of your beauty so deeply! What did you bring in your beautiful hands of a prophetess? Perhaps the blessings of a redeemer, such as infinity delegates to humankind from time to time. You might have consoled the exile of noble souls. Poor humanity, it will always be unaware of the loss it suffered in you. In any case, has it ever understood such losses? When Shakespeare died, how many wept? At Golgotha, how many wept for Jesus? Who, then, except for me, could remember your aborted grandeur, the grandeur manifested to me alone?

A torment has haunted me for a long time. Was your death my punishment? Was I temeritous in wanting to manipulate the redoubtable forces of the Word, wanting, as a man, to create like a God? At any rate, I have suffered the torture of Prometheus. On your tombstone, my daughter, to which my loins are riveted, the vulture of regret has lacerated my liver.

In life, I sense your soul illuminating mine with an interior radiation. *Irradiat haec anima meam.* And I await the hour of exit when you will come to fetch me for the mystery of Becoming, the hour when your hands, your beautiful hands of theophany, with a tutelary gesture, will open the supreme Golden Door to the soul of your father.

REGELINDE

by Remy de Gourmont

IT was in the times when the providential barbarians arrived
to liberate Europe from Roman tradition. The Goths were
fecundating slothful Spain. A new beauty sprang forth amid
the debris of vain temples: From Aphrodites shattered like the
stones once thrown by Deucalion, a new humanity was born
into the world, radiant with energy and naïvety, ingenuous and
violent, and from the dust of Ceres, ground by heavy millstones
accustomed to the docility of grain, the men of the North
kneaded an unknown bread, which gave to males the mystery
of the will, and to women the mystery of grace.

Regelinde was the daughter of a king: a jewel whose case
had been closed upon her on the day of her birth and never
re-opened. She lived in the palace and the royal gardens, alone
in her rank and alone in her essence, as unique as an amethyst
sculpted into a cup, from which her father had only drunk once,
mingling with the dark wine the fresh blood of a tributary rebellious to tribute.

Clad in a white robe decorated with a cross of jet, with a
crimson collar and the silver ring of a secret betrothal on her finger, she walked in silence. The officers fell silent as she went by
and bowed, their eyes veiled by their left hands in the Oriental

fashion imported to Hispalis[1] by Isidore, son of Gregory, the king's physician and a learned man.

No one ever spoke to Regelinde except her father, Rescaon, Bishop Majorian, and her nurse Ipa. None of her forty slaves would have dared to touch the hem of her dress without an order from her eyes or a sign from her finger; Regelinde was the daughter of a king: a princess, mutely adored by the people of the palace like an emanation or an incarnation of Iscratene, the boreal Sun, like Iscratene herself, the feminine Star which loves humans for six months and hates them for six months.

But Rescaon was a Christian, baptized in the snows by Abbas the Martyr, who, in order to inundate the child, master of the North, had used the heat of his hand to melt a piece of ice cut in the form of a crescent moon—and Regelinde, a Christian, did not believe in Iscratene, but the privileged daughter of the living God.

Humble at the feet of Bishop Majorian, meekly accepting his penitential speeches, and humble in the face of her father, ears open to his counsel, the princess rediscovered in solitude the pride of being the unique Regelinde and the joy of being loved by the One before whom kings were only dust and bishop's ash. God loved Rescaon; God loved Majorian; God loved Ipa—but God did not love Ipa, Majorian or Rescaon as he loved Regelinde; and that was true, as true as it is that there are seven planets in the firmament, as true as it is that thunder is a clamor of the sky, a warning that we have to weep for our sins.

One morning, Rescaon called his daughter and announced to her the impending arrival of the prince to which she was secretly betrothed. The courier had arrived in the night, preceding him by six days' march. She was instructed to prepare to receive as her lord the young king of Hippona,[2] Saran, who wore on his finger a silver ring exactly similar to Regelinde's ring.

---

1 Hispalis was the Roman name of the city now known as Seville.
2 The Roman city of Hippo Regius, which had several other names before becoming the modern Annaba.

Saran! She had often dreamed about Hippona and Saran; by dint of thinking about him when her nurse told her the story of her secret betrothal, she sometimes even pictured him in her imagination: similar to and as superb as Zinthe, the captain of the blue archers, who had a zigzag of lightning tattooed on his forehead, as superb, with a gaze as coldly mild, but more regal.

Saran! She was, therefore, to become a woman!

Regelinde meditated that mystery, but as she was very pure, it was in vain. Doubtless, the day after the wedding, instead of the white robe starred with the cross of jet, she would don a crimson robe, and when she became a mother, a robe of green fringed with red gold if she bore a son, or flax-blue if she bore a girl—but how would she become a mother?

Interrogated, Ipa raised her gray eyes to the heavens and said: "Iscratene, my mother, Christ, my savior, do you hear what she is asking?"

That was all. Then Regelinde commanded that Isidore, son of Gregory, should be summoned and left alone with her.

As well as being the king's physician and master of ceremonies, Isidore was a magician. He had studied under the most knowledgeable teachers in Thebes, Chrysopolis, Alexandria and, finally, in Erythraea, the city of the red sands, the inhabitants of which conversed freely with demons, and whose prince, Hucar, thrice resuscitated, used up more women in one day than there were clusters of grapes on a royal vine.

Isidore came in. He was neither young nor old but he appeared full of life, endowed with supernatural health.

"Princess Regelinde, the man with whom you, a virgin, seclude yourself, ought to be an old man."

Isidore collapsed all of a sudden, as if beneath the burden of centuries, and Regelinde spoke.

"Teach me the science of generation. Tell me how the Father engenders the Son; tell me what the conjugations of the stars are. Name the principles, the causes and the means. Who is the father of the fauns, and who is their mother? Teach me the norms and the ambigenies,[1] the genealogy of similarities and that of disparities, the creation of the human and that of the goat, that of the musimon,[2] and that of the angel. I'm listening."

"I shall say nothing," Isidore, the son of Gregory, replied, "but look."

And the infinity of worlds unfurled in space, like the links of a prodigious chain. Regelinde saw the succession of generations, the desires and the works, the acts of amour and the births.

She saw, at the commencement of things, the shadow of the Father, immense in the pale sky—and of the Father, as a surgeon, the son was produced.

She saw the amorous stars mingle their fluids—and new lights immediately populated the firmament.

She saw the Principle, which is a wheel whose hub is a diamond, whose spokes are the seven primordial stones, and whose rim is a unique alloy of all the pure metals—and she understood that the principle, the cause and the means are One.

She saw the creation of the angel, the brush of wings, the creation of the aegipan,[3] the pan-goat, the faun and the musimon.

She saw, finally, by what means humans receive life—but then the shame was then so strong in her pure heart, and the fear so violent in her chaste soul, that she suspended the mage Isidore's evocative arm, fell to her knees and cried:

"After having seen that, I do not want to see any more. May those images remain forever beneath my eyelids, and alone, in order to inform me that I ought not to be like other females, and that my pride ought to be different from the pride of all

---

1 This rare Latin term is approximately similar to the modern concept of hybridity, referring to dual parentage.

2 Musimon is an obsolete term for the animal now known as a mouflon, which was once thought to be a hybrid of a sheep and a goat.

3 It is not obvious how aegipans differ from fauns, the name Aegipan probably having originated as an alternative name for the god Pan.

other women and all other beasts. I want to be loved, I want to be fecundated, but only by superior methods, and not according to animal formulas; there is no point, since I possess henceforth the knowledge of the principle, the cause and the means. God, through the intermediary of the Mage, has instructed his daughter spiritually; the flesh is useless to me, and I deny its instincts.

"Saran, I shall not be your wife, for you would despise a beauty self-destroyed."

She removed the silver ring of the secret betrothal from her finger and gave it to Isidore, saying: "You must make me another, adding to that one its weight in gold, in order to signify the union of Regelinde and the Infinite."

Then she said: "Salvation is acting in negation of natural laws."

"That is so," agreed the Mage.

When he had gone, Regelinde put out her eyes.

THE PHILTER

by *Théodore de Banville*

ONE would search in vain for the slightest vestige of a romantic setting in the elegant and correct boudoir in which Madame Amann, the celebrated fortune teller, gave her consultations. As for the diviner herself, she had the costume and manners of a woman of the highest society, and apart from the gleam in her eyes and slightly tragic pallor of her face, one would not have found anything strange about her, except for the habit she conserved of not putting rice-powder on and washing her face with pure water.

One cold morning last October, Madame Amann saw a young woman entering her redoubt who was very similar to her, as pale as her with blazing eyes, but having as well a fine aristocratic appearance and the absolute self-confidence that an immense fortune gives.

"Madame," said the visitor, who had sat down in an armchair by the fireside, "take up your great game, your magic cards—and above all," she added, taking off her gloves, "look at my hand attentively, for I have to interrogate you about the gravest matters. Desirous of having confidence in you, however, I want to know first whether your art tells you who you are dealing with; so, commence by consulting the tarot cards on that matter!"

"Madame," said the diviner, "that would be a futile char-latanism, for I have the pretention of being a Parisienne, and what Parisienne does not know Madame Suzanne d'Autels? In sum, know that our art consists of observing Life far more than demanding solutions that are always uncertain from the science that we possess incompletely. So, Madame la duchesse, having been able to see you in the Bois, at the Opéra, and in church—in sum, everywhere that I have the right to penetrate—I have no need to torment the cards to divine your fortunate or unfortu-nate adventure, and to call by its name the frightful malady that is killing you."

"What do you know, then?" said the duchesse.

"I know," said the cartomancer, "that you adore madly young Comte Armand de Luz, and that he belongs to you, as you have wished. But despair and fever are devouring you, because you read in his heart better than he does itself, and although he has ceded to your charming seductions, and even more to the contagion of amour, you know that he does not love you and you sense only too well in the depths of your heart that he will never love you."

"Never!" aid Madame d'Autels, with a horribly desolate smile. "And why not? What is the obstacle? Tell me; I want to know."

"Well, Madame la duchesse," said the diviner, "are there not mysteries that defy science as well as intuition, and does amour have any other law than it's own existence? Believe me, struggle with the true legitimate arms of womanhood, with passion, with tenderness, and with your marvelous beauty, but don't seek to enter the unknown worlds in which one respires an icy air and from which one returns livid and stupefied."

"In any case," said Madame d'Autels, "whatever the obstacle is that I have to overcome, the cards can doubtless tell you what it is."

"Yes," replied Madame Amann, "and I'll consult them if you wish."

"In sum, you consent to follow your métier. Have all these preparations not been made with the goal of asking for a little more money? But what can have made you think that the Duchesse d'Autels is a miser?"

"Ah, Madame," said the diviner, "rather wish to Heaven that you had never entered my home and that the fatal gold does not pass from your beautiful hands to mine. But there is still time; quit me; go back, abandon a deadly design, accept the long, cruel suffering and don't bite the fruit of the forbidden science, which will only leave a rotten flesh and bitter ashes in your mouth."

"Come on, Madame," said the Duchesse d'Autels in an imperious tone, her black eyebrows frowning. "Pick up your cards!"

"Well," said Madame Amann, after having dealt the cards and read fluently what they dictated, "Monsieur de Luz will not love you because he is ineluctably destined to love another woman. See, Madame, everywhere and incessantly, the Queen of Spades—that's you—follows the Knave of Hearts; but he turns his back on the Queen of Spades in order to pursue the Queen of Hearts, and always the nine of hearts comes to place itself between them. Monsieur de Luz is fated to love a young woman whose life is linked to his; you will soon encounter that fortunate rival and you will recognize her immediately, for you will then sense within you a disastrous collapse, and you will be invaded by a mortal chill. Ah!" she continued, taking the hand of the duchesse, "born under Apollo's planet, you are condemned not to be loved by the man you love, and look at your abruptly broken heart line! Is your ineluctable destiny not visibly written there?"

"However," said the duchesse, whose features then took on a frightful expression, "I know that there are means of constraining the will, of forcing the heart of a man to that which it does not wish: philters that pour into a rebel lover an intoxication that fells him, and from which he cannot wake up! Now, these philters you know, for you are not what you seem to be; no mystery of science is foreign to you, and it is for that reason that I have come to you. I need the magic liquor whose flame burns the veins and awakens in the man who has drunk it a tyrannical and insatiable amour."

"Oh! No, not that!" said Madame Amann, whose lips became livid and who was visibly agitated by a convulsive tremor. "Not that, Madame! Think that you are imposing a culpable action on me, and eternal remorse; that you're asking for the loss of my repose—and," she added in a low voice, "my soul."

"I can pay for it," replied Madame d'Autels, proudly, placing a wad of banknotes on the table. "Since you know me, you know that I have in hand all the means necessary to persecute and destroy you, and that you cannot protect yourself against my hatred; obey, then, without putting up a futile resistance. When shall I have the philter?"

"Tomorrow," said the cartomancer, in a voice so low that the duchesse would not have been able to hear it if the bitter desire that was torturing her had not given her senses a strangely subtle acuity.

On the evening of that same day, Madame d'Autels, who was sleeping heavily and painfully, suddenly felt the diviner take her by the hand, and through a suddenly opened window they both fled through black, sinister space striped with horribly blue bands.

They were both naked, drawn by a black and icy hurricane, and the whistling wind made their loose hair a horizontal mass. They flew in a darkness so opaque and sinisterly thick that they could not see anything in front of them except grim obscurity; they were invaded by a chill that froze their blood, and the pale duchesse Suzanne found in that continuous suffering a bitter and painful sensuality.

Finally, they alighted on a deserted strand where the sea was moaning, and the diviner ordered her companion by signs to remain still and hold her breath. In the heart of the fog, bats, winged dragons and bizarre monsters were flying, scarcely distinguishable, and suddenly skimming and gliding over the phosphorescent sea.

Over a fire of an unknown color, three old women, entirely naked and emaciated, shaking thick white locks of hair on their smooth heads, were cooking in a cauldron and singing irritated stanzas to a monotonous rhythm. They were adding new ingredients incessantly, and the duchesse saw claws, hanks of hair, the teeth of wild beasts, reptiles and bloody debris in their bony hands. In the most profound darkness, on a red throne, she could vaguely make out a giant figure crowned with an iron diadem, around whom turbulent dancers with faces as white as snow were spinning, violently transported by a storm-wind.

Suddenly, she heard the supreme cry, the terrible sob, of a creature having its throat cut; one of the old women drew away, swiftly returned, and put into the cauldron something that the duchesse could not perceive; and immediately the flame, as if drunk with joy, rose up vertically and enveloped the cauldron; the philter was made. With the aid of a spigot open in the flank of the cauldron, one of the old women poured the red liquid into a golden flask; she held it out to Madame Amann, whose naked flesh and pale face then expressed such a terrible anguish that the Duchesse d'Autels felt a chill sliding rapidly into her heart, and she fell unconscious.

She woke up in her bed, as if from a dream; dawn had scarcely broken, and beside her was the frightfully pale diviner, who was holding the golden flask out to her.

"Madame la Duchesse," she said, "this is the philter you have demanded. Thanks to it, Comte Armand de Luz will burn for you with an ardent passion; but if a single day goes by without him having drunk this deadly liquor, his incessantly renascent desire will be replaced by an absolute and irremediable aversion."

Having spoken thus, Madame Amann withdrew, casting a long glance at the duchesse in which there was almost as much pity as hatred.

Madame d'Autels did not take long to make a trial of the philter on her young lover, and she soon saw that the cartomancer had not been mistaken. Previously so cold and indifferent with her, the Comte de Luz, now possessed in every drop of his blood, could no longer live without Suzanne's kisses and the perfume of her hair; he rolled at her feet, devoured her with caresses, followed her like a dog, suddenly carried her away in his arms like a prey, and even in a theater box or in a carriage in the pathways of the Bois he could not help kissing her eyes, her eyelashes, her ears and the stray hairs on the nape of her neck, madly. It seemed to him that he wanted to bruise, wear away and knead under his lips the flesh of that woman, who delivered herself to him with a triumphant joy, and of whom he never found enough, never being close enough to him. However, with the lucidity that genuine amour gives, the Duchesse d'Autels sensed very clearly—a horrible thing!—that in reality, Armand's soul remained completely foreign to those overwhelming intoxications and that he was obeying, unconsciously, an alien and artificial force.

One evening, when the two lovers were at the Opéra, a slender young woman with desolate blue eyes and an almost transparent face, of sublime beauty, went into a box, accompanied by an old man of the most grandiose appearance. They were Mademoiselle Julie d'Esplandes, an immensely rich orphan, and her guardian, the Marquis de Madiane. The duchesse heard them named around her, and by the violent blow that she felt in her heart, she understood that she had before her the rival announced by the cartomancer. In the same way, she only needed a single glance to know that Mademoiselle d'Esplandes loved Armand de Luz, and that, weak and defeated, she was languishing, dying of her ignored amour.

The most poignant thing for Suzanne, however, was that, at the moment that the young woman entered the hall, Armand, without even seeming to see her, was seized by a convulsive tremor. Finally, guided by the admiring murmurs in the hall, he saw her, and looked at her for a long time, like a madman or an invalid who, on emerging from a long crisis, seeks vainly to recognize a face whose features solicit his memory.

The Comte de Luz had never seen or remarked Mademoiselle d'Esplandes, but the amorous effluvia emanating from her invaded and took possession of his soul, without him being conscious of it, because the imperious will of the philter prevented him from understanding what was happening within him. From that moment on a struggle commenced, only visible for the Duchesse d'Autels, whom jealousy was lacerating with a thousand sharp points, although her lover was still curbed at her feet by the violence of irresistible Desire.

He kissed her arms, her hands, covered her with furious caresses; but suddenly, at the same moment and without any delay, he wanted to depart for the sea, for the Pyrenees, for some country retreat; no human power could have retained him. It was necessary for the duchesse to follow him, arriving at the place toward which Armand felt attracted as if by an invisible magnet; she was sure of encountering Mademoiselle d'Esplandes there on some excursion, so beautiful and so touching, and getting thinner from day to day by virtue of the decline that was drawing her toward the tomb. For the young woman, whose least caprices the Marquis de Madiane obeyed, wanted incessantly to flee Armand and his gaze, which was killing her; but she would not have been able to go far enough that he did not divine her, in order to search for her and follow her—and yet, when he saw her, he did not recognize her, blinded by the philter that communicated a material and savage delirium to him.

As for Madame d'Autels, she knew and understood everything; she knew that she possessed her lover like a booty, like a stolen treasure, but that if he could recover himself momentarily, freed from the somber enchantment that weighed upon him, he would have returned immediately to the gentle fiancée who turned her celestial eyes toward him desperately. Thus, while Armand served as a plaything for her deceptive folly, and Mademoiselle d'Esplandes, as white and tremulous as a drooping lily, felt her life and strength decreasing, the Duchesse d'Autels, burning with despair and hatred, was slowly consumed by a horrible fever.

Soon, the fits of that malady would become so intense that they would endanger her life; she would have furious rages, cerebral transports, long deliria, and in one of those crises, the violence of which exhausted her, Doctor Mélis, called in haste, would administer a powerful narcotic, which would plunge the duchesse into a long and heavy sleep.

An irremediable catastrophe! For necessarily, on that day, Suzanne could not, as usual, pour out the deceptive philter for her lover, and, suddenly awakening, uttering a great cry of rage and deliverance, running to where his heart drew him, abruptly inundated by a delicious flame, he arrived just in time to kneel beside the bed in which the beloved virgin was about to die. Already invaded by the supreme pallor, with the serenity of Heaven in her blue eyes, Mademoiselle d'Esplandes was hardly able to speak any longer, but in the hour that remained to her and when both of them could hear the divine words "I love you!" pronounced by an adored mouth, they had time to draw ineffable delights therefrom and to betrothe their souls for eternity.

On emerging from the house where the dear sleeper reposed, Comte Armand found his jealous mistress at the door, and rejected her with such an expression of scorn and disgust that she saw herself irrevocably doomed. Mad with dolor, she went stupidly to the cartomancer, in order to address vain and futile supplications to her.

"Oh, Madame la Duchesse," said Madame Amann, with a profound sigh, "why did you not cede to my prayers? Suffering is the very condition of our life, which cannot be avoided, and it is uselessly that, in order to flee, one has recourse to an impious science, the effort of which overturns the mysterious laws of nature and makes the Angels weep!"

TO AN UNKNOWN SISTER

by Joséphin Péladan

WHY are you hesitating? The heart is a good guide; one follows it weeping, but while weeping one lives and one climbs, wounded but heroic, toward the summit where the angel awaits us who will lift us up with his ocellated, quivering and sudden wings.

Stranger come from the land that I hate, what wind of fate has caused your swaddling-clothes to float away and what cross are you bearing to the terrestrial Calvary?

Your spirit has cried out to the mirrors that I have sculpted of the desired beyond, magical reflectors; your spirit has cried out and recognized its dream beneath the features of exception and subtlety that I borrow from da Vinci to dress my son of languorous light.

Glory be to God, who gave you an elevated soul; I am merely the bow of the enchanted violin, and if I have awakened the mystical sleepers and idealities lying within you, I am only a clarion of the celestial Diana, glory be to God,

Alas, as a son of Satan, a daimon, if I can sow amour and fire in my path, and give my sisters divine insomnia, an errant heart, a troubadour whose voice laments with the storm wind, God does not permit me to make those flames ardent, and the arms of my sisters, extended impotently, rowing vainly in the shadow in the night, cannot embrace me.

I am carrying toward the mountain whose location I do not know the Holy Grail of the ideas of my distant ancestors.

Dare I carry a sister with me in the fatal ride?

The chimera on which I am mounted, without a bit or bridle, is felonious; the Inferno from which it emerged is lying in wait for me and harassing me.

I no longer have anything but pride, the golden sword buried beneath the vase of a Delta. I no longer have anything but pride, the tiara crushed beneath the hoof of the great bull. I no longer have anything but pride, but I have retained power all the same, which has conquered you, predestined woman; I raise before God my hand, on which no ring signifies servitude, and, son of the first priests, I bless your gentle heart, which has beaten toward me, and I draw the graces of Heaven upon your head.

However, if you would be the virgin designated to refresh my eyes with your pure breath, and my forehead weighing upon your breasts could go to sleep; if you would be the fay whose golden wand opens a tranquil and sure path through the forests filled with terror by the wild beasts of the Real; if you would be the sister, consoling and mild; if you would be the woman sent by the angels in answer to my prayer; oh, be not her; I am carrying my misfortune; I would buckle under yours, and the order of destiny wants me alone and plaintive. Damned is whoever presents his heart to the shocks of existence, in order to make spring forth therefrom, before those whom instinct obscures, the spark ignited in the flank of Prometheus.

I would dearly like to see you, however, if only in image . . .

When autumn comes, melancholy and russet, I will go in order to collect myself to the land where you are, and spend a day, distracted or annoyed, beneath the tranquil balcony from which your dreams soar. Later—too late—when life has put barriers between us, will we be ashamed, timid and cold hearts, of only having provoked happiness in thought?

The contents of the cup that our angel or devil hands to us evaporate, or are poured away during hesitation. Before emptying it, we sound it for long time, only wanting it to be inexhaustible.

You dare not take my time, but I would dare to take your life! Forget, forget the hero in my glimpsed work, who resembles the Beloved, the passion that does not fill me would kill you.

Let us not join our lips; they are red, they are warm, founts of vertigo, doors of lust; but let us give a hand to the children of the same father we would have given ourselves.

Yours trembles; I can feel the artery beating the thin and lucid skin, and it is not by virtue of instinct that my veined temples are beating, it is not pleasure that incites and impels us; we, who seem to desire one another, my sister, recognize one another; listen to that voice, the voice of the blood that sings the glorious moment of the brother discovered, the sister encountered.

Yes, you are my sister, since you are reciting in a whisper the hymn of the unreal that I am singing at the top of my voice. Yes, you are my sister, for you have not granted the wishes of the mortal stammerers of amour and vulgar helpers of women. Yes, you are my sister, and you have withdrawn and retained your hand, in accordance with the royal tradition of the Race, from the hands extended from below. In order to encounter a heart, it would have been necessary for you to descend, and you have sensed mine without bending down. Yes, you are my sister, and duty demands that I pause in my chimerical path in order to kiss your heart, and then to close it like a holy tabernacle when the mass is concluded.

Sorority, incest, or virtue, or sin, assumption of the good fall, whatever is the fate of our nascent amour, whether a mystical aurora rises over us, or whether it carries the red and violet shadow of pathetic sunsets, we shall emerge in bloom from the dream, or purer from the sin.

Yes, purer. Noble souls in the athanator of passion free themselves from the matrix and sublimate themselves; and in passing though a heart orientated toward God, the muddiest current is purified.

The flesh becomes a trampoline and launches us, bewildered, beyond form, and the same spasm that brutifies Bottom projects the Oelohite[1] toward the stellar zone.

The vibration of amour was sonorous waves that rise into the azure turning blue or dying, from the erotic shock of two bodies in emotion two souls sometimes soar in ecstasy. *Felix culpa!*

Fortunate sin, but sin; on emergence from pleasure, vigilant dolor always demands its toll; the Dream cannot substantiate any soul; the Dream is a desire that, like the symbolic serpent, bites without joy.

Be my sister; and let us go through life hand in hand. If amour comes one day to join our lips, we shall have made the effort of a great duty and we shall have struggled, before the fall, against the earth and its instinctive force, we Oelohites, sons of Atlas and Aether.

---

1 An Oeholite, sometimes synonymous in Péladan's work with a Daimon, is a kind of demigod, or what Nietzsche called an *übermensch*: an attainable condition of transcendent being at which humans can and ought to aim.

LIKE CHILDREN WHO RUN AFTER A MASK

by Fréderic Boutet

> There are men for whom illusions are as
> necessary as life . . . When they approach the
> truth they draw away very quickly, like
> children who run after a mask, but flee if
> the mask turns round . . .
> —Nicolas Chamfort

YES, said the old man, it was somewhere near here. As I came around the great rocks that form the summit of the hill, on my way back from the Orient, the sunset was red and dusk was emerging slowly from the gorges, the idle precursor of night. When I reached the western slope, darkness already had its empire.

I descended through the darkness of a sycamore wood and halted on the edge of a plateau overlooking the valley. The moon's disk emerged from the profound horizon and rose into the back sky. Its green light bathed the jagged chain of the mountains and the plain at their feet.

Something was happening in the plain at the feet of the mountains.

Emerging from a narrow defile, a cortege was advancing slowly. First I saw a troop of halberdiers with shiny helmets. After them, came men in robes on horses under strict control, and then priests clad in black or white. Among them, preceded by a cleric holding up a silver crucifix, was a bishop with his mantle, crosier and miter. Then I saw two men who were isolated in the middle of the soldiers. One was the executioner and the other, bare-headed, gagged and chained, was the condemned man. They were walking side by side. More soldiers came next, in considerable numbers. Then there was a large crowd of people, sometimes silent, sometimes uttering deathly cries.

The goal of the procession was at the foot of the hill where I was standing. There was a gibbet waiting for them, with the gesture of its stiff arm.

Then, because such things interest me, I went down very rapidly, much lower, in order to get a better view.

The company had formed up around the machine of death, the priests in front with the judges, and then the soldiers and the common people.

The condemned man was brought to the foot of the ladder. The bishop approached with his crucifix, but the man turned his head away and I saw his pale forehead and the gleam of his eyes, although I was a long way away. Meanwhile, cries of anathema rose from the crowd. The condemned man climbed the steps toward death. The rope was placed around his neck, but then, raising his bowed head, he extended his bound arms toward the crowd, the soldiers, the judges and the priests, as if to bless and forgive them . . .

Already, without the executioner having touched him, he had abandoned the ladder and was hanging there, motionless—dead.

Now, all of those who were there looked at him for a moment, and then looked at one another, in silence; and it seemed that they were gripped by a great fear, for they fled in bewilderment.

They bumped into one another, were knocked down and trampled, and got up in order to flee more rapidly, without looking back. The soldiers dropped their weapons, the priests tore off their robes and the judges whipped their mounts, pitilessly bowling over any obstacle.

They disappeared pell-mell, and nothing remained but the hanged man and his scaffold, in the greenish glimmer of the moonlight.

I went down the steep slope, reached the plain and then the gibbet. I leaned toward the ground and I recognized, amid the dark grass, the presence of the magical plant known as the mandrake.

Turning toward the brilliant moon, the mother of incantations, I dismounted, knelt down, and, pronouncing the magical words, I tore the marvelous root from the ground, fearfully. A few drops of bloody sap sprang from my hand. I was not burned by it, and knew that was a beneficent augury.

I climbed the ladder that was still below the scaffold, seized the hanged man and lifted him up to the arm of the gibbet, which was a broad and sturdy beam.

I sat down with the body beside me. I untied the rope, removed the gag and freed the hands. Then I shouted loudly, toward the stars, the invocation of life that is found in the Book that comes from Nineveh[1] and nowhere else—a book more profound than any other. I shouted the invocation at the stars and I put the salutary root into the dead man's mouth.

The dead man's eyes opened, and the dead man sat up beside me under the gibbet. Then, casting the plant with the human form over his left shoulder he said: "That which had to be

---

1 Fragments of the *Enuma Elish*, containing the Babylonian Creation myth, allegedly the oldest book in the world, were found by Austen Layard in the ruins of Nineveh in 1849; a version was published by George Smith in 1876. The text acquired a reputation among nineteenth-century occultists as a repository of Hermetic secrets—supposedly contained, of course, in the bits that Layard did not find.

accomplished has been accomplished." And he added: "Why intervene in my destiny?"

"I saw you dead," I said, "and then I saw the fear of the executioners and their disorder. That told me that you were beyond ordinary human beings, and that there had been iniquity in your execution. Then I desired to know the cause of your martyrdom, and the measure of their injustice. I desired to know too, if you can tell me, what land you have traversed in going toward the Shadow. And that is why I dared to make use, on this propitious night, beneath the incantational moon, of the science that I acquired at the price of my very soul in the arcane of the profound Book of the Divines of Nineveh—the book more profound than any other. I beg you, if I have done wrong, to absolve me . . ."

"Yes," he said. "There are causes that you have been able to know, but another cause, coming from the Unknown, has engendered them, which is this: the things that must be accomplished, are accomplished. Now, that was engraved on the page of Time.

"For you, for as long as I can, I shall continue to speak. I shall tell you what I know about my terrestrial existence. About death, I shall tell you nothing, for it is not permitted that humans should see beyond, nor prior to, this momentary existence. But that country is not a country of shadows . . .

"I do not know my beginning. Always I have been similar. I have lived for many centuries and I have seen, as in a dream, things changing around me. I did not pay much attention to them, for I looked into my soul, preferably the soul of dead time. I have lived in the lands where the ancient sages lived. I understand all languages, I have read all books. I have plunged into the mystery of all religions, but Doubt remained my companion, with the cold light of its clairvoyance. It has never left me, and that was the burden of my hours . . .

"But I have thought so much, in silence and meditation—sometimes on the precept of the god engendered by the waters, with the fakirs that guard the pagodas on the Ganges; sometimes on the tenebrous hieroglyphics at the feet of sphinxes in the Egyptian deserts; sometimes on the books of sacred morality in the monasteries of the Middle Kingdom; sometimes inspiring myself with the belief of the Prophet in the shadow of a mosque; and finally in the solemn meditation of abbeys where the monks seem to be shadows exalting the maxims of the crucified Nazarene—I have thought so much that my mind has surpassed the ordinary limits of human understanding.

"With the aid of philosophers of all times I have acquired a perfect knowledge of the human heart, and I have also penetrated the arcane of the Rose-Cross, and fathomed the unique book of Hermes Trismegistus. I know all the secrets of Solomon and the science of the heavenly bodies, the recorders of terrestrial destinies . . .

"Now, as I found myself in the desert where Babylon was one night when I was dreaming, the cause of human evil was revealed to my soul; it was revealed to me in its entirety, at a stroke, and I learned at the same time, that which it was good to know, and the method of knowing it.

"Yes, I knew then, by virtue of a manifestation of eternal powers, that all the misery of life stems from this alone: that human beings are unaware of their duration. I also knew by what mathematics it was possible to calculate the number of days allocated to the existence of every human being.

"I began by calculating the end of my terrestrial destinies. The presages indicated the evening that is upon us. The presages also indicated that immediately afterwards, I would be resuscitated with a being torn from the earth.

"However, when I possessed the secret, I was aware that it was necessary for me to spread it through the world. I quit the solitudes and the society of the dead. I thought that I ought to choose an isolated city, create disciples and send them abroad bearing word of the Truth. After much research, I believed that the city behind those hills ought to be chosen among them all. I stopped there, and began work.

"I spoke in the streets, at the crossroads, in the schools and in the assemblies to announce what it was possible for me to teach humans. I spoke about the power I had. I represented the immense security in study and in action, in pleasures and in enterprises, that would emerge from knowledge. I spoke about the marvelous and tranquil certainty that would arise, with wisdom, in initiated hearts, permitting them, whatever their beliefs might be, to prepare for the inevitable end . . .

"I expressed these things, and as I know the words that induce complete conviction and the words that no one can doubt, everyone had faith in me. They were gripped by invincible curiosity and begged me to extract them from ignorance of the number of days that still lay before them, to unveil the hour and the instant when that which cannot be avoided or corrupted would extend its irresistible power over their destinies.

"They begged me, with the most forceful supplications, and I was obedient to their desire. They knew, with no possible illusion, and all of them were immediately plunged into despair. They lamented, struck their breasts, cursing me and deploring their misfortune, that of now knowing how little time they had to live—however long the indicated time might be. Their anguish increased by the minute; they were more unfortunate than they could say. I was astonished, but I thought that it was only the manifestation of human weakness before anything unknown, and that they would recover their spirits before long.

"Meanwhile, those who did not yet know fled from me in terror, in order not to know—but the power of curiosity brought them back. They interrogated me with a feverish hesitation. They emerged from doubt and, falling down in fright, called upon the deadliest spirits of the earth, the air and the sea to assail me. Far from thinking of distributing sagely the days that remained to them, they thought of nothing but pleasure, in order to stifle the voice of time in their hearts. Scholars abandoned their work, merchants their business, and all of them, in terror, rushed in cowardly fashion toward lust and intoxication, in which they sought oblivion, sobbing with horror. And unhappiness, shame and fear dominated the city.

"The judges assembled and the crowd came to denounce me. Soldiers were sent to bind me and to take me before the tribunal. The oldest of the judges, whose long white beard covered his breast, said to me: 'Listen to me, Man, we have examined your work in its causes and its results; we have examined it impartially and we have found it detestable. You say that you are a benefactor of humanity, when you are the worst of torturers. You said that if we knew the hour at which the supremely redoubtable one will extends its power over us, we would be able to await it with tranquility, and would be able, with wisdom, to prepare ourselves to receive it. That is false.

"'Look at what has become of those whom curiosity has gripped under the influence of your fallacious word. See their anguish and their torment, and recognize the fruits of your revelation. As they have found it, so will all those for whom the veil of fear is lifted find it. Now, we wish this to cease. We want to remain in salutary ignorance, in unconsciousness and indecision. Tomorrow frightens us and we adore the mystery that permits us still to believe in life. We are confined in hope, and we close our eyes, block our ears. However, the anxiety survives and no one can kill it completely.

"'What would happen, then, if we knew the law of our destinies, if we had to count every hour, every minute, every rapid temporary second, fleeing irrevocably? What torture could equal that of being able to say, with certainty: now, so many days, then so many, then so many . . . now it is in three days, now it is tomorrow . . . it is today, already, and what fate awaits us?

That is the true mystery that we do not know, in spite of our religions and our priests. That alone is what it is important for us to know, and which you do not tell us. You destroy what is good in our doubt and you leave horror to subsist.

"'And after all, what need do humans have to know anything whatsoever? We do not want any certainty that shackles our pleasures. We have bodies, and those bodies want to kill their soul in order to live in tranquility. It is necessary to abolish all looking forward. The future is troubled. We only want to see the present and to deny death even when it touches us with its terrible hand. We refuse to fathom anything. We want to enjoy possible enjoyments in peace. Spiritual science is the mother of unslaked desires, dolorous meditations and scorn for the sensuality that is the only thing that matters.

"'Ignorance, with its indifference, its idleness and its vices, is the best companion of human beings for their ambiguous destinies. We want to conserve it, and you shall die, you who want to extract us from it. You shall die. You shall be hanged. Don't try to respond; our ears are blocked with wax, for your voice is more dangerous than that of the sirens, and will infuse us with accursed curiosity. Tomorrow, you will be hanged. You will be declared an impostor and guilty of sacrilege, and everyone will believe it, in the joy that your predictions are belied.

"'Tomorrow, your science and your strength will be destroyed. That must be, for the happiness of human beings is not to know . . .'

"The judge fell silent, and I saw that I did not know the human soul very well, and that, for the science in question, humankind is the only book, and not books, of which I had not read enough . . .

"Thus, this evening, I was brought here and hanged, amid the howls of the multitude.

"Adieu. You know what you desired to know. The moon is high in the sky. This is the hour when I must return whence I came. My secret will go with me, for that is also written on the page of Time . . ."

He let himself slip from the arm of the scaffold and remained hanged at the end of his rope.

As for me, I took the ladder away, and then I left the plain forever, leaving the gibbet, its hanged man and the incantatory light of the green moon.

Ever since that time, however, which is very distant, my mind has been stubbornly tormented by a problem that I cannot resolve: that of knowing whose situation is worse—the situation of the hanged man, or the situation of those who hanged him.

THE EXTINCT PIPE

by Charles-Marie Torquet

I

WHEN the slab of the crypt had fallen back over the paternal coffin, finally liberated from banal handshakes and condolences, Denis Magalèse returned in all haste to the house, where he would be alone henceforth, and, no longer sustaining his pride, his hatred and his scorn for people, he abandoned himself to the savage manifestations of the most animal dolor.

For two days and two nights his forlorn bestial howls resounded in the vast empty abode. Finally, fatigue overwhelmed him, an emptiness stunned him and a long, irrepressible slumber, like that of a child falling asleep after a long chagrin, overtook him and enveloped him gently.

When he awoke, after a long dream, he ran to the dead man's study and with a last gaze that he wanted to be piercing and memorial, he embraced all its details, fixing their exact image in his mind; then, with the shutters and the door closed, he took away the key. Thus, no one could profane henceforth the obscure retreat that his creative genius had filled; the furniture, the books, and slightest implements of everyday labor, among which the master's existence had gradually flowed, would remain just as his departure had surprised them.

In the bosom of the mystical half-light that filtered through the laths of the shutters, in which the rays of light seemed to take on a personality and reveal their vivifying energy instinctively, there would be an intact and silent sanctuary The paternal soul could come to wander there, placidly, to revive spiritually the beloved life, to bathe in all sensuality in the effluvia of filial reverence.

II

Those duties fulfilled, he resumed his monotonous existence of a ministry employee, punctuated by comings and goings at fixed hours, with the same unconscious pauses before the same banal shops; an alternation of deathly chills and cordial sunlight, bleak dejection and juvenile hope, the insolent stupidity of citizens that it was necessary to venerate and the conscientious idiocy of his superiors.

As before, he passed for a "crackpot" in the eyes of his colleagues, interested neither in the monologues of some nor the dominoes of the others. Thinking a great deal, he spoke little, associating with no one and disdaining glasses of beer, locking himself away during his hours of liberty, "reading, writing and philosophizing," according to those messieurs, who detested him for his mutism and his feminine sensitivity.

And the years went by without attenuating Magalèse's regrets or his chagrin. He could not even abstract himself in the cherished studies and elevated philosophical research into which his father had initiated him from the lamentable thought and incessant remembrance that his only friend, the adored master, had departed.

Until the desired hour of death, deprived of the guide who had given him light, vigor and will, and rendered him great by enabling him to form concepts, he would drag himself along, solitary, groping in the darkness of his debilitated intellect. The sweetness of living, once savored so much, was no longer anything but despair and ennui.

He was decaying into total indifference.

III

After seven years, Denis realized that instead of being appeased at length, his grief seemed to be exacerbating, while a dull presentiment warned him of something new.

Often, in the midst of labor, a confused malaise suddenly agitated him; an anxiety gripped him, stupefying him in a kind of internal suspense, as if an opaque curtain had been drawn between his faculties and the occupations to which he was applying himself; and then the memory of the fatal day imposed itself, and for long hours, he contemplated obsessively the closed door of the study in which his father had died.

He saw him again, tall in stature, sustaining his pipe with an ample gesture, surrounded by the heavy undulations of his majestic puffs of smoke. Suddenly, the ringing of the bell had been heard, immediately followed by the sinister sound of a fall. People ran to lift Monsieur Magalèse up, his face grimacing, thick gray foam on his tumefied lips, and that hideous regular elevation of the cheek by exhalation, like the palpitation of a toad's throat! Monstrous and idiotic, he soon expired, devoid of consciousness and speech.

And, his eyes attached to the door, Denis was invaded by an immense desire to go in. His extraordinary imagination, his excessive and enthusiastic character having always consecrated him to suffering, he searched with a gluttonous instinct for sadness and affliction; he found a caressant bitterness in being unhappy, a muted enjoyment of a superior order that crucified him.

Thus abruptly rejuvenated, his memories procured him an indescribable emotion, enabled him to grasp again the presence of the beloved individual and the immediate laceration that his loss had caused.

Only one scruple retained him: was violating the solemn meditation in which the mausoleum slept not a sin?

IV

One Sunday afternoon when, all daylight blocked, he was working by lamplight—in prevention of the spleen of winter skies the occult perturbation interrupted him again, and, whatever determination he put into continuing his work, it was impossible for him to do so. Never had the desire to see again the place where the master had been struck down by apoplexy dominated him more tyrannically.

Forcefully attracted, as if inhaled, while detesting the action that solicited him, he no longer possessed the faculty of resistance.

He told himself then that he would inevitably have to satisfy his curiosity and gave himself reasons, trying to convince himself that his intentions were pure.

In truth, if his father was watching, how could he be irritated by such piety? Very respectfully, he would go in, look with all his strength, and when he had seen and seen well, he would be satisfied; then, as if sending toward the heavens a smoke of incense, he would allow a reaggregated and reconquered memory emanate toward Regret the mute prayer of his loving thought.

Afterwards, he would emerge, to return at long intervals to mediate thus, to steep himself again in the milieu that had fostered his intelligence, where the walls, the furniture and the most trivial trinkets would be impregnated, as if *charged*, with the generative power of his concepts.

Under the influence of such an ardent dilection, an intellectual tension toward the dead man, the ambience might emit in his favor a little of its accumulated force, comforting his sick and impotent mind by means of that transfusion.

Oh, to concentrate in oneself the virtuality of the paternal spirit!

V

Denis opened the door. A singular perfume stopped him on the threshold, asking what synthesis there was for him in that odor. Had not the permanently closed room contracted the vague reek of mildew that sacristies emit?

Everything was as it had been at the fatal moment: on the table, the journal that he had crumpled at the first spasm of the apoplexy; beside it his pipe, doubtless set down with a convulsive gesture, for a little cylinder of agglomerated ash still lay near the bowl.

Startled, he had risen to his feet, had abruptly pushed back the armchair and, already not seeing anything but myriads of golden stars trembling before his bulging eyes, had lunged toward the bell and had fallen heavily on that black buffalo hide with a sinister dull thud.

Mechanical and pensive, Denis sat down in the armchair and picked up the pipe so amorously stuffed by his father. Lovingly, he snuffed it, almost savoring the smell, and, having turned it around and examined it from all angles, he polished the pretty rhythmic object, the burned topaz of which was dotted with scintillations, with a flap of his jacket.

That pipe, which his father had clenched between his lips at the terrible and mysterious moment of his death had been extinguished at the same moment as its master, and the last puff of smoke had flown away with the last sigh of the man!

While he handled the object so intimately linked to his father's existence, that companion of blissful reveries and grave thoughts, a religious and fearful emotion invaded him; it seemed to him that a soul had also fled therefrom, and, imagining that he was only rolling between his fingers a sort of cadaver, he shivered, like a violator of a tomb, and quickly replaced it on the table with the instinctive horror of the living for the dead.

Ashamed of his childishness, he tried to stride back and forth in the room, and his footsteps caused the porcelains to resonate; he shivered again and turned round, as if at the sensation of a presence; then, reflecting that a feverish erethism rendered him inept that day to evoke those funereal thoughts, he fled.

VI

All week long, however, although he strove to distract himself, the memory of the pipe never quit him.

The idea of a narrow liaison, a concomitance, between the life of his father and that which he accorded to the utensil, had gripped his brain, even though he found it ridiculous and burst into nervous laughter more than once, arguing with himself and making fun of himself.

Nevertheless, it was the monstrously comical aspect, the extravagance of such a supposition, that seduced him and took possession of him in spite of himself.

It's evident that I'm mad, he thought. *The soul of a pipe! Where the devil have I picked up that crackpot notion? How many people pass for reasonable whose heads are filled with delirious phantasmagorias? Three quarters of supposedly commonsensical people are only lunatics, and I'm one of them, there's no doubt about it. The soul of a pipe? And yet, is it necessary for us to proclaim absurd what we don't understand? It's the dull tendency of a junior schoolteacher to deny* a priori *all notions outside of our range that has made those imbecile materialists, those narrow-minded and pedantic scholars . . .*

The consciousness of an object? Why not?

VII

The following Sunday, as his stubborn thoughts still recalled him to the pipe, Denis gasped with a sudden commotion.

Extinct, yes, but not empty! Was it not in his power to re-light it and finish it? To resuscitate the thing that had died in the teeth of his expiring father—what a rare and suggestive act!

Then he started to tremble at having thought of that. It was finished, lost, ensorcelled, he would be committing sacrilege . . . A sacrilege, but pregnant with unpolluted sensations, unconsidered ideas, with mystery . . . What shame! It was no longer a matter of filial reverence; he had unmasked himself, the execrable; it was to satisfy an odious curiosity of a sick man that he was about to tempt death!

He could no longer find the energy to extract himself from temptation. Convinced from then on of his weakness, and skill-ful in self-deception, he remembered his father repeating incessantly in his lessons the urgency of always learning, of knowing at any price, and, strong in his lie, he turned the key in the lock.

In the study, motionless for some time considering the pipe, suffering horribly from the internal combat and wondering why he was struggling since he now knew his incapacity to vanquish himself, since he would smoke it, he strove to reason on abstract subjects, to extirpate the obsession of his brain, with the entire certainty of the vanity of his efforts.

What horrible scenes were about to appear, what unknown cogitations to awaken? What spectacles never seen by a man were reserved for him, for the sinner who troubled the repose of the dead?

A torpor fogged his thoughts; slowly, automatically, he picked it up; the match clicked and orange-tinted blue gleams vaguely licked the panels that dusk was already darkening.

In the semi-darkness the puffs of smoke rose up, twisted into strange volutes, and gradually, Denis discovered that he understood them; an extraordinary and subtle perspicacity penetrated him with a continuous propagation—capillary, so to speak—and as the plastic and significant clouds rose up more compactly, his intuition extended immensely.

Soon, he perceived and saw growing the radiant dazzle of an ineffable living light that absorbed him, dissolved him and drank him.

Like it, he expanded in ubiquity; an enormous intoxication enraptured him in his infinite dispersion; he unfurled in harmonious waves in the radiance of an eternal smile.

The unveiled Universe opened up, brightened, translucent, melted into splendid golden floods, the contemplation of which was pure Happiness.

He knew the reason for things; he conceived the Inconceivable; he understood the Absolute, being Intelligence.

But now the universal vibration slackened, the sparkling splendor became a torrent of shadow, and then the compact darkness that drew him away with a formidable current,

As it had been gradually instilled in him, he felt the Force disintegrate, abandon him, flee from everywhere as though it were being sweated . . .

Immediately, the pipe was extinguished.

In a very low voice, but so distinct that it would have been perceptible through the most extraordinary din, he clamored three times: "Father! Father! Father!" and suddenly raised eyes that were bulging from their orbits; violently, he pushed back the armchair and with a dry click he placed the pipe on the table, which broke and vomited out a little cylinder of agglomerated ash.

His hands extended as if to repel some horrible vision, he took a step, stumbled and fell prostrate on to the buffalo-hide with a sinister dull thud.

LOVE AMONG THE STARS

by Camille Flammarion

"WHAT up with you this morning?" I exclaimed, on seeing André arrive in my study, with a disconcerted and desolate expression. His face was very pale, his eyes haggard, his hair unkempt and his step weary, as if he had come back from a long-distance run. "You obviously haven't spent the night stargazing, although the sky was as clear as I've seen it for a long time."

"On the contrary—yes, I spent a long time observing the sky last night; but I'm emerging from an unparalleled astonishment, and I certainly haven't slept a wink this morning. I'm still flabbergasted. But what you mistake for terror was only an agreeable and charming surprise, followed by a boundless regret—a surprise so great that I haven't recovered from it."

"Have you discovered a new star with a fantastic spectrum, a nebula of extravagant form, a comet with hectic tresses? Is it only the insomnia that succeeds a vivid excitement?"

"It's an adventure more extraordinary than any you could imagine. I dreamed about Dora—yes, Dora, my deceased beloved."

"Oh, your imagination! What tricks it plays on you! You've become the victim of hallucinations—you, whose mind is so calm and ponderous. Don't trust yourself! I've already told you that. It's a dangerous slope. You're too much a poet. I prefer mathematics—it's safer."

"I'm not arguing. Hallucination, dream, whatever you like; but I'm still overwhelmed by what I've seen and heard—and that's not unreasonable at all."

"Well, tell me your story. I don't doubt that it will be very interesting."

My friend André was a young man of twenty-five, an excellent observer of the sky, describing with great exactitude the planetary aspects of Mars, Jupiter or Saturn—to which his studies were preferentially devoted—but a trifle dreamy and mystical. A great and unforgettable distress had struck him, and since that time, which was still quite recent, he had been plunged into a constant melancholy.

He had fallen in love with a delightfully beautiful young woman, as dreamy as himself, ardent and passionate, whom he had suddenly lost after three months of adoration. And during the two years since the blow had struck him, he had thought of nothing but her, scarcely succeeding in forgetting her for a few moments in the scientific work that absorbed all his strength and energy.

Life without her was sad and colorless, and he had often wanted to die. He hoped to die soon, and in fact, his health, once so flourishing, was deteriorating insensibly. He believed in the survival of the soul and wondered incessantly where his beloved might be. Several times, he had told me that he thought he had sensed her presence nearby, and heard some kind of internal voice speaking to his soul. I had tried to deflect him away from these ideas, which seemed to me to be dangerous to his mental health, and I had believed that he was no longer thinking about them when he arrived that morning, so troubled and agitated by his vision.

He explained that at about two o'clock in the morning, while he was examining through his telescope a region of the Milky Way very rich in stars, he had, so to speak, swept the beautiful constellation of Cygnus with his instrument, and had paused on the admirable double star Albireo, composed of two suns, one golden yellow and the other sapphire.

While he trained a very powerful ocular lens on the blue star, and was preparing to observe it with a spectroscope in order to make a special study of its curious light, he had experienced a sort of dazzling in his eye, which he had initially attributed to the bright glare of the star, and had also felt a slight electric shock on his shoulder. He continued the observation nevertheless and fitted the spectroscope to the telescope. Either in consequence of the fatigue of the night's observation, however, or simply to rest momentarily, he had sat down in the large armchair in which, occasionally, after long observations, we had the habit of stretching ourselves out and going to sleep briefly.

The rays of moonlight entering through the cupola, forming a light streak of blue-tinted light, were caressing the apparatus, the globes and the maps. He tried to get up to carry out his spectroscopic observation, but very close to him, he had seen, with his naked eyes, the adored form of his beloved standing in the moonlight, and had simultaneously felt nailed to the armchair by a superior magnetic force.

I shall, however, leave it to André to tell the story, for what follows is exactly what he told me.

Dora was standing there before me. Above her shone Albireo. My beloved was even more beautiful than before, idealized and as if made translucent by a celestial clarity.

My first impression was amazement. I was not in the least afraid, and yet I felt a glacial frisson run from my feet to my head and I began to tremble. I remained sprawled in my armchair, as if my body were made of lead. She didn't come closer to me, and it seemed to me at first that I didn't want to approach her.

She looked at me tenderly with her large azure eyes, which always seemed to be opening on some new astonishment, and said to me eagerly: "Why haven't you come? I'm waiting for you. We haven't yet known love!"

The tone of her voice was the same as before, and as soon as I heard it, the apparition lost its strange character and became— for want of a better word—natural.

At that mild reproach, that regret and that avowal, all our hours of happiness reappeared before me, animatedly: our passionate intoxications, our delightful ecstasies, our endless kisses—and the very extravagance of our sensuality, all those enchanting scenes suddenly resuscitated in my brain, went through me like a lightning-flash of radiant joy.

I couldn't help replying: "What! We haven't known love?"

"Certainly not," she replied. "We've only had its gross sensations."

"Oh, but how exquisite!"

"Yes, for the Earth. How different it is here!"

"Where's here?"

"In the system of Albireo's azure star."

And she told me that she lived there, in the midst of a sort of angelic population. While I listened, I seemed to be living that new life with her. It was no longer death; it was life. I found myself with her again, as before.

"Yes," she added, "what a difference there is between the love one knows here and that which we tasted on Earth!"

I confess that I experienced a disagreeable sensation on hearing that confession.

"How do you know that?" I cried, piqued by a sudden bizarre resurgence of the thorn of jealousy.

"Foolish! Still foolish!" she replied, with her adorable smile. "Jealous of a dead woman!"

"But you're not dead, since you're talking to me about love, and claiming to experience joys unknown on Earth. No, I'm not jealous—but I still love you. Well, I'm capable of being reasonable. Explain yourself."

"On Earth, we only have five senses: sight, hearing, smell and touch each play a role in our sensations, although true love resides essentially in the attraction of souls toward one another. We only have five senses, or only four."

"How many more have you today, then?"

"Seventeen. And I repeat, I'm waiting for you. And of those seventeen, there's one that surpasses all others, worth as much as the rest put together, which on its own might be called the sense of love."

"Which is?"

"It's the electrical sense. In love, electricity plays a preponderant role, even in terrestrial organisms, which are so gross and obtuse. The human soul is a substantial entity, electrical in nature, which radiates far beyond our visible material body. That electricity emits invisible waves, which are very different from those of light."

"Yes, I know," I replied, my mathematical mind taking over. "Luminous waves are three ten-thousandths of a millimetre in length, while electrical waves are thirty centimetres."

"I didn't know that."

"I understand perfectly well what you're saying to me, therefore—that there's a radical difference between the magnitude of the vibrations that give birth to electrical or luminous effects."

"None of the five senses of the terrestrial body can perceive electrical waves. Among us, by contrast, it's the first of our seventeen senses. It's much more important than sight itself. Why does one love? Why does one experience sympathies and antipathies? Why does one remain different? That's a mystery unknown to you, although it's very simple for us, who perceive it so directly by means of a special sense.

"The soul, which is an electrical substance, emits into its surroundings electrical waves invisible to you but perceptible to us. You might compare these waves to the sound waves that emanate from the vibrating string of a violin, a harp or a piano. If these sonorous waves encounter in their passage another string able to vibrate harmonically with the first, the second string will emit a sound without anyone having touched it. It's an experiment that you can make at any time.

"If two souls vibrate in unison; or sometimes, better still, in harmonic accord, their mutual waves, one encountering another, associate and fuse, and the two beings are united with one another by a chain more solid than iron. It's not only their gazes that are knotted, it's their entire being. All that one might do to oppose that union would be wasted effort. It will be accomplished, if necessary, after death.

"If a cacophony results from the encounter of the vibrations, antipathy is the result, and the most beautiful reasoning can do nothing about it. That man is antipathetic to me; that woman gets on my nerves. Don't seek to correct the first impression; it will be wasted effort.

"Well, on Albireo, we see these vibrations of the soul, these etheric undulations, as you see by means of light; we perceive them by means of our electric sense, while they remain foreign to you. These electrical vibrations, which are like the very atmosphere of love, are unknown to you on Earth. You experience love much as the deaf experience music."

"Oh!" I said. "How ungrateful you are!"

"No, my adored one, I remember everything. But remember that love is the intimate union of two beings. In terrestrial amours, there is no entire melting into one another. But here, where the electric sense is entirely developed, our etheric bodies are like two electric charges that annihilate one another in lightning. The combination is so intense that of two beings who embrace, only one remains—like oxygen and hydrogen, which, in combining, lose their individuality to form a drop of water, a limpid pearl that contains the entire rainbow and summarizes the universe."

"But what happens afterwards?"

"Well, afterwards, one can recover oneself! I don't know how it happens, but one is resuscitated."

"That's not impossible. Electricity can dissociate a drop of water and separate once again the oxygen and hydrogen whose union formed it."

"You know how to explain everything scientifically."

"So," I added, "one goes as far as losing consciousness of one's existence—really dying—and being reborn?"

"Do you understand now that our seventeen senses, governed by the first among them, provide sensations compared with which the most vivid joys experienced on Earth are merely the coarse impressions of mollusks? And what light inundates us! What flowers! What perfumes! It's like a perpetual ecstasy. Of, if you came, if you were here!"

"Can't you take me?" I exclaimed, launching myself toward her.

"Come!"

I seized her in my arms, stuck my lips to hers, and suddenly saw, in the heart of a very soft and tender blue light, that Dora was bearing me away on immense wings. I was clinging to her body, lost in delight. Numerous beings, drifting like us in the atmosphere, had the form of dragonflies, with antennae, palps and aerial organs, which doubtless represented the new senses that she had mentioned to me.

I understood that I had been suddenly transported on to one of the planets of Albireo's azure sun. Cascades of blue water fell from the rocks and ran through an immense garden carpeted by brilliant flowers. Birds with bright plumage, seemingly luminous in themselves, filled the air with their songs.

"Let's go through this light," she said, "toward the evening horizon and descend into the palaces of night."

Having moved out of the illuminated hemisphere, we arrived in semi-darkness. All the rocks, all the vegetation and all the animals shone with a blue, green or roseate light, phosphorescent or fluorescent. The rocks undoubtedly possessed properties analogous to those of phosphates and sulfates of barytes, which store solar light received during the day and radiate it during the night. The flying creatures were similarly luminous, in the fashion of fireflies. Darkness, on this world, is never complete, firstly because of that curious phosphorescence of every body, secondly because of Albireo's second, golden sun, the distant light of which is almost never absent, and also because of a ring analogous to that of Saturn, which, lit by these half-suns of different colors, is sometimes blue, sometimes yellow and sometimes green, and distributes the strangest gleams through the semi-darkness.

How small a thing is our poor and minuscule terrestrial world, which we imagine to be everything, by comparison with those ultra-terrestrial marvels!

My beautiful and beloved Dora carried me lovingly between her wings, and we descended toward the shores of a lake, beneath an immense arborescent foliage, the vast leaves of which extended like a cradle of verdure over a carpet of moss strewn with a thousand little flowers.

"This is where I live," she said. "Let's rest."

In my delight and ecstasy, I wanted to seize her in my arms and savor on her lips the exquisite happiness of being loved by her—but scarcely had she touched the ground than her terrestrial form was instantly transformed into another, similar to the beings that we had encountered flying in the atmosphere. She was no longer my Dora. She was, however, even more beautiful and more radiant, and compared with her, I felt like an earthworm.

"To love me still, to love me forever," she said, "it's sufficient to die! Quit the Earth. Here, you will be mine."

"Have I not quit the Earth, then?" I replied, astonished.

"No—look."

She touched my lightly on the forehead with the tip of an antenna and I felt a sharp electric shock. I opened my eyes and found myself alone, sitting in the large armchair. My beloved had disappeared.

I no longer have any doubt that she really is living on that star in Cygnus. She is calling me there and I shall soon recover her. I love her more than ever!

Such was André's story. That apparition had had such a powerful impact on him that, from that day onwards, his mind appeared to be wandering far from the Earth. His poor health declined rapidly, but he lived happily in his dream, with the desire, the obsession to see it realized.

I was not surprised when, a few months after the adventure that has just been reported, I was told of the sudden death of my dear comrade.

On a beautiful summer night, perhaps haunted by the same vision, he had stretched himself out in the same armchair, next to the great equatorial telescope, aimed at Albireo, and, in the morning, he was thought to have fallen asleep there—but his cadaver was completely cold.

To his right, a little bottle containing hydrocyanic acid—one drop of which is sufficient to dissolve the bonds attaching the soul to the body—had fallen on to the floor.

THE STAR OF THE DEAD

by F. Jollivet Castelot

To Dr. Papus

A somber blood-red moon spreading mystic terror in strange reflections ...

A profound black sea with heavy, seemingly viscous waves; a sea set ablaze by lunar rats; and over the false thickness of that glaucous ocean, a light mist of phosphorescent molecules ...

The isle emerges from the bosom of the somber elements, a bleak, solitary isle whose red-brown soil proclaims the sickening spectral desolation ...

And through the chaotic waters, toward the isle, fly the souls of the planetary dead; over the red-black waters pass floating violet shadows, the doubles of those who have quit the Earth and whom the attraction of destiny has brought to these shores.

The phantoms wander, crowding the sad and solitary isle, rising toward the bloody star, vaguely luminous in their astral envelope ...

No speech cleaves this world's atmosphere, no sound resounds; the waves move without echoes; the mist always remains motionless.

At certain moments, following the direction taken slowly by the Red Moon, the spirits unite in processions, in groups

201

of mauve gleams, in families of amour or amity; together they flutter over the sea, still as black as ink; together they rise up toward the garnet moon; together they move through the eternal, eternally phosphoric mist; together they plunge their vaguely luminous bodies beneath the somber waves, and they dance, soundlessly, the macabre round of the dead over the mute waves that lick them with a reflection of incendiary reflections.

Then they head toward the isle. On the soil of the Ossuary they alight and settle, awaiting the return of the Vision . . .

Then, on the isle that was bleak and deserted, devoid of plants and trees, strange phenomena are produced, magical decors unfurl, innumerable scenes extend, displaying the succession of elapsed events; the Evocation of the Past, of anterior lives, is taking place; the sequence of images is depicted in a bizarre kind of dream, in a series of calm, melancholy, terrifying dreams.

All the souls present see their previous existence again, their active existence, their real planetary life; on the beach of dreams—on the shore of the beyond where their imperfect monads gather after terrestrial death—the souls contemplate cherished or detested scenes of which they were, with physical bodies, the heroes, the victims, or the actors.

And under the incendiary kiss of the Red Moon, the Moon of the dead, the panoramas succeed one another, varying, hastening in a kaleidoscopic march. Manors and châteaux loom up; ruins appear, surrounded by profound mysterious forests, parks, green and flowery meadows; a sunlit sky bursts forth with blue hues, tinted with an autumnal copper, in spite of the red light of the star that shines incessantly. All of that mingles, confounded as in dreams, but more precisely—and some phantoms recognize places in which they lived previously, the locations in which the stage of their journey was accomplished and their actions carried out . . . Here are the beings one perceived—women, men and animals—and souls rediscover, still at a distance: parents, friends, houses, cherished places; and they launch forward sobbing their pain and crying, untranslated by voices, their tenderness and their regrets, their amour and their desires, still persistent . . . but as they approach, the vision draws away; they are obliged to witness, impotently, the phantasmagoria of the past in akasic images.[1]

Ah! That crenellated château with florid, perfumed terraces, on which a young and beautiful woman is walking slowly—one spirit recognizes it, and also recognizes the woman, the adored mistress, the adulterous spouse, the lover stolen from the husband. The specter extends its arms, its astral body tortured by the same desires—beautiful or ugly—that assailed it during life, but even more refined, more completely pierced; and it calls to the beloved, runs to the pillars of the terrace, shakes the foundations of the edifice with its immaterial hands; it rises up, reaches for the beloved—but then the decor that it is pursuing recoils, slowly fading away and vanishing in the distance, a tempting mirage. An ardent, dolorous lust grips the specter, which watches the cherished being departing in the depths of the horizon, her lips extended for a kiss. The darling is doubtless dreaming about him in her château, dreaming on her planet, dreaming of the dead man she loved more than anything, more than her adoring spouse, more than her children, more than her lost honor. And in a dream in her slumber, she also finds him, borne toward him as he is toward her, but ignorant of his destiny and his misfortune . . .

That image is succeeded by another; a new scene unfurls, evoking another lived past; instead of fine actions read, frightful visions appear: images of blood, images of murder, of war, and

---

1 In Theosophical theory, Akashic, or Askasic, records form a compendium of events encoded on a hyperphysical plane of existence which are available for consultation by disembodied souls. Lifestyle fantasies often credited their revelations—especially those dealing with the remote past of lost continents—to the visionary consultation of Akashic records.

everyone judges their works and efforts therein, suffering even more before rising up—for thus Nature wishes it, which insists that each progress should be slowly gained by her children, at the price of multitudinous tortures and much suffering.

※

Here, the life of things unveils some of its mysteries, the Mathematics of the Kosmos is better understood, the Fatality of things is marked, the enchantment of phenomena is legible. Souls understand better that on the earths of exile the Determinism of their existence and the Ideal that they ought to pursue. Things participate in hominal life, influence actions, bring and add their occult energy to other fluids. The categories of beings appear; these are passionate, love their mistresses greatly, savor many lips; those remain agames[1]; others are faithful to their unique amour, and each, in his manner of being and trying out his ideal, is right in a way, for some see their ideal woman, so beautiful, so pure, so complex that they cannot encounter it in one alone, and several are necessary to compose an approximation of the glimpsed splendor. Who can describe the dolors of those who pursue the admirable vision in vain, the completely beautiful woman, the Callista of which he dreams? Who can describe the disappointments of each possession of an imperfect body, each kiss of mediocre fakes? And is that one not an artist, does he not love ardently the god Beauty?

And others, finally, do not rediscover or discover the beloved. Destiny, for a reason unknown to them, but necessary, prevents them from encountering the sister-soul, even the primitive and temporary sister-soul of the rapid carnal liaison.

---

1 The Theosophists in India associated with Madame Blavatsky's disciple Colonel Olcott used the term "agames," borrowed from Sinhalese, to refer to people belonging to a traditional religion, usually Christian, but Castelot seems to be using it idiosyncratically.

This love agames lack, weeping their lament, crying and sobbing toward the unknown of grand amour. Then they devote
themselves to their dream of amour: they sing it by means of
Art, Poetry, Music or Science. And do they not love ardently
the god Truth, the god Light?

Oh, it is because all of them, all beings, are conducted by
inflexible Destiny; it is because the phenomena of their life are
connected without them being able to react; will is a force very
latent in humans, an energy of Nature, of the Universe; humans
scarcely possess the seed of it. They can only struggle via Science
and study. Oh, how illusory is their free will—what a vain
word! And that's why God-Nature doesn't punish being, simply purifying it by means of suffering, disengaging souls from
their sheath of heavy matter formed by elementary particles, in
order that diamond-souls necessarily rise toward the Light; it is
by means of love that Nature tests souls, making them suffer in
order to render them brilliant and pure; the more inferior, the
heavier, the soul is, the longer it has to weep and to rise; the less
it contemplates Reason and Beauty.

So this isle, this ossuary with a blood red Moon is not a
place of great dolor devoid of hope. This Earth of the Dead,
this seemingly heavy planet—in reality an ethereal, astral planet—is a place of transition; spirits return there surrounded by
their astral envelope, the physical double; the souls of planets
go there—including those of our solar system—and in extraterrestrial, and hence indescribable, suffering, specters finish their
purification, ridding themselves of their corporeal double. In
this region of black sea, in this land of solitude and silence, with
a Red Moon, black moths in this land of dream, they meditate,
think, seek the goal to follow and comprehend the laws of the
Universe.

The Harmony of Nature appears to them; they know that all
is harmony, that everything, including evil, concurs in imprint-
ing the eternal melody, the song, the universal chorus. For they

are not unaware that life through Infinity can be compared to a book in which beings are the characters, the letters. Now, the characters differ and vary; some are great others small, some are better traced than others, but that has no influence on the book itself, on its Spirit, on its Idea. Every letter brings its personality to the work; every character has its part in the realization of the Idea of the Book. That Idea, the purpose of the book, vibrates through all its pages, all its words, and the phrases depicting the evil-shadow are no less necessary to the Unity of the Work, to its end, to its soul, to the contrast of images and the comprehension of the whole than the phrases describing the Good, which is to say the Light, Superiority, Clarity.

What responsibility do those incarnate letters bear, expressing Good and Evil? Has not the author of the volume placed them in accordance with inflexible laws in order to realize in style, in emanation, his own will? And do not all those words serve to elevate the Temple, to personify the general Harmony? Thus, individuals are the characters of the Great Book of Nature. Every being collaborates in the edification of the Ideal, sings one note, high or low, in the divine Hymn . . .

And over the black ocean, according to the sad but voluptuous vision, the Phantoms glide, the Fays of shadow.

The Star of the Dead, without pausing, caresses with mild red fluids the mute Angels that carry within themselves the exquisite Memory of the past of the Dream and the mad Hope of the Sidereal future.

O Amour, O Amour, you cradle with your ardor—on your wings of fire you sustain them—and you enrapture the angels with your celestial kisses, for they are awaiting the Sister-Soul.

BURN THIS

by Jules Lermina

I

O N the point of undertaking the most audacious work that a man has ever attempted, determined to go to the very threshold of Death, without being certain of not being obliged to pass over it, I want to study myself, to relive my entire past life, to consider as if with a microscope the infinitely small things that have led me to the limit of the infinitely large—in a word, to make my confession.

I have only resolved to make that confession, however, in the solitude of an egotistical meditation: I alone will ask the questions; I alone will answer them.

If, in writing it down, I give substance to this intimate enquiry, if my pen materializes this interrogation and draws up this report, it is, of course, because I want to employ a sort of mnemonic technique, for my own benefit, and not in order that these lines should fall under anyone else's eyes.

If I emerge alive from the ordeal I am about to undergo, I shall re-read these pages and I shall add to them, in a few strokes of the pen, the solution to the Problem; I shall write down the formula of the Secret. Then I shall consult myself. Should I destroy the manuscript, or, on the contrary, deliver it, with the

Supreme Law that it will contain, to human curiosity? I don't know. Ought the infinite power, the formula of which will be revealed at the same time as its existence, its mode of action and the procedure of its exercise, to be handed like a deposition to the seekers of Truth? I'm still hesitant.

In any case, I don't have to make that decision now, since it can only be posterior to what I am about to attempt.

It might transpire, however—so terrible are the risks to be run—that I shall perish in the accomplishment of the task on which I am determined. Whether that will happen prior to the act or whether I shall fall, like a soldier, on the cadaver of the enemy, I don't know. But it might be that, in one or a few days, having observed my absence, servants or friends will go into my room and find me inanimate and cold—dead—with the notebook in front of me in which I shall have inscribed an account of the battle fought, without my having been able to record the victory or the defeat. In that event, I don't want this to be read by profane imbeciles, who would be terrified or would mock, go mad or remain stupid.

Thus, before my departure—and I mean departure—I shall enclose these pages in a large envelope and I shall write, by way of an address, the two words: *Burn This.*

Ordinarily, these sorts of posthumous instructions are respected, and I have the further guarantee that, in the event, as always happens in cases of sudden or singular death, a magistrate will be consulted, who will see to it himself that my wishes are carried out.

I have another motive for acting in this manner.

Although, in the eyes of the vulgar, the action that I am about to carry out is criminal—and it is the character of the action in question that I shall study, in conducting a kind of analysis by means of the words and letters that will be its detailed representation—I am not wicked. The hatred that I experience against the individual against whom I shall mount a furious combat is, in reality, nothing but the notion of a right that belongs to me and which the individual is obstinate in misunderstanding. I lay claim to my right; that is justice, since there has been a rupture of equilibrium, to my detriment. But that right, I do not recognize against all humankind.

Now, I know that the Secret, acquired by me at the price of so much effort and a reasoned perseverance of which very few would be capable, would be an agent of evil in the hands of the ignorant, deleterious to the individual and mortal to society, precisely by virtue of the distance that separates the present—considered normal—state of science and real knowledge of the Mystery of life and death.

If everyone knew the possible objective, everyone would rush toward it, blindly and madly, not understanding that the route must be followed slowly, one step at a time, lest deviations, derailments and falls lead to a universal upheaval. Humankind will always resemble a novice rider launched forth on a spirited horse, which he does not know how to master or steer, and which, soon carrying him away, will throw him and fracture his skull with its shoe.

I do not have the courage to assume that responsibility.

I am one of the first, and perhaps the only one in the Occidental world, to have had sufficient mastery of himself to arrive, without any cerebral lesion, on the threshold of the mystery; the only one who has been able, in the plenitude of his reason, with the mathematics of common sense, to take accurate account of the road followed—and, having reached the abyss, to measure its awful depth. In preparing to hurl myself into it, I know what I am doing; I know the peril; in that duel with the infinite, I have a firm hold on the weapon that might grant me victory.

And yet, am I not mad? I would be wrong to say no, since I have not been able to abstract myself completely enough from my animality to resist the passion that might perhaps kill me and by which I am allowing myself to be drawn . . .

It's getting dark. I'm alone. My lamp is enveloping the place where I'm working in light, while all around it is in profound darkness.

I'm writing.

II

I am French at heart and by reason. If it were not prideful, I would say more than French: Gallic, Parisian. I was born into a family of petty merchants, whose name has been found at the head of many invoices for several hundred years. Their horizon had always been limited by the Rues Saint-Denis and Saint-Martin. One alone had thrust forth as far as the Rue Vivienne, but he had returned to his natural center, the Rue Turbigo, where he died.[1] That was my father. He was a tailor.

He was a small, nervous man with a colorless complexion, very active, who ran around Paris every morning, his clothes under his arm, intelligent in business, very honest and very obliging. He knew how to divine a trustworthy client, and did not refuse him credit, but was hard on anyone who tried to take advantage of him.

He was, moreover, the incarnation of reason; he was sober and chaste. As a true Parisian, he adored the theater, and a late-paying client could soften him considerably with the gift of a complimentary ticket. He appeared to have no imagination, and the sole cerebral debauchery that he permitted himself was the interest that he took in the imaginary adventures of the stage. A drama impassioned him; he sincerely hated the traitor and wept naïvely over the fate of the juvenile lead.

---

1 The writer names the Rue Vivienne to signify that his father once had ambitions toward self-education because it is the site of the Bibliothéque Nationale. The Rue Turbigo is in a commercialized district not far from Les Halles.

I knew him to have but one vanity: his surname figured on the register of the conquerors of the Bastille and on the Colonne de Juillet.[1] They were the family's titles of nobility, and he clung to them. His political opinions were, moreover, in harmony with his well-poised character. He went as far as the extreme limits of liberalism, but refused to exceed them. Critics of authority amused him, and he laughed heartily at the witty gibes they directed against the government, but at the slightest hint of active violence he became serious again, demanding before all else that he be allowed to work in peace.

In sum, he was placid. I remember wondering, frequently, whether there was, beneath his banal appearance, the fabric of a profound philosophy. When I was a child, I was sometimes struck, while he was working contentedly in the back of his shop, by the gleam that I saw filtering beneath his lowered eyelids. I know that he was highly esteemed, not only for his probity, but above all for the rectitude of his judgment, and also for an education that I could not judge, but which—in certain details that I recall—was evidently superior to his station.

He had a clientele of professors and young scientists, to whom he gladly rendered inappreciable services that permitted a turn-out indispensable to debuts. When a timid individual, armed with a recommendation, came to attempt what he called "a frock-coat coup," my father, with his slightly sly simplicity, knew how to make the neophyte talk; more than one, taken by surprise, gave evidence of an unequivocal respect for the petty merchant who thought and spoke soundly, even about questions entirely beyond his probable competence.

One day, one of them exclaimed, while laughing, but not without a hint of esteem: "But you're subjecting me to a veritable examination, Monsieur!"

---

1 The taking of the Bastille was the initial insurrection that launched the Revolution of 1789; the Colonne de Juillet was raised in the Place de la Bastille to commemorate the Revolution of July 1830. A name thus doubly figured would therefore have very solid Republican credentials.

"Bah!" said my father. "A Parisian ought to know a little about everything."

The fact is that he read a great deal, especially in the evening, never going out to the café.

All in all, he was a good man—and his conduct toward my mother was that of an angelic being.

I knew how he had come to marry my mother. In a house in which he was resident, and in which he exercised his profession, a tenant he did not know had committed suicide—a crack-brained eccentric, it was said in the neighborhood, who lived alone, devoting himself to what good folk call "the Devil's work." In fact, he was doubtless one of those disdained savants, endowed with more education than reason, who pursue too lofty a dream without being resolved to climb the steps that might lead them to it. He had taken out several patents, but had exhausted all his resources without being able to exploit them usefully; my understanding was that he had directed his research in the field of electricity, or, rather, of magnetism. At any rate, the unfortunate, having run out of money and energy, had poisoned himself, not without first having destroyed all his manuscripts, as well as the apparatus he had used in his experiments.

Only one sheet of paper had escaped that auto-da-fé; I still have it. It bears the strange title: *The Life of the Dead*.

I don't know how my father learned that this man, who was believed to be an old bachelor, was a widower and had a daughter, brought up in a boarding-school some leagues from Paris. The child was fourteen years of age; the death of her father—who, it appeared, had always paid her fees regularly—necessitated the cessation of her studies, and also delivered the poor girl to all the hazards of a life of poverty.

My father was still a bachelor at the age of forty. It pleased him to take an interest in that unknown girl, and he substituted himself for the absent father. The girl was pretty and intelligent;

she was grateful, and when she turned eighteen, my father married her.

A year later, I was born.

About myself, and my early childhood, I will talk in due course.

The union of my father and my mother was one of the happiest for eight years, but at the age of twenty-six my mother contracted an illness that led her to the grave five years later.

I have before my eyes a letter written by my father, addressed to a man who is pleased to call himself one of the masters of modern science; I shall transcribe it in its entirety in order to penetrate its terminology, evidently incomprehensible to the person whose help it was requesting, but which no one is more qualified than I am to translate.

I notice within it, above all, the rationalist and positivist tendencies of my father's mind, which mistook the singularity of a poorly-observed condition, by reason of preconceived ideas that opposed their examination.

This is the letter:

Monsieur de Docteur, as you have authorized me to do so, I shall acquaint you with the circumstances that I have observed in my poor wife's malady. I beg you to excuse me, if these observations seem obscure to you; I am recording the facts that I can see, or believe that I can see, and, being unable to explain them, am doubtless describing them badly—but I can assure you that everything that follows is the absolute expression of the truth, as it appears to me.

It was two years ago that I first noticed the initial symptom. One evening, at about ten o'clock, the child had been put to bed and I was putting my books in order. I was with my wife in the room that serves us as both a living-room and a dining-room. It is lit by a lamp suspended from the ceiling. Adèle was sewing, and not talking to me—which was no cause for surprise, for she was often silent and thoughtful. Suddenly, I heard a sliding sound. I raised my head immediately and saw my wife slumped against the back of her chair, her eyes closed, as pale as a dead woman.

I launched myself toward her, seized her in my arms, and laid her down on the settee, then ran to my bedroom and came back with vinegar and smelling-salts. For more than a quarter of an hour, however, all my efforts were fruitless. Her heartbeat was feeble, her pulse sensibly slowed, but still regular. I dared not leave her to seek help, fearful of a mortal crisis.

Suddenly, though, I saw her face take on color again; her pulse, which I consulted immediately, recovered its vigor. She took a deep breath, opened her eyes and began to speak, initially in an incoherent fashion. She talked about the child who was in the next room. He was fast asleep *now*. Then she apologized for having worried me, saying that it was no more than a slight illness. She went to bed and went peacefully to sleep. I ought to note that, by a singular coincidence, young Paul, when he woke up the following morning, thanked his mother for coming to kiss him during the night. He had evidently been dreaming.

That crisis was not renewed for six months, but at the end of that time, it reappeared, in almost identical conditions, but more intensely and more alarmingly. During the faint, which lasted an hour, her body became cold, her face was covered by the mask of death, and momentarily, it seemed to me that her heart was no longer beating. Terrified, I shouted for help. Neighbors came running—but Adèle woke up again, as she had the first time. The fit was completely dissipated, without leaving any appreciable traces.

I called a doctor, who did not attach any importance to these symptoms and gave me a banal explanation, further belied by my wife's character and temperament. As for her, when I questioned her about what happened during these fainting fits, she replied with explanations so bizarre that I have not yet dared to impart them to you. Today, I need to tell you everything.

She tells me that suddenly, at the moment when she least expects it, she feels that a force she is unable to resist draws her outside herself—that is her own expression. It is, she says, as if a cupping-glass were applied to her heart, creating a vacuum within her entire being. Finally, she added—and here I appeal to your indulgence for my unscientific language—something that is her life (doubtless her vital force) is exhaled outside her, condensing in a vaporous state, and drifts through the apartment . . . what do I know? Naturally, I attribute these illusions to an unhealthy condition; it is something akin to the hallucinations of fever, and I would not attach to these tales any other value than that which they merit as symptoms of a temporary condition, if, unfortunately, the fits were not becoming increasingly frequent.

Today, I can say that lethargy is the poor woman's normal condition, and that rational and active wakefulness is only the exception.

For an average of four days a week, Adèle is plunged in sleep, without taking any nourishment. She never seems to be suffering, except at the beginning and end of the crisis. I shall explain. When she is about to fall into the state in question, I am alerted to it by the play of her physiognomy: first surprise, then anxiety. There is an anguish in her eyes that sometimes has a fearful character, which I can only compare to the terrified alarm of a child from whom a dentist is about to extract a tooth, and who has seen the steel instrument approaching his mouth. Then, to continue the comparison, one might say that the operation takes place instantaneously. There follows an immediate relief, but, at the same time, as if the blood were flowing from some invisible wound, the face becomes colorless, the cheeks become hollow, the forehead because taut and the lips become thin.

Throughout the crisis, the face remains impassive. There are never any contractions in the limbs, nor convulsive movements.

If the expression employed by my dear Adèle did not awaken near-fantastic ideas—against which my reason protests—I would say that I have before my eyes nothing but a body, whose soul is temporarily absent.

What is perhaps even more striking is the mode of resurrection. Forgive me for employing that word, but my first priority is to make myself understood.

After sixteen to twenty-four hours of immobility, I suddenly see my wife lift her hand to her heart—never her head, although that seems to me to be the seat of the illness. She then pushes her torso forwards as if, in the heart thus presented, she were offering to receive the breath of life again. Then again, a quiver of anguish troubles her physiognomy, but it is instantaneous, and from that moment on, life re-enters her; her limbs become flexible; her eyes and mouth open.

Except that the lassitude, non-existent after the first fits of this strange illness, is becoming increasingly overwhelming. To be sure, she lives through these intermittences, but her pulse is weak, her respiration scarcely perceptible. She speaks in hushed tones, half-closing her eyes as if daylight might harm them; her movements are slow and she is incapable of manual work, her hands have so little strength. The slightest locomotion, even crossing the room, exhausts her.

Then, as I told you, what frightens me the most is her smile, soft, resigned and continuous. If I question her, with all necessary precautions, she replies with generosity, as if she were gladly making me a concession. She no longer explains her sensations. It's my fault; she has glimpsed a few signs of incredulity in my face, while she was telling me about her visions.

And yet, can I deny that she had told me about events that were occurring in the shop while she was lying motionless in her room? Can I deny that she has repeated words I have spoken outside her presence, which she could not have heard? Can I deny—crazy as it is—having found around my son's neck a locket that was shut in a drawer, which she did not go near?

But I will stop there, for you might perhaps think me insane, although my reason has never been firmer. I can no longer believe in the exact science of which you are one of the most illustrious representatives. I beg you, come to the aid of my dear wife. Save her!

III

My mother loved me passionately. She had, as I've said, received a good education and had attempted to stimulate my intelligent faculties from my earliest childhood.

It's necessary that I analyze here what I felt, from the earliest times of my life onwards, because, in contrast to so many others, my memories of extreme infancy are, in certain respects, very clear and easily graspable. If this were destined for public view, I would abstain, for I would be accused of lying and perhaps madness, as my father feared, when he recoiled before a confession of the "anti-scientific" truth.

To myself alone I say this: I was scarcely two years old when, during the most profound sleep, I knew that my mother was watching over me and thinking about me. On that notification of the invisible, I woke myself and waited. Listening with all ears, I did not hear any sound. Then, gradually, I perceived the sound of a sigh, of a suppressed yawn; she got up, bare-footed, and came to my crib. I opened my eyes slightly, not enough for her to think that I was awake, and she seemed to me to be surrounded by a shiny mist.

She kissed me and I fell back into a deep sleep.

Later, and before she was visibly affected by the illness—I employ the conventional term—that would kill her, I had sensed the following impression: I was sitting a few feet away from her, playing; she was gazing at me lovingly; then, on my forehead and in my hair, I felt a very soft breath, an ethereal but material caress. I was not astonished, not knowing as yet that I ought to be astonished by it.

I felt the impression of her arms before they had enfolded me, the kiss of her lips before they had touched my forehead.

On other occasions, when I had not gone near her for some time, I suddenly felt a slight friction, as if someone had touched me on the shoulder to solicit my attention; then a magnetic attraction drew me toward her; I went to kiss her, and she did not seem astonished either. She had wanted me to do it and I had obeyed—nothing more.

Why be astonished? My mother had carried me; she had nourished me with her milk. The most natural of all bonds connected us. That the connection was of a superior degree, I don't deny. There are instruments whose harmonic tuning is exceptional. But it was me most of all of whom the old saying was true: *A child is a plant incessantly watered by maternity.*

If I fell ill, my mother enveloped me with herself, not figuratively, but in the full sense of the term. Her love emanated from her, to spread around me like a warm vapor. If I bumped into some item of furniture, I ran to her so that she could kiss the bruise—and the pain disappeared. If I had a toothache, she passed her finger over my gums, and the ache ceased: maternal magic whose effects we see every day, but which pass unnoticed! Who will write down its rituals?

In truth, even when I was weaned, my mother continued to nourish me with her substance. I believe—and this is not an insult to my father's memory—that all that marriage comprised for my mother were the joys of maternity; she had an expansive nature that fitted badly with the calm equilibrium of my father—the paradigm example of a reasonable man, twenty-five years older than her, and too much a friend to be a lover.

She had a vivid imagination and told me stories at night that she made up herself, and which showed me sunlit regions in an exquisite light. I remember that I sometimes asked her for

218

a pearl-grey tale, sometimes a mauve tale, sometimes a golden tale. The enunciation of color summarized for me the particular emotion that each of her tales aroused in me. My father remained serious while listening to them. He was not very pleased that my mind was being disturbed in that way. The rather gross magicality of booted cats, ogres and donkey-skins appeared to him to be less dangerous to the imagination than those vague and paradisal evocations. My mother understood, and fell silent—but what she no longer told me aloud, I still listened to in her gaze, in the caress of her hands and the rhythm of her feet drumming on the carpet.

I was weak, nervous and irritable. My father took me in hand, attempting to correct my faults by means of daily education. He made me take iron and tonics. He was a great believer in gymnastics. My mother, for her part, combated my weakness by infusing me with her strength, calmed my nerves by breathing on me, defused my anger with the radiance of her exquisite placidity.

I know—I am convinced—that I only lived because of my mother, and I know too that it was of me that she died. In the perpetual surge of her maternity she expended herself, gave herself entirely . . . I know, as I say, because I saw . . .

Yes—and no one in the world has heard that word emerge from my lips—I *saw*, on the days and nights when my mother was immobile in her crises, *I saw* her form approach me, felt her life penetrate me, her vitality combine with mine. And it was in that incessant effort to pour herself into me, by virtue of a sublime and adorable endosmosis, that she exhausted herself, drained herself, ran herself dry, and died.

I said that my father's conduct was angelic. No expression can better describe the generosity, patience and maternity of which he gave proof in his turn during my mother's long prostration. He would certainly have given his life for her, if he had known how. There were terrible combats in that sage rationality, which

I can now divine—for I have found out since that he went in secret to consult specialists who were no less worthy than the physicians, but who, alas, were no less ignorant, alarming his bourgeois Voltairean common sense with the mystical confusion of their pronouncements. I found a heap of books in his home that he must have studied and re-read a hundred times over—but he was endowed, above all, with the typically French mind that demands precision and clarity, and only wants to act judiciously. Whatever one may say, the French mind is eminently mathematical; it requires deduction that nothing can interrupt, a thread that nothing can tangle or break.

If he had understood what was happening to my mother—as I understand it, who am, perhaps, going to die of hatred as she died of love—he would undoubtedly have saved her. But who could have explained it to him? Between ignorant orthodoxy and mystical charlatanry, he gave preference to the former, and was not, all things considered, mistaken.

I was twelve when my mother died.

I subsequently suffered a long and painful illness, during which my father cared for me with a devotion that did not falter for a single minute.

I have said that I remember impressions of my youth. There is one that I have not forgotten—that I cannot forget, and whose truth I shall analyze with all rigor. Oh, how they would laugh if they knew that!

The physicians diagnosed in me a complete exhaustion, an anemia that had reached its final phase, complicated by gastralgia, neuralgia and so on. My weakness was such that I was always lying down, either on my bed or a chaise longue. I had ringing in my ears, visual disturbances, and an infinite need for immobility. The slightest movement was suffering to me, and caused irritations throughout my being that were translated into veritable fits of fury.

In sum, it was a normal, catalogued malady whose natural termination was anticipated before long. Maternal heredity, said the earnest bonzes.

One night, my state of weakness had taken on such proportions that my father stationed himself beside my bed. I saw him as if through a veil, and yet I remember that he was weeping. In reality, I felt that I was dying—which is to say that something was escaping from my entire being that I did not even try to retain. Although my heart was scarcely beating, I felt the dull impact of each of the pulsations by means of which it was attempting to launch the regenerative oxygen into circulation.

Suddenly, my father, gripped by a sort of frenzy, got up, leaned over me, and shouted at me, with a voice that resounded through my body like a clarion call: "But I don't want you to die! I beg you, my boy, my dear child, make an effort . . . react . . . have the will to live . . ."

And all of a sudden, I understood that word: *will*. Something passed through me that was both instantaneous and formidable. I didn't make any movement; I didn't stiffen in any visible effort; but I felt that an enormous intensity of energy was concentrated in my brain . . . I *willed* . . .

And I lived.

This time, I lived because of my father, who, in an unconscious exclamation, had taught me will-power. In him, that cry had been the instinctive expression of a sort of appeal for a miracle, and that miracle had come to pass, by awakening in me an as-yet-unfamiliar notion, constraining me to a centralization of force, the triggering of a mechanism that altered the plane of my vital being, a modification of equilibrium that worked to my benefit. I was saved!

But I can also say that I was lost, for I had, according to the Biblical expression, plucked the fruit of the tree of knowledge that is the Will.

And it is Will that might soon kill me.

IV

As soon as I was better, my father, not wishing to expose me to the hygienic perils of boarding-school, made me follow the curriculum at the lycée.[1] In the evenings, a tutor—one of his clients—consented to give me private lessons.

I was well-endowed; I had my mother's imagination, and her curiosity in matters of intelligence. At the same time, by virtue of a rather remarkable hereditary equilibrium, I possessed my father's sense of order. My teacher called it the sequencing faculty, and in truth, the expression was accurate. Whether it was a matter of literary work or a mathematical calculation, I always had to proceed systematically and methodically, always commencing the edifice at the base and superimposing materials symmetrically. To every enunciation I replied with a question, then another, until I sensed that I was supported by a solid foundation. Only then did I permit imagination or invention even to enter the stage.

Moreover, I conserved in my innermost depths that notion of Will to which I knew I owed my life. By an instinct singular in a young man, still little more than a boy, I did not squander it. On the contrary, I hoarded it thriftily, in order to project it in its entirety with irresistible impulsion, when the moment came, toward the desired end.

By my success at university,[2] I gave my father the only joy that he had experienced since my mother's death. To second it, I won first prize for Latin translation in the open competition.

---

1 The Rue Turbigo is the location of the Lycée Turgot, named after the first author of the modern philosophy of progress.

2 The narrator presumably attended the open lectures put on in the Salle Gerson at the Sorbonne, even though he was not old enough at this stage of his story to attend university as a student; he makes subsequent reference to the competition to which this passage refers being held in the hall.

There again my will had intervened in interesting circumstances. The set text was from Tacitus. I had translated it, so to speak, at the speed of the pen, with the exception of one four-word phrase that was exceedingly obscure, by virtue of its conciseness and the allusion it contained to a little-known historical fact.

I did not worry about it unduly, and was thinking about something else—writing verse or fully extrapolating the amazing combinations that can be extracted from a simple Pythagorean table.[1] Suddenly, the first signal was given, indicating that no more than a quarter of an hour remained to hand in the copy. I immediately started copying out my rough draft in my best handwriting, when I noticed that the four words in question still remained inexplicable.

The second signal was given: five minutes to go.

Then I understood that, unless it was complete, my translation was only good for the waste-paper basket. I experienced something akin to an electric shock; then, instantaneously, I sensed that I was now only alive at a single point, the profound—or, rather sharp—attention that was being brought to bear on Tacitus' phrase. At the same time—I was completely conscious of it—an impulse of my entire being concentrated my vital force on the enigma, and the translated words sprang from my pen, without my taking account of their correctness. I handed in my copy without re-reading it.

When I stood up, I was stunned and had difficulty walking in a straight line. I was so pale that my comrades made fun of me, supposing that I had examination nerves.

A few minutes later, leaving the Salle Gerson, the avidly-breathed air restored my equilibrium. I remembered the Latin words, and the translation. It was perfection itself.

---

1 A Pythagorean table is a list of opposites; at least one of the dichotomies in the supposed original (one/many) gave rise to much philosophical debate.

I won the prize. My father, who held university education in the highest possible esteem, embraced me more effusively than usual—and yet I could not help noticing how his hug lacked the enveloping warmth that had once characterized my mother's caresses. Alas, the kiss too was lacking.

The day after the awarding of the prizes, my father had a fall in the street, which had the most disastrous consequences. His head had struck the angle of a sidewalk, and he was brought to the house unconscious. The cerebral shock had been so violent that it caused a haemorrhage.

That same night, his death-throes began. I was beside him, as he had once been beside me, at the moment when life was about to abandon me—and on an instinctive impulse, I cried out to him, repeating his own words: "I beg you, father, dear father, make an effort . . . react . . . have the will to live!"

He turned his lethargic and vitreous eyes toward me. It seemed to me, judging by the contraction of his lips, that he made an effort—but a raucous breath, abruptly cut short, emerged from his breast. He was dead.

Often, since then, I have reproached myself for not having substituted my will for his and not having compelled his life to obey me. But I was not yet sufficiently master of myself in the exercise of my will to abstract myself from purely reflex instincts. My first impulse had been to address to him the adjuration that had saved me.

I had acted recklessly, without any method. I know that now.

V

Now commences a period in my life over which I can pass quite rapidly, for it marks a pause in my cerebral evolution.

I was an orphan, devoid of relatives who had any interest in me. My father had left me, if not a fortune, at least a very reasonable income of about ten thousand livres per annum.

One of my father's clients, Monsieur Charvet, a professor at the Collège de France, doubtless impressed by my evident aptitude, accepted from the justice of the peace the role of surrogate guardian, took charge of my patrimony, and advised me to continue my studies.

I consented meekly. I did not feel any urge to live freely then. Far from it; the boarding-establishment to which I had to resign myself did not appear to me to be burdensome. I was then in a singular state of mind; far from aspiring to independence, I had, on the contrary, a vague desire for claustration. A biography of the Abbé de Rancé, which had fallen into my hands, had turned my ideas toward monasticism.[1] I had read with avidity the lives of the great hermits, the Christian legends of St. Paul of the Thebaïd, Saint Anthony and Simon Stylites, and those examples had given rise in me to a contemplative passion.

In the evenings, studying by the tempered light of lamps, surrounding myself with a rampart of books, I succeeded in abstracting myself so completely from my environment that I created an artificial solitude for myself; I then experienced an infinite joy, losing myself in vague reveries, more hollow than profound. Gradually, I yielded to a sort of hypnotism—which, of course, I neither observed nor analyzed at the time, and which only dissipated when the signal was given to stop work.

I accustomed myself to that state as to a daily bout of intoxication; I took a thousand precautions to make sure that my assigned work was finished, in order to reserve myself that hour—or half an hour, at least—of supreme placidity.

Once a fortnight I went out, and spent the day with my guardian.

He was a man of about forty-five, who had occupied himself with Orientalist studies since his youth. He was a widower with

---

1 Armand-Jean Le Bouthillier de Rancé (1626-1700) was the founder of the Trappist Cistercians. There are several accounts of his life, but the one that the narrator read is almost certainly the one published by Louis Dubois in 1869.

two children, a son two years older than me, who was preparing for the École Polytechnique, and a daughter . . .

I don't want to think about her yet. She was a child. She was scarcely twelve years old.

As for the son, he was subject to a very singular phenomenon.

Monsieur Charvet, as I said, had devoted his life to the study of Hindu languages; he was one of the most assiduous collaborators of Max Müller and continued the work of Burnouf in France.[1] By virtue of an entirely natural tendency, all of his interior décor bore the stamp of Hindu ornamentation. His study, especially, was cluttered with statuettes, the stumps of columns and stones of all shapes and sizes recalling the studies to which he devoted himself, all scattered randomly but forming a strange and gripping collection. He was tall, blond and—to sum him up in a word—insipid; with his long hair, his white plump face, his irremovable spectacles, he resembled a *privat docent*[2] in a German university.

His son, whose name was Georges, had dark, curly hair and a nascent beard that separated into two points. His eyes, exceedingly dark and widely-separated, with a slight tendency to pretemporal protrusion, had a singular softness, like a moist limpidity in which the gaze drowned. In brief, with his mat complexion, he seemed to me to represent the archetype of a man born on the shore of the Ganges. That impression was instinctive, but it seemed to me that his physiognomy harmonized perfectly with the oriental frame in which it appeared to me—and what was most curious of all is that my observation was exact, for his comrades had given him, jokingly, the nickname of Buddha.

---

1 Max Müller (1823-1900) was the most famous linguist of his day, who did extensive work in Orientalism, anthropology and various other human sciences. The work of the notable Orientalist Emile Burnouf (1801-1852) was also continued by other members of his family.

2 A *privat docent*, or *privatdozent*, was a lecturer in a German university who made his income from fees paid directly by students rather than by drawing a salary from the institution.

He was very gentle, a good fellow, and showed me a genuine sympathy. We often spent the day together, usually strolling through Paris. He chatted economically, and seemed very attentive to my loquaciousness, which he underlined with his habitual smile.

A year passed thus; I started to study philosophy.

Georges was accepted by the École Polytechnique, but—to my great surprise—declared himself satisfied with that success and declined to take advantage of it. He stayed with his father, whose secretary and collaborator he became.

That year, the bad winter weather obliged me to spend several Sundays at Monsieur Charvet's house. I noticed then that Georges only went out with me to oblige me. Evidently, my verbosity bored him; I had the exuberance of silly and pretentious speech that characterizes the age at which one knows nothing, and cannot be told anything. Newly embarked on formal philosophy, I spouted endlessly about the most abstract questions, taking my memory for science; I was unbearable, and I sensed it.

By contrast, Georges—Buddha—was coolly passionate about his father's work, and I divined that it was painful to him to be snatched away from it to serve me as a benevolent interlocutor. I took offense; feigning, in my turn, to be weary of futile perambulations, I asked permission to spend a few days in "the pagoda," as I called the Orientalist's study. There was a certain pity in Monsieur Charvet's tone when he told me that I would be "very bored." I protested all the more strongly. I would install myself therein, at a table, and study my Descartes.

Thus it was done, and the two savants soon forgot my presence.

In that era, with the exception of a few moments of auto-magnetization to which I devoted myself every evening, I had returned to a normal state of mind. I had completely lost the notion of the effects I had once felt next to my mother, as well as appeals to will that were more instinctive than reasoned.

I had resigned myself to being a pupil of moderate ability—one of those called "conscientious."

It was, therefore, purely out of curiosity that I lent an ear to the conversation of the father and son, who were deciphering a manuscript and exchanging their observations. I heard the full and grave sound of a language that I did not understand, in which the *a*s were modulated with strange harmonies, in which the consonants had slippages, aspirations, bizarre rotundities and despotic gutturalities.

Then they stopped and talked in French, punctuating their sentences with words that were new to me and which had all the attraction of a secret grimoire.

I still remember, as if it were yesterday, this exchange of remarks: "These fakirs," said Monsieur Charvet, "are merely skillful conjurors."

"I don't think so, Father," Georges replied. "Everything can be explained by the projection of Linga-Sharira . . ."[1]

"But Linga-Sharira is itself inexplicable."

"Why? Linga-Sharira is to Sthula-Sharira what Buddhi is to Atma . . ."

To be sure, I didn't understand a single word of this discourse, but either by reason of the melody of the language—Sanskrit, as I later discovered—or that disposition common to us all which is the attraction of the unknown, I listened thus for several hours, without a gesture or a movement, besotted with

---

1 The Sanskrit-derived term Linga-Sharira was popularized during the French Occult revival by Madame Blavatsky's Theosophical writings, where it refers to the "astral body" or "double" that every human being supposedly possesses. The original term refers to the "characteristic mark" or essence of the transmigrating entity that is serially reincarnated in a physical form, the Sthula-Sharira, another term much bandied about in neo-Rosicrucian circles. The approximate equivalent to Linga-Sharira in Buddhist thought is the *atman* [self], but that term was rendered as Atma when it was appropriated by Madame Blavatsky into her syncretic description of the "Septenary" (sevenfold) nature of man, along with Buddhi, the two terms previously cited, Prana, Manas and Kamarupa.

sounds that offered no meaning to my reason, ideas that I could not grasp but which produced exactly the same effect on my nerves as that of a tambourine struck with a dull and monotonous rhythm upon the whirling dervishes of Constantinople. I arrived at an ecstatic numbness, a weighty and exquisite charm.

The session came to an end, and I almost regretted hearing the two men, who had seemed to me to be mysterious beings for several hours, chatting like mere mortals about mundane matters. I dared not urge them to return to their favorite studies, however, and went back to school, prey to an intense preoccupation.

The next time I went out, I employed all my diplomacy to obtain a further session, and succeeded easily—for, in truth, I had not been any trouble. And for three months, once a week, I was able to procure myself that inexplicable joy, which had no other motive than the ingestion of mystery. By force of paying attention, however, I had succeeded in finding out, first that it was a matter of a Sanskrit language—Devanagari[1]—and then that the two savants were trying to explain the prodigies effected by privileged individuals, yogis or fakirs: burial prolonged for months and followed by resurrection; trees born from a seed and growing in two hours; phenomena of levitation or suspension in mid-air.

Monsieur Charvet was incredulous; Georges thought it possible.

As soon as that notion had penetrated my brain, I paid the greatest attention to the discussions of the father and the son. I have always enjoyed exceptionally keen hearing—not only in the sense of hearing at long distances or the perception of the faintest sounds, but above all from the viewpoint of the notation of the sounds heard. As soon as I paid attention to them, the words whose significance escaped me were seized by

---

1 Devanagari was in Lermina's day, and still is, the most common script used to represent Sanskrit in printed texts.

my memory like the notes of a song, and once alone, I could transcribe them with their exact pronunciation, if not their real orthography, well enough that I solved the problem of speaking Sanskrit before understanding it.

At the same time, though, and by virtue of a perfectly natural correction, I was gripped by an intense desire to learn it. My aim was certainly not purely philological. For me, the possession of the language implied the possibility of a miracle; I considered it as a magical formula, thanks to which it would be possible to effect prodigies. There was one of them, in particular, that became the aim of my most ardent desire. A hundred times, while asleep, I had sensed myself rising up into the air, flying like a bird, rising up to prodigious heights, and simultaneously experiencing in that levitation an exquisite sensation. Since the fakirs were able to levitate while awake, why should I not do the same? I persuaded myself that the pronunciation of certain Sanskrit words, in conditions as yet unknown to me, but which I would be able to discover, communicated occult powers to human beings.

I would not have confessed that fantasy to my guardian or his son for anything in the world.

More than anything I feared a sign of disdain. It was therefore necessary for me to put myself to work, alone. I bought dictionaries by Desgranges and Oppert,[1] which I hid with the care that some of my peers put into hiding novels, and, renouncing my hypnotization by study, I set to work doggedly. I was surprised to observe how the entirely mechanical work of pronunciation to which I had devoted myself facilitated my task. After three months, I was able to read a page of printed text fluently. As for the translation, that was another matter. Sanskrit is to modern languages what algebra is to arithmetic.

---

1 Lermina has "J. Desgranges" but he means Alix Desgranges (1793-1854), who published his *Grammaire sanscrite-français* in 1845. Julius Oppert (1825-1905) published his *Grammaire sanscrite* in 1859.

It's necessary to find the key to understand its almost mathematical combinations.

It was then that the idea occurred to me to make use of the will-power that had, in various circumstances, got me out of difficulty.

To my great annoyance, however, I found that it was impossible to deploy once again those concentrations of energy that had once been produced, as it were, spontaneously. In fact, I had become a normal, balanced, mediocre individual, like almost all the rest of humankind.

I became irritated, and abandoned my Sanskrit books.

Then I started my law course, and, the sudden death of my guardian having put me in possession of my capital, thanks to an emancipation that advanced my majority by a few months, I suddenly changed direction. Intoxicated by my liberty, I launched myself full tilt into pleasures of which, until then, I had not even conceived the idea.

To tell the truth, I became an abominable scapegrace, and yet—such is the power of heredity—even in the most stupid extravagances, even when my companions in pleasure overstimulated the vanity of my wealth, as they say, and even when I obeyed the caprices of those creatures who exploit our foolishness, my father's sense of order survived, or rather revived, in me. I did not spend more than my income, a little less than a thousand francs a month—which constituted a regal civil list in the Latin Quarter.

Five years passed in this way. I paid little heed to my studies in law, and only passed my examinations reluctantly.

What would become of me? I gave little thought to it.

Would it not have been better, in any case, for me to remain in that mire, in which I would gradually become torpid as I sank, than to have been violently torn away from it to rise again, so high that today I have only one more step to take to attain omnipotence . . . or death?

What decided my future was a ridiculous quarrel over a girl that began in an all-night restaurant between myself and a student, which escalated to such a pitch of violence and threat that we were thrown out of the establishment. We—my adversary, myself, my companions and the women—found ourselves on the sidewalk.

My adversary continued to insult me. He was a colossus, a Provençal with enormous shoulders and muscles of steel. I was the first to raise my hand, though. We rushed at one another. In the blink of an eye, he had grabbed me around the waist, and I felt as if I had been gripped by a circle that would crush my ribs and break my back.

Then, by a cerebral effort identical to the one that had once revealed the meaning of a phrase by Tacitus to me, all my vigor was concentrated in my hands, forearms and biceps. I struck out—or, rather, something emerged from me that was more than me—and the man uttered a strangled cry and fell . . .

I too collapsed in a heap, inanimate, half-dead from exhaustion and effort.

There ended the first part of my life. I can say that, although only six years have elapsed since that catastrophe, in those six years I have lived more than in the previous twenty-five . . . I'm now thirty-one. I could be fifty. And besides, isn't it only on the eve of a battle that one knows how old one is? Real age is one's proximity to death.

VI

I came round after three days, during which I did not have any notion of the exterior world for a single instant—and yet I knew that I was alive. Everything in me—body and mind—was merely bound in the inextricable network of a torpidity that did not permit me thought or movement.

The first external impression that reached me was the sound of two voices. One was male, contained and serious; the other soft, exquisitely musical, so penetrating and, so to speak, all-conquering that it seemed to me that my being was a harp vibrating in harmony with it.

Then, instantaneously, I experienced in the location of my heart the sensation of a rapid breath, which, coming from without, entered into me, so violently that it was almost painful at first. At the same time, however, that something—still indefinable for me—expanded throughout my entire being, seething with a vitality that titillated my fibers and the extremities of my brain. Then I was gripped by a kind of intoxication: an overheating of my entire organism, a flood of words, an incoherence of movement. In fact, my equilibrium was not yet established—the equilibrium that is both health and consciousness.

Gradually, sedation took effect, as in a bowl in which a liquid, suddenly agitated, resumes its level. As if making a decisive grab for the external world, I opened my eyes. At that moment, I was half-lying on my side, and my gaze took in the whole of the room in which I found myself.

It was winter; a fire, not very ardent, set a reddish light in the hearth, against which two seated shadows were outlined, leaning toward one another. Through my curtains, I also made out the glow of a night-light.

They were unaware of my awakening, and were talking in low voices. I recognized one of the two voices, already overheard in the course of my resurrection. Now I knew that it was that of Georges Charvet. How had I come to be there? I didn't know.

He was speaking. "This crisis," he said, "is doubtless the last. As I've explained to you, he has natural dispositions that are truly astonishing. The state in which we've seen him recalls, make no mistake about it, that of the bizarre individuals I've told you about. I'm convinced that he will come out of it safe and sound; the only danger is that, because his lethargy was not the result of a voluntary action, but an accident, he has not taken any of the precautions that the Hindus use, so that the return to life might take place with a violence so brutal that his body will be unable to support it."

Then the other voice said: "Oh, he's young and strong!"

That was all—and yet, that second decided my entire life. We Occidentals are ignorant of the unheeded power of sound. We pass by the strangest phenomena without even affording them the favor of our attention. For example, we suddenly hear the windows of a room vibrate strongly when a violinist plays his instrument, without being astonished that almost all of the notes produced by the bow are uninvolved in that effect, while one alone—and not always the sharpest—has suddenly determined the quivering in question. Thus it is that a particular combination of chords within a tune penetrates us to the utmost depths of our being, putting a sob in our throat or squeezing our heart, without it being possible for us to say what the chord was, which has passed rapidly and fleetingly. Thus it is, also, that a scientist has discovered today, in the production of certain sonorities, a force compared with which even those of steam and electricity, as they are known today, are what an infantile flick is to the hammer-blow of a giant.

Thus it was, in sum, that the voice in question made all the fibers of my being vibrate like a violin-string beneath the bow, penetrating my bone-marrow, filling my heart, circulating throughout my body—so that, impassioned and exalted, I sat up, crying: "Who said that?"

Georges bounded toward me, and I felt something like a surge of rage—for, at that moment, he hid from me that which I wanted to see. Did he divine that fury in my first glance? I think so, for he stood aside before having touched my bed and said: "Sister, he's saved!"

His sister! The one whose name I had often heard pronounced—a strange name that only the whim of an Orientalist could explain—Sita,[1] the young woman I had scarcely glimpsed until then, and who had suddenly appeared to me as if evoked by my call, at twenty years of age, admirably beautiful, with her high, slightly bulbous forehead, her large, profoundly soft dark eyes, her hieratic profile and her mysterious priestess's smile!

Oh, why stir up those memories within me? Why dig down into the ground beneath which I attempted to bury them so long ago? Why revive in my being the fire that burned my life? I need to, though, for it is from them alone that my present resolution and strength derive!

She went out, leaving me alone with Georges.

I had suddenly recovered all my composure, only retaining within me the echo—never extinct thereafter—of that voice, which would be my joy and my torment forever. I only heard what Georges said, just as I heard all other noises, through a sort of crystalline veil that melted every sound into the unique pitch by which I was penetrated, or rather enveloped.

First he told me how I came to be in his house. When I had fallen down, none of those who were present—chance companions—knew where I lived, but someone had remembered Charvet's name, and, aided by anxiety and the fear of being involved in a brawl that might have serious consequences, someone had been sent to fetch him. He had come running, and had me transported to his house, while my adversary's friends placed him in a cab, unconscious, and took him away.

Fortunately, the police had not intervened—but for two days, Georges' anxiety had been great, as much because of my lethargic state as because my adversary's life seemed to be in peril.

Then he told me something that seemed incredible, but which was nevertheless true, as I now know. My adversary had

1 In the *Ramayana*, Sita is the wife of Rama, whose abduction by Ravana, the king of what is now Sri Lanka, precipitated a war between that island and the Indian mainland.

been in the comatose state that follows a blow received full on the cranium, and yet, he bore no trace of the impact, no swelling or bruise. And—this, in particular, seemed to enter the domain of the implausible—all the witnesses of the scene affirmed in the most peremptory fashion that I had not struck out, that my hand had not even brushed him, and that at the moment when he collapsed, it seemed that he had been laid low by an impact whose instrument had remained invisible. For that reason, the pseudo-scientists and students in the company believed that he had suffered a sudden cerebral haemorrhage caused by the excess of his own anger.

That was manifestly false, since he had been completely restored to health the next day, without experiencing any of the symptoms that necessarily follow an internal cerebral disturbance. Then again, I knew perfectly well that I had struck out, if not with my fist, at least with something that had sprung forth from me . . .

"Well then!" Georges said to me, laughing. "So you know Sanskrit, too?"

"Why do you ask?" I said, blushing slightly.

"Because, in the intermittences of the lethargy, when the vital force made an effort to re-enter into you, you pronounced several phrases, perfectly correctly . . . it was my sister who noticed them . . ."

"Her!"

"Oh, you don't know—there's no way you could. Since my poor father's death, Sita has come to live with me, and has manifested such an extraordinary aptitude for the study of Oriental languages that I was obliged to consent to her collaboration in our work . . . and after two years, it seems to me that I'm no longer anything but a schoolboy by comparison with her. She hasn't so much learned as remembered, I'm certain of it; there's a very singular case of atavism in our family, which revealed itself for the first time in my father's aptitudes. Until then, no one in our family, at least as far back as we can trace its past, seems to have been associated with the Orient—but then, in my father and myself, the desire to learn manifested itself unexpectedly, and, to tell the truth, without any involvement of our will.

"Now my sister, whom I had naturally kept apart from those studies until recently, suddenly revealed herself, in the space of a few weeks, to be the most profound, most intelligent and, so to speak, most intuitive interpreter of the languages of southern India. There, where, for my father and myself, impenetrable obscurities remained hidden, in the literal sense of the word—where, in its philological form, the philosophical spirit escaped us—Sita has more prescience than science. The unintelligible seems to be clear to her, the unfathomable opens up . . . oh, my friend, if you knew what a boundless world she has drawn me into in her wake . . . a sublime world of which our purest mental enjoyments are but a scarcely-perceptible reflection . . ."

And while he spoke, I saw enthusiasm light up his face like a glow radiated from some unknown hearth . . .

From that moment on, my resolution was formed. I too had an intuitive desire for that knowledge, and I persuaded myself that in me, as in them, there existed some sort of atavistic predestination. Did Georges not admit himself that it was surprising that I had, by myself, so easily acquired the rudiments of a language that still remained in the domain of erudition? Was not my very patience a proof of my innate aptitude?

Georges was good, and also weak, so he welcomed my plan joyfully. He had always considered me as a younger brother, and it pleased him—especially after my long absence—to reassert his quasi-elder-brotherly rights in my respect—the right of protection and also of surveillance. I had spent the early years of my youth foolishly, no path had opened before me; I had not manifested any taste for the law or for medicine. Why oppose the tendency that resembled a vocation?

"Except," he told me, "that it's necessary to obtain my sister's agreement."

I looked at him in surprise. What reasonable objection could she oppose to my desire?

"You don't know Sita," he replied. "She's the guardian of the temple."

I didn't attach as much importance to that phrase as the literal meaning seemed to imply. Besides, was it not the case that, while I affirmed to the brother the express desire to instruct myself in the Hindu sciences, I was thinking above all of the sister: the one whose voice had overwhelmed and conquered me; the one whom I already loved so violently that my entire life, my entire energy and my entire ambition converged upon her alone.

To live in her atmosphere, to bathe in the waves of her voice, in the exquisite fluidity of her gaze—that was my dream ... and she might refuse me that happiness. Why would she?

VII

I didn't see her for twenty-four hours.

I was completely recovered; in fact, never had I felt so strong, so ardent. I felt the vital force circulating within me, warm and vibrant.

Georges came to find me in my room, to take me to the dining room where Sita was waiting for us.

"Have you talked to your sister about me?" I asked him, in the casual manner of a man sure in advance of success.

He shook his head and did not reply. My heart lurched and I went pale. I had the sensation then of an unknown danger, with which I was impotent to contend. It was like a jealousy whose actual object escaped me, but which caused me intolerable suffering.

I went in. Sita was standing up, and then, even better than in the first disturbance of awakening, I saw the adorable perfection of that creature, who could only be characterized by the word pronounced by her brother: a priestess.

In the slenderness of her supple figure, the lines of her shoulders, neck and bosom, the rectitude softened by the folds of her dress, there was a kind of religious placidity that was both disturbing and attractive. Her black hair, by virtue of an uncontrived arrangement, made a mystical band of her forehead, and in her profound, soft eyes, the gaze became lost, as it is at night when, lying on one's back, one plunges imaginatively into the gulfs of the nocturnal immensity.

She didn't extend her hand to me, and I didn't offer her mine; I did not have the courage of banality.

When we were seated, I waited for her to speak, certain of retrieving in the first word spoken the note whose echo I had conserved within me.

"Monsieur," she said to me, "my brother, who loves you very much, has consulted me in your regard. Is it really true that you are determined to participate in our studies and endeavors?"

I hesitated to reply. I had just noticed something new. Her voice—the voice that might have been that of the Sphinx speaking to Oedipus—was in counterpoint, as if in a sort of third, with that of her brother, and I suddenly sensed that mine, intervening, would sound false—and that conviction, which was correct, imposed itself upon me so strongly that I nodded my head, without pronouncing a word.

"Would you permit me," she continued, "to acquaint you with my impression, in all frankness? I hope that you will not be hurt by it, since, in reality, my objections are addressed less to you personally than to the French race to which you belong..."

"But are you not as French as I am?" I exclaimed, in bewilderment, addressing myself to Georges.

He smiled and touched me lightly on the arm. "Listen to my sister," he said.

"We are, indeed, French," Sita went on, "but who knows exactly what their ancestry is? At this moment, it's not a matter of us, but only of you. Well, I believe that your innate qualities, inherent in your entirely Gallic, entirely Parisian origin, are a considerable obstacle to your desires. In the studies that attract you, you see primarily the philological aspect . . . and, if I can judge by certain words that escaped you during your lethargy, you are particularly motivated by the curiosity innate in every man, the curiosity of mystery, of the occult . . .

"Answer me frankly, do you not imagine, perchance, that a profound knowledge of Oriental languages might give adepts access to a supernatural world, where one might acquire powers that are . . . magical? And tell me, is that not the true reason for your neophytic ardor?"

At that moment, her eyes were fixed upon me, and it seemed to me, singular as it might be, that I felt on my forehead and my temples, the real, material, tangible and substantial effluvia of that gaze. My emotion was such that I replied, swiftly: "Can you read my mind, then?" I stopped abruptly then, irritated by the discordant vibration of my own voice.

She lowered her eyelids, and continued softly: "You see that you are already attributing a supernatural power to me—I don't know why. For whatever reason, my observation has touched a nerve . . ."

"Is it a crime, then," I exclaimed, "to dream of enlarging the faculties with which nature has endowed you?"

"Certainly not," said Sita. "The duty of a human being is to become better, and all that is good is powerful. But if that power can be acquired—which I neither affirm nor deny, of course, conscious as I am of my ignorance—it only has value by reason of the desired result. Suppose for a moment that you were endowed with a superior power, in sufficient proportion to permit

240

you to change the order of the world to some degree; suppose that you could, for instance, transport yourself instantaneously from one place to another, penetrate material bodies or even discover hidden treasures . . . what do I know? I'm searching the legendary actions of magicians for whatever might suit my thesis . . . I wonder what use you would make of that power?"

I stammered, unable to find an appropriate answer.

"You would employ your power," Sita went on, "to acquire glory . . . you would want to be powerful among the powerful . . . I'm not just talking about wealth, luxury, material satisfactions. You might be generous enough to scorn them . . . but wouldn't you experience an infinite happiness in becoming the idol of your contemporaries, in dominating them with the full height of your energy, of hearing yourself called Master, King . . . can't you imagine in your mind the immense joy of accepted, respected power . . . of universal acclamation saluting you as you pass by, of the enthusiastic salute of an entire people? Tell me, can you repel that dream?"

"If it required my life to obtain its realization," I cried, in a transport that I could not master, "I would be ready to give it . . ."

And, shivering, carried away by the splendid and imperious vision, I looked at Sita boldly, as if to offer to share that power with her . . .

"The knowledge that you seek," she continued, more coldly, "imposes on human beings the most absolute abnegation, the complete, irrevocable renunciation of all ambition and egotism. Its acquisition has, for its first condition, the conception of charity, the love of others: sacrifice, in the most profound sense of the term. All knowledge bestows power; that is axiomatic. Ours only bestows power for good . . . the good of humankind entire. If it should happen—which is impossible—that one of those possessing it were to conserve any thought of personal interest, by virtue of that fact alone, he would be no longer be anything but ignorant, and he would fall back to a station lower than the lowest of pariahs and slaves . . .

"That is what you did not know, Monsieur, when you asked my brother whether you might share in our work; that is what requires me to advise you to give yourself a better warning than I can give you. Reflect, then, and once again, forgive me . . ."

"Reflect!" I cried. "You haven't understood me, then! Do I know only what I desire? In my turn, don't be offended if I tell you that you've set a trap for me. What man could glimpse, without a thrill of passion, the scene that you painted for me just now . . . when you hurled me into images of glory and power in which the soul feels dizzy? And of that power, which you say that I should only dream, from now on, in a rapid vision, of using for the good of others . . . but I don't want to argue. I was misled; I bumped into the obstacle that you placed in front of me yourself . . . I recognize my error, I confess it, I deplore it. The way that I want to take leads elsewhere; I accept it, with its sufferings, its renunciations . . . its martyrdom, if necessary.

"As you have said, I'm a neophyte, and apprentice, a child . . . but since both of you are learning charity, essential generosity, why do you reject my good will and my sincere resolution? I beg you . . . Georges knows that I have no aim in life. I feel drawn towards these endeavors by a powerful attraction. Wherever your path might lead, I want to follow it . . . and if I encounter only suffering and disillusionment, well, you will abandon me, and without a sigh, without any reproach, I shall watch you depart alone for the luminous regions into which I shall be unable to follow you!"

"Poet!" said Georges, laughing.

Poet perhaps, but above all . . . shall I say amorous? No, the word doesn't convey the exquisite and poignant sentiment that was increasingly overwhelming me. I no longer belonged to myself; I felt as humble before Sita as a valet trembling at the prospect of dismissal. Oh, I loved her, I adored her . . . as I love her and adore her at this moment, when, having extracted nothing from her treasure of knowledge but an accursed fragment, I am about to confront death in order to get closer to her!

To that romantic tirade, Sita had made no response, but I had seen a veil of indescribable sadness spread over her face. Fearing that I had wounded her with some excessively sharp expression—which I tried in vain to recover from my memory—I fell silent in my turn.

Georges, however, divining my preoccupation, changed the subject of conversation, and we talked about my childhood, while Sita, still silent, seemed absorbed in an intimate meditation.

Suddenly, to the side or above us—I couldn't tell then where it came from—a clear but extremely soft ringing sound became audible; it was as if the blade of a knife had lightly tapped the rim of an exceptionally delicate glass, but combined with another, purer and more Aeolian, sound.

Sita and her brother turned their heads abruptly, and looked at one another. The young woman was a trifle pale. She seemed to be interrogating Georges with her eyes.

All that he said was: "Yes, yes . . . go!"

Sita got up; as if by an instinctive movement, her two hands formed a cross over her breast, and she left the room, with a slow but firm step.

Georges had followed her with his gaze, and I read a sort of anxiety in his expression.

"What was that ringing sound, then?" I asked him. "A summons?"

He looked at me, as if he had not understood my question at first. Then he replied: "Yes, a summons . . ."

"I would have sworn," I added, "that the bell was ringing within this very room, in the air that surrounds us . . ."

Georges took my hand and, in a more serious tone than usual, said: "It's a summons. I can't tell you anything more."

And silence fell between us again; he was darting his eyes toward the door by which Sita had left; I was motionless and oppressed, as if I had suddenly found myself on the threshold of the unknown.

A quarter of an hour went by, which seemed like a whole day to me.

Then, from outside, Sita called through the door to her brother, who got up and disappeared in his turn.

Left alone, I let my head fall into my hands. What was Sita saying to her brother? Had she guessed my secret, and was she about to pronounce my sentence of exile? At that thought, I experienced such pain that I thought I was dying. Had I given myself away so soon, so foolishly? What young woman would not have been offended by a confession so abrupt—so brutal, to put it more accurately?

Alas, I still did not know her, and did not know the extent to which my dread was shaped by stupid vanity.

Georges soon returned and said: "Sita will stay in her room all day. If you want, we can go for a walk, as we used to, when my father was alive . . ."

"Yes," I said, "but will you permit me to ask you a question?"

"What is it?"

"Has my request been conclusively rejected?"

He fixed his gentle and benevolent gaze upon me. "Tomorrow," he said, "you may commence your studies."

I uttered a cry of joy, and thanked him effusively.

"Don't be in too much of a hurry to rejoice," he added. "Who knows whether you might not regret having obtained that consent for as long as you live?"

Oh, I wasn't listening to him; I didn't hear him. She had welcomed me; she had not sent me away. I was about to live her life, twenty-four hours a day!

Now, I know that Georges was right . . .

I don't regret anything at all—but I'm doomed!

VIII

My installation was rapidly effected. An apartment on the same floor proved to be vacant. I took up residence immediately. It was agreed, to my great joy, that we would take our meals together. Our studies were to take up all our time. In sum, I was Georges' guest and only went home at night.

Then began a year that was, for me, all delight; I had accepted in reality the role of pupil that I had solicited: a pupil of both Georges and Sita, the former taking particular responsibility for the overall supervision of my studies. To be sure, any Parisian who had arrived unexpectedly in that apartment, where two young men and a young woman spent almost all of every day, would have been very surprised. Next door to the library where Sita was most often to be found, studying manuscripts, taking notes, getting to the bottom of the knowledge of the ancient Aryans, Georges gave me lessons like a schoolboy, in a study where there was nothing but two desks and a few chairs.

To begin with, he had insisted that I learn English, not only its current vocabulary but especially its scientific and metaphysical terminology. In spite of the fearsome aridity of the task, I carried it out with a joyful ardor. The modern Hindus, Sita had explained to me, comment in the language of their oppressors on ancient writings whose originals, hidden in the temples of southern India, have not yet been made available to the public. It is therefore important, in order to penetrate the arcana of the sacred science more rapidly, to understand the occidental expressions into which they translate the philosophical idiocies whose meaning may escape us *a priori*. And, in fact, although I had succeeded within six months—so great was my perseverance—in being able to read any English text fluently, as soon as I opened a book written by a Hindu about Buddhist theories, I seemed to be going into an unknown world in which everything was utterly cloudy.

I understood then what Sita had meant when she had opposed to my desire my Frenchness; there is in us a clarity of deduction, a mathematics of common sense, that finds it difficult to accommodate the tenuousness of metaphysical arguments, the delicacy of the thread linking one idea to another; having the genius of assimilation, by virtue of that very fact, we lack the patience of slow argument.

From time to time, it seemed to me that I understood, in its entirety, the cosmogonic and historical system of the Hindus—and I explained it, victoriously, in a flood of words that were linked together, I thought, according to the rules of an inflexible logic.

Then Sita intervened. It was evening, when the active work had come to an end, and all three of us required of the conversation a release from our quotidian silence. I spoke, proud of myself, intending to prove that I had set foot on the threshold of the temple into which—as I imagined—I would enter triumphantly, with Her. And then, with a word, Sita threw me back into the depths of my ignorance. I listened to her, delighting even in her criticisms, savoring the voice that was my life. Need I admit it? I heard the melody, noting its delicacies one by one, its rhythms, its musical arabesques, which charmed me and intoxicated me . . . and of the other science, I perceived very little.

Gradually, however, enlightenment dawned in me; I had taken a first step, for I had lost the conviction that modern science—I mean that of Occidentals, a purely materialistic, positivistic science that sets aside all metaphysical speculation—was the last word in human knowledge. My horizons had suddenly broadened and I had admitted the possibility of a higher science, concerned with the destiny of Beings; I had glimpsed—not without a certain alarm—the sublime cycle of Matter and Spirit in which life moves, from its grossest manifestation to its most infinitesimal dilatation, toward Unity.

Was that science not still in its infancy, and would it not continue growing when purely material science had solved its final equation? I now perceived, by absorbing Hindu manuscripts, the existence of mysterious individuals, adepts of pure science endowed with powers that, without exceeding the faculties of humankind, constitute, on the contrary, their development, extrapolated to limits that we are not able to attain in the materialistic state of civilization in which we live.

I was struck then by the light suddenly cast on the world of spiritual forces by the phenomena of hypnotism, suggestion, and the effects of medicine at a distance that our professors are studying today in hospitals. That was, for me, a striking demonstration of psychic power, the effects of which, submitted to rigorous experimentation, might and ought to be formidable.

Were Hindu adepts—those designated by the title of Mahatmas—in possession of the totality of these Forces, of which we have only acquired a few fragments? Be that as it may, I had the conviction that it permitted them to accomplish feats that seemed miraculous to my eyes, but which were, however, explicable in terms of the superior development of fluidic or psychic power.

When I submitted these ideas to Sita, she tried to deflect me away from them—not that she denied their accuracy, at least with certain reservations, but she said: "My friend, if you are working with us to acquire power, you are following a false path."

"What's your objective, then?" I exclaimed.

"The good of all," she replied, fixing her huge dark eyes upon me.

"But don't I know myself that you already possess superior faculties, attained by your perseverance? Don't I know that you're in communication, by means of a sort of psychic telegraphy, with the Adepts of India? Don't I know that, if some communication needs to be made to you, you're alerted by a sort of aerial bell? Don't I know, finally, that certain letters, addressed by you to India, receive replies without any routine, material or human delay? And isn't it only natural that I should desire to obtain that multiplication of faculties myself?"

"Which is to say," Sita continued, smiling, "that you take me for a magician and want to become a magician yourself..."

"Why not? In you, nothing can be criminal . . . it's virtuous to imitate you and follow you . . ."

And in talking to her, I tried to put my entire soul into my lips. Did she understand the profound love that I had conceived for her? Did she understand why I had submitted to that claustration, why I reduced myself to the role of a disciple to whom knowledge is measured out, as if he were incapable of supporting it, and why, finally, I wanted—yes, I wanted it, now—to possess the power that I divined . . . and which would make me her equal, if not her master?

Oh, what would I not have given to see her in her turn, attentive to my lessons, testifying by her attention to her affectionate admiration! What a torture it was for me, when I expanded myself in theories that seemed sublime to me, to glimpse an amicably ironic smile in the corner of her mouth.

That evening, taking advantage of the familiarity that had gradually developed between us, I persisted. I reproached her for her pride. Why did she not think me worthy to launch myself, like her and her brother, into the higher spheres of metaphysics? Did I want to deny, or even dispute the principles that I had acquired from her? Did I not admit as a verity the existence of a spiritual force independent of physical form and able, by meditation, study and will, to purify itself further and further? Did I not accept the existence, apart from that physical form and that vital force, of consciousness, the supreme expression, as regards organized human beings, of the psychic force linked to the body? Did I refuse to admit the existence of species superior to ours, purely spiritual, rising by an admirable evolution toward the fusion of the individual Mind with the Universal and undifferentiated Mind?

I said all that, passionately, as if every word had but one meaning: Love! As if, in deifying her science, I had deified her.

And she didn't answer me, absorbed in a meditation that put a dolorous furrow in her forehead. Doubtless I caused her to feel pity!

I became irritated then; I got carried away; I accused her of egotism and insensitivity. I was, after all, no longer a child to whom one teaches his lesson, a scamp at whom one directs lectures. I knew enough now to have the right to the whole science ... and I claimed it ... I demanded it ...

"Not yet," said Sita.

"But why not? Why not?"

She got up, looked me in the face, and replied: "Because you aren't good!"

I recoiled, thunderstruck not only by the horrible assertion, but by the radiation of her gaze, which chilled my brain. I clutched my face with my hands to shield myself from that effect, and after a few seconds, during which it seemed to me that I endured the agonies of death, I looked up again. She had disappeared.

Georges took my hands, trying to calm me down. His intervention only exasperated me further. I vented my anger on him, in furious reproaches. It was to his influence that I owed his sister's hatred. Besides, was it not a crime to condemn a young woman to these arid and pointless studies? Was that a woman's role in life? Even if he, personally, was under the influence of charlatans whom I neither knew nor wanted to know, had he the right to deliver the soul and intelligence of Sita to them? Was it necessary for me to attribute to him I knew not what egotistical ambitions, for the satisfaction of which his sister was nothing but an instrument?

Georges stopped me with a gesture.

"Listen," he said. "I won't repeat my sister's last words to you. I'd like to hope that she's mistaken. Don't force me to believe her. When you asked to study with us, you were carefully and sincerely warned. Science is a weapon that has two uses, according to the hands that wield it: an archangel's bow or an assassin's dagger. Think about that. The myth of Hercules hesitating at the crossroads is profoundly human: two paths are open before you, one of which—ours—leads to the supreme Bounty, the Good . . . the other, I leave it to you to imagine where it leads . . .[1]

"Just remember that, according to the path chosen, you must either follow us or . . . separate yourself from us."

IX

Oh, how atrocious that night was, in which I interrogated myself, face to face—and what I write here is not an empty metaphor.

Yes, that night I had a positive and indisputable notion of the phenomenon that I have studied so intently since, and whose realization I shall shortly pursue to the supreme limit, where Life and Death are only separated from one another by a mathematical point.

So, I went back to my apartment, enervated and feverish, sensing in my breast a blaze of anger that did not expand outside, but whose flame, on the contrary, I felt burning my entire being, the heat coursing through my every fiber, penetrating

1 The image of Hercules at the crossroads became familiar in Classical art as an allegory of moral choice, perhaps best-known in a 1748 painting by Pompeo Batoni, in which the hero is confronted by Venus, symbolizing the path of sensuality and self-indulgence (*voluptas*) and Minerva, symbolizing responsibility and virtue (*virtus*). The parallel drawn with Paul's situation is, however, inexact. In choosing the path of *virtus*, Hercules goes on to win glory, which is precisely the lure that Paul fails to avoid. The point of the story is to contrast two kinds of wisdom.

every cranny of my body. At that moment, I was like a boiler that carries its fire inside, and has no safety-valve. My entire physique was, in a sense, distended by an excessive pressure. My vital force accumulated within me, under the overheated production of my thoughts.

I did not speak, nor did I cry. All my life was in my brain, whose lobes were functioning with an extraordinary activity.

Immobile, as if electrocuted, I was not reflecting, for reflection implies the mental employment of linguistic forms. I was subject to a sequence of unformulated impressions, which were like the imagined representation of my sensations. I saw Sita standing before me, and without even thinking the words "I love you!" I enveloped her with my love. Her anger and scorn—for that was what I obtained from her—weighed upon me, crushed me, broke me. A moment came when, in a mad hallucination, I thought I sensed that she was killing me—and the surge of terror and pain was such that I made a violent effort to escape her, or rather to overcome her, to vanquish her.

In that impulse of my entire being to go to her, I experienced a sort of tear in the region of the heart, and suddenly, it seemed to me that my life was flowing out through it, as though a wound. Suddenly, my brain had gone cold, as if half-empty, at the same time as a sensation of breath—which was not unfamiliar to me, but which went this time from within to without, from inside my breast to the ambient air—caused me a sort of suffocation. Thus the cylinder of a pneumatic machine would suffer, if it were an organic body, at the thrust of the piston that expels the air from it.

Far from resisting, moreover, I lent myself to it; I assisted that flight of my vital force with all my might; I found therein the enjoyment of an exquisite numbness, a singular intoxication, like that which precedes a definitive loss of consciousness. But I did not go so far! My senses were not abolished, my intelligence was still functioning, my eyes seeing . . . and seeing this.

Two steps away from me, a white form was standing, so feeble in color that I could hardly see it, a cloudy, sidereal silhouette of my own being. Although it had no features or physiognomy, I recognized it. It really was me that I had before me; it was the very essence of my life, materialized—and I suddenly remembered that mediums were able to double themselves in that way. Until then, I had laughed, like so many others, at the experiments of William Crookes, studying apparitions by means of precise instruments, scrupulously noting their material influences, even photographing them, doubting his senses and checking them by means of automatic verification.

But what appeared to me to be singular was that, as I reasoned, the form faded, as if the vital force that constituted it were flowing back into me; if, on the contrary, I succeeded in stopping thinking, it became sharper and its contours became firmer.

Momentarily, it even became so clear that I felt frightened, as before a fantastic manifestation; my fear was translated into a violent mental effort and I fell backwards, inanimate.

When I came to, three hours had passed. I was extraordinarily tired, but my ideas had recovered their clarity.

I reasoned.

One point was, for me, beyond doubt. I had felt, I had seen. I was not mad; I had not been the victim of a hallucination.

Aided by the elementary knowledge already acquired during that year of study, I posed the terms of the problem thus. Recalling the accidents of my childhood, the projections of will—or vital fluid—of which I had had indisputable proof on several occasions, I concluded that, thanks to my exceptional organization, I had the ability to launch outside myself all or part of what constituted my individuality, my energy, my life. That something, although impalpable and diluted, nevertheless had its own entity; and I remembered then the expression of the occultists of India: the *astral body*, which is to the body what steam is to the engine that it fills, what electricity is to the apparatus that it causes to act.

The information received was suddenly clarified. The human ternary appeared to be composed of the physical body, the astral body or vital force, which causes it to act physically, and the will or consciousness, which exercises its effect on both elements. Thus, master by virtue of my will of my physical body, I was similarly master of my astral body, which the Hindus call Linga-Sharira. Curiously enough, that was one of the first Sanskrit words that had struck me and had given me the desire to study it. Was that not akin to a predestination?

And I found in that concept the explanation of the fluid of the magnetizers, and the pretended miracles accomplished by mediums. I divined that my will would be able to direct that force issuing from myself, impose certain actions upon it—and I already felt possessed by an immense pride, in thinking of the marvellous and secret power that I certainly did not intend to squander in the fashion of conjurers, but to employ entirely in the realization of my desires.

From that moment on, a profound calm spread through me. I was sure of my strength; I was in complete possession of myself. I would reckon with all resistance, no matter what form it might take.

And Sita, would Sita be able to refuse her admiration, when she observed that I had conquered, by myself, with my energy alone, the power that she attributed to the Adepts that hid themselves away in the solitudes of the Himalayas? Would I not finally be her master, her spouse, her king? Would I not hear her say to me one day, like the Sita of the Ramayana, whose name she had borrowed:

"I will go where you go. Separated from you, I would no longer wish to inhabit the same Heaven; I swear it to you by your love, by your life! Paradise without you would be an odious abode to me; the inferno, if we shared it together, would be worth more to me than Heaven!"

Ineffable joys! Triumphant hopes!

Alas, of all that, what will soon remain?

X

The following day, I declared my surrender. I implored my forgiveness.

Was it not excusable, after all, to have had too much ambition? I was young, ardent, enthusiastic. In the aridity of the work to which I had dedicated myself, was it criminal to dream of approaching the ultimate wellspring? Yes, I was only a pupil, a child, a catechumen. I bowed down.

Georges embraced me gladly. Sita replied with her enigmatic smile. And the labor recommenced—but this time, my path was mapped out. I knew where I was going.

My friends' Oriental library was at my disposal; I could choose the books that held a special interest for me. It was then that I understood how useful it had been for me to learn the English language, with the perseverance that had been imposed on me.

I also devoted myself to Sanskrit with a new ardor, and by the light of my personal experience, I rapidly pierced all the obscurities with which the texts had thus far seemed to me to be enveloped. The *Upanishads* and the *Bhagavad-gita* became easy reading for me. In addition, I gradually exercised the play of my will. I was able at certain moments to concentrate it, to put it in action, to multiply it tenfold for a time—still very short, but which I gradually prolonged, by means of the acuity of my comprehension.

My friends, of course, had no suspicion of the intense labor that I was investing in myself.

I had understood that, whatever the cost, I had to develop the exercise of my psychic strength progressively, by insensible degrees. That way, after a year or two of continuous and carefully-measured effort, I would be certain of victory.

Sita was in the full bloom of her youth and beauty. The sympathy that my assiduousness and docility would attract on her part would facilitate my task considerably. I was patient, because I was fearless. No man ever crossed the threshold of the house; there was no rival to dread. Then again, I esteemed Sita's intelligence too highly to suppose that she could abandon herself to any vulgar affection for a man unworthy of her. The key that would open that heart would have to be made of gold, and that gold would be my knowledge and my power.

I experienced a kind of joy that was simultaneously delicate and sharp in observing the reserve with which she never ceased to treat me, after the day of our argument. She did not trust me, that was evident; she had hoped to find more abnegation in me, more renunciation of human ambition. What did it matter? I was certain, when the moment came, of enveloping her so completely with my strength, of penetrating her so intimately with my influence, of subjecting her so passively to my will—in a word, of conquering her so completely—that she would no longer have the slightest notion of resistance . . .

And then, she would be carried away by me into the sphere of the dominations, above all terrestrial creatures.

What dream could be superior to that in her eyes?

To that question, I was to receive a response like a thunderbolt . . .

The second year of my apparent training had just concluded, and I was advancing slowly but surely along my path.

I had been able, by paying careful attention to my words and deeds, to attenuate Sita's suspicions. Little by little—so I believed, at least—I had penetrated her heart and won her sympathy. Certain of my docility, she gave more and more of herself, opening to me the treasures of her intelligence, the depth of which would have frightened me had I not known that my strength would soon be equal to hers.

My love was transformed into adoration; for some time, her physiognomy had been illuminated by a new gleam. Her face was a soul, her gaze a thought, her smile a brightness. Was the woman awakening within the maid? Sometimes, I seemed to glimpse the signs of a languor that worried me, but if I addressed a question to her timidly, she seemed to wake up abruptly. "I've never felt as strong or as happy," she replied, while a spark sprang from her eyes.

Sometimes, I succeeded in imagining that she had divined the passion that was burning my heart; I attributed the pallors and oppressions that I noticed to her resistance, to a nascent love. I would have liked her to say something, to encourage me. And why could I not constrain her to do so? My will-power, in consequence of the reasoned training to which I devoted myself, was beginning to acquire the expected development.

I had already carried out several experiments in the street or at the theater. If I fixed my stare on a passer-by, I saw him, at my mental command, slow down and come to a halt. The effect produced by my mental effort being known to me, my psychic force projected externally gripped the individual and forced him to obey me. Thus, in an auditorium, I could force the most attentive audience member to turn his gaze away from the stage and look at me.

I had gone further. One day, as I passed in front of a department store, I saw a crowd gathered at the door; a man who had stolen something from the display had just been arrested. As he had had time to get rid of the product of his larceny, though, he was denying it energetically, so forcefully that doubt was beginning to enter the minds of the watchers.

I went forward and observed, by virtue of the man's pallor and a certain facial tic of which he did not appear to be conscious, that I was looking at an alcoholic and a neurotic. Without addressing a word to him, I looked at him fixedly, not in the face but from behind, and by a mental effort, I ordered him to confess his misdeed and tell the whole truth. Instantaneously, he was shaken by a convulsive tremor, and started to weep. Under the undeniable influence of a nervous shock, he confessed his guilt and pointed out the accomplice to whom he had handed the stolen item.

I was, therefore, no longer able to doubt: my power existed, but still—I had to admit—in very modest proportions. When I had made such an effort, several days passed without my being able to repeat it. The nervous influx that I had expended in a few seconds was only slowly reconstituted.

I had also attempted other experiments, on material objects. By touching them, I had, of course, been able to produce in inanimate objects such as a table or the back of a chair, cracking sounds and jolts that I could even, to a certain point, direct at my whim by imparting a rhythm to them and limiting their number—but that was child's play, and was insufficient for me.

For some time, every night, I spent an hour attempting to exercise that influence at a distance. I succeeded in projecting externally a quantity of psychic force—a fragment of my astral body, my vital force—and directing it toward an object: an item of furniture, a penholder or a piece of paper. Thus far, however, the effects produced had been almost negligible. As my will was only exercised in conditions of absolute calm, it had none of the impulsion that I would have obtained by projecting it in a state of anger or passion. The smallest object could scarcely be displaced by a few millimeters. I had even doubted myself and had set up a measuring device that registered the movements graphically. They were real, and thus capable of augmentation—and that observation was sufficient, since it proved both the reality of the phenomena and the progressive effects obtained by my studies.

I had, in any case, surpassed the initial phase of incredulity and mistrust—and in what I had learned of the powers of the adepts of Hindustan, nothing any longer appeared to me to be impossible.

Why not admit, in fact, that humans, relegated for many centuries to mysterious solitudes, could have acquired and conserved, by transmitting it under the seal of mystery, a science that would be to the science of electricity what electricity itself is to the notions of force we possessed a hundred years ago? Anyone in the court of Henri III who had talked about communicating speech from Paris to Brussels in a matter of seconds would have been taken for a madman. Why, in another hundred years, should the transmission of thought, of will, from one human being to another, by means of an as-yet-unknown etheric vehicle, not become a banal matter? Why should the vital force, thus far unstudied and undeveloped, not produce effects that today seem magical, but which, once harnessed and channelled, so to speak, will merely be instruments of civilization and well-being?

Anyway, what need was there for reasoning? The facts were, for me, patent and indisputable. What did the future matter to me? What did tomorrow's humankind matter to me? For me, one sole objective existed: Sita's love; and to that end I would sacrifice anything, including my life.

Already I was dreaming of subjugating her; it seemed to me that I was strong enough; and once, when I saw her pensive, a few feet away from me, her eyes half-closed, I tried to read her thoughts or to constrain her to impregnate herself with mine. Oh, what would I not have given to be able to decipher the enigma that was concealed beneath that blank forehead, behind those pure eyes!

But in vain I concentrated all the energy of my will into a sort of beam; it seemed to me that she was surrounded by an unbreachable circle, an armor against which my strength buckled, like the stem of a reed on a steel plate. She was alerted to my attempt, however, and turned her surprised eyes toward me, blushing as if my hand had brushed hers—and I went pale, ashamed of myself, vanquished by that mute expression of innocent reproach.

She was, then, protected against me. Would that always be the case? No, no! For I was in the process of acquiring the necessary power.

Oh, if I had hesitated again, if I had recoiled from the supreme struggle, it would have been sufficient to vanquish my scruples, to remember what had happened on one accursed day!

All three of us—Sita, Georges and myself—were together in the library. Like the hero of Edgar Poe's *Raven* I was reading a few old books of forgotten legends. Georges was writing. Sita was sitting with her head resting on the back of her armchair, deep in thought, her pale and slender hands extended on her knees.

Suddenly—and this only seems a prodigy to the eyes of the ignorant—from the air above our heads, not even from the ceiling, a shower of rose petals descended upon her. She uttered an exclamation of surprise and stood up.

I had already been a witness to similar phenomena, and I knew that they were only produced when one of the Mahatmas of India—the one that Sita called her master—was alerting her to some imminent communication.

I became livid, feeling an unbearable pressure on my heart. Slowly, Sita headed for her room and went in.

"What's happening, Georges?" I exclaimed. "I want to know—I'm afraid!"

"Is it the seeming miracle that troubles you?" he replied. "Haven't your studies taken you beyond surprise? If the Mahatmas can address words or messages over long distances by psychic telegraphy, why wouldn't they be able to send flowers?"

"But I don't dispute or doubt that!"

"What's troubling you," Georges went on, appearing not to notice my agitation, "is that the Adepts have the power to make matter pass through matter, rose petals through walls. Don't you know that everything that exists is merely an aggregate of infinitesimal molecules, the momentary dissociation of which is possible. It's not the roses in their integral form that have passed through the materials of the house, but the dissociated elements of flowers, which the Mahatma has subsequently reconstituted . . ."

What did all that matter to me? What frightened me was the science itself, the power that I sensed in suspension around Sita, enveloping her, penetrating her, conquering her. What was my strength compared to that? I was afraid of defeat; I hated the adversary, the enemy . . .

Suddenly, Sita reappeared.

Never—no, in truth, never—had she been so ideally beautiful. Even her clothing seemed impregnated with light. In the black hair curling over her forehead there was a kind of diamond dust. I recoiled, breathlessly, as before an apparition.

That sublime transfiguration terrified me and delighted me at the same time.

She took a step toward me and held out her hands, and—how did I not die on hearing it?—she said: "Rejoice, friend, for the great joy so long awaited is finally to be realized. You can testify that I have neglected nothing that might render my Masters favorable; my brother and I, docile to instructions, have striven to master the laws of the Superior Science—not yet to the extent of the supreme initiation, alas, which is given to so few, but at least to gain access to the portico of the Temple of Truth . . . and our Masters have finally responded favorably to our respectful requests, so often solicited . . ."

I looked at her wildly, as stupid as an infant to whom one is speaking in an unknown language.

She continued, softly, as if transported by an ecstatic rapture: "I shall therefore be able, with Georges, to devote myself entirely to the sublime work that is to establish the chain of union between the past and the future, between the Orient and the Occident, between our incomplete civilization and future societies, to attempt to attain the superior plane of consciousness, of spirituality; to elevate myself as far as Prana![1] Oh, my friend, my brother, I shall open to you the great and broad way to the supreme virtue—and who knows whether, one day, you might not be called to join us?"

"You're *leaving*!" I cried, finding none but that single word, in which all my despair was concentrated.

"Tomorrow," she said, simply.

"You're leaving!" I repeated. "For what country? For how long?"

"In two days," she replied, "we shall embark on the steamer that will take us to Madras. It is not permitted to me to say any more." With an ineffable smile, she added: "The duration of our absence? How can I guess? Out there, in the solitudes, where pure Science reigns as mistress, where it will perhaps be granted to me to understand the sublime Secret of Nature, of Unity, the principle and goal, the initial and final point of being, where perhaps I shall see resolved, in the magnificent synthesis of All, the Scattered and Purified Forces, shall I eventually be ordered to return to the milieu of my Occidental Brothers, to bring them a ray of that enlightenment? That is still in doubt, that is the ultimate anguish . . . but I shall obey my Masters!"

I said nothing more, having the poignant constriction of strangulation in my throat. Sita was standing, with one hand on the mantelpiece, tall, sublime and divine. She made a sign to Georges, who went out . . .

I was alone with her.

---

1 Prana is sometimes translated, quasi-metaphorically, as "breath" or "vitality"; in Vedic philosophy it is one of the five "organs" or "modes" of sensation, but when the term was adopted by Madame Blavatsky into her Septenary model of human being it took on a more grandiose significance— hence the reference to it here as a kind of final phase of spiritual advancement.

Then, in a paroxysm of despair and anger, my entire over-excited being shuddered; I felt a formidable surge of blood rise from my heart, through my breast to my brain, and I cried: "Wretched woman! So you dare to tell me—me!—that you're leaving, abandoning me, letting go of me! So, with all your false science, all your demonic illusions, you haven't understood, haven't guessed! Your Science, the Future of Humankind, the eternal Unity . . . do I know nothing of that myself? My own science, my future, my goal . . . is you and you alone! The Alpha and Omega of my life is but one word: Love!"

She raised her head slightly, but without ceasing to smile.

Then my fury increased further. "Yes, I love you! I only have thoughts, energy, will, because I love you! And some Hindu sorcerers, charlatans or crooks are going to snatch you away from me! Oh, there's nothing out there but fortune-hunters . . . for you're rich, of course, and the monasteries of the Himalayas are avid for that windfall! And you think that I will permit that . . . ?"

Then, suddenly lowering my voice, I continued in a concentrated tone, my clenched teeth scarcely letting my hissing voice filter through: "Beware, Sita. Sita, you don't know that I too am strong, that I too am powerful . . . and if I wished . . . !"

In saying that, I lied. For once again, at the outset of that fit of rage, I had attempted to subjugate her, and all my violence had broken against an envelope of marble!

"Well, no . . . I'm not threatening, I'm begging! Sita, I'm offering you my life—take it. Oh, what does the Supreme Science matter to you? There's nothing in it but loving, and being loved. It's not true that you aspire to the Eternal Nirvana . . . the union of the individual soul with the universal soul, at the price of the true, present, active union of two human souls! What is the impersonal It compared with the You and the Me, living and thinking? Sita, I love you! I love you! Don't leave me, don't send me away . . . You're not answering . . . you want to go! Well, take me with you . . . I'll be your slave . . . is that not enough? Your dog!"

It seemed to me that she was shaken. Then, more ardently still, I continued: "Have pity on me, Sita! Stay, stay! Besides, can such conjuring tricks impose themselves on your intelligence, so sure and proud? What are these people saying, who are the guardians of lost Sciences? What Sciences? From what sources do they emanate? They're endowed with faculties that seem surprising to us . . . but there's nothing supernatural about them. Here too, by means of hard work, we shall conquer them . . . yes, Sita, I know that, having already mastered the majority of their secrets. Leave these thaumaturges escaped from the ancient temples of Eleusis, tricksters who impose nothing but ignorance, where they are . . . and the power, insofar as it is real, and practical, we shall possess so completely that by means of it we shall elevate ourselves above the stupid crowd . . . we shall be masters of will, we shall break all resistance, no obstacle shall block our flight . . . and we shall act like those men, whom you claim so passionately for humanity and who are nothing, after all, but egotists . . . yes egotists! For, if it is true that they possess these powers, why conserve them for themselves alone? Why, if they have the Truth in their hand, does that hand remain obstinately closed? Prideful and misanthropic, that's what they are! And it's those creatures, dressed up with sonorous and grotesque names, who will tear you away from me, who will kill me! Sita, you shan't leave!"

She had stood still throughout, not even interrupting me with a gesture.

I stopped, as if, after the signification of my final will, all resistance was impossible—but into that silence, her voice suddenly rose: the voice that was her greatest strength, which vanquished me and broke me.

"Friend," she said, "I forgive you. Live, and seek generosity."

And without adding another word, she set off for her room.

I leapt in front of her, ready for any violence, my arms extended to stop her, to seize her, perhaps to carry her off . . . but without her hand touching me, without even her dress having brushed me, I was forced to step back—and I saw her pass in front of me, saddened, to reach the door, which opened, and closed behind her.

I rushed at that door, hammering it with my fists, madly, furiously, crying out, calling, choking.

Suddenly, I felt a hand come down on my shoulder. I turned round abruptly. A man I did not know was in front of me: tall, brown-skinned, in the prime of life.

I divined, instantaneously, that it was Sita's abductor. How had he got in? By what doorway? I had seen nothing, heard nothing! What did it matter, anyway? He was the enemy; he was the accursed Mage whose infernal power was ruining my life . . .

In a paroxysm of fury, I made as if to leap upon him.

"My brother . . ." he said.

And at that word, and the sound of his voice, as some kind of vibration was manifest in my skull, with stupefying suddenness, I felt my nerves relax, my anger abate, my overexcitement crumble, as it were—and while he spoke, I remained standing, motionless, respectful, vanquished, devoid of fight, numbed into a submissive acceptance.

"My brother," he repeated, "you are on the threshold of Evil. Listen to me. I want, in a few words, to initiate you into the truth. You are a crooked instrument that I shall straighten, and attempt to utilize for the work of the Good. In us you see nothing but science. You're mistaken. In us, you see magicians. You're mistaken. You accuse us of egotism. You're mistaken.

"In times whose distance in the past seems improbable to you, there existed a civilization other than this one. Your poets have divined its existence, your philosophers have recovered its memory. Plato and Herodotus named it Atlantis. More recently, your scientists have found in your own soil undeniable proof of the existence of a continent that linked Europe and America.

"Suppose for a moment that this continent—Atlantis, or whatever you care to call it—has existed, that human beings have lived there for a period of centuries compared to which what you call historical times would be scarcely an hour.

"Suppose also that those humans have enjoyed a civilization superior to the one of which you are so proud—equal, for instance, to that which your successors on Earth will enjoy in ten or twenty thousand years . . . for why limit the Future?

"Suppose, too, that the forces with which you are familiar—heat, electricity and light—have been studied and analyzed to the extent of the discovery of the primal Force that is their essence . . . that the other phenomenal manifestations that you group under the names of hypnotism, magnetism and suggestive action, have been recognized in their principles . . . that all these powers, some of which are physical in the present sense of the word, and others immaterial—still according to your modern language—have been summarized in one unique force, similar to the one that Bulwer has designated under the fantastic name of Vril in his *Coming Race*.

"Suppose, finally, that a frightful cosmic cataclysm suddenly swallows up the inhabited lands, overturns the continents, destroys the human race . . . what would then remain of your civilization, however perfect it might be? Nothing but silence and oblivion . . .

"But then, suppose once again that a few people have escaped that cataclysm and are, in consequence, alone in possession of the secrets of that perfected civilization. Around them, evolution would recommence, slow and measured, seeking its path. Would they put at the service of that new, infantile, ignorant, fearful race, the science, now terrible and frightfully dangerous, of which they alone would be the sole custodians? Would you not deem it an odious crime to put a stick of melinite[1] in the hands of a child?

"No, those people would not surrender any secret. Patiently, through the centuries, spent in silence and meditation, they would conserve and transmit the mystery of psychic force—of Vril, if that expression without precise significance appears more acceptable to you. From generation to generation, disciples and masters, pupils and initiates, sages and Mahatmas alike, they would set themselves the arid and truly humane task of waiting for the moment when it would be possible to put back into the hands of humankind the heritage of their forefathers, intact.

"Why, you asked a little while ago of the woman we have judged worthy of being one of the heirs and guardians of the secrets of the past, do we not reveal ourselves boldly and frankly to everyone, in broad daylight? Out of pride? Would we not, on the contrary, have a thousand opportunities, in the vain display of our knowledge, to provoke astonishment and win glory?

"Out of misanthropy? It's the opposite that is true . . .

"For we refuse to give you power, you who would only make use of it for the satisfaction of egoistic passions—do you dare to assert the contrary, you who would sacrifice humankind to one of your caprices? Who would take possession of it? The exploiters who would find in it a new means of crushing the poor and oppressing the weak!

"Does that mean that we intend to keep it forever? Not at all, for we are merely custodians—but faithful custodians. As soon as civilization, repudiating its traditions of violence and oppression, has entered the path of true Humanity, of universal

---

1 This oft-quoted analogy usually refers to a stick of dynamite or a loaded gun, but Lermina's is a patriotic version, because the French government had chosen melinite (picric acid) as the explosive of choice for both civilian and military purposes in 1887, two years after Eugène Turpin had patented a method of incorporating it into blasting charges. It was not an ideal choice, because the acid tended to corrode its containers, sometimes leading to dangerous instability.

access to well-being, of true altruism, we shall not wait for a single hour to return to human beings the deposit that we have faithfully conserved.

"And even then, it will not be without a certain anxiety, for it was by the excessive exercise of those very forces, whose secret we shall reveal in its entirety, that the ancient civilization perished. But we shall invest our hope in the Eternal Justice that is Equilibrium.

"One more word: the time of revelation, though not immediate, is nevertheless drawing near; that is why, for some years, we have consented to allow a few disciples to come to us. But with what precautions! The one we call *Chela*[1]—the pupil—must successively renounce all egotistical passions, extinguish in himself the slightest desire for glory, for fortune, for material satisfaction. The renunciation is nullified if regret persists. Only then, when we have acquired the proof that the initiate will only make use of the revealed forces for the good of humankind entire, may he glimpse the door of the temple.

"Have you understood, my brother? If, sometimes, we permit ourselves a manifestation that is surprising—in the present state of your knowledge—to attract human attention, we do so with extreme prudence, and in favour of those in whom we hope to find subsequent devoted collaborators, impregnated solely with a love of Humanity.

"Certain people, like you, are endowed with faculties that render the study of our mysteries easier, more comprehensible, but, more often than not, they become prideful of what they call their force—an infinitely petty emanation of the True Force—and have neither Generosity not Patience. They remain what they are, simple temporary oddities. You, my friend, must beware: you have arrived at the knowledge of the second degree of the human septenary; what you call the astral body. Certainly

1 In Sanskrit, *Chela* means "slave" or "servant", but the term was modified in Hindi to refer to a disciple of a guru, and that was the meaning that became familiar in English, largely thanks to its adoption by Madame Blavatsky.

there is reason to esteem in you the perseverance and the method of the effort. If you persist, you will succeed in developing in your astral body the faculties of motility, even of action, which you consider as a power. But for what will you employ it, except to satisfy your *Tanha*,[1] your unsated desire to live, and your egotism? Take care that the force in question, inexpertly manipulated, does not turn against you and cause your ruin.

"I have spoken. Your submissiveness in hearing me is itself proof—in your eyes—that we have the power of the good, and also the will. Farewell, my brother. Sita and her brother are coming with me to the regions of Science. I hope that they will come back one day to bring the world the lesson of universal Charity. We shall be glad if you become worthy to follow them . . .

"Now, go to sleep!"

XI

Three years have gone by: three years in which I have suffered every torment. I am not a sage. I am a living, vibrant being, in whom passion takes on a frightful intensity.

I came round three days after the mysterious being had pronounced his final words, which were a command. Oh, he was stronger than me, an initiate of all psychic actions, and he had overcome my resistance as easily as a child's.

I had slept for three days—a heavy and dreamless sleep—and when I awoke, I ran, like a madman, to Sita's apartment. Gone! They had gone! A letter was waiting for me, containing a farewell . . . and what a farewell! Banal consolations, hypocritical advice and burlesque adjurations. Become good! Devote myself to humanity! When I had but one desire, which was to feel strong enough to take the world in my hand and crush it between my fingers!

1 The literal meaning of *Tanha* is "thirst", but it was widely used in Buddhist teachings to mean a kind of unwholesome craving for material satisfaction, and was adopted therefrom into Theosophist jargon.

Those dreams touched me deeply. What did I care for the happiness of peoples? In truth, I laughed at all that, and I'm still laughing today, when, possessing the power, I shall concentrate it entirely in the supreme effort . . . of hatred, of evil. Well, yes, the Mahatma was right! If all the secrets were revealed to us, we would use them wickedly against this wicked world . . . and as my hatreds have, after all, a single fixed objective, and I shall not feel any joy in doing harm to those I disdain, I shall burn this confession, the memento of my work and my suffering.

The following day, I was on the shore of the Mediterranean. No ship had left for India. I ran around Marseilles like a lunatic. I discovered neither Sita, nor her brother. I supposed then that they must have left for England. What good would it do to search the continent for them, anyhow? Had they not got a long start on me? Without thinking it through, I took passage on the first departing steamship.

And I spent six months in India, searching the valleys, scaling the peaks, on the track of those accursed adepts who had stolen my soul. When I questioned them, the English answered incredulously, with jeering laughter. The indigenes gravely pretended not to understand, or seemed to be waiting for some password that I didn't know. Did the detested impostors even exist? Had Sita been the victim of some immense imposture, to which her brother might perhaps have been an accomplice?

My anger increased with my lack of success.

Then I resolved to employ that very anger, passionate and inextinguishable, to the solution of the irritating problem that I had set myself. I reasoned coldly, for, outside of my love—can I say my love?—I felt perfectly in control of myself.

I knew—the Hindu had admitted it himself—that I was already in possession of an exceptional force. I could attempt feats forbidden to any other human. I was not a medium; I was more than that, since I could gradually develop my psychic power and conserve its direction. Had I not seen in India those fakirs who, under the radiation of their concentrated astral force, could cause a seed consigned to the earth to germinate in a few hours, and those yogis who succeeded in suspending their animation and were buried for two months, subsequently emerging from their graves alive and well?

And there was nothing supernatural in that—reasoning proved it, with the support of my own experience. Had I not died several times myself, when I had fallen into lethargy during a sudden and excessive projection of my will?

In brief, I started from the principle that, by a reasoned effort, I could abstract myself from the rules of normal life. And then, pitching power against power, I would engage resolutely in battle against the villain who had taken Sita away from me!

I returned to France, and there, in the most absolute solitude, I resumed the course of my studies, without haste, without leaving anything to chance, with inflexible method.

I had drawn up a plan in advance, from which I was determined not to deviate. Since I had been unable, in my material body, to find any trace of Sita, it would be necessary for me to create a new existence for myself, in an imponderable body— astral, as they say. By that means I would be able to travel long distances, penetrate into the most hidden retreats, insinuate myself close to her . . . and then avenge myself. Oh yes, avenge myself! For it was that, and that alone, that I wanted, that I still want. Deceiving the vigilance of her guardians, I shall go into the sanctuary where she is hiding, and there I shall say but one thing—*it's me!*—and I shall strike!

I have measured in myself the frightful difficulty presented by the projection outside my material body of the vital fluid. There was, at first, terrible suffering, like the thrust of a stiletto full in my heart. I set to work, forcing myself, in absolute immobility, by exercising upon my entire being a pressure of will in infinitesimal quantities, to annihilate that pain, whose worst result until then had been to withhold the free disposition of the force I emitted.

The pain was a distraction; it was necessary, little by little, to eliminate any sensation, which, by monopolizing my attention, or suggesting a single thought to me, might use up my mental energy, in no matter how small a quantity.

I also perceived that the needs of the organism were an evil subjection. The anchorites alone were able to achieve ecstasy, and little by little, I suppressed hunger and thirst. I composed aliments for myself strictly measured to restore equilibrium to the quotidian and physical losses, at the same time as, by abstaining from any unnecessary movement and any effort that did not end directly to my goal, I diminished the organic expense to the point of rendering it almost non-existent.

I renounced everything: curiosity, interest, desire. I was able to walk my body around Paris like an inert machine, without any external impression troubling its purely mechanical action. My eyes no longer saw, my ears no longer heard, except in the strict proportion that was necessary to avoid any accident.

Then, I deemed that these very ambulations, initially useful to maintain my circulation, were no longer indispensable. I made them shorter, gradually diminishing their range, until, in the end, I no longer went out of my apartment.

By contrast, my spiritual self acquired an increasingly great lucidity and acuity. I felt that I was mentally disengaged from the shackles of matter, and that my psychic force was becoming increasingly refined.

It was then that I made a serious start on the decisive task.

I had succeeded, without overmuch effort, in further realizing the effect that had already been produced, without the aid of my will: the vague external materialization of my vital fluid. But at the very moment when I wanted to reinforce that vague entity, to give it a more concrete existence, there occurred, on the contrary—or, rather the cerebral effort of reasoning to which I devoted himself caused—an evaporation of the form obtained, or I fell into torpor during which the work continued without my being aware of it.

I established this latter point by means of a photographic apparatus that I set up in the following manner. I worked in the dark in order not even to have the distraction of light. Lying on a settee, I provoked the emergence of the vital fluid. Then, by means of a clockwork mechanism, the photographic apparatus was started up, steadily unrolling a sheet of sensitized paper. Another mechanism ignited a magnesium wire at ten-second intervals. When I fell unconscious, the apparatus continued in operation for a determined time, after which a switch caused a bell to ring, which recalled me to reality.

I have the prints here, before my eyes. I shall attach them to this manuscript. Either they will burn with it, or I shall recover them . . . if I come back.

On these prints—which do not lie—I can follow the progress of the operation.

To begin with, there is a jet of grey vapor at the location of the heart, so tenuous that it is almost invisible; then a shallow spiral that rises at first, then rotates around its axis, interlacing, becomes heavier and gradually falls back in a line resembling a strip of white cloth. Then, while the vital source is still running, the thread broadens, as if spreading out, enlarging and initially becoming diluted, as if filling a mold, soon thickening by degrees—relatively, that is, without arriving at opacity. Soon, that vapor takes on a form: mine.

It was at that moment that, for six months, I had myself awakened by the bell. I had employed that long delay in gradually pushing back the moment when I fell unconscious, which I had only been able to obtain by infinitesimal fractions of a second. At the end of that period, though, I had succeeded in remaining awake until the perfect production of my external form. Furthermore, I no longer had to dread the scattering of my will; it was concentrated entirely in the materialization obtained.

It was then that I devoted myself to perfecting the form in question and, having given it existence, giving it force. First, it was necessary that it should be able to move, although, materially, I remained motionless.

It took a long time for me to determine that movements created in my brain were represented in my double and executed with as much precision as I if had carried them out myself, bodily. By means of a cerebral action I created a gesture, distinctly represented in a clear image, and my form accomplished that gesture, hesitantly at first, but soon with a perfect precision. Thus, little by little, I was able to extend its arms, move its legs, wave, move it away or bring it closer to me.

I was often interrupted by falling unconscious, but, being able to anticipate it, I activated the photographic apparatus, and I acquired the proof that my form obeyed me even so.

It was necessary for me then to give it purchase on the material objects surrounding me—that is to say, to make it an active and submissive slave. But the progress I had made was such that the attempt cost me no great fatigue. The procedure was still the same: I created in my mind the quadruple movement of approaching a bookshelf, reaching out for a book, taking hold of it and bringing it to me. If I fell into a torpor before the act was completely accomplished, I found the book beside me when I woke up.

Finally, three months ago, for the first time, I was able to tell myself that I had fully succeeded: I no longer experienced any painful sensation, only a little lassitude when the effort was prolonged for too long. The fainting fits became rarer and rarer, and were only determined by further progress.

Thus it was that I risked my life in the following experiment.

That form, composed of atoms so tenuous that they did not even have the consistency of the molecules making up a gas, ought, in my view, to pass through the densest bodies—through their pores, as it were—and subsequently recover its integrity of composition.

In order to make certain, I surrounded myself with a sort of wall, made of wood five centimeters thick; then, on the other side, where I could not see with my material eyes, I placed the photographic apparatus.

I projected my form, concentrating all my will-power upon it, and tried to oblige it to pass through the obstacle. Not only was I unable to succeed, but, in persisting against the resistance, I provoked a kind of reactionary shock that, rebounding on my brain, threw me into a kind of lethargy that lasted for several hours.

I had a moment of discouragement. Had I come so far only to come up suddenly against the impossible? I meditated for some time, and logic finally came to my aid. I created in my brain the act of passing through the board, I objectified it mentally. The form disappeared from my sight. I called it back by the same means, and had the joy of observing that the photographic print proved my success.

Gradually, I was able to give my form a more distinct physiognomy, almost to the extent of a perfect identity with my material body. I dressed it in my clothes, animated it with my thoughts and my will.

There was one fact that I could not deny, however, which was that the link attaching my vital force to me became weaker as I gave more distinction to it. When it thought, there only remained in me, so to speak, the distant echo of the thought, a shadow scarcely aware of the will. Were the link by which I called it back to me to break, it would be death.

I hardened myself against that anguish, however, and today I am, with as much human certainty as there can be, beyond all peril.

Why am I writing these words, when my conviction is the opposite?

I have certainly been able, in recent times, to dispose of my form like another self. I have been able, while lying on a settee in a state of complete motionlessness, to project it out of my apartment, out of my house. I know—because it has my thoughts and my memory—that it has been able to travel the streets in my perfect appearance, to be seen by people who know me, that it has replied to greetings addressed to it. I know that it has raised itself up from the sidewalk beneath my window, coming back into this room through the wall. I also know that the distance that separates me from it is unimportant, and that it is not by distance that the vital link might be broken.

What is it, then?

Here I am, alone, firm in my decision to attempt the supreme proof. Soon, I shall lie down there on my settee and I shall project my form. I shall order it to cross the continents, the seas, to go out there, into India, to find Sita's trail, and to approach her . . .

It will obey me, I have no doubt.

But at the moment when it takes the final step toward the woman that I hate—that I love! that I love!—how can I tell whether the commotion might be so violent that the link will be broken . . . and then . . . !

Well, am I afraid? There have been three years during which, not for a single minute, not for a single second, has a single one of my thoughts tended to any other goal than the one that I am now approaching.

Will I hesitate? No! Have I not a profound pride in my work? Am I not the strongest of the strong, the most powerful of the powerful?

Am I mad? Come on! Could a madman have a brain as lucid, a pulse as firm?

Sita! Sita! In your profound peace, it is you who have everything to fear. For my will is threatening you, for my force—which you mocked—is about to launch itself toward you with the speed of lightning! Sita, I love you ... and I have condemned you to death!

I am no longer hesitant!

Stand up, slowly, slowly, mysterious form which is my will and my life! Go, free of the chains that retain my abject body here; go Linga-Sharira! (Oh, how softly she pronounced those words!) Go accomplish the accursed work ... and come back to give my mortal heart the joy of hatred assuaged, of love avenged!

There you are, my messenger of death! Greetings! Absorb all my force into you, drink my life, drink the fluid of my breast and my brain ...

I can't write any more. I have to seal this envelope. I must ... so that no one will know ... the secret. I must write ... *burn this* ... ah!

Epilogue

Read in the *Nouvelliste Parisien*:

For several days, the tenants and concierge of house no. * in the Rue *** had seen no sign of the eccentric Louis de S****, who lived in a sort of absolute claustration. They decided to alert the police. The magistrate who ordered the opening of the doors established that the unfortunate man was dead. The time of death seemed to have been some forty-eight hours earlier. The cadaver seemed to be absolutely exsanguinated and presented the peculiarity that it was in a state of perfect preservation. The physicians concluded that death was due to a cerebral aneurism.

On a table next to the cadaver an unsealed envelope was found, in which there was a manuscript written in a feverish, almost illegible hand, which seemed to be full of incoherent divagations.[1]

---

1 Readers are presumably supposed to draw their own conclusions from the fact that there is no mention here of the photographs allegedly appended to

Louis de S**** had devoted himself, we believe, to the practises of magnetism, and was prey to mental disorder. As he enjoyed a certain wealth, his house has been sealed.

The body has been transported to the Morgue.

Postscriptum. At the moment of going to press, we have learned that the autopsy has invalidated the diagnosis of the physicians who initially examined Monsieur de S****'s cadaver. The unfortunate committed suicide by piercing his heart with a needle of such slenderness that it left no external trace of a wound.

Singularly, this morning, when the employees went into the room where the body had been deposited, they found the shroud strewn with rose petals. No one has been able to say who came to render this pious homage to the mortal remains.

---

the manuscript.

APPENDIX:
THE TWENTIETH-CENTURY
LEGACY

THE TEMPLE

by Gabriel de Lautrec

"THERE'S a step," said Lucia.

She was standing on the threshold with a torch in her hand. The door was at the bottom of a slope on the side of the villa. The entire house, save for that retreat, was plunged in silence and obscurity. There was no silver stripe in the gaps of the shutters to divulge the interior life. A trellis embroidered with ivy surmounted the triangular wall near the door to the tunnel, and the moon, aided by the nocturnal breeze, made the sharp and dreamlike shadow of the foliage tremble on the white façade. Lucia's torch was also trembling, and paling in the pale air. The young woman, clad in a long black robe, evoked the image of welcome at the entrance to the catacombs. Saint-Maur saluted her with a smile over which a vertical finger put a cross of complicity. Then, making his companion the same sign to be quiet, he drew him inside.

There were ancient high-ceilinged cellars beneath the house. From outside, their existence could not be suspected, because the foundations of the house left no visible opening. Doubtless the ventilation of that part of the dwelling was enabled by secret passages, and lamps must have burned there continuously. Such enclosed solitudes were found in the neighborhood of large cities, which served as the habitation of the mysteries. Every human city is ringed by houses for phantoms. With a divination of that vicinity, the dead too are sent into fraternal suburbs.

They were under the somber vault, and the door immediately closed behind them, as if invisible hands had been awaiting the signal. The two young men shivered at the sudden impact, but Lucia made a sign that they should follow her. Their silhouettes danced in the torchlight over their footsteps in the corridor, sometimes following them with the blackness of their movements, sometimes elongating over the vault, cut or twisted by the projection of a ledge. They passed several closed doors barred with iron, and two or three bays guarded by grilles, behind which stairways plunged into the darkness. At the turning of the steps down below, a night-light fanned the walls with a dubious light. Then the route went round a bend, and Jean Derève perceived the entrance to a vaulted room, into which their guide introduced them. She designated seats next to a table surmounted by candelabra, and disappeared.

Once alone, the young men consulted one another with their gaze, exchanging mute impressions. The fashion in which they had been brought was strange. A carriage had awaited them at the exit from Saint-Maur's house, with a companion they recognized by means of words agreed in advance. They had been asked to permit their eyes to be blindfolded. That was the obligatory ceremony of excursions of this sort.

They remembered the vehicle going through the evening streets then, by roundabout routes deflecting all conjecture, and eventually rolling along a road that appeared to them to be outside the city, without them being able to determine in which direction they were going. A fleeting impression when they got down in front of the house and the blindfold had been removed had enabled them to suppose that they were at the end of some deserted avenue, near a wood. Perhaps all the twists and turns had not taken them very far, and the city was hiding close by, behind two or three curtains of trees.

They also knew that after their introduction, having made an oath of silence, they would be left at liberty to find the way back. That mystery, not of long duration, did not trouble them.

For the moment, they were solicited by the aspect of the place. They saw a kind of narrow cell, which must have been made for waiting, only furnished by dark wooden seats and a table. The walls, like those of the corridor, were made of stone separated by lines of cement; it was the décor of church walls and cloisters. That geometric disposition was the only ornamentation. They could have believed that they were in an Egyptian hypogeum, inhabited by a population of silent mummies gilded by immortality, or one of the chambers located inside pyramids, linked by long dark corridors, over which the mass of triangular granite weighs, while outside were clouds of sand stirred up by the desert wind, the sun and the cries of birds.

There are mysteries that require lugubrious clearings in the forest, with the rustle of leaves and the pale face of Hecate through the black branches and the frightened howling of shepherds' dogs. Others are celebrated underground, fleeing the gaze of the blue sky, where the intermediation of gnomes or vagabond sylphs is invoked.

No rumor came from the rooms that must be nearby, separated from one another by the walls of the foundations. A few minutes went by. Jean Derève became discouraged. He had only accepted the initial precautions with great difficulty. An anxious desire had caused him, after successive vain experiments, to entrust himself to Saint-Maur. Like many others, he was in search of a formula for life, but his desire had become an impatience. Why were these delays and veils of ceremony always disposed at the entrance to the sanctuary? Would the truth not have gained from being shown suddenly, stark naked? The memory returned to his mind of other initiations whose exterior preparations had only been romantic jugglery devoid of purpose. He did not think that mystery belonged equally to the rites of wisdom and error. It was appropriate that different things had similar appearances, in order that one could employ reasoning.

"We have to resign ourselves," Saint-Maur said, "to finding veils everywhere. Isis is always under the mantle. You're complaining about a darkness whose contrast alone makes light. The High Priest of Jerusalem only entered the Holy of Holies once a year. It would not have been the Holy of Holies if the crowd had had the leisure to penetrate it every day. Think of the cavern of Arabian tales in which the precious gems and sacks of gold are heaped up, the door of which only opens to those who know the magic word.

"You think that deceptive forms have duped us too frequently by their appearances. A fine knight of adventures, truly, the man who is astonished to encounter enchantments, monsters and mirages in the forest, and who would like to see the hospitable threshold of the castle appear at the first bend, without going astray. You know that the chatelaine ought only to be smiling, that the pages ought only to be walking clad in gold and lace, and the brass trumpets ought only to be sounding to welcome the weary and sad visitor whose mantle is torn by all the thorn-bushes. But even if the ritual walls that loom up before you only have symbolic value, they must be accepted.

"The winner of the ancient games penetrated his natal city on his return by means of a breach made in the wall. Honor is signified by effort. Pythagoras spent thirty years in silence and study before being initiated into the Egyptian mysteries. All things being equal, one can at least approve of the ceremonies that remind us of the difficulties. Anyway, I can hear voices through the thickness of the walls."

An invisible bay opened nearby, and Lucia returned. She was holding two red cloaks over her arm. The two companions put them on and followed her into the corridor. Other turnings, cleverly adapted into the restricted space of the subterrains, formed a veritable labyrinth, the extremity of which, for the range of voices and light, was a long way from the exterior. A corner crossed showed them, in a square niche in the wall, a statue that they recognized as that of Harpocrates, the god of silence.[1]

Lucia glided ahead of them; her black robe with moving pleats put bat-like shadows around her. One right-angled corridor was so narrow that they had to pass through it sideways one by one. It was a souvenir of epochs in which the research of obscure things had been regarded as a crime and the friends of the occult had been obliged to defend their dwelling. There are images that represent a vanished necessity. Events disappear but forms endure. Many present rituals have that significance.

Lucia knocked on a door that was suddenly perceptible, which had a resonance of heavy wood. It swung on its hinges soundlessly, however. A bright light struck their faces, at the same time as perfumes and the sound of voices, and the visitors had the sanctuary before them.

It was a vast subterrain in the form of a hemicycle, with a much higher ceiling than the corridors. Only a few steps led to the lower level. The entrance on the threshold of which the young men were standing occupied the left of the diameter. They saw a bare room with the same regular design of stones. An odorous smoke blurred all the details. On each of the five arched walls with apparent ridges that formed the semicircle, wrought iron fittings bore yellow candles. Another, central light was coming from the long opposed wall; Saint-Maur and Derève supposed a hearth set back in its depth from the line.

In the low middle of the room, gray swirls of perfume were tinted with red light, rising like an exhalation toward the ceiling. The latter, posed over the bare walls, was painted pale blue, on which faint golden figures—lines, orbits and spheres—depicted

1 Harpocrates was a Greek adaptation of the Egyptian god Horus specific to Alexandria; that origin allowed his subsequent association by modern occultists with the supposed Gnostic phase of the Hermetic tradition.

the various systems of the world, with planets and comets, according to Copernicus, Ptolemy and the primitives. Around the subterrain men were standing clad in cloaks similar to those of the visitors, who remained on the threshold, somewhat nonplussed, awaiting a summons.

One member of the audience separated from the semicircle, conferred momentarily in a low voice with someone who could not be seen, hidden by a projection of the wall at the top of the staircase, and then came toward the young men. His face, like all the others, was almost entirely hidden by a vast hood, which the two newcomers did not have. There is no impression more anguishing than that of finding oneself with one's face uncovered, in a gathering of unknown and dissimulated persons.

The greeter, once having reached the highest step, said: "You do not know us, but we know you who you are. Before it is permitted for you to witness our sessions, swear to keep silent about everything you might hear and everything you might see. We shall leave you to return to our midst or to leave forever, as you wish. Everyone decides. But if you leave, you must forget, and never take the road that leads here with a profane. Make the oath."

"By what is it necessary to swear?" asked Saint-Maur.

"By the goddess."

They attested to the goddess that they would keep the secret.

The introducer took them by the hand and led them down the steps. Then they were taken to the center of the assembly. A man with his back turned to the hearth was in front of then, and in shadow, but the light was behind him, so he symbolized the obscure conductor toward it.

"What do you request?" he said. His voice was clear with a resonant timbre, enabling the supposition of a young man. His tone was reassuring.

Saint-Maur, instructed in advance, spoke first. "We request the light."

The interrogator added: "What do you know?"

"Our ignorance," said Saint-Maur.

"You will still be ignorant, since you are human, and for humans, to understand is to be brought back to humanity. You will still see with your eyes and you will hear with your ears. No one can even conjecture what things are in themselves. In order to know them in their essence, it would be necessary to be at the center of everything and each individual thing in particular. Have you even penetrated the nature of your soul and its place in infinity? But there is no real center. The true world only exists in the vision of an intelligence; enable your mind to become a center. You will have found the absolute when you know that everything is relative and you know more relationships.

"Forms are held together and summon one another by a mysterious bond. The universe is like a sumptuous fabric. As soon as one seizes it, it unfurls entirely, embroidered with signs in gold and crimson. You will never lift, even in moments of ecstasy, the sacred veil of Isis, but you might surprise, at any moment, a different movement of the goddess and find her present everywhere. The name under which you worship the universal law is unimportant; it has no name and no face. The supreme thought that is manifest will only ever exist for you in its manifestations. The sole objective of science is to attain unity.

"The value of the word is purely that of a symbol. A sign of the identical unknown that we perceive in everything, it marks the front with an emblem that reminds us of that identity. Seek to know the laws, instead of asking in a puerile manner whether their creator exists, and under what form imitative of human form, and whether his name is Zeus or Jehovah. Astronomers know that it is only for us that the stars are named Aldebaran, Cassiopeia and Sirius.

"That is why you must refrain from mistaking the formula of our research for a reality. If anyone tells you that we worship fire, believe it, while not believing it. You are in the sanctuary of the most ancient religion. It is the one from which all the others have come. They have preserved some of its rites, mingled with crude and new superstitions, but all flames and all candles are lit at the same altar. We have chosen the symbol that appears to us to be the most venerable and the best. In order to speak to humans it is necessary to speak human language. All things are signs, however, and signs of other signs. After having seen, you can only conjecture."

The man who had spoken appeared to be the high priest, or at least the initiator. When he fell silent, all the members of the audience sat down in chairs, the high backs of which bore figures engraved in the wood. They were arranged against the wall; the assembly thus formed the magical semicircle. The high priest occupied the center. The hearth was now visible in front of which he was standing: a vast niche hollowed out in the wall, arched in form, floored with paving stones, with a flue above it.

The flames of the burning wood, almost a furnace, shone violently, The pellicle of gray dust, the image of cooling stars, did not have time to form over the ardor of red embers. A perpetual breath of air stimulated them. To each side of the hearth, on the wall of the room, there were two fountains with the heads of chimeras in green bronze, pouring water into two round stone basins set on the floor. Everything seemed made to be interpreted.

The assembled audience no longer formed a perfect circle. That is a figure that represents the absolute, and the most fortunate image by which we can express our impotence to express it. However, like all definitions of the world or of God, it is a sterile formula. One cannot enclose being—or, to put it another way, becoming—within a closed line. Circumference indicates repose and achievement. Life is movement and perpetual exchange. But the semicircle preserves the possibility of the beyond. It is continued by two parallel lines that extend into the distance and whose appeal is prolonged to the limits of supposed space. And if we are, in our inferior nature, the reflection of a higher nature, as Plato thought, the semicircle aspires to completion by another, actual or created by us, but situated in infinity. The focal point placed in its axis is also the reflection of another focal point.

Those thoughts were engendered, confusedly, in the minds of the visitors. They had the impression of living, momentarily, in a milieu haunted by symbols. But symbolism is all of literature, all of art and all of religion. It is the reduction of things to unity, the discovery of the same rhythm in the diversity of planes. Christ only spoke in parables, and everything is similar. The secrets of ancient science and magic are enveloped in legend, like transparent veils. Great poets are those who encounter unexpected and accurate images—which is to say, new relationships.

The décor differed here from the usual banality, or rather, it had the perfect banality that is a harmony. Only the red cloaks, the color of which was a natural concession in the sanctuary of fire, put a romantic note into that discreet concert. Jean Derève evoked other séances. He reviewed the various initiatory interiors previously traversed, in which the cult of Isis, as well as that of the Great Architect,[1] was adorned with faded garments and cabalistic figures in gilded cardboard. How many temples had the sole aim of permitting the priests to live on the credulity of the fervent! He remembered naked swords crossed over the heads of the audacious, and Hebrew words pronounced on the threshold of equivocal sanctuaries by people so ignorant that they pronounced them purely because to them, they were Hebrew.

But perhaps, he thought, sadly, that was the foundation of everything, and images are always required to amuse the human

---

1 The Great Architect (of the Universe) is the deity of freemasonry, within which tradition Martinism and modern Rosicrucianism evolved before separating therefrom.

child; the most delicate require more artistry in the line and the color.

Meanwhile, the high priest continued:

"Do not form a judgment of what you have seen before having meditated. All forms can only suggest, without representing, the unknown gods. The mages of all times have sought the unique principle. Some have believed that they had found it, and the result was the same, for the truth is revealed under one or other of its appearances to those who invoke it with a pious heart. There is no futile prayer, and sincere errors are errant on the route of the absolute. The act of faith to the veritable deity is composed of multiple invocations to all strange idols, and the name of the Supreme Being consists of the numerous syllables that denominate the numerous false gods. That is why, and to appease the secondary demons as well as the transitory powers, we have accepted as a departure the rite of the four elements. The quaternary is sacred. What does it matter whether we address our preliminary homage to mobile water, with Thales, to subtle air, with Anaximander, or to the earth, mother of humans, since everything is resolved in fire. Worship with us the four elements."

Immediately, the faithful rose to their feet and started to march around the room, stopping at the third circuit. One of them went into a neighboring room to fetch a light column whose superior tablet was broad and covered by a black veil. The irregular pleats of the veil hid objects of worship.

"This black veil," said the High Priest, will be for you the somber chaos in which all the elements are buried. What a powerful hand it required to bring them out of primal chaos!"

He lifted the cloth, a cup appeared, full of water, which was water, a vase full of salt, which was earth, and a rose, to signify the perfumes of the air.

Then everyone remained silent. The High Priest had thrown the veil into the hearth. The elements were created. The somber object flew away into the chimney like a crimson flag. There were a few minutes of slight anguish. Then, slowly, in the calm air, a voice rose that appeared to come from the depths of the earth. Afterwards the accompaniment of an organ also very distant, commenced. And, changing the words in a minor key, the subterranean voice pronounced the orison of the water elementals:

Masters of the ocean and all the shores
Who hold in power the moving ground of the waves,
Kings of caverns, the rain and clouds
Whom spring summons to the doors of enclosures,
You who come to open the source of springs,
And fecundate the bushes and the powerful oak,
Enabling to circulate in the network of veins
The limpid water changed into their sap and blood,
We here salute your magical power,
And your voice speaks to us with the sound of great waters,
But we also understand you in the music
Of the summer spring that cradles the birds.
Heights that reflect the profound immensity,
Depths that exhale you into the heights,
Give us the true sense of life and the world
In which eternal exchange is the true creator.
Pour into our hearts the love of sacrifice,
In order that, having become better and wiser,
For the divine redemption of error and vice,
We can offer you water, blood and tears.[1]

---

1 The four parts of this invocation had previously appeared in the literary section of the November 1900 issue of *L'Initiation*. A similar ritual is described in Victor-Émile Michelet's "Holwennioul," published in his occult periodical *L'Humanité Nouvelle* in 1899, although that ritual also includes the swords treated dismissively here.

The voice fell silent. The hierophant took the cup and poured a few drops of the ground, in libation. The cup passed from hand to hand, until the last. It was replaced, empty, on the sacred column.

Meanwhile the organ rumbled, and the sanctuary was surrounded by a tumult similar to that of great waters. The voice rose up again, but it appeared to be coming from a profound retreat. It was the earth elementals that it invoked:

> *O you who haunt the human vault beneath our feet,*
> *And make it tremble over its profound gulfs,*
> *In the name of the seven torches of the sovereign night*
> *Lead us toward the light of which we dream.*
> *Reveal to our eyes fixed on the mystery*
> *The lost talismans of the holy city,*
> *Which you keep hidden in the bosom of the earth*
> *Under the seal of silence and obscurity.*
> *Master of nocturnal laborers whose task*
> *Is to reunite the gold of the dispersed veins,*
> *As soon as we have labored relentlessly*
> *With the sure hope of being recompensed,*
> *Magnify our hearts for future labors,*
> *You who inspire us with the occult and its desire,*
> *And who wear, reigning over obscure splendors,*
> *The sky on a finger, like a sapphire ring.*

As he had done for the water, the priest lifted the vase, took a grain of salt and placed it on his lips. The members of the audience did likewise, and the voice continued, imploring the elementals of the air:

> *You whose breath creates and destroys all form,*
> *Spirit who travels borne on the wings of the wind,*
> *Your respiration populates enormous space,*

Life is like a shadow to your moving gaze.
You guide, alternated beneath a magical power,
The ravens of night and the doves of day,
Enable, with the light of your mystic soul,
The breath of amour to penetrate our depths.
One day, to the eternal movements of this world
All wanderers will be encountered by others,
And, dreams mutated into profound verity,
Roses will grow on the branches of cypresses.
Like shipwreck victims battered by the tempest,
We are struggling in the horror and error of dusk,
But our hearts have known the preparatory calm,
And the dawn is as odorous as a censer.
Vast sigh that silenced the ancient creator,
Mouth of shadow exhaling the eternal mystery,
By means of perfumes, colors and music,
Baptize us in the subtle and fraternal air.

Everyone respired the rose. The sacred objects were taken away; the assembly formed the circle again and, all is members prostrate, listened to the orison of the salamanders, the demons of the inferior fire.

Eternal, uncreated Father of all things,
Whose triumphal chariot rolls over the world,
Real fire of Eternity, Cause of causes,
Inspire us with the prayers to be offered to you.
The throne where you sit dominates the expanse,
Nothing escapes the immense gaze of your eyes.
Every word pronounced is heard.
Grant our prayers, you who hide behind the gods!
Compared with your splendor, the stars are mere ash,
You shine in the height of the sky as within us,
Into our obscurity deign to send down

The light of which the suns are jealous.
Reign over us by means of heat and light,
Cold shadow is the mortal sister of the void,
Every ray surging from the primal source
Creates a new world in the gaping abyss.
We know that from your unique power are born
Souls, desire and amour, the golden torch,
Beneath the vain formula and the ancient image,
It is always you that humans have adored.
All the sacred mantles are only shrouds
In which form and the only God resuscitate,
And lamps are on the threshold of various sanctuaries,
As witnesses of the true worship, that of fire.

For it was appropriate to invoke the supreme element with more solemnity, and to implore it first in its humblest manifestation. Terrestrial and perishable fire, to the surveillance of which the salamanders are appointed, is only the least reflection, in the distant obscurity, of the immortal and primitive fire. The latter respires the infinite. On the road that leads to it, as the highest image visible for us, is the Sun.

And that was the prayer to fire. The same servant stood up, and went to take from a cupboard firmed by a hollow in the wall, a red book, which he brought piously to the middle of the room.

He deposited it on a light and high table and opened it. The letters were black, arched in form. The yellow paper was tinted with nuances in which the appearances of smoke and flame were recognizable. The reader chanted:

"I salute you, Ignis, Agni, lamb of fire, Ormuz. Osiris, Mithra, who are manifest by way of Yama, the thunder, and by way of Athene, the lightning. Father of Phobos and Hephaestos, it is to you alone, under various names, that humans render homage, to you alone, O our god."

A response ran through the religiously attentive audience: "*Soli deo, deo soli!*"

"I salute you, you who are born and die at the solstice and emerge from the sepulcher on the third day, Adonis, Adonai, Jesus, god of the pyre and the cross. Merciful and cruel God, Moloch requiring victims, brazen bull with ardent flanks, eye that shines at the center of the triangle and flame that it summarizes, angel that appeared in the bush. I shall turn my gaze toward the Orient, where you triumph incessantly, and from which you rise toward the zenith, to succumb in the Occident. By your fall, the glorious sea is illuminated in its depths. The glaucous and somber populations that its abysms contain, have your revelation every evening. On your sparkling tracks people and humanity go.

"I shall turn my eyes toward the Occident where you flee in order to carry life beyond. The watchers look out for your approach, and the mountains are crowned by temples consecrated to you, O Helios, Saint Hélie.[1] Rising sun, surrounded by a cortege of hours in roseate robes, pouring flowers of joy from their hands. Flame of the heart above the earth, lightning-flash, star in the sky, fire that consumes offerings and divine fire that receives them, shadow of the ineffable cause, blinding for mortal eyes, you who are born of two mothers and who have your cradle for a tomb, it is in you alone that we ought to believe and to whom we should sacrifice; to you alone, O solar god!"

The voice of the recitation was impregnated with fervor. Then it fell silent.

Perfumes poured from bronze cups over the red embers emerged slowly in dense white swirls of smoke, toward the vault, like the columns of an unreal temple.

A different voice continued:

---

1 The reference is not to Saint Hélie of Lyon, but rather to the Abrahamic prophet usually known in English as Elijah, sometimes called Élie or Hélie in French; the author prefers the latter term in order to forge the link with Helios.

"And I salute you also, among humans, the discoverer of fire, Prometheus!

"What unjust forgetfulness spreads its shroud over you, father and creator?

"It was a crime to want to posses the god. Had he truly made humans in an hour of wrath, that he was irritated by your theft? But bow down before his jealous fury, for he has allowed you to keep the shreds of the mantle, crimson and gold, that you stole. Everything that he wants is just and good. He has not chained you to your rock for eternity. The thrust of the sword causes a spark to spring from the rock, and you climb up again toward the gods to perpetuate your memory by means of the lamps that watch over the various altars. True Adam, you rediscovered the sacred fire lost by the first Adam. It is your story that all the sibylline books contain.

"O Prometheus!

"We have been the slaves of the clouds and the wind. Do you recall human life before the invention of fire? But he came to soften the curbed forms of iron for weapons and the plow. The earth gave wheat. Flame hollowed out trees and the first ship floated. Let it cry humankind! It conquered the face of night. When the god disappeared in the decreasing crimson of the horizon, having become blue again, instead of invoking the pale moon or obscure goddesses by means of incantations, we stimulated, in order to render homage to him, the shining shadows of the sun.

"Lamp!

"Vacillating torch of the miner who plunges, by way of sloping subterrains, into the region of heavy air.

"Lamp of the laborer curbed by night over the blank sheet or the page of a book; the light is in his soul as well as around him.

"Lamp of amour that fearful Psyche approached to the unknown!

"Spark come from above, what poet of works in the fabulous vanished night pronounced the breathless emotion of the first undulation of your blue flame?

"Glimmers of summer hidden in the hollows of old trees, from which we make them surge forth, like ancient shepherds, by striking two white stones, enabling the nymph with the golden hair to appear from the centenarian oak.

"Take homages in your hands, like garlands of red roses, and rise again toward the solar god."

Silence reigned again; but it was troubled. Indistinct noises were coming from the door. Moans and sobs were heard. All of them directed their gazes toward . . .

"The adoration of fire," said a voice.

The perfumes of cups flowered myrrh and aloes. An odorous smoke misted the room and oppressed hearts. The torches gleamed beneath a veil. A religious torpor almost suffocated the members of the audience, and in the atmosphere, in which red and fleeting gleams enlaced, fatigued eyes were ready to see the strangest forms, by means of the fantasy of evocation.

Meanwhile, the sobs continued on the other side of the wall. They were mingled with ecstatic plaints. A new pity seemed to be begging to be received. The High Priest headed toward the entrance and the visitor.

The door opened, and a man appeared: an old man with twisted limbs, a grimacing face furrowed by deep wrinkles, he evoked the supreme limits of age. His appearance was sudden and bizarre. A black robe with wide sleeves, secured at the waist by a rope, dressed ineptly a dwarfish and disproportionate body, with an enormous head covered in gray hair. One might have thought, on seeing the gaze of his green eyes, that he was a veritable gnome emerged from some fantastic realm. It is certain that envoys from the neighboring world live among us. The entire person of the old man inspired alarm.

He was seen to descend the steps jerkily, hopping from one foot to the other. He could not aid himself with the walls. His hands were hidden over his breast by a flap of his robe. With crawling movements, turning from one side to the other, he came all the way to the middle of the room. Each of his movements was accompanied by the same sobs, marks of madness or emotion. Suddenly, however, having reached the center of the curved line formed by the initiates, as if at a real focal point, he straightened up and was almost august. His arms were disengaged from the folds of the robes, and the young men perceived a small object shining in his hands, raised and joined.

In the midst of bewildered starts and acclamations, Jean Derève, aided by his companion's smile, sensed present impressions fusing with a vanished memory. He knew the talisman that the clenched fingers were holding aloft. Curious about occult things, he had been amused by the story, as a poetic legend; but he had to believe it now.

No jewel approaches for beauty a fragment of an ardent furnace. Red is the color of blood and life; but precious stones are like dead beauties. If fire did not pale and fall into ash, if it could remain as it is in the heart of a hearth it would be the most splendid of rubies. No rajah of fabulous India possesses anything similar in his treasures. Tradition requires the existence of that impossible jewel to be accepted.

A mineral whose nature could not be precisely determined served as a pretext for all that worship, and its mysterious nature was not in contradiction with the new suppositions that stupefied science sees realized every day. The properties of substances differ. That means that each contains and reveals a form of energy. Some are luminous. Others can, with brightness, produce a constant heat. In the midst of adorations and ritual precautions, they kept the fiery stone discovered by a Bohemian, whom the poetic imagination had made into a messenger of the sun. For, with the brightness of the most beautiful rubies, it was also a perpetual ardent coal. It burned without being consumed, and its redness, which passed from vivid to dark, for the various joy of the eyes, was not a deceptive symbol. Visible Fire, at its approach all hands, including those of the most pious, became profane. One could no more grasp it than a firebrand. It was intangible, like flame, lightning and mystery. That is a religious quality, for our corporeal person. And certainly, with the love of the extraordinary that is human, such an object can sustain astonishment better than fetishes of wood or stone. It has not always required as much for people to make a god.

It could be compared to the philosopher's stone, or the ember placed by an angel on the lips of Moses. According to the legend, the talisman had been conserved in a sanctuary in India, sheltered in a hollow granite container sculpted in a triangular form to signify the pure fire represented by the pyramids, and then, after several voyages, transported to Europe. A faithful follower, doubtless one of the last descendants of Asiatic worshipers, a guardian of the occult tradition, jealous of exposing it to the gaze of his brethren and of making it the occasion of ceremonies, had undertaken to set the jewel in a metal bezel. It is appropriate that every idol can be presented by the priest above the prostrate crowd, to receive prayers and vows. The discovery of a metal capable of retaining the stone without being damaged by the contact had demanded patience and an entire lifetime. Now, the man to whom its pious care had been entrusted elevated in his hands a light reliquary, from the heart of which it cast its durable fires around. But by virtue of keeping the talisman captive in its metal circle during the hours of religious penalty, the hands of the worker, gloriously burned, were deformed and mutilated. It was said that they could no longer serve any other purpose than holding the reliquary in a definitive grip. Black and twisted, they retained the indestructible marks of the wounds made by the god.

Meanwhile, the uninterrupted groans of the old man were mingled with the invocations of the entire audience. Some, standing in various parts of the room, in ecstatic poses, seemed to be challenging the idol. Others, fallen to their knees, their heads buried under their cloaks, were sobbing hectically. Appeals in all languages were overlapping, for there were doubtless initiates in the modern city who had come from the most diverse regions, united by a common faith.

The scene became tragic. The red smoke undulated, making bodies appear, at the whim of the flames, in strange attitudes, like the forms that one dreams for a subterranean inferno. The High Priest remained motionless, sitting in his chair in the middle of that human swell, his eyes on the stone and the old man. He represented, in a fleeting vision, the bleak master of the Sabbat seen in ancient prints, his hand on his chin and his elbow on his knee.

The young men, nonplussed, and understanding that those men were unaware henceforth of the presence of strangers, feared some unexpected development. As they took refuge by the door, it opened slightly, and the silhouette of Lucia made a shadow. She beckoned to them from outside.

When they were in the vestibule, she closed the door behind them, through which clamors were now audible. They traversed the narrow and winding passages again. Jean Derève and Saint-Maur reached the room where they deposited their red cloaks. Then Lucia conducted them, in the diminishing echo of distant voices, to the external threshold.

She saluted them with a smile and the same gesture of silence. They had the bewilderment of a sudden contrast. Trees of all shades of green were agitating in the breeze. The sun was nascent in its freshness, and there was a slight joy in respiring, while mist was rising from the landscape in order to vanish impalpably, like another incense, toward the red disk on the horizon.

TSADÉ[1]

by Renée Dunan

NO! No one has ever seen, and perhaps ever will see, the prodigious metapsychical, hyperphysical and panpsychical experiments that I have been able to witness, and in which I have participated. On several occasions, they have given me a thrill that no human event, even if it were as vast as a continent, as disastrous as a war, as tragic as . . . but any comparison would be vain. What I have seen, mark my words, is beyond them all . . .

I have been in contact with beings from worlds transcending ours. The realities that have overcome me do not originate from any terrestrial logic or reasoning. They were . . . they were . . .

I was then the secretary of the beautiful and strange seeress who called herself Madame Palmyre. She lived near the Étoile in Paris, in a huge apartment extended through three buildings, on two floors of each of them.

---

1 I have retained Dunan's idiosyncratic spelling of this section-heading in the volume entitled *Baal*, one of four, all of which are letters of various Semitic alphabets, whose alternative spellings vary considerably from one language to another, and in different reference-books. Tsadé is the eighteenth letter of the alphabets in question, Iod the tenth, Samech the eighteenth and Beth the second; they correspond approximately to the letters Z, I, S and B. They are presumably employed in order to imply some Kabbalistic significance, perhaps to represent the four levels of engagement described in the *Zo'har* (direct, allegorical, inquisitive and mystery), although the four letters conventionally used to designate those modes are P, R, D and S.

One day, when I was in the personal service of Tony Dreyse, the banker, I had expressed my boredom with his invoices, his bonds, his share prices, his brokerage, and, above all, the invincible stupidity of his clientele, to whom I had to feed financial claptrap on daily basis. Dreyse said to me: "Well then, I'll use Marthe Knoberg, whom you've trained so admirably—I say that without any malice—and you'll be able to try another profession. Here!—Palmyre needs a secretary. Go to her!"

I knew Palmyre—a personal friend of Tony Dreyse's—and I went to see her.

She was an extraordinary woman, not easily comprehensible, full of secrets and strange vices. She knew the entire planet, had bewildering physical and psychic powers at her disposal, and concealed imperial ambitions—and she was beautiful too, proudly wearing a Greek mask, svelte, firm, despotic and endowed with a fascinating ubiquity.

She ruled, with a rod of iron, a clientele of politicians, bankers, writers, ponderous and skeptical men, who buckled before her like reeds. All the women of the theater, wealth and fashionable society had had recourse to Palmyre, once or a hundred times over. She had abused them and treated them harshly, but even the most spiteful nevertheless spoke of her tenderly—and the men even more so.

She predicted the most mysterious futures, brought the most hostile lovers together, and *magnetized*, for various and preposterous reasons, pens, pajamas, bracelets, nightshirts, writing-paper, love-poems, armchairs or objects too delicate to name . . .

She taught heirs to cast spells from a distance on relatives overly attached to life, caused people to win on horses or at baccarat, sold love-potions, potions to increase will-power and potions to wreak vengeance, performed black masses and malefic ceremonies of every sort; in sum, she had resuscitated all of medieval magic.

She made a lot of money, demanding ten thousand francs for a five-minute consultation and veritable fortunes for all the amorous sorceries in which she excelled. No one ever refused them.

I did not believe in any of the secrets of occultism in which Palmyre traded. All that nonsense delighted me nevertheless, as evidence of public credulity. I only admitted that the witch's correspondence was very flavorsome. A psychologist would have discovered treasures therein, for a sorceress's male and female clients never lie. All the same, I was often astonished that Palmyre's predictions were so accurate. Hazard is not so exact . . .

Also, I marveled at the fact that she was able to achieve everything she attempted. She reunited separated lovers, ensured vengeances, brought complex projects to a conclusion—in sum, seemed as skillful and as much a mistress of her activity *as if it were really true.*

One day, shortly after noon, we were conversing in one of the private rooms. I gathered that she was not feeling well, and her obsidian eyes seemed to be resorbing the light. Her thin red mouth was smiling with a kind of malignity.

"Renée," she said to me, "we're in danger."

I looked at her, with a powerful urge to laugh. "Of course. The whole world is in danger of earthquakes, like the one in Japan."

She shook her head slowly. "I'm not talking about natural hazards, Renée—I mean that there's an external, unknown will that is directed against me, and which might do a great deal of harm."

I assumed an ingenuous expression. "You have too much business sense not to have taken precautions."

"Precautions! What precautions?"

"Against danger, naturally. I don't see that the gentlemen of the Lady with the Scales . . ."

She looked at me in astonishment. "What are you talking about, child?"

"The Pointed Tower, of course."

"Oh! You were able to think that I was worried about those individuals. In truth, Renée, you think like a child. What do judges and jurists matter to me? They're in the palm of my hand—like this!"

She made a fist, extending her thumb and little finger, and laughed.

"I don't understand the danger, then."

"You haven't been targeted, Renée—at least, I don't think so—but I . . ."

"Targeted by whom, pray? It's as if we were speaking two different languages."

She got up, took three indolent steps across the room, and threw up her bare arms and slender hands toward the ceiling. I saw the swollen hollows of her shaved armpits, and the creases of the long black satin sheath-dress she was wearing were accentuated all the way to the groin.

She came back to me. "There's a force, Renée, an Occult Force, perhaps familiar, that has become hostile to me . . . very!"

"An occult force? My word! I must tell you that I don't know about that. Since I've been here, I've seen many things, but occult forces . . ."

"Come on, Renée—did you think that I don't know anything about the profession I practice?"

"All things considered, I consider the profession as an astonishing farce . . . that you have, however, brought to a prodigious degree of perfection."

"But it exists, my child!"

"What exists?"

"What I say and do . . ."

"No, I pray you, don't take me for a potential client for cartomancy. When you asked Lucette de Lantz, the dancer, for three thousand francs to magnetize the writing-paper on which she wrote to the lover she wanted to get rid of, you expected me to swallow . . . the writing-pad in question was one I bought in a sale at the Louvre department store. Come on!"

Palmyre laughed. She sat down and crossed her legs, then slowly lit a cigarette. I could see her thin ankles and the plane of the tibia, to which her black silk stockings were clinging. Finally, she said: "You've calmed me down by reminding me about Lantz. Yes, that's a trick, the business with the magnetic paper . . ."

"And the talisman on virgin parchment that you sold for twelve hundred francs to the senator, Paul Maysonnés?"

"Oh! That, Renée, is another matter . . ."

"And the dagger—or stiletto, rather—to kill Giovan Balassio, the rich Sicilian merchant by plunging it into the heart of a wax statuette?"

"But you know perfectly well, child, that it worked."

"Oh, he was undoubtedly ill. He died. Agreed—but the stiletto had nothing to do with it."

Palmyre stood up again and went to root about in a cup for a sort of curved triangular needle.

"Put your hand on your knee, Renée."

She sat down a short distance away, holding the needle between her thumb and middle finger, point down.

"Well?"

"Your hand is four meters from the needle, isn't it, Renée?"

"Approximately. Do we need to measure?"

"Shut up, or I'll . . . look! As I lower the needle, it will pass through your hand. Do you feel it?"

"My word—yes!"

"And what else?"

"Why, it's bleeding!"

"And?"

"Oh—but that's really hurting!"

"Good! Would you like me to take hold of you by the nose without coming any closer?"

"No thanks!"

"Are you convinced?"

"Hmm!"

"Oh, you're a stubborn denier. If I were malicious, I'd convince you well enough. Do you see that incense-burner with the birds?"

It was a block of carved hollow bronze, extraordinarily beautiful. Palmyre raised both her middle fingers, simultaneously, toward the incense-burner.

The heavy bronze rose up from the sideboard and floated in mid-air.

"I'll put it on your head!"

It came to rest against my forehead.

"I'll send it outside . . ."

The door opened then, with a brutal click, and the incense-burner went out, floating a meter above the ground. I sat there, horrified.

"Oh! Right!"

"You're beginning to marvel, my child. Come on to the balcony; I'll do something remarkable to teach you . . ."

We went through the fencing studio filled with Japanese sabers, and the print studio, where admirable occult designs and prodigious canvases by Odilon Redon were on display.

In the third room, which was almost bare, with only an ebony chair in the middle, there was a vast bay instead of a window, which Palmyre opened. We were at the corner of the Avenue Victor Hugo.

"Do you want us to make that woman who's doing what we're doing, over there, fall from her balcony?" Palmyre said to me.

"Make her fall from her balcony? I don't understand."

"Look, Renée," she said—and suddenly began addressing me in the familiar mode, "you're going to understand. Stand aside—and look down there!"

I moved to the right after seeing Palmyre sit down on the ebony chair, from which she could see the minuscule form of a woman in pink occupied in watching the passers-by. We were at least a hundred and fifty meters away. I could no longer see the witch, but my heart suddenly leapt in my breast, and an unknown emotion shook me from head to toe.

Within two seconds, without anything to indicate how it had happened, I saw the decorative wrought iron of the distant balcony crumble like plaster. The woman in pink seemed to vanish, but I suddenly rediscovered her whirling downwards, falling... falling...

I thought I could hear within me the imperceptible impact of that human body crashing into the ground. And almost immediately, as I was leaning against the wall, Palmyre's balcony, less than a meter in front of me, cracked.

The echo resounded like a hammer-blow among the metal ornaments. At the same instant, Palmyre emerged and took me by the arm.

"Come!"

I went back into the room with the ebony chair. We went back through the studios, and, two minutes later, we were in the armchairs where the conversation had begun. Palmyre was incredibly pale.

"Do you believe, Renée?" She always used the intimate form of address is moments of excitement.

"Believe! What?"

"That I have powers at my disposal... mighty ones."

"It seems to me, indeed..."

"Well, I told you at the outset that there's a contrary force targeting me."

"Human?"

"I hope so—but I don't know yet."

"What does this force want with you? Are there conscious forces outside the world, then?"

"I don't know whether they're conscious, but yes, they act as if they have our kind of consciousness."

"There are, according to you, several types of consciousness?"

"Of course! Consciousness is the perception of a difference between object and subject, between perceived matter and the observer. There are as many consciousnesses as there are possible relationships between being and non-being, which might itself be the being of a sub-non-being, as the absolute is the perfection of a mode of relativity . . ."

"You're a metaphysician worthy of that Hedwige, who once shut Casanova's trap in Geneva,[1] even though he was an expert debater—which is to say, an Italian."

She laughed ambiguously. "It's impossible for you to be serious, Renée!"

"Listen, I already know you as a prodigious businesswoman. You suddenly reveal yourself to be a philosopher, a female fakir, a sorceress—that bewilders me, and as Père Hugo said, in bewilderment, there's laughter . . ."

"You shouldn't joke, Renée. There's an unknown force against me. It's not very active, but it's dangerous, and you might fall victim to it—for, participating in the life of the beyond by virtue of all my operations, I'm within range of the mysterious enemy, and you live so close to the sun . . ."

"Really?"

"But you've just seen it. My action, in breaking the guardrail of the woman in pink's balcony over there, was immediately followed by a reaction that broke mine. If you had been leaning

---

1 Casanova's memoirs record that in 1762 he had a brief affair with Hedwige, the daughter of a Protestant minister, while he was posing as an occultist in order to extract money from Madame d'Urfé—a scheme that allegedly went awry because his confederate, Marianne Corticelli, sold him out, forcing him to leave Geneva in a hurry.

on it, you would have plunged down, six floors. Mere pulp, my poor Renée!"

"You want me to believe that at the moment when you murdered the woman in pink . . ."

"She isn't dead, and won't die."

"You know that?"

"Yes. She fell on to the awning of a café."

"You want me I believe that, at that exact moment, someone tried to play the same trick on us? That's like something from a feuilleton novel . . ."

"Child! I'm the one who destroyed my own balcony. That's how enemies in the occult world operate. They reflect dangerous influences back on the person who sends them. With a certain degree of mental leverage on another mind, one can even contrive that malign wishes, evil intentions and ungenerous desires fall back on the person who gave birth to them. Thus, she tortures herself by wishing ill upon others."

"That doesn't seem to me to be unjust . . ."

"Oh, Renée, 'justice' is something that demands precautions before the word's pronunciation . . ."

"But in any case, a person who only has good wishes for all around her does not run into the danger that is threatening you?"

"Good! *Good!* Who knows what that is? There may be evil moralized, but good, never. It engenders pride, and pride is perhaps the worst of all moral evils. Pride tends to become action—which is to say, domination; which is to say, calamity. It is the most beautiful, the heaviest and the most colorful part of good that is evil."

"Evil is good, then?" I murmured.

"Sometimes, Renée. In evil, there is a saving humility. Villon is very righteous, and Baudelaire is a saint!"

I mulled over that Manichean doctrine confusedly. Palmyre, her head tilted back, sphinx-like and voluptuous, watched me

through half-closed eyelids. Her mouth curled into an uniden-
tifiable expression: a smile, a threat, an appeal, an invocation or
a curse.

I left that ethical terrain replete with potholes. "What about
your enemy?"

"I don't think he hopes to moralize me by threats, for I'm
not at all docile."

"What, then?"

"There will be a fight. I have my moments of weakness, but
you've reinvigorated me. Nevertheless you ought not to be unaware of the danger."

"I believe that I've proved—again—that fear and I never
share the same bed."

"You talk well! We'll give the finger to the hostile entity. If
it's another sorcerer, let him beware! If it's a being or a force
from beyond, I'll devise traps—and the Triple Hecate"—she
laughed—"will serve me."[1]

"The famous female toad of the Eleusinians?"

"Oh, you know that? Yes, she's the Astarte of the initiates of
old, the daughter and enemy of Baal."

The doorbell of the apartment sounded its discordant and
fluid notes.

"Let's not lose sight of the clientele, Renée. Come with me,
and always remain to the visitor's left."

---

1 The phrase "triple Hecate," popularized by Shakespeare in *A Midsummer
Night's Dream*, recognizes that the original Thracian deity—who probably
was featured in various mystic rites, though not as a toad—was fused with
other Graeco-Roman goddesses, becoming identified with the earthly
Artemis/Diana, the lunar Selene/Phoebe and the queen of the Underworld,
Persephone/Proserpine. Hesiod identifies her as a daughter of Zeus and
benevolent goddess, but her name became associated with witchcraft in
Greek and Roman literature, perhaps by virtue of confusion with another
mythical individual of the same name, the daughter of Perses, who was a
notorious magician and poisoner. Shakespeare (who might, unlike Palmyre,
have been able to distinguish the two) refers to the other Hecate as "pale
Hecate" in *Macbeth*, representing her as the patroness of sorceresses.

*

It was a gracious woman, young and irrational, who had come to seek Palmyre's help. Her lover, after having shown her unequivocal signs of love for three months, had already shown slight signs of coldness; now he was utterly icy. She wanted a talisman to bring him back and to ensure that he would never leave her.

Palmyre listened patiently to the young woman's tangled explanations. In a voice that appeared to disconcert her clients, so cold and indifferent was it, she said: "Give me your hand."

The woman extended her right hand.

"The left!"

Palmyre affected scorn. She darted a malevolent glance at the interlacing lines covering the smooth and perfumed palm; then, extending her arm nonchalantly to reach behind her, she picked up a little triangular dagger, extremely slender with a needle-sharp point. She followed the lines with the point.

"Parallelism here, rupture there, the two lines confused. An accident here, two or three months . . ."

The young woman, whose hand was trembling under the contact of the sharpened steel manipulated by the witch, seemingly inattentively, started in approving astonishment. "An automobile accident."

Sharply, Palmyre commanded: "Keep your hand still, I beg you. This dagger is poisoned, and you'll hurt yourself."

Petrified, the client turned the color of old wax, her nostrils fluttering.

Then Palmyre got up, threw the dagger forwards, over the head of the terrified young woman, and when it fixed itself in a block of wood with a biting sound, she said, authoritatively: "Two thousand francs. Within five days he'll be your lover again. Four thousand, and I'll assure you four years of love, during which he'll be impotent with any other woman than you." She signaled to me to come with her. "In two minutes, Madame, a servant will come to bring you to the laboratory, where we shall do what is necessary."

We went out. As soon as we were outside, Palmyre burst out laughing. "What a hold one has over them, eh, the clients? She'll go ahead, and we'll perform a little mechanical magic. You'll see things you haven't seen before, Renée."

We waited for three minutes in what Palmyre called "the laboratory." It was pentagonal, oak-paneled all the way to the ceiling, with five chairs made of different woods and various strange objects that might have been a physicist's machines. The servant bought the four thousand francs, which Palmre put into her pocket, and the client was introduced.

The witch made a sign bidding her to sit on a rosewood chair, then looked her in the face as she drew nearer to her, with a kind of fascinatory authority.

"Do you want to see your friend?"

"Yes." She spoke with a fearful and sensual timidity.

"Look!"

Palmyre's hand—closed, save for the raised index finger, which bore a ring with a black pearl—described a rapid gesture in the air. It was a closed elliptical curve, inclined at forty-five degrees to the floor. The gaze of the amorous young woman plunged directly into it.

Suddenly, to my infinite amazement, the oval seemed to fill with darkness. The air within it condensed into a dense opaque mass; one might have thought that it was a liquid dancing in a shaken vase. At first, the liquid was dark in color; it brightened, becoming paler, and seemed to solidify under a strange silver light and finally settled into immobility, flat and profound.

It was a mirror.

Forms were born in the mirror: a bachelor apartment, with hunting prints on the walls, divans laden with cushions in pastel colors, and feminine lingerie thrown negligently over a blue footstool.

A man came in, tall, slim and smiling. He was clad to the waist in pink pajama trousers, with a naked torso. He sat down and lit a cigarette.

"It's him," said the young woman, with a lascivious terror. One might have thought that she was about to throw herself at the man with the bare torso, who settled down comfortably among the cushions.

But the scene took on a new aspect. Clad only in flesh-colored stockings, ardent blonde hair and a pearl necklace with three strands, a pretty girl appeared, nimble and benevolent, with a glass in her hand. She drank a dark red liquid, quickly set the glass down, and came to lie down on the divan that was already occupied . . .

At first, the two lovers played innocent games; then . . .

The deceived lover was spluttering with fury. She was still immobilized by superstitious dread, but I saw her shaking like a tree in a storm. Doubtless, no woman had ever seen and contemplated the frolics of her own lover with another in that fashion. Thirty seconds passed, slowly; then, becoming incapable of resisting her wrath, the deceived lover got to her feet and rushed at the magic mirror. She plunged her hands into it wildly, as if she intended to avenge herself upon the interlaced couple . . .

Palmyre stood up, with a cry. Too late! Caught by the mysterious surface that her hands had suddenly disturbed, the young woman seemed to sink into the evocative oval and disappear into it.

What an extraordinary sensation, absurd and yet real, was recorded by my brain, without credence, while my retinas received that testimony. A meter in front of me, an individual quietly vanished. I saw the body disappear; then there was the head, which turned terrified eyes toward me. Eventually, everything evaporated!

Shocked by horror, I perceived, without any doubt, that Palmyre's client had exited our world, our three-dimensional space, our knowable domain . . .

The mysterious oval, luminescent and agitated, congealed then, and became a bright white color. Nothing any longer survived of the young woman, who had been alive in my presence twenty seconds before.

I looked up. Backed up against the partition wall, Palmyre, arms extended, had a forehead gashed by two vertical wrinkles. I sensed that she was as tense as a bowstring. In a hissing whisper, she said: "Don't move, Renée. Don't move!"

I remained motionless, curious and frightened.

Suddenly, I distinctly saw the face of the visitor reappear in the oval, with enormous round eyes—the eyes of a nocturnal bird of prey. Then it disappeared again, after which a kind of hideous form was generated at the center of the mirror. It stretched itself out there, underwent violent contortions, and then materialized, in five seconds, and fell on to the floor. The mirror had vanished.

I recoiled against the wall, nauseated by terror.

What was there, in front of me? It was impossible to describe precisely. One might have thought that it was a cephalopod; a sort of round and convex body, to which tentacles were attached.

Two reddish eyes with large green corneas were visible in the middle of the body. The tentacles were innumerable. They seemed to be generating and vanishing incessantly. From the center of the body to the periphery the degree of reality tended toward zero. A spindle-shaped gleam was emitted along a line dividing "the thing," passing between the eyes. One might have thought that a regular spasmodic contraction was tormenting the object, the beast, the being, the body—what name could one give it? At equal intervals, the light faded and then intensified, passing from an unknown color to a degraded and liquid violet, then to a dull and effervescent red. Beneath the form, the carpet began to burn.

In a soft voice, Palmyre said: "Get out, Renée. Go as quickly as you can to the poison room"—that was a room in which one saw, quite frankly, a painting representing Brinvilliers[1] preparing her death-philters—"pick up the glass flask marked *omega* and bring it here . . ."

The door was to my left. I went out like lightning and ran to get the *omega* flask.

My mind was in a bizarre state. A curious and slightly fearful anxiety was mingled within me with a need to deny everything that I had just seen. To deny in advance, without reflection, in order subsequently to be at ease in an eventual discussion . . .

I was, however, accustomed to exact studies. If I had chosen to be a witch's secretary, rather than do something completely different, it is because I love the unexpected and the picturesque. Abel Levystar had often asked me to work for him. The experience I had already had with Dreyse was sufficient for me. Men of finance seem, at a distance, to be practicing an almost metaphysical profession, but fundamentally, it's grocery. A witch—that is someone who can add spice to quotidian labor! But with my collection of degrees, in letters, sciences, oriental languages, and so on, I could do anything I pleased. All the same, no matter how accustomed one is only to reasoning, out of respect for one's own intelligence, according to narrowly realistic principles, must one therefore deny the authentic testimony of

---

1 Marie d'Aubray, Marquise de Brinvilliers (1630-1676) was convicted of poisoning her father and two brothers, in association with her lover, in order to obtain their inheritance. The affair caused a flutter of panic that grew into a storm when the fortune-tellers of Paris were rounded up and put to the torture, one of them obliging her tormentors with a highly fanciful tale of murder and black magic, which implicated numerous courtiers, including one of the king's mistresses, and generated one of the great scandals of the era. Several literary and dramatic works were based on the case, including one by Alexandre Dumas.

the senses if it is too distressing? For those extravagant things, I had seen, seen, seen . . .

I found the flask. It was half-full of a golden yellow liquid. I grasped its rounded form and returned at a run . . .

I opened the door . . .

Where was Palmyre?

A strange scene appeared to me. At the place where the sorceress had been flattened against that wall two minutes earlier, there was no longer anything but a bright violet "aura" outlining the witch's silhouette. That aura was pulsating like a fearful heart. Violently projected into the middle of the location where Palmyre had been—where perhaps she still was—I saw three tentacles curved in opposite directions, bluish grey in color, departing from the body of the being, the beast, the form born of the mirror, the eyes of which had disappeared.

The tentacles occupied the summits of an inverted isosceles triangle, the base of which was the line connecting the breasts.

I gazed at it stupidly. The carpet was burning with short flames curved toward the door; the form, gathered together and incomprehensible, now resembled a grey-blue spindle whose limiting curves extended beyond the apartment by courtesy of the illegibility of the immediate space.

It was impossible for me to separate the real from the imaginary in the spectacle that I had before me—but was there anything real there, and what imagination was making me see that the beast was *holding* Palmyre?

I took a step forward. My foot extinguished a tongue of fire, and I felt the heat of the slowly-burning carpet rising up beneath my skirt.

I raised the flask. My hand clung to the vessel by means of a violent inward effort. I lowered my arm. The neck of the flask collided with a pentagonal mahogany table, at the center of which a hypnotic sphere was shining. The neck broke and the liquid spilled out in two spurts, which reminded me, cruelly, of two jets of blood escaping from the carotid arteries of a decapitated individual. The yellow liquid turned red as it spurted . . . and suddenly volatilized, expanding in nimbuses of rutilant vapor, with the same odor as nitric acid vapor.

I leapt backwards, sneezing. Nothing in the room had changed, and yet an instinct—a kind of knowledge emanating from the secret crypts of my conscience—told me that something mysterious was happening in front of me.

The nitrogenous, or seemingly-nitrogenous, vapors flowed in two currents that I could see clearly, one curving inwards, coming from the ground, the other horizontal, coming from straight ahead, in which I could no longer make out the wall, the aura or the tentacles.

Brutally, like the blow of a fist, I heard something heavy and soft fall, a meter away from me; then the vapors melted into the air, dissolving with incredible rapidity, and . . .

I perceived Palmyre, still pressed against the wall, eyes closed, with one arm upraised and the other twisted at the height of her groin. Her face expressed a tragic dolor.

And in front of me, lying on the floor, was the young client who had melted into the magic mirror a short while before.

The monster had evaporated.

All that bewildered me to an extent surpassing what one might call, even in the fullest sense, astonishment. Before certain spectacles, the brain records without belief, and one remains stunned before the testimony of the most certain of the five senses. That was my situation.

Meanwhile, I ran to Palmyre. The client, lying on the floor, attracted neither pity nor curiosity, but the witch, her face twisted, moved me prodigiously.

I took her by the hands. She was rigid and cold. I pulled her away from the wall, and her leg moved forward of its own accord. She retained a sense of normal progression. I guided her to the door, making sure not to trip over the foot of the supine woman.

I led Palmyre to her private studio. There I sat her down. I observed then that from the breasts down her black silk dress was burned a star shape—a burn similar to those on the carpet over which "the beast" had been crawling a little while ago.

I knew where to find a cordial that Palmyre had told me to use in her times of depression. I searched for it, took it in hand, and filled a glass, which I brought to the witch's lips. She drank, with difficulty, and then opened her eyes. I recognized that she had returned to normality, or nearly so. The contortion in her pain-stricken mouth eased.

"Renée," she said to me, "go and lock all the doors to the corridors leading to the room back there."

I went to do that without waiting for any further instruction. It was evidently necessary to prevent the servants from entering the pentagon in which the client was lying.

When I came back, Palmyre, naked save for white crepe underwear, was putting on a new dress similar to the one that she had been wearing before. I saw that her breasts were scored with white-tipped scratches.

Without hiding my astonishment, I said: "That needs some liniment . . ."

She nodded affirmatively and murmured: "Bring me the little pharmaceutical box in black wood. The small one—the one in the large laboratory."

I brought the box. Palmyre took out an unguent and some cotton wool. She dressed her wounds.

"It's nothing! Five days at the most. If you'd been two minutes later, mind . . ."

I had twenty, fifty, a hundred questions on my lips. I did not know how to start, and gazed at her with loving curiosity.

"Will you get me another glass of cordial?"

I did as she asked.

"Drink some yourself."

I drank.

"There! We'll be able to talk about what you've seen. You're frightened, aren't you?"

I formed a half-smile of agreement, then said: "What about her, back there?"

Palmyre raised an index-finger and shook her head. "Finished!"

"But . . ."

"Don't worry, Renée. She can no longer truly resume a durable and ordinary existence, but there's still enough life in her for me to send her away on her own, like a thinking being. The street, the carriages, the tramway . . . she won't die here . . ."

An icy cold descended from the top of my head to my temples, and from there to my jaws and shoulders. The manner in which Palmyre spoke seemed to me so atrociously criminal that I lowered my eyes, for fear that she would read my sentiment therein. She breathed in slowly, smiled at some unknown idea, and then turned to the window where dusk was falling. Out there, near the gable of a building, a massive moon was visible, with the hue of pale flesh. Palmyre pointed at it. "My protectress!"

There was a brief silence.

Softly, she said: "Baal! Baal!" To that name she added unknown words that sounded like a prayer. Then she reverted to comprehensible speech. "Renée, have you ever seen or imagined that a being from a plane other than ours, our world of three-dimensions, folded by time . . . have you ever imagined that an occult, magical, extraterrestrial being might love a mortal?"

I made no reply.

"Well, as the Bible says—and all other religions too—it happens. You've just seen a monster from beyond attempt to . . . yes, Renée, you saved me! I don't know what would have happened without you. I can't know. We're entering here into a domain in which my mode of comprehension ceases to be valid. That . . . love . . . still remains a mystery to me. That's what explains the occult hatred that is following me. In this matter, though, what one explains remains inexplicable.

"What is this being? What is it doing here? What does it want from me? Is it even a being? Is it a product of the Earth or is it returning thereto? So many questions. That's what is multiplying these serial echoes of my will that initiates call repercussions. But why? How did I come to be known and indentified by it . . . or him?

"It took advantage of the magic mirror to act on our plane. That's evidence of a sort of intelligence equal to ours . . . except that no other being—so far as I know—has found, by inverse operation, a means of passing into our world from the world of the superior dimension."

"But what does the mirror do, here?" I said.

"The mirror is a reality, Renée—a reality that emerges from the normal dimensions. Do you understand? It participates in two worlds—a looking-glass into the beyond."

"I don't know whether I understand . . ."

"Listen. If you cut a line, the section of the line is a point; if you cut a plane, the section is a line; if you cut a volume, the section is a surface; if you cut . . . a four-dimensional reality . . . the section is a volume, but a volume with two of our dimensions and one of the beyond. If you place that volume in the time axis, you have the magic mirror. It's sufficient that it be polarized according to the secret thought of the person to whom you offer it for you to be able to see . . . in space and time . . ."

"How can I picture a volume that creates a section of a superior space in the time axis? It's obscure!"

"But Renée, outside of the three dimensions, it's thought alone that is action and reality. Placing it in the time axis is simply giving it the movement of thought . . ."

I remained mute. The explanation seemed deceptive in its simplicity.

Palmyre went on: "Imagine that the volume which is the section of a plane by a four-dimensional surface is, in human terms, a plane—which is the mirror—and at the same time a volume, which is to say, a fragment of space limited by the imaginative extension of a human thought obedient to duration. Its third dimension isn't terrestrial."

"But what is our seducer—the other-worldly individual who wants to take you as a man might—doing? How can the notion of love extend unchanged beyond conceivable reality?"

"You're accumulating too many questions, Renée. The individual, as you put it, appears to belong to a dimension of space superior to ours, and must also live in time, but I know nothing about it. Perhaps it's transversal to time..."

"Then Einstein, and his equations in which t is the fourth dimension...?"

"Don't digress, Renée! I'm far from knowing everything, and perhaps the word *know* signifies nothing in this respect. In any case, the magic mirror gave the entity you call my 'seducer' a means of passing from its own world to ours. It took advantage of it."

"How?"

"By virtue of the imbecility of the little woman who threw herself at her lover, at the actual image of her lover. The being captured the poor woman's vital force—her existence, her life—in the intermediary space and immediately manifested itself, as it was able to do, in the form, the aspect and the elements that it was able to extract from that human reality, momentarily dissolved and transported between two worlds, which it recreated in its own fashion."

"Then it's not that sort of octopus, as we saw it, in its life outside the world?"

"No—the octopus was, in a sense, the three-dimensional section of that life-form from an external dimension. In sum, that cephalopod with a hundred tentacles, real as it was—and

I'm fully aware of its reality, since it . . . the octopus in question is a sort of symbol, a concept. Over and above three dimensions, the reality that lives beyond can only be, materially, an idea, if I might put it that way. A nominal reality . . . the words are lacking, Renée . . ."

"But which can make love—sexual love—in a matter more abstract, in spite of its concrete verity, than the most transcendental mathematics?"

"Oh, Renée, that's what I don't know. There are many hypotheses—if that word can even be employed here—but the two most acceptable are, firstly, that the creatures of the hypercosmos have already participated in human life and retained violent passions by virtue of having known them—which is explicable in terms of metempsychosis, or the alternative supposition that the 'beast' has desires and the power to satisfy them, tragically—and secondly, that sexuality might be conceived as a phenomenon so absolute, so philosophical, that the entities of the superior worlds participate in it . . . and all its consequences. It's difficult to admit, but . . ."

"Sexuality isn't love. Besides, Freud has clearly established the origin of the sexual in the genital. Amorous pleasure is linked to the organism; it's inconceivable that without the *ad hoc* organs . . ."

"Yes. But what can I say? Each of our actions undoubtedly has cosmic repercussions, especially the act that humans repeat indefatigably without wearying of it—the act of love. Perhaps, therefore, our sexual enjoyment corresponds to a creation, or to a formation in unknown worlds in which it echoes. Who knows its essence? Who has penetrated its mystery? No one! Thus I might imagine that there is always a sensual vibrato in the beyond, a subtle, effervescent and profound burning sensation that is perhaps not unconnected with the universal activity of things, to atomic feverishness, to that incomprehensible Brownian motion, to radioactivity, to . . . where does it end,

Renée? Perhaps a hectic lover, flexing in the grip and delirium of joy in her fever, is setting fire to distant suns and causing them to rotate."

"What folly! Moving from possibility to possibility, one ends up with formulae whose reasoned connection is ungraspable . . ."

"Everything and nothing is ungraspable, Renée. Love, which so many imbeciles—generations of imbeciles—have tried to localize and hide, in the body as in the mind, is undoubtedly the sole reality that dominates the real, which explains it, and which emerges from the life of absurdity founded on fabricated antinomies. Besides, I've always believed that intelligence is a sexual phenomenon, a form of the joy that closes the act . . .

"Perhaps there's nothing else, fundamentally, in our world and beyond. Like the shadows in Plato's cave, everything would then be a moving, formless, changing reflection of love—not of the idea of love, which is nothing, but of the act of love, of contacts that give birth to the extenuating folly around which, in spite of the social lie, all societies live, and which persists after the death of individuals."

"Tell me, then, is the cult of Priapus the only one that humans have conceived in conformity with the absolute?" I smiled—but Palmyre remained serious.

"Renée, I don't seek explanations in religion. *Everyone worships Priapus*, without intending to, spontaneously. But I'm trying, by means of observations whose fragility is as apparent to me as to you, to verbalize an outline of things—an outline in conformity with what I know better than others, which takes account of what I have seen, and what I imagine as I gaze through the mysterious portals that I almost passed through a little while ago . . ."

"We're both accumulating—for I'm following you closely in these crazy ideas—and piling up what rational people call contradictory ideas. Aren't we making a sort of mythology? I'd like to be able to explain what just happened without trampling all reason, all logic and all causal connection."

Palmyre got to her feet. In her white face, the lips were a passionate and luminescent red. She sat down on a table, her legs dangling and swinging.

"So, Renée, you, who are an educated woman, continue to accept the vain prejudices that have been baptized as reason? You believe that human logic is an entity, not a game, like the rules of poker?"

I picked out the word *prejudices*. "All the same, the principle of identity isn't a prejudice, wouldn't you say?"

She laughed, applying her hands to her burned breasts. She was beautiful, attractive and demonic. A kind of lasciviousness emanated from all the gestures with which she emphasized the most abstract formulae. Ideas fell from her supple mouth like kisses.

"Oh, René, you're fit for whipping, for burning alive—but everything in the mind is prejudice! What? The idea has never occurred to you, while reading *The Critique of Pure Reason*, that the famous categories of understanding, of space and time, can't be homogeneous . . . but if space and time aren't homogeneous—and they certainly aren't—what becomes of knowledge of the world? And is the world itself definable?

"Look, suppose that the world is a sphere in which time, duration, follows the law of extension—of surfaces or volumes, or anything you please—and that duration follows a law of reduction of activity like that of Newtonian universal attraction. What would a spherical world thus realized be like? It would disconcert all laws. You see, if you take two points, A and B, on a radius of that sphere, the distance measured in duration would not be the same from A to B as from B to A. Please note here the disappearance of your cherished principle of identity. Note too that from the center, where duration is fixed, to the periphery, where duration is infinite, one ought to conceive of the radius as a circular symbol, for infinite duration is equal to zero duration. In consequence, the radius of my sphere is a curve. How many dimensions would a being living on that sphere have? Three, four, six?"

She laughed joyfully, and I saw her abdomen oscillate along with the relaxations of her diaphragm.

"Do you think, Renée, that it's sufficient to find a rational application of the rather bold concepts of metaphysical mathematics to kill all the old so-called scientific prejudices? Oh, the heterogeneity of time and space—what curious things! And the notion of continuity too, when attacked, makes people despair. And yet, the notion of continuity and that of homogeneity, if one reduces them, abolish all geometry, the science that is, in a sense, the very criterion of evidence. No, Renée, today's science is not a science. It is to that of the future what ours was twenty thousand years ago. Personally, I anticipate that it will soon be necessary to introduce the notion of quality into that of space, which is nothing but quantity by definition, according to the stupid: the notions of degree and order are necessary in space and time, and that of displacement, or of groups in duration. Then, the absurdities of magic, stripped in advance of their anthropomorphism, will become normal, and no one will any longer laugh at the possibility of a living and passionate being issuing from transcendental spaces and appearing to us here, just as no one today laughs at the most paradoxical laws of optics or hydrostatics."

Suddenly, though, her laughter froze. She stood up.

"I need to get rid of the late client. Stay here, Renée. It will take me twenty minutes—it's a terrible and dangerous business. I'd rather you didn't see it."

She went out, tranquil and indolent. Immediately, I caught sight of the satin sheath-dress with the triangular burns. The irregular stars of the burns were quite clear. They were slightly red on the underside; a little blood had leaked out beneath them.

I sat down to reflect. Discussion with Palmyre could not lead to any conclusion, for, entrenched in the undergrowth of transcendences, she could defy all assaults. But I did not have her facility in dealing with the Chinese puzzles of metaphysics, and preferred to restrict myself to what I had seen. It was necessary to accommodate all of it within the customary framework of my reason.

Had I actually seen those things? Yes! There was no possible hesitation. I had seen; I had not had a hallucination, nor had I been plunged into one of those "secondary states" that remove all value from testimony.

Suddenly—without, I presume, anyone touching the door through which Palmyre had gone out—I saw the heavy panel open, as if powerfully pushed. A gust of air surrounded me with a cold contact. My blood experienced the flight from the skin toward the heart produced by a cold shower, and with an indescribable emotion, of an overwhelming violence, I came to my feet . . .

A sort of icy cascade descended along my spine. On my head I felt exactly what the word "horripilation" signifies, and a girdle tightened about my waist, rising upwards.

At the door, an apparition became manifest: a sort of pale and transparent shadow that was—that had to be—Palmyre. The electric light went out at the same time, and silence fell: a new silence, an otherworldly silence, which covered up the anterior human silence.

No matter how self-controlled one is, there are spectacles that give one gooseflesh. I stood there panting, in front of the open doorway, blocked by the phantom, which stood out against the faint glare of the corridor, itself illuminated by the light of a transverse corridor in which two lamps were hanging from the ceiling in front of two neighboring doors to the right and the left. Then, in the corridor, emerging from the invisible part, and clearly illuminated. I saw Palmyre's "client" leaving . . .

Horrified, I tucked in my elbows and my knees, as a sort of contractile terror gripped me, during which, with an automatic tread, the young dead woman disappeared again into the corridor that intersected the one facing me at right angles. I had, however, had the time to read on her face, forever mute, that the thinking being, the life—the secret and mysterious thing that animates all earthly existence, in sum—had disappeared from the body that a demonic power maintained upright and in motion, as if . . .

Behind the marching body, Palmyre appeared—a Palmyre that I had never seen before, clad in a sort of clinging white coat of mail, with a luminous emanation at the ends of her arms, extended toward the woman's back.

Palmyre did not look at me. She disappeared immediately into the transverse corridor—but a luminous wake followed her. I thought I could detect the profile of the mysterious monster: the cephalopod with the obscure eyes; the strange being that had come from the other world to possess the frightening and satanic witch. Was it still following her?

That idea made me retreat to the closed window. I opened it with a reflexive gesture, to get out of that crazed atmosphere . . .

The air came in, gentle and fluid. I breathed it in voluptuously.

Then, in the bitumen sky effaced by cloud, the moon appeared. It was red, bloated and heavy. It seemed to me to be an obscene and malevolent idol.

In the avenue, launching its wild and quavering cry at the moon, a dog began to howl . . .

THE SECT OF ETERNAL OLD MEN

by René Thimmy

IT was a Sunday afternoon. Eleuthère had given me a rendez-vous and I knew, in addition, that he was interrupting his studies that day and consecrating it to repose, like a good little employee.

"I'm going to take advantage of the good weather," he told me, "to show you that even around the most ordinary things, in the most frequented places, mystery doesn't lose its rights. It's all a matter of revealing its presence."

Monsieur K*** had taken his hat and he knotted his silk scarf over his breast carefully.

"I'm like the Comte de Saint-Germain," he told me. "I at-tach great importance to cold and try to protect myself from it."

"The Comte de Saint-Germain?"

"Yes, the immortal Saint-Germain The Comte de Sant-Germain has only been able to attain the very advanced age at which he has arrived"—at this point Eleuthère K*** counted on his fingers and appeared to reflect—"two hundred and fifty-six years, almost exactly, because he has constantly protected him-self against cold with meticulous care. There is no science and no method of respiration that prevents the lungs being fragile."

"You think that the Comte de Saint-Germain is still alive?" I asked, eagerly, for I had always been passionately interested in that curious historical figure, who has already become legendary.

Eleuthère K***'s only response was a smile. "One of these days I'll tell you what I know about him, and as chance would have it, I know a great deal."

I saw him put on his spectacles and unhook a calendar that was hanging on the wall. He looked at the table of the phases of the moon.

"Ah! You're in luck. It's the evening of the full moon."

I was about to ask him what connection there was between my luck and the evolutions of the moon in the sky, but he drew me outside.

"We're going to the Bois," he said.

We were not pressed for time. We climbed into an autobus, and then another, and when we arrived at the Porte Dauphine we mingled with a crowd of people.

While chatting, Monsieur K*** drew me toward a determined goal.

I dared not ask my guide too many questions. What the devil were we going to do in the Bois? Like every Parisian I knew that very profane mysteries are practiced there, or were practiced there before the intervention of the police, but they did not belong to the genre that interested me.

"Patience!" whispered Eleuthère K***, who divined my curiosity. "You're going to see that the fount of youth can sometimes be replaced by the trees of youth.

"You can see verdant trees around you," he continued, "And you might think that they all have the same value, the same power, from the human point of view? Well, nothing of the sort. Among those trees there are leaders and masters, and there's the ordinary crowd. There are also some that are a source of life for the human race, from which one can draw health, even longevity, and which give it directly. At last, there are people who claim that . . ."

"Vegetables do, indeed, furnish remedies . . ."

"No, no, it's not a matter of that. It's not for the exposition of such a simple truth that I've bought you under the acacias of the Bois de Boulogne. I want to show you the trees of life, the god-trees."

I thought immediately about some worship rendered to trees. I pronounced the name of the druids.

Monsieur K*** shrugged his shoulders.

"People only think about the future life as a luxury. The immortality of the soul is a luxury. In reality, they only think about this life, the life in which they eat and drink, and they only think about prolonging it for as long as possible. Life! Everything is there. Everyone wants to live for as long as he can, and for that, they're ready for the most insensate practices."

We had reached the lake and were going along it on the right. We covered another two hundred meters in the midst of innumerable strollers attracted by the mildness of the spring sunshine. To the left there is an immense fir tree surrounded by iron railings, and then a meadow with a wood of lindens that seem to have been planted in the same epoch, for their size is almost identical.

"You see those linden trees," said Monsieur K***. "They're perfectly ordinary trees, at least in appearance. And yet, they're magical trees."

"They don't have the appearance of it, and those children playing at their feet don't appear to have the slightest consciousness of their supernatural influence, if they have one."

"We're unaware of it," replied Monsieur K***. "We don't know the occult reason that brought them here."

Children were running hither and yon.

"Anyway," said Monsieur K***, "it's not a matter of all that youth, but rather of old men."

He drew me a few paces further on. "Consider that centenarian aspen that has two young oaks beside it, and those chestnut trees to the right and the left. There's mistletoe on the aspen. The centenarian aspen, the oaks and the chestnuts could, strictly speaking, with a little good will, form the design of a cross. Evidently, it would be better if it were well-designed. It isn't; but it's very difficult to find trees forming a regular cross in the Bois de Boulogne."

I was surprised, and, above all, disappointed. Monsieur K*** took me to the Porte Dauphine.

"Yes, that's all, for the moment. But wait; we'll doubtless come back this evening if, as I suppose, special rites are practiced in this place. I wanted to enable you to see, beforehand, the décor of the ceremony, to show you how ordinary it is and that it doesn't reveal any particularity in itself."

It was agreed that we would dine together and that, in the evening, Monsieur K*** would take me to the center of a sect to which he gave the name, familiarly, of the sect of eternal old men. That was what they called themselves intimately, but they were known to a small number of initiates by the name of vitalists.

It was a rare and special favor to take me there, for the sect was secret, in principle, and only comprised seven members.

"Seven eternal old men, seven trees," K*** told me, with a smile that I did not know how to interpret, for there was both doubt and a hint of respect on his lips. "Oh, life! How attached men are to life! There are some who, like those, consecrate all their activity to it, all their thoughts to the prolongation of an existence that is sometimes very unhappy. Some have confidence in amour, in medicine, what do I know? These make their entire life depend on trees."

"Are you part of this sect?" I asked, while we dined in a restaurant in the Place Clichy.

"No, certainly not; firstly, because I don't believe sufficiently in the initial principle that directs them. I don't believe in it, and yet . . . Secondly, I don't have sufficient love of life to make as many sacrifices. Then again, there's an inconvenience, a strange inconvenience. Look at the hand and neck of the person to whose house we're going; and if she shows him to us, look at her child, the youngest one, very carefully."

I knew that K***, in spite of his great seriousness, did not detest surprises, and that he took pleasure in contriving little *coups de théâtre* that he had prepared.

"It's eight o'clock," he said to me, "and the vitalists go to bed early when the care of their life permits them to go to bed. But I think that this evening—the evening of the full moon—they'll stay up late."

We went up the Rue Lepic, turned right, climbed the stairway of a house and stopped at a third floor that had nothing remarkable about it.

Monsieur Durand—he bore a name very similar to that one—came to open the door, a lamp in his hand.

While K*** exchanged amicable words with him and tried, by making an eulogy of my erudition in occultism, to excuse himself for having brought me. I remembered his recommendation and studied the hand that was holding the lamp.

I nearly uttered an exclamation of surprise. Monsieur Durand was prodigiously hairy, as hairy as few men can be. The entire external part of his hand was covered with a long black down, and long hairs were protruding from his sleeves and invading his wrists.

A second sufficed to perceive all the details of a strange thing. I noticed that the hairs covering Monsieur Durand's wrists and hand had a very peculiar characteristic. They were not normal human hairs. They had a sort of vegetable appearance.

At the same moment, a door opened and a lady, who was carrying a very young child, appeared in the doorway and disappeared again, without having been able to suppress a gesture of astonishment at the sight of us. Before then, however, I had perceived the child—by surprise, doubtless, for his mother must not have heard us ring the doorbell. He was entirely covered in a light down, a down that did not belong to that of hair, a down that made one think of plant growth, the growth of thick grass.

We were taken into a modest dining room and invited to sit down, with an extreme politeness.

Monsieur Durand must have attained sixty years of age. His face was clean shaven with an extreme care that betrayed a desperate struggle in itself. Looking at him with great attention, I was able to observe that he must have shaved his forehead, and even his nose.

At K***'s request he turned to me and talked about his group without any embarrassment.

"We're not a secret society," he told me—Monsieur K*** smiled—"we're a society that has limited the number of its members to seven: seven old men who simply have in common their desire to prolong their lives . . . which is quite natural, isn't it? And as there is a very knowledgeable biologist among us, and two physicians, and we all have curious minds, they make us party to their research, their discoveries and their hypotheses."

"And that's all?"

"Almost. I said seven old men; that's not entirely accurate. There's a young man among us. He's the son of our friend and master, the great V***."

His voice had taken on a hint of respect. I interrogated his eyes. "The members of your group can die, then?" I said, smiling.

"Yes, they can. We don't hope, at least for the moment, to avoid death entirely. We only struggle to delay it, but we hope—and, of course, we impart of that hope to a small number of people capable of understanding us—to arrive at delaying it almost indefinitely.

There was undoubtedly a dubious expression on my face.

"Why not?" Durand went on. "The human body is normally organized to attain two centuries, or two and a half. If we don't attain that number of years it's because we don't live in accordance with natural law. Monsieur K*** must have talked to you about masters who live in Tibet, the founders of the theosophical society, whose existence is not in doubt, having been attested by a host of people of good faith who have known them. Several have arrived at two hundred years of existence without having any of the inconveniences or failings of old age."

"Yes, but you're talking about sages with a rule of life very different from ours. Can one, in the vibrant atmosphere of Paris . . . ?"

"Evidently; and that is our secret. Thanks to our method, the method discovered by the master V***, who was unfortunately unable to perfect it while he was alive, we think we can prolong human life to unexpected limits, even in Paris, even without leading a special life of privations and asceticism."

At that moment, someone rang. Monsieur Durand got up in order to open the door, and I heard several people arriving at the same time. There were murmurs and deliberations in the antechamber.

The doorbell resounded again, and in a few minutes all the members of what K*** called the sect of eternal old men had gathered in the dining room, where we were. They were all bearded and hairy, but those beards and hair had a hint of brushwood about them, which differentiated them from ordinary pilosity.

The vitalists were taciturn, and scrupulously polite in my regard. The general conversation was interrupted by heavy silences. They talked about their method of vitalism, which they depicted as an ordinary procedure analogous to those of Doctor Durville or Mazdaznan.[1] That method, they said, had

---

1 The first reference is probably to the occultist and magnetizer Hector Durville (1849-1923), the director of the *Journal of Magnetism* and founder of the Eudiaque Order, a society whose initiates allegedly worked toward the "magnification" of human being. His three sons, Henri, Gaston, and André, carried on his work, publishing abundantly in the field of "naturist healing" and founding the magazine *La Vie Sage*. Mazdaznan is a religion invented

for a principle the force of solar radiation and the decomposition of those rays, individually adapted.

All that had nothing very new. One of the bearded men, more ingenious than the others, let himself go momentarily in talking about the influence of lunar rays. Imperceptible signs and irritated glances informed him that he had just embarked on a path forbidden to the profane. He lowered his head and did not say anything more.

The embarrassment increased. In order to dissipate it, Monsieur Durand offered us an old walnut liqueur that reminded me of the provincial evenings of my childhood.

Habituated as I might be by my profession as a journalist to vanquish ill humor caused by obligatory indiscretions, I understood that it was necessary to leave. I made a sign to K***, who got up immediately.

Everyone then became amiable again. We took our leave and departed.

I was disappointed, but K*** immediately put his hand on my shoulder.

"Nothing is lost," he said. "You've seen the seven eternal old men—six old men and one young one. I hoped that they would expose their theories and their rites to you; they haven't done that. I'll summarize the theory briefly and in a moment, you'll see it put into practice."

He hailed a taxi, which deposited us in the Bois, on the road going alongside the lake to the left, a little before the entrance to the restaurant pavilion, now closed. It must have been shortly after midnight. K*** looked at the sky several times.

---

during the Occult Revival by one Otto Hansch, alias Ottoman Zar-Adushi Ha'nish, and supposedly reviving a sixth-century variant of the Zoroastrian religion, which promotes vegetarianism and physical and breathing exercises in the promotion of health and longevity. The cult continued to thrive after its founder's death in 1936, and enjoyed a new surge of fashionability in California in the heyday of the late-sixties "counter-culture."

"The moon will soon be at its zenith. It's an indispensable condition for the seven old men to accomplish their ceremonies efficaciously. And that won't be without some complication for them. It's necessary that the place be deserted and that no one comes to ask them to explain what they're doing."

We walked back and forth for a good half hour. At that time of night, the Bois is entirely deserted. It is only troubled, in general, by the kind of demi-orgy that recalls, in the heart of the twentieth century, the frolics of ancient mythology. As they require a rather elevated temperature, which that mild spring night did not yet provide, everything was tranquil in the amicable lunar silence.

"There they are!" exclaimed K***, suddenly.

He drew me to the right side of the road immediately adjacent to the lake.

"They" were, indeed, arriving, in small groups. Two of them had taken a taxi, whose engine we could hear purring some distance away. They had assembled rapidly not far from the centenarian aspen covered with mistletoe that K*** had pointed out to me during the afternoon.

To begin with, they darted anxious circular glances around; but the surroundings were deserted. K*** and I were hiding as best we could.

That went on for some time. Then, finally reassured, the vitalists gathered around the aspen. They had a slight alarm then. Voices resounded some distance way, and two cyclists glided slowly along the path. That provoked a temporary dispersal on the part of the vitalists; but the newcomers, doubtless thinking that it was a matter of nocturnal prowlers, accelerated rapidly.

I looked in the direction of the old aspen. The seven old men—one of whom was young—had disposed themselves in a cross and I seemed to recognize the one in the middle, thanks to his small stature, as Monsieur Durand.

Then I thought I perceived a few sounds, a murmur of alternated words, like a chanted prayer—a prayer sometimes punctuated by a suppliant cry—and I saw that the seven men had begun to walk slowly around the trees.

Gradually, their pace increased, as the prayer became more rhythmic.

"Let's move closer," I said to K***.

And, like redskins on the warpath, we slid from tree to tree. The road was deserted. The vitalists were favored by chance.

"Do you know what they're chanting?" I asked.

"I believe it's a prayer in the Phoenician language, very ancient, the exact meaning of which they don't know. It's a prayer to the moon, to ask it to give its strength to the vegetal realm and permit that strength to be transferred to humans."

"Phoenician?"

"I've had the text before my eyes. Perhaps it's the primitive language of the first Carthaginians. I've been able to recover myself the traces of a Carthaginian magic that reposes on the more or less transmissible strength of trees. The African coasts of the Mediterranean were once covered by immense forests, and the rites that were celebrated then at the water's edge not far from Carthage, under the fabulous trees about which Pliny talks, can't have lacked grandeur.

I remarked to K*** that in the infinitely more modest frame of the Bois de Boulogne, seven bearded and hairy men, marching in the light of the full moon and singing a bizarre chant in an unknown language, presented, if not grandeur, at least something uncommonly picturesque.

But the seven men were going increasingly rapidly. Sometimes they stopped, and I saw them embrace, by turns, the aspen, the two oaks that were next to them, and the four chestnut trees whose ensemble made the design of a cross.

We were doing our best to stay hidden. No one passed by. The chant became faster, and suddenly, the seven voices were only one. A strange sound, profound and almost desperate, emerged from the seven throats. It was a long, dolorous note, which, because of the place and the solitude, became terrible.

"Baloeth! Baloeth!" I seemed to hear.

K*** whispered in my ear: "The power of sound! It's the rhythm contained in the syllables of the name of the moon that causes the force of the planet to descend—at least, the members of the sect are convinced of it—and its action upon the trees."

The seven old men were no longer moving. K*** tugged my sleeve.

"That's all. We have nothing more to do but go. Even if they perceive our silhouettes, they won't risk following us in order to determine our identity."

We walked in silence to the Porte Dauphine.

"I'd like to know," I said, "in what exact measure the seven vitalist old men are working to become eternal by spending the nights of the full moon in that strange fashion. Do these ceremonies correspond to something real, and do those who practice them have chances of living much longer than you or me? What's your opinion?"

"I can't respond to you exactly. Does one ever know the ultimate cause and the succession of effects? For a start, the imagination plays such a great role! A man who thinks about the prolongation of his life and performs rites for that, in which he has confidence, will certainly succeed in extending his life by virtue of that confidence. Perhaps the seven old men would have the same chance of eternity by circling around telegraph poles at midnight."

"I share that opinion."

"Wait. For the case that concerns us, there is nevertheless one particular, certain and visible fact, which is that all the members of the sect are hairy, in an abnormal fashion, and that the hairs of their beard and tresses have a vegetal character that bears a closer resemblance to grass than ordinary hair and beards. Monsieur Durand became the parent of the child that you saw three yeas ago, immediately after he began to practice the method of Monsieur V***. That's at least significant. Now, if we consider the magic in which all the philosophers of antiquity believed, why should we not think that the vitalists have a method that permits, in a certain measure, the transfusion into them of life?

"Think about it. The seven of them form a perfect magical chain. Thanks to a rite unknown to us, they create between seven determined trees another magical chain. They connect the two chains and, by means of the force of appeal, at the moment when the moon is at its zenith and at its greatest power of action, they obtain the descent of its force. It is that force which ought to cause vegetal life to flow into human life. In addition, that sect has a sister sect that seeks by other methods to attain the prolongation of existence by means of animal vitality."

K*** must have seen my gaze shining with interest. He stopped, and reflected for a few seconds.

"The sect of which I speak is not limited in its number to seven, and I believe that its practices are horrible; so it is secret. I don't know whether the full moon plays a role, but what I do know is that the principle consists of drinking the blood of a living animal, the blood that flows from a lacerated body. There is a magical chant that must be chanted while the blood is being drunk. That sect existed before the other and that its center in an artist's studio situated in the former Passage Gourdon,[1] now baptized differently, and which opens on to the Faubourg Saint-Jacques. Does it still exist? That's what I can't tell you . . ."

---

1 The Passage Gourdon, built on top of one of the many quarries forming the so-called catacombs of Paris, famously collapsed in 1879. The Villa Saint-Jacques, now a restaurant, was built on the site.

ABOUT THE AUTHORS

THÉODORE DE BANVILLE (1823-1891) was a greatly respected poet who published his early work before the 1848 Revolution, and then joined forces with Catulle Mendès to stimulate a Romantic revival after the damage inflicted on the Movement during the Second Empire. He also wrote plays, but in order to make a living became a prolific writer of short fiction for *Gil Blas*, one of the new newspapers that multiplied after 1880, when new technologies of printing and paper-making facilitated a boom. Most of his work in that medium was naturalistic, but he contributed a notable series of fifty *contes fantastiques* in 1880-81, reprinted in book form as *Contes féeriques* (1882; tr. as *Magical Tales*) Most of them featured his own brand of *fées*, but he also recruited many other motifs that were later to become standardized, inevitably borrowing ideas from occultists and previous works of occult fiction, always seeking to reassess the ideas they contained in his own idiosyncratic fashion.

JULES BOIS (1868-1943), who sometimes rendered his name as Henri-Antoine Jules-Bois, first obtained literary success with the "esoteric drama" *Les Noces de Sathan* (1890), and his further ventures in occultism included a survey of *Le Satanisme et la magie* (1896). His feminist works, including *L'Eve nouvelle* (1894), anticipate an end of anthropocentrism and the genesis of a new woman. He published extensively in *La Nouvelle Revue* whose founder and first editor, Juliette Adam (1836-1936), wrote on occult subjects herself; Papus reprinted her *Un Rêve sur le divin* (1888) in *L'Initiation*. Bois' contributions included the serial novel *Le Vaisseau des caresses* (1907; book 1908). "Le Succube," was first published in the 13 February 1893 issue of the newspaper *Gil Blas*; the translation appears here for the first time.

FRÉDÉRIC BOUTET (1874-1941) became one of the most prolific writers of short fiction for newspapers, following in the tracks first laid down by Théodore de Banville, often venturing into fantastic fiction in the early stages of his career and similarly becoming a significant but unsung precursor of surrealism. He was one of the consultants listed in the literary section of *L'Initiation* and his first collection of short fiction, *Contes dans a nuit* (1898; tr. in *The Antisocial Man and Other Strange Stories*, 2013), from which "Like Children Who Run After a Mask" is taken, was issued by the specialist occult publisher Chamuel. Although his involvement with occultism appears to have been brief and his engagement with fantastic fiction did not long survive the ebb-tide of fashion that largely banished such material from newspapers after the turn of the century, his contributions to the genre are admirably inventive; further examples are translated in *The Voyage of Julius Pingouin and Other Strange Stories* (2013) and *Claude Mercoeur's Reflection and Other Strange Stories* (2013).

ÉDOUARD DUJARDIN (1861-1949) is nowadays remembered as one of the pioneers of "stream-of-conciousness" narrative, in his novel *Les Lauriers sont coupé* (tr. as *We'll to the Woods No More*), serialized in 1887 in the *Revue Indépendante* shortly after he acquired the co-editorship of the periodical with Téodor de Wyzewa, and foreshadowed in the short stories collected in *Les Hantises* (1886; tr. as *Hauntngs*), from which "The Dharana" is taken. Dujardin's literary productivity slackened considerably when he inherited his father's fortune, when he became a celebrated Parisian dandy, but he retained to his interest in unorthodox scholarship in several popularizations of the thesis that the Christ of the New Testament was a mythical invention, elaborated in *Histoire ancien du dieu Jésus* (1927; tr. as *The Ancient History of the God Jesus*), the thesis of which he had previously dramatized in two plays.

RENÉE DUNAN (1892-1936) was a prolific and versatile journalist and novelist, who employed several other known pseudonyms and was sometimes suspected of being pseudonymous herself (or, if certain unproven posthumous allegations made by one George Dunan can be trusted, himself). She was very active in the 1920s, when she corresponded with André Breton and thus associated herself with the advent of surrealism. *Baal, ou la magicienne passionnée* (1924; tr. in *Baal; The Devil's Lovers*), from which "Tsadé" is taken, was one of the earliest publications bearing her principal signature. Her interest in the occult sciences appears to have been primarily academic in spite of the fervor of the novelettes assembled in *Baal*, and its manifestations in her other novels is rather peripheral, although *Les Amants du diable* (1929; tr. as "The Devil's Lovers") is an interesting Micheletesque study of the witch-panic.

NICOLAS CAMILLE FLAMMARION (1842-1925), the older brother of the publisher Ernest Flammarion, was a professional astronomer who became the leading popularizer of that science and an assiduous spiritist whose hosted séances attended by many scientists and artists. He was a member of the Theosophical Society and the Society for Psychical Research. It was in his salon that Charles Cros proposed a method for communicating with Mars that was adopted in several scientific romances, and the playwright Victorian Sardou produced a series of allegedly-spirit-inspired drawings of souls reincarnated on other worlds—a notion of which Flammarion, under the inspiration of Jean Reynaud, was particularly fond; he popularized it in the essays collected in *Lumen* (1864-55; first book version 1872), the best-selling *Uranie* (1889), the novel *Stella* (1897) and the present short story, which first appeared in the 15 February 1896 issue of *La Nouvelle Revue*; the translation first appeared in *The World Above the World and Other French Scientific Romances* (2011). The idea was appropriated by several other writers associated with the occult revival, including Jean de La Vaudère.

REMY DE GOURMONT (1858-1915) was one of the co-founders of the *Mercure de France*, where much of his short fiction and criticism was published, and he became one of the principal commentators on the Symbolist Movement as well as one of its principal participants. He lived for some years with Berthe Courrière, whose interest in occultism he shared, but his own brand of mysticism was far from the Satanic one that his friend Joris-Karl Huysmans credited to the character based on her in *Là-Bas* (1891), celebrating a milder reverence for pagan philosophy. His mysticism underlies much of his supernatural short fiction, especially the items collected in *Histoires magiques* (1895; tr. as "Studies of Fascination" in *The Angels of Perversity*), from which the present story is taken, and *D'un pays lointain* (1898; tr. as *From a Faraway Land*).

FRANÇOIS JOLLIVET-CASTELOT (1874-1937) became an enthusiastic convert to neo-Rosicrucianism, a practicing alchemist—developing his own theoretical "hyperchemistry"— and a utopian philosopher in the socialist tradition of Henri de Saint-Simon and Charles Fourier; he was a key member of the coterie associated with Papus and was also a correspondent of the radical writer August Strindberg, influencing the ideas in some of the latter's more surreal works, some of which were written in French. Jollivet-Castelot published a "mystical novel," *Au Carmel* and an "esoteric novel," *Le Destin, ou Les Fils d'Hermès* (both 1920), but the majority of his publications were on the subjects of alchemical hyperchemistry and "spiritualist Communism." The present prose-poem, written in his youth, appeared in *L'Initiation* in 1892; the translation is original to the anthology.

GABRIEL DE LAUTREC (1867-1938) was, for a while, one of the more flamboyant lifestyle fantasists of the *fin-de-siècle*, advertising his occult interests, his friendship with Paul Verlaine and his fondness for hashish in his literary works, his dandyism and in the décor of his apartment, but he worked by day as a schoolteacher, and eventually toned his act down considerably, becoming a prolific proto-surrealist humorist under the influence of Alphonse Allais and aiming most of his later publications at the juvenile market. The series of quasi-autobiographical items published in *L'Initiation* in 1907-8 under the collective title *Le Feu sacré*, to which the present piece belongs, was translated in *The Sacred Fire* (2019), along with those of his *Poèmes en prose* (1898) not included in *The Vengeance of the Oval Portrait and Other Stories* (2011). Although fictionalized and hallucinatory, the series provides a valuable document of the neo-Martinist phase of the Revival.

JULES LERMINA (1839-1915) was a radical journalist arrested more than once for subversion; he was in prison when the siege of Paris began in 1870, but appears to have been offered release if he would join the National Guard; he agreed, and was sent out of Paris to fight the Germans, thus being unable to join the Commune and avoiding subsequent transportation to New Caledonia. Chastened by the experience, he returned to Paris and journalism, becoming a successful writer of action-adventure *feuilletons*. When his daughter Marie-Pauline married

the occult bookseller Henri Chacornac, Lermina became involved with the Occult Revival, writing several stories based on
ideas fed to him by Papus, including the present novella, first
published as a pamphlet in 1889; the translation first appeared
in the collection that was supposed to be called *The Zippelius
Secret and Other Stories*, although it was altered by the publisher to *The Secret of Zippelius and Other Stories* (2011). Lermina
introduced occult elements into numerous stories, usually for
purely melodramatic purposes, but his prestige as a writer was
sufficient to prompt Papus to ask him to chair the Congress of
Occult societies that he assembled in 1889.

VICTOR-ÉMILE MICHELET (1861-1938) was a childhood friend of Stanlias de Guaita, and collaborated with him
and Papus in the formation of their new Martinist Order;
he was also a fervent admirer of Édouard Schuré. He shared
Joséphin Pelandan's interest in Symbolist Art and his first book
was *De l'ésoterisisme dans l'Art* (1890), published more than ten
years before his first collection of poetry, *La Porte d'or* (1903),
although the material therein mostly dated from long before;
his collection of fantastic short stories and prose poems, *Contes
surhumains* (1900; tr. with additional material as *Superhuman
Tales*), from which the present story is taken, beat it into print,
as did its companion volume *Contes aventureux* (1900), but
they too recycled material from the 1890s.

JOSÉPHIN PÉLADAN (1858-1918) was the most prominent French Occultist of the 1880s and 1890s, relentless in his
self-promotion, and featuring regularly in newspaper gossip
columns. Primarily a lifestyle fantasist and a literary fantasist
rather than a scholarly fantasist, most of the ideas he promoted
were second-hand, but his Salon de la Rose + Croix, held annu-
ally between 1892 and 1897, became an important showcase
for Symbolist artists. He was already a successful novelist by

then, although the increasingly esoteric and didactic series of volumes collectively entitled *La Décadence Latine*, with which he followed *Le Vice supreme* (1884) did not match its success, their relentless promotion of the idea of the androgyne as a culmination of human evolution seeming excessively bizarre to many readers, and many of their rhapsodic interludes seeming incomprehensible—probably deliberately so. The prose poem "A un soeur inconnu" first appeared in volume five of the series, *Istar* (1888), and was separately published in Areséne Houssaye's *La Grande Revue: Paris et Saint Petersburg* in November of the same year. The translation first appeared in *Volupté*, the journal of the British Association for Decadence Studies, in 2019.

GILBERT-AUGUSTIN THIERRY (1843-1915) changed his signature to Gilbert Augustin-Thierry late in life to emphasize his kinship with his paternal uncle, the famous historian Augustin Thierry. His father Amédée Thierry was also a historian, who was forced to make a living from journalism when sacked from his academic post during the Bourbon Restoration because of his Republican opinions. Gilbert followed closely in his footsteps, becoming a pillar of the *Revue des Deux Mondes*. That periodical picked up a series of stories launched in the *Nouvelle Revue* under the title "Histoires de Mort et de Vivant," of which the present story was the second. This translation first appeared in the collection *Reincarnation and Redemption* (1919), which was followed by two volumes aggregating four later items in the series, *The Blonde Tress and the Mask* (2021) and *Stigma and the Pompeiian Fresco*. The intensively-researched historical backgrounds of the stories, most of which are short novels, and their earnest tone, entitle the later ones to consideration as some of the finest examples of nineteenth-century occult fiction. An earlier novel in the same vein was *L'Aventure d'une âme en peine* [The Adventure of a Soul in Torment] (1875).

CHARLES ERHARDT DE SIVRY (1848-1900) was much better known as a composer, primarily of operettas, a musician and an orchestra conductor than as a writer; in the late 1860s he was a regular at Nina de Villard's salon—dubbed the "mental breakdown factory" by Edmond de Goncourt—where many future Communards gathered and prodigious quantities of absinthe were allegedly drunk, and at the Chat Noir in the 1880s a friend of many of the "decadent" writers who gathered there. He was one of the consultants for the literary section of Papus' *L'Initiation*, in which the present story first appeared in 1891; it was reprinted with a selection of his other fantastic stories in the collection *Les Mauvais sous*, published by Les Âmes d'Atala in 2014. The translation is original to the present volume.

"RENÉ THIMMY" was the pseudonym of Maurice Magre (1877-1941), which he employed for two books, the first of which, *La Magie à Paris* (1934) offered a mock-journalistic account of the contemporary residuum of the Parisian occult underworld, to which Magre had been introduced by Gabriel de Lautrec around the turn of the century. The authorship of the book was long unknown, confused by the fact that Magre appears in the text as a character, thus distancing himself from the unnamed narrator, but Magre's biographer, Jean-Jacques Bedu, has established his authorship beyond any reasonable doubt. Magre's active involvement with practicing occultists appears to have been brief, but it made a very deep impression, which influenced his subsequent conversion to a variant of Buddhism, and which he drew upon in many of his novels, beginning with *L'Appel de la bête* (1920; tr. in *The Call of the Beast*) and continuing with *Priscilla d'Alexandrie* (1929; tr. as *Priscilla of Alexandria*), *La Vie amoureuse de Messaline* (1925: tr. as "The Love Life of Messalina" in *The Angel of Lust*), *La Luxure de Grenade* (1926; tr. as the title story of *The Angel of Lust*), *Le Mystère du tigre* (1927; tr. as *The Mystery of the Tiger*),

Lucifer (1929; tr. as *Lucifer*), *La Trésor des Albigeois* (1938; tr. as *The Albigensian Treasure*), *Jean de Fodoas* (1939; tr. as *Jean de Fodoas*) and *Mélusine, ou le Secret de Solitude* (1941; tr. as *Melusine*). Collectively, those novels amount to the most impressive body of work in the genre of occult fiction produced in the twentieth century. Many of them are fervently quasi-autobiographical, but are extravagantly fantasized, as is the present story, whose translation is original to the anthology.

CHARLES-MARIE TORQUET (1864-1938), was the younger brother of Eugène Torquet, author of the hallucinatory fantasy *Force Ennemie* (1903, signed Jean-Antoine Nau), the winner of the first Prix Goncourt. A journalist who edited a number of periodicals, he described life on Mars in a Flammarionesque speculative article in *Je Sais Tout* in 1906. He had a number of one-act plays produced, including at least one at the Grand-Guignol. He published a great deal of short fiction in the newspaper *Excelsior*, including "Les Messes noires de la Rue Louis-Blanc" (1928). The present story, signed Ch.-M. Torquet—although he subsequently used the signature "Charles Torquet"—appeared in *L'Initiation* in 1891; the translation is original to the present volume.

JANE DE LA VAUDÈRE (1857-1908) was baptized Jeanne Scrive, the daughter of the Surgeon-General of the Army, but lost both her parents while she was a child; she was raised in a convent and married off by her relatives soon after she completed her education to Gaston Crapez, who inherited the Château de La Vaudère from his mother and added its name to his own. His wife also adopted it, retaining it when she left the family home to live in Paris, where she attempted to seek fame as an artist before switching her attention to poetry, drama and eventually to fiction. Her early publications include a good deal of material based on her experiences in the occult underworld of

Paris, much of it—including the present story—published in translation in the collection *The Double Star and Other Occult Fantasies* (2018), part of a series that also includes several other occult novels, including the best-selling *Le Mystère de Kama* (1901; tr. in *The Mysteries of Kama and Brahma's Courtesans*, 1919), *Le Harem de Syta* (1904; tr. in *Syta's Harem and Pharaoh's Lover*, 2020) and *La Sorcière d'Ecbatane* (1906; tr. in *The Witch of Ecbatana and the Virgin of Israel*, 2021). "Reincarnation" was first published in book form in *L'Anarchiste* (1893). Always a controversial figure in Parisian society, La Vaudère's fame did not long survive her premature death, and her reputation was undermined by her prolific production, but she was an enterprising writer who deserves considerable credit for her contributions to fantastic melodrama.

"CLAUDE VIGNON" was the pseudonym of Marie-Noémi Cadiot (1828?-1888), who married Alphonse-Louis Constant, later known as Éliphas Lévi, in 1848, and had at least one child before they separated. She subsequently lived with the Marquis de Montferrier, the brother-in-law of a prominent Polish Messianic philosopher, and then married the politician and future prime minister of France Maurice Rouvier after Constant's death. She took her pseudonym from a character in Balzac's *Comédie humaine*, although it was also the name of a notable painter active in the early seventeenth century. Her first book of fiction, following several articles of art criticism, *Minuit!!* (1856), from which the present story is taken, was banned by the censors in Paris but published in Belgium, and reprinted the following year in abridged form as *Contes à faire peur*. Her subsequent literary work was much more restrained. "The Dead Avenge Themselves" is original to the present volume.

www.ingramcontent.com/pod-product-compliance
Lightning Source LLC
Chambersburg PA
CBHW050512110726
47899CB00005B/1427